THE RED HAT

RALPH McINERNY

THE RED HAT

A NOVEL

IGNATIUS PRESS   SAN FRANCISCO

MAY 0 6 2002

Cover illustration by Christopher J. Pelicano
Cover design by Riz Boncan Marsella

For Marvin O'Connell, old friend

"The distinction between historian and poet is not in the one writing prose and the other verse. . . . It consists really in this, that the one describes the thing that has been, and the other a kind of thing that might be."   — *Aristotle*

PROLOGUE

Julian slipped away from the studio to his office, where he changed into the black suit for which he had paid twelve hundred dollars. He left the collar of his shirt open, took the briefcase from the back of the closet, and headed for the rear exit.

"Julian?"

He turned to see Peggy standing at the end of the hall, a silhouette, except for her face, which was illumined by a cone of light descending from a recessed lamp in the ceiling. Her expression was puzzled. Julian had the sense of being caught. He hastily waved, turned, and pushed out into late-afternoon sunlight.

He drove through heavy traffic to LAX, where he put his car in long-term parking, took the shuttle to the terminal, and headed for a men's room. In a stall, he carefully removed his jacket and hung it on a hook behind the door. He had placed his briefcase on the toilet. He snapped it open, removed a garment, and shook it out. He put on the Roman collar and adjusted the vest-like dickey over his shirt before snapping it tight. He then put on his jacket. On the way out he looked into the mirror for a glimpse of the priest he should have been.

At the Avis counter, using an Ohio driver's license that would expire in two weeks, he rented a car. The girl behind the counter could not seem to lift her eyes above his Roman collar. Julian's expression was otherworldly, as if he were immune to her charms because of his calling. He asked directions to Huntington Beach, and she tore a map from a tablet and traced the route with a ballpoint. He thanked her.

"You're welcome, Father."

So she was Catholic. Why so shy? Perhaps he had stirred up feelings of guilt in her. On another occasion, he might have sought to arrange a meeting, to give her spiritual direction.

"God bless."

In the shuttle to the Avis lot, an elderly couple faced him across the aisle. Her mouth was a thin, disapproving line, and her husband, who seemed to be resting his stomach on his knees, tilted his head back and looked sceptically at Julian. Julian ignored them.

When he drove out of the lot in the rented Toyota, he did not turn south toward Huntington Beach but north onto I-110. He joined I-405 and then got onto 101, his destination Thousand Oaks. From time to time, he tipped the rearview mirror to get a look at himself as a priest.

He was thirty-six years old and had supported his mortally ill father for seven years after graduating from Bowling Green University. Major, classics. During those seven years, he had worked at a Minneapolis television station, advancing from gopher through cameraman to floor director. He had not considered it a career. It was only a way to make money until he was free to enter the seminary.

While he tended his dying father, he taught himself what he would have been learning in the seminary, philosophy first, then theology. He knew the sixteen documents of Vatican II like the back of his hand; he read every magisterial document out of Rome. He subscribed to *Origins, Catholic World Report, Fidelity, Crisis,* and the *Wanderer.* The turmoil in the Church did not affect him; he ignored it. Let theologians dissent, let nuns complain, let priests go over the wall. Julian's own sights were firmly set. He was what he would learn to call an ultramontane. After his father's death, Julian applied to the bishop of Toledo. He wanted to start an entirely new life in a new place.

Trouble began his first year in the seminary. He was older than his classmates and had the assurance of someone who had made his way in the world. He found it difficult not to question what his professors taught. When he could no longer ignore how heterodox their teaching was, he resolved to keep a buttoned lip and tough it out until ordination. Perhaps he might have succeeded in this if he had not had one teacher after his own heart. Father Leach was openly critical of the curriculum, bewailed the mode of living in the house, condemned the whole tone of the seminary. He was witty and bitter and universally loathed. Unwisely, in bull sessions, Julian succumbed to the temptation to come to Leach's defense. He became a pariah by participation. After Leach was transferred to Washington, things settled down, and Julian made every effort to blend in. But it was too late.

He was interviewed by a committee of the faculty after his second year. The atmosphere was congenial; the panel seemed genuinely interested in his views. What did he think of the role of women in the Church?

"I have a great devotion to St. Teresa of Avila as well as to Edith Stein."

"What about ordination?"

"For women?"

They nodded, smiling encouragement. He summarized the document with which Pope John Paul II had hoped to end the discussion.

On sexual morality, he said that he felt it had been a practical mistake for the Church to accept a distinction between orientation and practice. A mistake repeated in the *Catechism*.

"Homosexuality is always sinful?"

"Yes."

Two weeks later he received a letter telling him that he

could not return to the seminary in the fall. He was given a number to call should he want to discuss the matter.

"The general thought was that you're too rigid, Julian. There seemed to be no element of compassion or caring in your discussion of problems. We all foresaw trouble ahead for you in the pastoral sphere."

"When can I come back?"

"I think you should look into another vocation."

He realized later that he had nothing in writing, and that it was no accident. It was clear to him that he was barred from the priesthood because he was too Catholic. As far as he could see he was only as Catholic as the Church. He told himself that the Pope himself could not be admitted to that seminary.

His bishop refused to see him. "He will never second-guess his seminary faculty", Father Leach said over the phone. He seemed almost pleased to hear Julian's bad news. "Any other outcome would have been unimaginable."

"Any suggestions?"

He said his suggestions would be as worthless as any recommendation he might write for Julian. "You have been spared a life of crucifixion. It only gets worse after ordination. This is the way it must have been in the fourth century—for non-Arians."

Julian would have preferred more sympathy. Compassion. But Leach was devoid of the pastoral touch. For Julian the priesthood was more remote than it had been during the seven years he waited to get into the seminary. He indulged in fantasies about Fr. Julian O'Keefe holding a congregation in thrall; he imagined himself on television, reaching out to millions in a plain, effective style. Meanwhile, he went back into television, migrating to California where he eventually became an independent producer—of commercials. He had cashed in on the infomercial boom, half-hour imitations of studio shows. Peggy had shown up one day with a small resumé and large hopes, and he was certain she would photograph well. She did. In the small lucrative world he inhabited, he made her a star. She was younger than he was; he kept it Platonic despite her obvious willingness to make it more; he became her confidant. His dream of the priesthood entailed celibacy. But they became friends, and she told him about her mother, Karen.

"She's a single mom. My grandmother raised me, really."

"Where?"

"Minneapolis."

"I'm from Minneapolis."

"It's fate", she said, leaning toward him. He gave her a fatherly kiss on the forehead.

"I never met my father. No wonder", she continued.

"Why?"

She sat back as if to get a good view of his reaction. "He was a priest."

It was destiny. More than either of them knew. Finding out who Peggy's father was became a project for Julian, although he did not reveal this to Peggy. Later she told him she was glad that he hadn't reacted when she told him about her father.

"I don't know what to think of it myself."

"Why think of it at all."

"My mother keeps bringing it up. I think she's proud of it."

Disappointment at his thwarted clerical career turned to bitterness, and Julian longed to punish the Church that had rejected him. Sometimes, wearing clerical clothes, he would stop at parishes north of San Francisco, arriving just before the pastor was scheduled to say Mass.

"Could I concelebrate, Father? I'm visiting relatives."

"What diocese you from?"

"St. Paul."

Chances were California priests knew there was such a place

but had never met a priest from there. Vested, standing to the left and a step back from the celebrant, looking out at the meager weekday congregation, Julian told God he did not intend to make a mockery of holy orders. "Make me a priest", he prayed. "Make me a real priest." As concelebrant, he was beckoned forward to read the commemorations. At the consecration of the bread and wine, he extended his hand in an ineffectual gesture. Sometimes he thought that he no longer believed any of it. But if that had been true, he would have been able to just forget it, get serious about Peggy, accept the life that was his.

The road turned away from the sea and flowed like a concrete river through the parched hills of autumn. California was apocalyptic, with its peculiar four horsemen of flood, fire, quake, and mudslide. The gospel injunction against building on sand was universally ignored, and million-dollar homes seasonally tilted and slipped down the eroding hills on which they had been erected. Or they burned. Or were shaken apart by the querulous earth. No wonder ad hoc religious cults sprang up everywhere.

He reached Thousand Oaks and turned off to the development in which Karen Christiansen had a condo. A remark of Peggy's had suggested her mother would not be home. His clerical attire was meant to gain him entry if the information was wrong.

"She's a fanatic", Peggy replied, when he asked if her mother still practiced her religion. "She's been to Medjugorje three times, when the war was on! She's had a whee of a life, and now she wants to make up for it."

She would be susceptible to a priest seeking to interest her in Marian apparitions. She was already interested. But had she heard of the Seer of Viterbo?

In the end, she was not home, and he admitted himself, slipped on latex gloves, and began systematically to search the apartment. What he wanted were any papers, photographs, letters that might provide a clue to the identity of Peggy's father. If the man was still alive, still a priest, Julian meant to expose the hypocrite. It was unbearable that he himself could not become a priest while an ordained priest had carried on as Peggy's father had. What was he doing now?

The living room had the unoccupied look of a studio set; there was no sign of its inhabitant, no personal mark. The kitchen was somewhat distinctive, but it was the den that began to seem like a home. A television set with a vast screen, shelves of videos, all of them religious, accounts of Lourdes, of Fatima, of the weeping Madonna of Japan. Sermons, instructions, video records of papal visits. In the bedroom was a shrine. A statue of Mary four feet high stood on a pedestal before which an abundance of potted plants were set. And a kneeler. It must be chiefly here that Karen Christiansen sought to do penance for the sins of her past life.

Julian went through the den systematically, looking behind books and videos, examining each drawer of the desk, looking under the pad, turning over the chair to see if perhaps something was concealed there. He turned back the carpet, looked under the cushions of the sofa and easy chairs. After half an hour, he was certain that what he sought was not in the den. There was of course the possibility that she kept such papers elsewhere, in a safe deposit box. If he had to cultivate her in order to find out who had fathered her daughter, he would. He was in this for the long haul.

He found what he wanted in a box beneath the bed, a flimsy pasteboard carton from a department store. The cover buckled when he took it off. There were photographs on top, and he went through them carefully, immediately putting two into his jacket pocket. The letters proved to be from Peggy's grandmother, a small bundle from a residence for the aged in Minneapolis. The birth certificate was a bit of a surprise. Peggy was only five years younger than he was. But then the photograph of Peggy and her mother in the den indicated that Karen Christiansen too looked far younger than she was.

The contents of the box formed geological layers; the deeper he dug the farther into the past he went. A newspaper clipping had a photograph of a man in clerical clothing. The same man figured in several other clippings, the stories tracing his rise in the Church.

"What are you doing!"

She stood in the doorway of the bedroom, angry, but terrified too. He rose to his feet and saw the ambiguous effect of his priestly attire on her.

"Didn't Peggy call you?"

"Peggy!"

She wanted to be reassured. If the circumstances were not so damning, he might have been able to tell a plausible story, explaining why he was in her bedroom rummaging through her most intimate keepsakes. He started toward the door, trying to hold her in place with a reassuring smile, but her mouth opened, and she tried to cry out. He clamped a hand over her mouth before any sound could emerge and pulled her back into the bedroom, getting an arm around her neck. She tried to bite at his hand as his arm closed on her throat, and in a panic he increased the pressure. She mustn't yell. The enormity of what he had done, breaking into a home, suddenly struck him. He almost forgot his burden until she went limp in his arms and her weight pulled him down as he eased her to the floor. Good God, she seemed to have stopped breathing.

He bent over her, his hands on the floor on either side of her body and put his ear to her mouth. There was no sign of breathing, but his own heart was beating so wildly it might have drowned out the sound. He drew back and looked down at her. Her eyes were not fully closed; her mouth, so much like Peggy's, was open. He did not know how but he decided he would try to give her respiration. As he lowered his mouth to hers, her eyes popped open, filled with terror.

She rolled to the side and began again to scream. Terrified himself, he struck her, once and then again, but she twisted and rolled and continued screaming. He grabbed a cushion from the couch and pressed it over her mouth, to shut her up. If she would just shut up, he would leave. The silence was so welcome that he pressed the pillow more tightly against her face. Finally she stopped struggling, and he removed the pillow.

Everything would have been all right if only she hadn't screamed. She should have reacted differently when she saw the way he was dressed. It became very important for him to think that what had happened to her was her fault. He had not wanted to harm her.

He began to take selected papers from the box. He would not take everything. He was certain that only Karen had known what the box contained. Then he stopped and thought for a moment. He returned what he had taken from the box, carefully replaced the cover, and then tucked the box under his arm.

He stepped over the body but in the doorway turned. She lay on her side; her blonde hair fanned out from her head. When she was found, it would be said that she had surprised an intruder and paid the price. She wore a pale green dress with a pleated skirt; her purse lay beside her.

He put down the box and knelt beside her. He opened the purse and began to pull things from it—Kleenex, a rosary, a lipstick—scattering them about. The wallet he tucked into his pocket. Then he pulled up her skirt, grabbed the top of her panties and tugged them off her hips, jerking them down her legs to her ankles. He arranged her legs in an immodest pose.

In the doorway again, holding the box, he surveyed the scene. No need to check the den; he had left it exactly as he

15

had found it. With his heart in this throat, he stripped off the gloves and put them into his trouser pocket, then let himself out of the apartment.

He encountered no one when he went out to his rented car. Before he began the drive back to Los Angeles, he took the two snapshots from his jacket pocket and studied them. The girl with the young priest could have been Peggy.

PART ONE

CHAPTER ONE

I

From his office window high in the building its critics were calling the Taj Mahal ever since the success of Jim Morrow's book, Archbishop Thomas Lannan looked down on Massachusetts Avenue, where a pick-up truck festooned with campaign posters honked triumphantly as it waited for the light to change. Faintly, the sound of answering horns rose to his ears. "Honk if you like Hank": This bumper-sticker invitation had made the District an arena of battling horns for months. "Blast Hank!" had been the response of the opposite party. Well, more people had honked for young Hank than had blasted him, and the improbable South Carolina man, whose presidency began with the millennium, had won a new four-year lease on the White House. Did this mean that the reactionary mood of the country had been reversed? Lannan felt that his own career was somehow tied up with the answer to that question.

Behind him his secretary Gene Wales made his presence known by a deferential clearing of the throat. Lannan turned from the window.

"Getting through that traffic would take some doing, Gene. What's on?"

"Oh, we can stay right here, Archbishop. There's nothing pressing."

"Here" was his office as current president of the National Conference of Catholic Bishops, also known as the NCCB. The phone rang, and Monsignor Wales picked it up. "Archbishop Lannan's office." A pause. "Could I tell him who's calling?" Wales' face was expressionless as he processed the response through the rolodex of his mind. Apparently without positive result. He shrugged and mouthed the name: Miss-is Kil-mar-tin. The name drew a blank from Lannan too, but he took the phone.

"Archbishop Lannan."

"Tom?"

"What can I do for you?" he asked against the grain of his annoyance. It had been a mistake not to let Wales handle this. "Mrs. Kilmartin, is it?"

"Of course that name means nothing to you. This is Maureen, Tom. Maureen Bailey, Frank's sister. Minneapolis, thousands of years ago?"

"Maureen", Lannan repeated and indicated to Wales that it was all right. The monsignor left the office while Lannan settled behind his desk. "Where on earth are you?"

"Immobilized at Dupont Circle. So much for my idea that I would just pop in on you. Can I see you?"

"Of course."

"What is all the excitement about?"

"There's been an election. Didn't you vote?"

"I'm just back in the country late yesterday!"

"Are you free for lunch?" He should check with Wales before making appointments, but this of course was different.

"That was the plan. I'll pick you up, if we ever break out of this mess."

"Do you have the address?"

"The driver does."

"I'm in my office at the NCCB."

"Where I just phoned you?" And across the years he could see her head tip to the side as she made a face.

"I'll just wait here for you."

"I have no idea how long that might be, Tom. And this was such a grand idea, to surprise you."

"Oh, you've certainly succeeded in doing that, Mo."

He hung up in wonderment at how that nickname had come spontaneously to his lips after all these years.

He rose and returned to the window, but his gaze was now reflective. He could still summon surprise at what he had become. The Most Reverend Thomas Lannan, archbishop of Washington. Slightly over six feet tall, he gave the impression of being taller because of his trimness. The lack of episcopal flab was no accident; every other day he put in twenty minutes on the treadmill he had irreverently dubbed the *via dolorosa*. His baldness did not suggest an absence; indeed it took an effort to imagine his well-shaped head with hair. His hair had been gone by the age of thirty, and he seemed hardly to have aged in the twenty-five years since. His skin was naturally tanned, a gift from his maternal German grandmother, and his eyes were large, dark brown, their gaze memorable, even if, at the moment, retrospective. The prospect of seeing Mo Bailey after all these years brought home to him the distance he had come since that long-ago time in Minneapolis. To the perks and aggravations of high office in the Church.

He started at the ringing of the phone and waited until Monsignor Wales answered it. The prospect that it might be Maureen calling back to say she could not make it through this traffic filled him with disappointment. Wales stood in the doorway.

"Who was it?"

"Janet Fortin. The girl at the White House."

He nodded. The young woman was the administration's liaison with religious leaders, a delicate task at any time but particularly so during the recent campaign, given her boss' knack for annoying what should have been his natural constituency. Hank Whitney either got very bad advice or was another instance of the Bill Moyers' syndrome, the Southern boy who longs to be a Yankee and ends up as the kind of liberal now all but universally disliked.

"Her message was that they owe you one."

"For what?"

"Justice Norman."

Leslie Norman's nomination to the Supreme Court had encountered no difficulties in the Senate hearings and only pro forma opposition from political primitives who had objected to another Catholic on the bench. But a month after being sworn in, with the President's reelection campaign under way, Justice Norman was suddenly in the eye of a self-created storm. *Lei,* the women's fashion magazine, published a fawning profile of the new justice and her lover Jackie. The two women had been living together ever since Norman's appointment to the court of appeals several years before. Jackie, a former nun, spoke of how much their faith had contributed to making theirs a stable, loving relationship. The following Sunday their pastor in Arlington refused them Communion.

"He is saying that Jesus rejects us", Jackie told a media team that happened to be waiting outside the church.

"Why do they have to announce these things?" Lannan had asked Wales. The justice might be trouble for the President, but she was more trouble for Thomas Lannan, who came under fierce pressure from conservatives to back up the Arlington pastor. From Milwaukee, Maud Erickson, a woman "priest" who claimed to have been ordained by the former archbishop, expressed solidarity with the two women. There seemed to be

22

no way that the NCCB could stay out of it, and Thomas Lannan was caught in the kind of dilemma he had spent his life avoiding. No matter what he did, he would be in the wrong. Doing nothing seemed, if not a solution, at any rate, the least costly course.

"Arlington isn't in your jurisdiction", Scanlan of Detroit said.

"They are contacting me as president of the Conference, Gerry."

"And what do you tell them?"

"I'm not taking their calls."

A chortle on the line. "*Si tacuisses*, eh?" Silence is the best policy.

The temperature had been raised when New York's Cardinal Guevara condemned the justice's perverted sexual life from the pulpit of St. Patrick's. Later that day, a mob of militants began tearing up the cathedral. Guevara himself removed the Blessed Sacrament, to prevent desecration, and was cursed and spat upon as he hurried off to his residence with the ciborium full of consecrated hosts.

This brought Frank Bailey into the battle, though not publicly, as would have been the case in his zenith as dean of dissident theologians. He could always be counted on to oppose noisily any authoritative move. Once, his counterblasts had been magnified by the media far beyond the dimensions of the original outrage. But of late, as the old Pope lived on and on, Bailey, an aging liberal, had sunk into despair, convinced that all his efforts on behalf of what he considered the spirit of Vatican II had been in vain. Lannan, as a gesture to his boyhood friend, had returned Bailey's call.

"Frank, how goes the battle?"

But Bailey went right to the point. "You've got to go on the offensive, Tom", he said in his raspy, excited voice. "Don't let Guevara speak for the Church."

"He is cardinal archbishop of New York, Frank."

"Is Arlington, Virginia, part of his archdiocese?" Bailey apparently wanted Lannan to defend the lifestyle of Justice Norman. "Tom, it's time we got on the right side of some these issues."

"That's the left side."

Lannan was about as likely to defend Justice Norman as he was to condemn her, and he sensed that Frank Bailey knew it. But that very reluctance suggested how he could handle the matter.

From the pulpit of St. Matthew's, he gave a restrained homily to a packed church. He began by saying he was certain that they were all as grieved as he by recent events.

"But to those who would condemn, exclude, alienate, judge, I offer the simple Gospel account of Jesus and the woman taken in adultery. Our Lord was more severe with those who came to censure and condemn and to use religion as a weapon against those no more sinful than themselves. Perhaps less sinful."

He read the account in John. He made no further allusion to events beyond the liturgy he was conducting. When he descended from the pulpit and walked slowly to his throne, he affected to lean on his crosier for support, his mitered head bowed, the great church hushed. He sat for two minutes in silence before rising, spreading his hand and saying, "We believe in God..."

As if in relief, the congregation rose and recited the Creed with an unwonted fervor. Lannan felt a solidarity with his people that was new to him. He the shepherd, they the flock. Not an image he would have voiced, of course; one had to be careful not to give offense, but it did seem to cover the occasion.

The Catholic News Service sent a version of the sermon out on its wire, and Nathaniel Patch followed it a week later with a summary of reactions. The diocesan press was favorable in a lukewarm way, but the powerful conservative media lambasted him for missing the point of the Gospel passage he had invoked. *The Wanderer* accused him of heresy; *Fidelity* carried letters from informants who had allegedly heard the sermon and claimed it was worse than reported. Well, different. If he had thought about it, Lannan would have counted on this reaction. Sometimes it seemed as if every angry Catholic with a little money had started his own publication to harass the hierarchy. But the response was good where it counted.

L'Osservatore Romano published Lannan's sermon side by side with Guevara's condemnation, and Ambrose Frawley at the North American College called to tell him it had made a tremendous impression.

"Guevara came through as a Pharisee."

"Any word on you know what?"

Frawley, a former protégé at the Conference who felt, not entirely without reason, that he owed his appointment as rector of the North American College to Lannan, was one of the archbishop's main sources of Roman gossip. The occupant of the see of Washington was almost always created cardinal, but sometimes only years after his installation. But this had not yet happened to Thomas Lannan, who had no intention of suffering the fate that had befallen Borders in Baltimore and Mays in St. Louis.

"Whenever Benedetto brings it up, the old man nods assent, but he does nothing."

"Is he still..."

"*Compos mentis?* Rumor claims he's as sharp as he ever was."

Lannan smiled, imagining what Frank Bailey would say to that. The scrappy theologian had once encouraged a campaign to gather signatures of those who wanted the Holy Father to abdicate and let a younger man with a clearer mind take over. Frawley had reported that rumors of this effort stopped all retirement talk in the papal apartments.

"I wonder if Rossi read my sermon."

"Haven't you heard from him?"

Frawley was a bright young man, but he had never learned how to avoid the awkward remark.

"Not yet", Lannan said meaningfully.

After a pause, Frawley said, "Right. I'll see what I can do."

Lannan closed his eyes in pain. To be patronized by his protégé! Ah, well. The important thing was that Frawley should make Cardinal Rossi of Milan know how the archbishop of Washington had handled a very delicate situation.

To be created cardinal was Thomas Lannan's ultimate ambition. After the red hat had been bestowed on him he could relax. Years ago, people had snickered when Joe Bernardin, appointed to Chicago and certain to become a cardinal, announced that he was now going to turn to Jesus and concentrate on his spiritual life. What had the man been doing up till then? But Lannan understood what Joe meant. Short of the big enchilada itself, out of reach for an American, becoming a member of the College of Cardinals was as far as any cleric could go. Lannan would not have said it aloud as Bernardin indiscreetly had, but once he had the red hat, he was going to become a new man. The old dream of sanctity could take precedence once more. He told himself that his ambition was impersonal; the elevation was something owed the archdiocese rather than himself. It would be a tribute to the Church in the United States.

He was ready, but nothing happened. The delay was increasingly difficult to bear. If it was explained by the advanced age of the Pope, whose silver anniversary in the chair of Peter had been celebrated with great pomp a year ago, well, the old man could go at any moment. The thought caused panic. Not yet, not yet, was Lannan's prayer at this alarming prospect. He wanted to be a member of the consistory that elected the next pope. Only cardinals under the age of eighty were electors.

It was not from President Whitney that he had expected gratitude for the way he had handled the Norman contretemps, and the message Wales passed on from Janet Fortin at the White House irked him.

"They owe me one, do they? Does he intend to withdraw the Death Bill?"

This piece of legislation invoked the privacy principle to cover physician-assisted suicide, a ploy that had not met with success in the courts. The NCCB had of course opposed the bill, assuming that this would be the common reaction, but the bishops had been taken aback by the widespread approval the measure seemed to command. Of course there were theologians like Bailey eager to explain that the position of the NCCB was not binding on Catholics and was of dubious weight in any case.

"That's just what I asked Janet", Wales said.

"And what did she say?" Was it possible that the President would be the means of triumphing over dissident theologians? Such a reversal on his part would be dramatic, but Whitney being Whitney, it was not unthinkable.

"She said she wished we wouldn't refer to it as the Death Bill."

"What else could he offer?"

Wales hesitated, as if unsure how he himself regarded the suggestion. "The ambassadorship to the Vatican."

Lannan laughed. Once Catholics had regarded this post as conferring great prestige on the faith, an acknowledgment of the nation's significant Catholic population. And there had been opposition because others too thought it was a significant matter. Not even the legendary Franklin Roosevelt at the height of his power had dared send anything more than a personal envoy to the Vatican. Truman had tried to appoint General Mark Clark, the hero of Anzio, but the Protestants had put a stop to that. But with Reagan the post became a routine appointment. In the years since, it had faded from public consciousness, and few realized that the country even had an ambassador to the Vatican. Most of the appointees had been Catholic, but neither priest nor politician now regarded the post as important.

"I wonder if Mrs. Kilmartin is going to make it through that traffic, Gene."

2

Nate Patch took the Metro to the CUA station, where the escalator was out of order, and he had to mount the unmoving steps on his own power. He bent forward as he climbed, trying to ease the pressure on the disc that pinched the nerve that turned his left leg into a thermometer of pain. Memories of long-ago physical ordeals in Navy bootcamp came to him, and he tried unsuccessfully to rid his mind of them. It would not do to feel at any disadvantage when interviewing Archbishop Lannan.

If he got to interview him.

If the current president of the National Conference of Catholic Bishops was even in his office.

Patch had called the archbishop's residence and learned that he was not there, but given the election news, he might be down at the White House rather than in his office at the NCCB.

People pushed past Patch on the narrow stairway. He wanted nothing more than to stop and find some position that would stop the pain in his lower back and leg. Maybe this was what St. Paul had meant by a thorn in the flesh. It was enough to try the patience of a saint, but, while Nate Patch hoped to be in their number in the final march, he had no illusions about his present condition.

He had washed out of the Navy because he could not swim. He relied on public transportation because he could not drive. And now that Lorraine had moved out, he was without a wife as well. It sounded like three strikes. He reached the top of the stairs and stepped out of the traffic the better to take off the jacket of his seersucker suit.

Nate Patch, Catholic journalist. Strike four? He had come to Washington from the Milwaukee diocesan paper, joining the Catholic News Service with dreams of being sent to Rome. That assignment hadn't exactly been promised, but it was dangled before him as an inducement to start at the bottom in Washington. It took him awhile to realize that the point of it all was to make room in Milwaukee for a protégé of the chancery office, not to advance the career of Nate Patch. He had also learned that the difference between the bottom and the top at the CNS was not discernible to the naked eye.

Getting his jacket off while hanging onto his briefcase proved to be impossible. Finally, he clamped the plastic briefcase between his knees and, while he stripped the jacket off his sweat-drenched shirt, began to sidle toward a bench. Several people turned to look at him, but he was beyond embarrassment.

His breath came in gasps after he lowered himself onto the bench. He stopped his hand on its way to the pocket of his shirt and the pack of Camels. He was overweight and out of shape. Lorraine was a freelance writer who had come to specialize in health items, ecological jeremiads, and, finally, feminism. The end was in sight as soon as her consciousness began to rise. She was earning more than he did and never let him forget it.

"Quit", she urged. "Get out of there and into the real world."

"I'm having difficulty deciding among my many offers."

"You've got to go out and look for them. Be aggressive."

"Assertive."

She took umbrage at that. The course in assertiveness had turned her into a bitch, at least with him. She practiced at home, and when she got the hang of it she planned to treat other people badly too. They fought and then made up, over and over, and it would have been difficult to say which of them was the more contrite.

"We should have kids", he said.

"Kids!"

"Well, one at a time."

"I'm not ready yet."

Lorraine was then thirty-two. Now he thanked God they hadn't had any kids. He had asked her to keep quiet about being on the pill.

"Why?" she demanded angrily, looking beyond him as if a platoon of archbishops had whispered the suggestion in his ear.

"It's bad ecology."

She thought about that. She did research. She got four articles out of it, each paying more than the previous one. And she went on taking the pill. You would have thought that meant she was ready for him night and day. Forget it. Some clergy knew more of the pleasures of the flesh than he did. The fact was, he had lost interest, more or less. He might be overweight, but Lorraine was no Miss America either. Besides, their marriage became something like the Middle East peace process—neither war nor peace. Lorraine's bitching had turned his discontent with his job into smoldering resentment. He had no idea where the Catholic Church was going, and he didn't think anyone in the bishops' conference did either.

"To the dogs", Lorraine had said. "Read Morrow's book."

Professor James Morrow, a hitherto obscure historian from Notre Dame, had written *The Decline and Fall of the American*

Catholic Church, a book that chronicled the chaos in the Church following the Second Vatican Council, which ended in 1965. It was a pretty convincing case. Unaccountably, it became a bestseller. Book clubs adopted it; news magazines featured it; Morrow appeared on several talk shows but then refused further invitations, and that turned him into a mystery figure. Articles asking "Who is James Morrow?" began to appear. The stance of the NCCB toward the book and its author was silence. The whole country was talking about it, but in the church bureaucracy in Washington mum was the word. Finegan, his boss, had spiked the mild story Patch had done, less on the book than on reaction to it.

"Maybe we ought to burn a few copies."

Finegan smiled, but it was his stomach. It was Finegan who had told Patch that Archbishop Lannan and Morrow had been boys together, back in Minneapolis.

"Morrow was in the minor seminary out there."

Patch spent a week of his vacation in Minnesota, researching it, talking with people. A priest who had been director of the Catholic Youth Center in Minneapolis was particularly voluble.

"The three of them worked for me one summer."

"Three?"

"Morrow, Lannan, and Bailey."

"Frank Bailey!"

The priest grinned at the effect he had created. When Patch talked to Bailey, the aging dissident was ambivalent.

"Don't give Morrow's book any more publicity", he growled.

"Because he criticized the Church?"

Bailey cocked an eye at him. The theologian had made a career out of savaging the Church, taking exception to every document that came out of Rome.

"You were kids together, weren't you?"

"Yeah."

"Along with Archbishop Lannan?"

Bailey teetered for a moment on the edge of talking but checked himself. "Lannan's your boss, isn't he?"

A threat? No matter. Patch turned the material over to Lorraine, and she did a piece called "Three Church Mice".

"We'll split", she said.

"We already have."

"I mean what they're going to pay me."

He said forget it, until she told him it was ten thousand dollars. If he had resented his role as Catholic journalist before, that did it. If Lorraine could make that kind of money, with material he gave her, what might he not do himself?

"Do something on the sex life of priests, Nate. No one knows more about it than you do."

"How do you mean that?"

She pursed her lips and wrinkled her nose. He was only half-tempted by the idea. Of course, he would only do it if he were prepared to move on from Catholic journalism. Lorraine was wrong if she thought he had any hot gossip. But who knew what a little digging might do?

Meanwhile, he rose from the bench, put a little pressure on his left foot, found that the sciatica had subsided, and began to walk up Massachusetts Avenue. The traffic was a mess, horns blasting all around him. Of course they were ecstatic in the District with the results of the election. The Great White Father was still in power, and the cornucopia would continue to overflow.

Archbishop Lannan and the NCCB could also claim to have a friend in the nation's reelected chief executive. And vice versa.

3

Roman traffic was notorious, but Maureen Kilmartin had never been completely immobilized like this in the Eternal City. And here everyone was relatively patient. She sat back in the limousine that had been provided for her from the Irish Embassy by Francis Russell, who had been a dear friend of Sean's. They treated her as one of themselves, as if immigration were going in the opposite direction nowadays. There was no point in talking with the driver; she couldn't understand a word he said. She wished she had kept Tom Lannan on the phone.

The traffic and the electoral excitement she could not share gave her second thoughts about breaking her journey home to Minneapolis here in Washington. Third thoughts would be more like it. Until she talked to Karen's mother about the letter she had sent Maureen, it would not do to mention it to Tom Lannan. Archbishop Thomas Lannan. Even if the accusation were true, what difference did it make, after all these years?

She found that she did not doubt it was true. As she read the letter, she felt that in some recess of her mind she had known it all along. At least that it was possible. Memories of the summer they had all worked at the Catholic Youth Center in Minneapolis marched across her mind—Tom, Karen, herself. Karen had been drawn toward the forbidden territory of the seminarian, a man whose future was celibacy. That might have been tolerable if he hadn't been good-looking.

"Is he good-looking?" Maureen had asked, trying to see Tom in this light. She had known him for years, but he was a classmate of her brother Frank's: he was going to be a priest.

"Come on."

"He's losing his hair."

Karen had waved away this undeniable fact. It was something Frank and Jim Morrow kidded him about—Tom's natural tonsure.

What had seemed only Karen's foolishness was soon matched by Tom's. Maureen had known little enough about men to be surprised by his susceptibility to Karen's dumb blond act. If it was an act. Maureen hadn't known that much about girls either, and she was astounded by Karen's revelations after her dates.

"I want to feel his lips on mine", she had said with half-closed eyes. "I want to open mine to his."

"How did you end up in a summer job here?"

"I understand kids."

Now, years later, Karen was dead, but the letter from her mother spelled possible trouble for Tom Lannan, and Maureen had felt a duty to warn him. But, as the car began to move, she was glad she had a fallback reason for calling Tom Lannan.

Ever since a guarded conversation with Cardinal Benedetto, she had considered having a talk with Tom Lannan, wanting to be of help to an old friend. The letter she had received from Margaret Christiansen, the mother of Karen, a friend of her girlhood, decided her. There was no way of telling whether what the letter said was true: the wavering spidery hand seemed dubiously connected with a clear mind. But what Cardinal Benedetto had said was clear, however obliquely he had put it.

The driver pressed the horn in response to those of the cars around them, then turned and grinned. Maureen nodded in complicity. He probably thought she was a foreigner. Well, in a way she was. It had been twenty years since she had felt like a real American.

Going off to Europe after the divorce had been meant to be a dramatic break with the tumultuous marriage she had endured for a decade. The irony was that the divorce turned out to have been unnecessary. She and the kids had hardly settled in the apartment on Monte Parioli in Rome when she got the news of Ray's death in the crash of a company jet. So much for all the acrimonious bickering over the settlement. After a legal skirmish with his sister, all Ray's money had come to her and the girls. Just like that, she was one of Rome's wealthy widows from elsewhere, rather than a member of the band of divorcées who at that time haunted Babington's Tea Room at the foot of the Spanish Steps.

Memories of her first widowhood came with difficulty now. There were photographs attesting that the girls had indeed gone to Marymount; albums recorded that she had dutifully taken them to all the sights: the Villa d'Este, Hadrian's Villa, the Circus Maximus. Soon Teresa and Jennie knew the city like natives, and it was Maureen who received instruction. That was all the more memorable because when the girls went back to the States for college, they shuffled off their Roman personae entirely, their Italian grew rusty from disuse, and they wrinkled their noses when she asked them to come spend the summer with her.

Of course Rome was aswarm with tourists in the summer, but that wasn't the reason. Maureen had met and married Sean Kilmartin and had been inducted into the closed little society of the Vatican diplomatic corps. It was then that her real Roman life had begun, and soon everyone assumed that she was as Irish as her husband.

"I hardly recognize you on the phone, Mom", Jennie complained.

"I can hear you fine." The cable connection had long since given way to satellites, and her daughter might have been in the next room.

"I mean your accent."

"What accent?"

"You sound just like him."

"Him" was Sean. Teresa resented her marrying again even more than Jennie did. She didn't really blame them. Her life had entered a phase that did not include them, no matter the regular visits to the States that Sean had insisted she make. He was quintessentially charming, not as a professional accomplishment, but simply because he was. He had been everything that Ray was not, witty and considerate and full of stories, which were partly Irish bull but which, more fundamentally, caught the sweet and melancholy undertow in people's lives.

"The *lacrimae rerum*", he had called it, the inherent sadness of life.

And she had waited. He learned to accept that, despite her extensive and expensive education, she was all but illiterate. Being married to him had been an education by osmosis, above all in the faith. Once he had called himself a spoiled priest, and, not knowing the phrase, she half-feared he had been ordained, but he hadn't even been near Maynooth.

"I thought about it; boys in Ireland do. Often it is reading Joyce that sweeps it all away, the more's the pity. Joyce was the spoiledest priest of all." And he began to recite: *I shall forge in the smithy of my soul the uncreated conscience of my race.* There was mockery as well as reverence in his tone, for he loved the music of the words.

He told her all about Joyce and a Jesuit education and reading Virgil as a boy and understanding only that there was so much of it he did not yet understand.

"Aeneas' affair with Dido, now, we thought we understood that. 'Love 'em and leave 'em' is your phrase for it."

"My phrase?"

He let it go. That was his way. Had they ever argued?

"*Agnosco veteris vestigia flammae.* It's the source of the phrase 'an old flame'. But the sadness of the line lies in the fact that Aeneas, sailing away, looks ashore and sees the fire and smoke of the pyre on which the heartbroken Dido has immolated herself."

Softly he said the Virgilian line again, speaking as a priest speaks at the altar. He taught her Latin. She became a schoolgirl again, working through Caesar and Virgil and Horace, even Catullus, but they were married by then, so it was all right. More than all right. Dear God, how she missed the touch and warmth of him. To this day, tears welled up in her eyes at the memories of making love with that sweet, dear man. At first he had dreamt of children, though she laughed aloud like Sarah when he voiced the hope. That was not to be, of course.

"Ah well", he said in sacerdotal tones, his hand on her thigh. "There is always the unitive meaning of the conjugal act."

It was her previous self she could no longer recall after being transformed by marriage with Sean Kilmartin. Once there had been a woman raised in Minneapolis, whose closest male friends had been her brother's fellow seminarians. On Wednesday and Saturday afternoons they would come to the Bailey house just across the Lake Street bridge and sit on the porch and talk about the strange life they led as they studied for the priesthood. Her brother Frank and Tom Lannan and for a while Jim Morrow too. There were others, but her memory had dwindled to those three.

Frank and Tom were duly ordained, and she was given in marriage to the enormously successful Raymond Barrett, became the mother of two girls, became brittle and bitter because of Ray's single-minded pursuit of power and money and every other known substitute for happiness. And then he had asked her for a divorce!

It seemed grievously unfair to her daughters that all her memories of the marriage of which they were the fruit had faded almost entirely away. By comparison, her memories of growing up in Minneapolis were vivid. Memories of Frank and his classmates, first at Nazareth Hall, then at the major seminary just across the river in St. Paul. Had Jim Morrow gone on to the major seminary from the Hall? Tom Lannan had spent two years there and then been sent off to the Greg in Rome. He had been ordained in St. Mary Major, but somehow Maureen could never imagine him as part of the Roman scene she had later come to know so well. But then he really hadn't been part of it, being a seminarian and later a student priest pursuing a doctorate in theology.

How many years had it been since they had seen one another?

But when the car swept up the drive to the building and the tall cleric came through the revolving doors, she knew immediately it was Tom Lannan. How unchanged he looked when he bent, peered into the backseat, and then smiled. He pulled open the door, got in, and leaned toward her. When his lips were on her cheek she remembered again the long-ago ambition of Karen Christiansen.

"All this excitement caught me by surprise, Tom", she said, sitting back against the door so she could get a good look at him.

"The election?"

The last time she had voted was in the American consulate in Rome, and she couldn't even remember what the occasion was. Another presidential election? Perhaps. Had she really thought her expatriate vote would matter? She was no longer registered now and felt total indifference to the course of government in her native land.

"And for whom should I have voted?"

"I never give political advice."

"At least you can tell me your choice."

The driver's manner had changed since an archbishop had gotten into his car. The traffic was less congested now, and the powerful car made swift progress through the broad streets of the city.

"You should be riding up front with the driver, you know."

There was a pause before the laughter came. "Rudy!" he cried. "How on earth did you remember a thing like that?"

"It's the sort of thing that sticks in a girl's mind. It gave me a sense of power."

"Power to lead astray."

"That too."

The Reverend Rudolph G. Bandas, rector of the seminary, had addressed the student body once a week. During a memorable spring, he gave a series of lectures on conduct appropriate to a priest.

"Scandal, gentlemen", he keened. "Scandal."

Everyone did an imitation of the rector, a hand laid upon the cheek, the little finger fluttering before the mouth and coming to rest on the lower lip as eyes widened with significance.

"It is necessary that scandal come, gentlemen, but woe to him through whom it comes."

The rector, it emerged—and it was this that entered into the lasting lore of the institution—the rector would not permit even his mother to ride beside him in his car. He placed her squarely in the middle of the back seat. No one could mistake their excursions for anything other than what they were.

"His mother!"

They decided that his sister, if he had one, rode on the back bumper and that unrelated females must be consigned to a trailer pulled behind the car.

Maureen had surprised herself by bringing up that memory.

Perhaps it had been elicited by the sight of Tom Lannan darting out of the entrance of the building and pulling open the back door.

"It's been ages since I've been kissed by an archbishop."

"The kiss of peace."

"*Osculum pacis.*"

His brows lifted in delighted surprise. "I thought the vernacular had triumphed."

At the embassy she had been told of Bruno's in Arlington, a place he didn't know, thus conferring on her the freedom of the neighborhood.

"Fitzgerald", she explained.

"Hmmm?"

"F. Scott. In *Gatsby.*"

"Ah, yes. I had forgotten your St. Catherine's education."

During her sophomore year, Maureen had read St. Paul's famous author and made the tour of the houses in which he had lived.

The restaurant in Arlington was noisy and young, not at all what Maureen had been led to expect by the recommendation it had received. She suggested they go somewhere else, but Tom took as a challenge the hostess' doubtful look when Maureen asked how long it would be before they got a table. Whatever he pressed into her palm settled that, and another donation saved them from having to wait at the bar.

"I'm sorry", she said, when they were seated at a table perhaps four feet square and placed dangerously close to the route waiters took to and from the kitchen.

"I like it."

"You know you don't."

"I wouldn't have worn clericals, that's all."

So he was aware of the attention his Roman collar drew, the reactions ranging from surprise through curiosity to disdain or indifference. Why did he seem an improbable witness to the faith in the post–Christian atmosphere of the Arlington restaurant?

"What other nuggets besides Rudy can you drag up out of the past?"

Because of the letter she had recently received from Karen's ancient mother, the summer Tom had worked at the Catholic Youth Center occurred to her. For him it was meant to be a little foretaste of the ministry to come. The apostolate to the libidinous young. Maureen had been a regular at the center throughout high school and worked part time for Fr. Parente since her sophomore year at St. Kate's. Would Tom Lannan need any help in remembering Karen?

"Do you remember our campaign against going steady?"

Going steady! A drumbeat of warning against dating one person exclusively had come from Joe Parente. The practice was seen as hastening the process of courtship and encouraging a premature pairing off that was a kind of engagement. Delicately touched on was the danger of intimacy, by which would have been meant at most prolonged kissing and a little timid groping while fully clothed. Maureen could have cried out at the innocence of those days. Only they hadn't always been innocent. Think of Karen.

"What was that all about?" Tom asked.

"Don't you remember?"

"I am trying to remember the director. The Italian priest?"

"Parente."

"Are you sure?"

"Yes."

It was Fr. Parente who had confronted Tom about Karen, speaking to him as priest to seminarian, as older man to younger.

"What I remember are summer evenings on the porch at your parents' house. Frank, Jim Morrow, myself. And you, of course."

"When you were all at Nazareth Hall."

"Jim has written a book."

"Oh, I know. In Rome it is studied as the key to the American enigma."

"Do they find us enigmatic?"

A harried waitress came to a stop beside them, puffed away a strand of hair that had fallen across her forehead, and asked what they wanted. Tom had only glanced at the menu, but he rattled off an order without hesitation.

"Okay?" he asked Maureen.

"Okay."

"Any hesitation and we might not have seen her again for hours."

Maureen was no longer interested in Memory Lane. Thoughts of Tom and Karen brought back the more recent memory of the letter from Karen's mother. Facing him in the busy restaurant, she wanted to believe that Mrs. Christiansen's claim was incredible.

"Tell me all about the archbishop of Washington."

"We should have gotten together before this. I get to Rome rather frequently, you know."

"How would I know?"

"Of course you wouldn't. Those trips are not a barrel of laughs. Appointments, cajoling, bootlicking, then out to Fiumicino and home."

"No time to call old friends."

"I'll make a point of it from now on."

"Oh, don't be too apologetic. Jim Morrow never called me either. After the fact, I learned that he had spent extended periods in Rome."

"With his family."

"While he was working on his book."

"He lost his wife a year ago."

"I hadn't heard." Why hadn't Frank told her? Out of consideration of her own loss? "I never met her."

"You would have liked her."

"Have the two of you kept in touch?"

"Until recently."

"Tom, it's a very good book."

"A well-told tale. Of course it is. Written as only Jim could write it. Some critics say it is merely a more eloquent version of what a dozen strident volumes have said."

"Are you one of those critics?"

He shook his head slowly. "No. No. Style and substance are not that separable. It is a very convincing and generally fair indictment. It puts me and quite a few others in the dock. You'll understand that it is not pleasant to read that you have been selling out the Church in order to ready her for the twenty-first century."

"I'd like to see him again."

"Give him a call. Go see him"

"In Indiana? It's hard enough to get back to Minnesota."

"Do you still have family there? I mean, besides Frank."

"Both of my daughters live there."

"Tell me about them."

His interest in Teresa and Jennie and their families seemed unfeigned. Maureen felt guilty at how feeble her own interest was. What kind of mother would begrudge a few hours' flying time to be with her children and grandchildren?

"They never really knew Sean."

Tom fell silent, and she was grateful. She could not bear to think about it now. "That's something you and Jim have in common, Maureen. You're both widowed."

Later she would wonder what subterranean association of ideas had led him to tell her then of the White House request that he advise them on a new ambassador to the Vatican. He seemed to think the overture was a sop, unworthy of what the administration owed the Church.

"Not that my intention in the Norman case was to influence the election. If I did. What I said was reprinted in *L'Osservatore Romano*."

"I saw it."

"Well?"

He leaned toward her, clearly expecting praise, and for a moment she was inclined to oblige him, for old time's sake, but it was really more friendly to tell him how many in Rome had seen his reply to Guevara as undercutting the Church and its teaching. Tom was clearly not prepared to learn that his sermon had seemed mushy and sentimental, an obscuring of moral doctrine. His decision not to argue the point clearly followed a brief struggle with himself.

"It's the bane of these times, Maureen. There are always labels, sides, factions. One has to be this or that."

"Hot or cold?"

"Ouch."

"You are a liberal, Tom."

"Am I? I'll tell you a secret. I cannot stand liberals, as a group. But then I can't stand conservatives either. And don't say that is being lukewarm. These partisan divisions are a result of politicizing the Church."

"One of Jim Morrow's major themes."

"And he's right."

"*He* should be your ambassadorial appointment, Tom!"

"Come on."

"I'm serious." She leaned toward him across the table. "This is an inspiration. They would love it in Rome. And it would not hurt you either, you know."

"Jim Morrow, diplomat?"

Maureen had surprised herself when she made the suggestion, but now, as Tom Lannan himself was doing, she turned it over in her mind, and it seemed an inspiration indeed.

"If you were instrumental in putting him there, your stock at the Vatican would go up where it is currently low."

"Jim would never leave the academic life."

"You could find out."

CHAPTER TWO

I

Monsignor Eugene Wales was having trouble getting an answer from the number for James Morrow he had extracted from the secretary of his academic department, a persistently inquisitive woman reluctant to divulge the information without some clue as to the reason for the call from Washington.

Does NEH mean anything to you?" he finally asked.

"Aha."

To himself he explained that they were the first three letters in the family name of Jawaharal Nehru. He jotted down the number she gave him in a confidential stage whisper.

"That's his lake place."

"Aha."

Meanwhile, the ineffable Fr. Leach slid into the office with the disjointed agility of a Dr. Seuss character. He folded himself into a chair and held his mug of coffee with both hands, his eyes traveling over the desktop.

"I have been perusing the book."

"The book."

Leach threw back his head and spoke theatrically. "*The Decline and Fall of the American Catholic Church.*"

"Just getting around to it?"

"The time is propitious, wouldn't you say?" God only knew

what Leach had heard, if anything. "This is the day the Lord has made... He gets most of it in, of course." Leach made this sound like a concession.

"You sound hesitant."

"The devil is not in the details. What do they add up to, that's the thing."

"You don't like the book."

Leach's brow rose, then his eyes, then his head. "He is a traitor to his class."

"How so?" This was a surprise. Wales would have thought that Leach, if he had picked up some rumor about Morrow, would have been overjoyed.

"The phrase, you may not recall, was used of Franklin Delano Roosevelt by his patrician Duchess County neighbors. When he became the ally of the unions and the foe of self-reliant citizens."

"What does Morrow have to say about unions?"

Leach made a face. "An analogy, Monsignor, requires that the mind see the similarity between dissimilar things. James Morrow has long been thought to be a conservative, that is, on the side of the theologically orthodox."

"Thought to be? Whoever thought otherwise?"

"He gave every indication that is what he was, true. One or two of his things will stand the test of time. This book will not. He waffles. He brokers differences where this cannot be done, where the differences are irreconcilable. One could almost believe that he is extending the olive branch to people like yourself and our beloved Archbishop Lannan."

Wales decided that somehow Leach had learned of what was afoot. "What would you think of Morrow as ambassador to the Vatican?"

Leach was incapable of expressing surprise, but something in his expression suggested that he had not expected the question. Regret for letting the cat out of the bag was overwhelmed by the pleasure of telling Leach what he had apparently never even guessed. But Leach had begun to nod his head in rhythm with his thinking. "It might be his salvation. Yes, yes. An ultramontane belongs on the far side of the mountain."

That was a dubious theory, as Wales undertook to tell him, relying on a passage in Morrow's book in which the historian pointed out that a common factor in the lives of the most prominent dissenting theologians was that they had studied in Rome and received Roman degrees, and not always from the Jesuit Gregorian University.

"Remember Luther, Father."

Leach's eyes widened. "A moment ago you refused to follow a simple analogy. How on earth did you get to Luther?"

The allusion had been Morrow's. The future reformer's visit to Rome had left an indelible impression.

"Another reason not to like this book", Leach said. "Schism is not justified because of the abuses of others."

Leach's reaction was Wales' first direct experience with conservative discontent with a one-time hero. Morrow's history of the Church in the United States since the Second Vatican Council, so long awaited by his peers, despite its title, had turned out to be an almost evenhanded account rather than a wholesale condemnation of the changes, reforms, and new directions that had come about since 1965. Had Morrow suspected that most people were bored with the extended controversy? Perhaps it was best to think of these past decades as a shakedown cruise of the newly refitted barque of Peter. There had been causalities, of course, and there had been mistakes. Undeniably, there had been scandals. They were all there in Morrow's book, but they did not stand starkly alone on the narrative horizon. He had balanced them with accounts of genuine renewal and signs of hope. Wales laid this out for the cadaverous Leach.

"I would not take much comfort from that if I were you, Monsignor Wales. Would you yourself base a claim that the postconciliar Church is redeemed because Opus Dei and the Legionaries of Christ flourish in it?"

"Maybe we should discuss the book after you finish it."

"I am not sure that I will."

A thought began to grow in Wales' mind that there could be overt conservative opposition to Morrow's nomination as Vatican ambassador. That could assure smooth sailing and gain credit from all sides for Thomas Lannan once his role in the matter was discreetly divulged.

When Wales finally got through to Morrow at his Michigan retreat, he switched the call to the archbishop, but stayed on the phone. This was his usual practice as secretary unless it was made clear that the call was to be entirely private.

"Jim, how would you like to be American ambassador to the Vatican?"

There was silence on the other end of the line.

"Are you there, Jim?"

"Why do you ask the question?"

"Once I have your answer, I will make another important phone call."

"Is it in your gift?"

"That would be putting it strongly."

"Too strongly?"

"No. I don't think so."

"Well."

"Jim, you would adorn the post. And I know it would be a great consolation to you to be your country's representative to the Holy Father."

"Why me?"

"Why not? would be a better question. You've finished your book. It has been received with a great deal of acclaim, and deservedly so."

"And a great deal of criticism."

"You're not concerned about getting a leave of absence, I hope."

Listening in, Wales was struck by the way Morrow held back. Imagine someone hesitating to let his name go forward for such a sinecure. Under the pad on Lannan's desk was Wales' memo listing possible candidates, and Morrow's name had not been on it. Any of the others would crawl through the wire to accept the nomination. All liberals, of course, or progressives, as Lannan preferred to call himself and his friends. What would be their reaction to Morrow's nomination? What would the champions of Maud Erickson say?

"Tom, I appreciate your thinking of me for this, but I have to confess I am surprised. You're not getting sentimental in your dotage, are you? If you do have a say in this appointment, I should think you'd be pushing Maud Erickson."

Reviewers had considered Morrow's treatment of women to be the great weakness of his book. Clearly the author had not participated in the great consciousness-raising that had taken place in the last quarter of the twentieth century. The section entitled "Come Into the Garden, Maud" had lampooned Erickson's dismissal of original sin as a sexist myth to subjugate women. She refused, she said, to rest her conception of the human race on a story about a naked couple stealing apples in a garden.

"Jim, you're my choice."

"But surely not your first choice."

What was this? Did Morrow imagine that others had turned down the nomination and Lannan was coming to him in desperation?

"My very first."

"When do you have to know?"

Wales could sense displeasure in Lannan's silence even if Morrow did not. Who could blame the archbishop now if he backed away from the idea? From those who learned of the offer, he would get credit for his magnanimity without having to confront the reaction to the nomination on the part of those who would feel betrayed.

"How much time would you like?"

"I'll call on Monday."

Monday! This was Wednesday. That meant days during which sponsors of other nominees would be exerting pressure on friends in the bishops' conference and in its sister organization, the United States Catholic Conference (USCC).

"Monday's fine", Lannan said brightly, not a trace of irony in his voice. "But why don't I call you?"

"As you like."

"Will you be at this number?"

"Yes, I'll be staying here."

2

James Morrow felt only half-guilty for not having voted in the presidential election. Whatever interest he might have had in the campaign did not survive the summer conventions. On the first Tuesday of November he had been at his summer place on Lake Powderhorn half-hoping he would be marooned by an early snow. Now on Wednesday, after the call from Tom Lannan, he sat at his computer as if he had an obligation to show that he did not regard his book as the last word.

Every writer writes with a particular reader in mind, whether imaginary or real, and the reader Jim Morrow had before his mind's eye during the decade he had been at work on *The Decline and Fall of the American Catholic Church* was old "Ibid" Cady, who had been his mentor as a graduate student at the Catholic University and the conscience of the American Catholic Historical Association until his death. He had been alive and alert when the early chapters of the book were written, and he was critical of Morrow's treatment of Modernism in what became the prologue, which traced the origins of the Council.

"Pius X called Modernism the sum of all heresies", Cady had said.

"I think I pointed that out."

"Of course you did. But do you believe it?"

"Yes."

"Your reader would never guess it."

Morrow decided to take pride in that. If Cady's baleful eye was always upon him as he wrote, he did not write exclusively for him. The division in the Church between conservatives and progressives had reached a point where it did not seem excessive to speak of a de facto schism. But Morrow wanted his ideological foes to accept the accuracy of what he wrote. Through 2,300 manuscript pages he sought to earn the mild disapproval of Cady because that would mean he could be read by anyone.

On the few occasions that he had published a portion of a chapter as an article or made use of his manuscript in preparing a paper for a conference, he had been whiplashed between the two sides. His fellow conservatives thought he was catering to dissenters, and the progressives were certain, no matter his current moderateness, that when the magnum opus finally appeared it would be an attack on them: this dictated the tactic of assuming that he meant what he had not said. He did not blame his enemies, though he intended to earn their grudging concession that he had gotten it right. And he began to take morose delectation in the dissatisfaction of his friends with what he was doing.

"How do you yourself see these events?" Jordan Boone the Dominican had asked him.

"I am trying to make them visible to others."

"But what do you take them to mean?"

"I am a historian, not a theologian."

"Meaning what?"

"I am trying to provide the basis for the kind of judgment you're asking me for. Has the direction the Church taken been for the good or for the bad, or is it a little bit of each? That is not for me to decide, not in this book."

"So you think that history is independent of and prior to appraisal?"

"I hope to lay out the sweep of events. I plan a final section that will cover the last ten years."

"Will that account be neutral too?"

"I will treat the last decade in the same way I did the Council— give as accurate and fair an account of events as I can. Of course, I will indicate how the actors themselves appraised what was happening. That will provide in part what you find missing."

Jordan developed the view that the very selection of events to narrate, the presentation of representatives of the "sides"— Boone did not himself consider that there were sides to these events—is itself appraisal. "If you attempt to treat them that way, events as they are prior to this or that interpretation, you have already taken a point of view, and I must add a dangerous one, on those events."

"What if I should say that I want to put a summary of events before the reader in somewhat the same way in which Aquinas put a survey of Christian doctrine before his reader in the *Summa theologiae*?"

"I would think you were making a bad joke. The *Summa* is an invitation to believers to reenact the thinking it conveys, a thinking that is already committed to the truth of Christian revelation. The dialectical appropriation of this is controlled by what has been revealed along with the authoritative interpretations and development of the *depositum fidei*. But your joke would be an important one, Jim, if you actually told it. It would make my point. Is the history of the Church to be written according to the same canons as secular history? Can the historian overlook the significance those events have for the believer—that is, their true significance?"

Morrow felt that he had indeed delivered himself into Jordan Boone's hands. Never argue theology with a Thomist, particularly when he is also a Dominican. Boone asked if Jim's ideal of history was the encyclopedia article, that is, the desire to know without knowing.

"A universal, neutral presentation by we know not whom?" Boone stopped himself. "Of course I am only a theologian, not a historian."

"Touché."

Jim Morrow had always had a limited appetite for the philosophy of history. Collingwood, Toynbee, and Spengler seemed slightly mad to him. Better the Tolstoy of *War and Peace* to those confident claims to discern the underlying pattern of events. The singular events themselves, the irreplaceable actors, the unpredictability of outcome—these are what fascinated him. Could he confidently see the big picture? The title of his book had been the suggestion of an editor, made first as a kind of joke, but then it had caught hold until he himself began to refer to the work in progress under that rubric. Yet his professional neutrality, to take Boone's word for it, went hand in hand with his personal conviction that in the wake of the Second Vatican Council the church in the United States had become gradually and all but imperceptibly Protestant. The parallel between the sixteenth century and postconciliar Germany,

54

which the great historian Hubert Jedin drew in a letter to the German bishops, seemed to Morrow the simple truth.

For that matter, in his heart of hearts, he conceded nothing to Cady and Boone and all the others. He was as ardent a papist as any of them, ultramontane in fact, and would have been content, like W. G. Ward, to have a fresh encyclical every morning with his breakfast. He had watched with dread the drift from Rome on the part of theologians, the secularization of the great Catholic institutions of higher learning, the defections from the priesthood and religious life, the scandals. His favorite writer on such matters was E. Michael Jones, the Savonarola of South Bend, whose jeremiads he savored as an adolescent might pornography. But he would never write that way himself. That was the style of the journalist, not the historian whose task was at once exacting and modest.

His apologia found its way into his preface. "Arguments reach conclusions but history never does. Its beginnings and endings are contrivances within which one must be as accurate as the subject permits."

Hegel might confuse his account with God's providence, but such Prussian presumption was repugnant to Morrow, and he was willing to suffer the criticism of his friends and the wariness of his foes.

Wolsey began to lick his hand, and Morrow patted the spaniel's narrow head. The dog had been a puppy when Morrow embarked on his great project. Like his master, he had grown old in the task: the eyes, sad from birth, seemed sadder now with a painfully acquired canine wisdom, and his muzzle sagged. There was nothing fancied in the arthritic slowness of the dog who, it was clear, wanted out.

Morrow pushed back from his desk, put on a jacket and a cap with "ND" emblazoned on it. No sun shone outside, and the fallen leaves looked simply dead. A stand of pine, non-deciduous, still obscured the view of the lake. At this season the lake might belong to him alone. All the other cottages along the shore were shut up now, buttoned down for winter.

"Are you up to a hike around the lake, Wolsey?"

The wagging tail engaged his rear end as well, and Wolsey almost scampered to the door.

Lake Powderhorn was in lower Michigan and large for these parts, though considerably smaller than Higgins Lake to the north of it. The owners' association that had been formed at the same time as the boat club had managed to prevent happening to Powderhorn what had happened to so many lakes within an hour's drive of the Indiana line. Others might be ringed by lots scarcely wider than a man's arm span, but here each cottage stood on lake frontage of two hundred feet and averaged an acre in area. Selfish, perhaps, forcing others farther north to other shores or to those grids off Lake Michigan where it took an act of faith to believe one was in proximity to water. The association had banned all motors from the lake, including auxiliary motors on sailboats. As a result, the lake had retained the air of a rural retreat. It was here that at least two-thirds of his book had been written.

Once outside, Wolsey made a quick tour of his territory, policing its borders, lifting a leg from time to time to seal again his claim. Morrow turned to look back at the cottage.

It had been a quarter of a century since he and Mabel had built it. The three children had been children indeed then, only Mary in school, Ken and Susan preschoolers. How easily he could imagine them at play there in the yard, down on the dock, in the water. And Mabel still somewhere inside doing the hundreds of things that women do.

Mabel had been dead three years, and his children were grown and gone. He had lived in the unspoken certainty that Mabel would outlive him and had been wholly unprepared when she fell ill and within a month was dead. Mary and her husband lived in Chicago, Susan was in her first job in a Minneapolis bank, Ken was a junior at Notre Dame. After the ordeal of the funeral that had brought out the solidarity of his colleagues and briefly made his children seem closer than ever before, he found himself definitively alone. Ken lived on campus; the house in South Bend seemed abandoned, not just empty. He dreaded the place, preferring his campus office or coming here to his summer cottage, which had always seemed haunted in the off season.

"You weren't meant to live alone, Dad", Mary said with the no-nonsense air she had inherited from her mother.

"I've heard that somewhere before."

"Oh?" Mary was miffed that she had not been the first to raise the issue.

"From God in Genesis."

Even her reaction to his faded professorial humor was her mother's. Throughout their married life, Mabel had conveyed the impression that they were really not permanent residents of South Bend. She preferred to think of it as exile, a sentence to be served, after which they would be paroled back to Minneapolis where they belonged. That conviction had somehow made it easier for her to accept death, as if dying in South Bend could not really be the end of one's life.

But it had been. Tom Lannan had flown out to say her funeral Mass, to the enormous astonishment of the administration.

"We were kids together" was all Morrow told the provost, who seemed to have drawn the assignment of finding out why one of the most liberal members of the hierarchy had come to mourn with a notorious campus conservative.

Tom had called this place Lake Vomit because of a visit during their first or second summer in which all the kids as well as Tom came down with flu. Jim alone had been spared, and he had lain in a hammock under the cottonwood reading Newman's *Apologia*. From time to time, a haggard Lannan would come to the screen door of the porch and look reproachfully at him.

"Why aren't you sick like a decent host?"

"I'm too weak to support germs."

Behind Tom in the cottage there was a scampering sound and then the slam of the bathroom door. There had been just the one bathroom then for everyone to be sick in, and that perhaps prolonged and certainly emphasized the ailment. Tom had come for ten days, but only the final four were what they had hoped for.

"This lake reminds me of Johanna, Jim."

"There's no resemblance at all, except that they're both full of water."

"Isn't that an island out there?"

It was. The two lakes did have that in common, although the island at Johanna was separated from shore by scarcely more than a distinction of reason and a footbridge, whereas Powderhorn's island was a hundred yards offshore.

Nazareth Hall, where they had been classmates, stood on the shore of Lake Johanna in what had then been a rural area north of St. Paul. The preparatory seminary of the archdiocese, it had been built in 1920 from the same plans as the Maryknoll seminary at Ossining, minus the pagoda-like flourishes on its tower. It comprised four years of high school and two of college, representing half of the twelve-year-long preparation for the priesthood. The other six years, two of philosophy and four of theology, were done in town at the major seminary built by Archbishop John Ireland at the foot of Summit Avenue on the banks of the Mississippi. Lannan and Morrow and Bailey had been thirteen years old when they entered Nazareth Hall. Lannan and Bailey had gone through the whole program to ordination, though they studied theology in Rome rather than in St. Paul. Jim Morrow, having decided after the college years at the Hall that he was not meant for the priesthood, left the major seminary to work for his doctorate at the University of Minnesota.

Jim too had thought of Lake Johanna when he and Mabel first looked at this property. The reason he discouraged Tom's comparison was that his old friend had by then adopted what was to become a widespread condemnation of the preconciliar seminary system.

"Imagine taking kids away from their families at thirteen."

"You survived."

"But at who knows what psychic cost?"

"Oh, come on. You were happy as a lark." Tom had settled into institutional life without difficulty. "You even defended the food."

"The food was good. Because of the slave labor in the kitchen."

Tom was not referring to the fact that students took turns waiting on tables, serving a week at a time and eating after the rest had risen and prayed and gone. In those days there were three hundred students in residence. Tom meant the German nuns whose convent was a wing that opened off the kitchen.

Jim Morrow was willing to admit that his own memories of those years at the Hall were unrealistically positive, but he simply did not recognize the school that Lannan and Bailey remembered in the horrified tones of survivors of the Bataan death march. But then, during and after the Council, the devastation of seminary education had to be justified, and the preferred way was to suggest that the questionable new was supplanting something unimaginably worse. Had his reaction to such revisionism been the beginning of his desire to chronicle the postconciliar Church?

He began to collect clippings, to photocopy articles, and to read the various accounts of the conciliar sessions, accounts which had taken such an adversarial tone. He had no intention, at first, of treating the subject professionally. Church history was not his area of scholarly competence. He was an Americanist with a solid book on the Federalist Papers, an annotated edition of *Notes on Virginia*, and a grant to work on American colonial history. Keeping track of what was happening in the Catholic Church began as a hobby, a personal as opposed to a professional interest. Eventually he acknowledged to himself that it had become more than an avocation; it was now a consuming interest. Still, he kept what he was doing from friends and colleagues, something that would later be cited as the mask behind which he interviewed unsuspecting victims. An article in *Commonweal* in which he praised features of the preconciliar Church in an effort to counter the growing assumption that the thirties and forties and fifties had constituted a Dark Ages, caused a stir. He found himself described as a foe of the spirit of Vatican II.

The eventual label was conservative. He resented that, at first, having always thought of himself as liberal. He had read *Commonweal* since high school, for heaven's sake. Its editors had printed the article that became controversial, yet they now considered him a conservative for recalling the noble preconciliar times that had produced, among other things, *Commonweal*. Eventually nearly all the eminent liberals of the preconciliar period would find themselves transmuted into conservatives—Maritain, Bouyer, von Hildebrand, de Lubac, Danielou, Hans Urs von Balthasar, Flannery O'Connor. By comparison with such giants, his own case was a minor instance of a seismic shift.

It was possible to circle Lake Powderhorn on the path that ringed it: each cottage provided easement; no walls or fences extended to the water's edge. The lake itself looked metallic and cold, its surface seeming to waver between liquid and solid. They had hardly begun their walk when he heard the ringing of a telephone. Wolsey also heard it and stopped. Why did they both think it was his phone that rang? It could be any number of others. Wolsey regarded him with sad eyes, seeming to ask if their walk was to be canceled.

"Come on", Morrow said, resuming his walk.

The wind at his back was brisk and penetrating and bore with it the sound of that ringing telephone until a turn in the shoreline cut it off. The path he was on took him back to Rome.

During the 1990–1991 school year, he had been on sabbatical in Rome, working mornings in the Vatican library, enjoying Rome with Mabel the rest of the day. The girls were enrolled in Marymount, and Ken went to Notre Dame International, and that left the days to them. They would settle down to an extended Roman lunch at an outdoor table, often at Sabitini's, across from the porched, imposing Santa Maria de Trastevere that dominated the square. Cats slithered beneath the tables; a wandering musician played soulfully on the hauteboy he had carefully assembled, drawing expectant attention from some diners, being ignored by most. He was careful not to catch the eye of a waiter, lest he be sent on his way.

What had he played? Jim Morrow had no ear for music and almost no memory for it. It was the sense of well-being, of contentment and peace, that came back to him. Theirs had not been a perfect marriage, of course. There had been memorable quarrels in Rome itself. Once Mabel had dumped a cup of coffee into his lap when he had ignored her directions and turned into a street that grew progressively narrower until the sides of the van were almost scraping the buildings that lined it. With this ultimate proof that he had taken the wrong street yet stubbornly kept going on, he got a cup of warmish coffee in his lap as Q.E.D.

Mabel was as surprised by what she had done as he was. In

the back, the kids waited, horrified. And then he had burst out laughing. He had been angry—close to swinging at her—yet out of nowhere that laughter had come, and soon the kids were whooping it up and Mabel was dabbing away at his trousers while people came to look through the windshield at these crazy foreigners.

What would it be like to return to Rome as his country's ambassador to the Holy See? He had been far more surprised by Tom Lannan's question than he had let on. Surprised and—how to put it? Insulted, was too strong; perhaps resentful. He was not really flattered by a purely ceremonial post. It smacked of patronage and deals, particularly because of Lannan's role in it. God knows what favor Tom had done for the administration to be granted a say in this appointment. Morrow had favored Whitney's opponent, George Astor. At least the man saw abortion as a moral as well as a political issue. Morrow had lent his name to a "Catholics for Astor" committee, completely honorific, but still not something that should commend him to the administration.

Walking beside the lake with Wolsey, he remembered that Jacques Maritain had served as French ambassador to the Vatican after World War II, but that did not seem precedent enough when he recalled who else would be his predecessors in the post. The French had a distinguished history of diplomats who were more than diplomats, St. John Perse, Claudel. In the nineteenth century, men of letters had sought to serve as American consuls, among them both Hawthorne and Howells. To let his name go forward would be a kind of selling out; he would become a chip played by the NCCB, and his conservative critics would doubtless see this as a payoff for the lack of *anathema sit*'s in *The Decline and Fall of the American Catholic Church.*

The woman who called on Friday identified herself as a friend of his daughter Mary. "Janet Fortin. I work at the White House."

"The White House!"

"I have just landed in Grand Rapids, and I'd like to drive down and talk with you."

"This place isn't easy to find."

"I'll find it. What's the best way?"

There were maps Mabel had made to guide guests to the cottage, but they were of help only to those coming from the south, west, or east. He didn't mention the maps, certain she would ask him to fax her a copy. She repeated the instructions he gave her and asked him what the mileage was.

"I should be there in an hour then. Is that okay?"

"I'll be looking for you."

An hour did not seem much time in which to ponder what most certainly was her mission. The call from Tom Lannan had come out of the blue, but this one was less of a surprise. Not that he had expected to hear from anyone else before he called Lannan on Monday. He had wanted the weekend for reflection, but he realized he had already made up his mind.

Speak Italian like a diplomat? He would rather just get by as he always had. The thought of being in Rome was attractive, certainly, though not as attractive as it would have been if Mabel were still alive. What would have been her reaction?

It was the thought that he would somehow be Lannan's creature if he let his name go forward that decided him.

3

Janet Fortin's first reaction when Gene Wales mentioned Morrow's name was surprise, but almost immediately she saw the shrewdness of the suggestion. Nothing coming from the office of the current president of the National Conference of Catholic Bishops wore its meaning on its face. Proposing Morrow seemed unlikely, but refreshing her mind on the professor gave Janet the beginning of a glimmer of Lannan's motive. And talking to Gene Wales helped.

Initially, reasons not to nominate Morrow leapt from the page, whether you thought of him as Lannan's nominee or the President's. Morrow's conservatism was not just ecclesiastical, so he qualified as an enemy of both the archbishop and Whitney. When is it to your advantage to honor an enemy? Janet had first heard Morrow's name when she was a student at Georgetown, but that was because his daughter Mary was her classmate and eventual debating opponent on political matters. They had been on different sides on the student health clinic brouhaha. What else could the daughter of James Morrow be but a conservative?

"What do you think of his book?" she asked Wales, watching for the dimpling of the corners of his mouth before he spoke.

"It's fair."

"That's faint praise."

"I would call it high praise. It could signal the end of advocacy history, at least among Church historians."

"You mean he didn't rough you guys up as much as you feared?"

"Didn't he? Read what he wrote on the NCCB and USCC. If he had his way, we would be disbanded, our assets returned to the people, and our headquarters turned over to the D.C. government for public housing."

"He's not very consistent then, wanting to bolster the welfare state."

"I doubt that politics interests him at all. Secular politics. His criticisms take their cue from Ratzinger."

"You're giving me reasons why Archbishop Lannan would not suggest his name to the President."

"He hit the conservatives too, and almost as hard. The important thing is that he found positive things to say. The criticism was meant to clear the way for something better, not just score points."

Gene gave her the number at Morrow's Michigan retreat. "No need to call him before Monday."

"Monday!"

The administration's intention was to make this one of the first announcements in an effort to get the second term off on a different foot. The Vatican post had been vacant since July, but the President had been persuaded not to act on it before reelection. If he had been defeated, his nominee might very well have withdrawn, adding another minor embarrassment to defeat.

"He wants time to think."

Janet took a deep breath, the better to put the question calmly. "Are you saying that you've already spoken to him about it?"

Monsignor Wales immediately saw the reason for her question. The corners of his mouth dimpled. "He's an old friend of Archbishop Lannan's."

"I hope he didn't offer him the post."

"He wouldn't want to make such a surprising suggestion without getting some inkling of how the proposed nominee would react."

That of course was Janet's job, but it was not the matter of turf that concerned her. When Wales told her of the call Lannan had made to his old friend, alarm bells went off in her head. All the administration needed to take the air out of the post-election euphoria was to have word go out that the National Conference of Catholic Bishops was appointing the new American ambassador to the Vatican. The thin hope of a successful second term, despite the margin of victory that had firmed at slightly more than 100,000 votes, would begin to evaporate before inauguration.

65

In Janet's experience, nominees consulted their friends, the word got out, there was no way to stop it. If this got to the media before the President had even heard of the suggestion, she would be the target of justified anger for preempting his decision. With the prospect of four more years, the long knives would be out, and she had no illusions about job security in the White House Annex. She came around her desk and took Monsignor Wales by the elbow.

"Thanks for letting me know right away."

"Does that mean you like the idea?"

It meant she had some fast consulting to do before she got out to Morrow's Michigan lake place. When Gene Wales had looked into her office ten minutes before, she had the thought they might have dinner together, but that was out of the question now.

She zapped through a memo on her computer to the appointments secretary's secretary and then got the travel office.

"Powderhorn, Michigan? Where the hell is that?"

"You're the travel agent."

She was booked through Chicago and legged back to Grand Rapids, where she could pick up a rental car. On the flight out, she studied a map of lower Michigan and flipped around in *The Decline and Fall of the American Catholic Church.*

It was the account of the Church prior to the Council that fascinated Janet. This was the Church her parents had known, and Morrow's pages on those times made them seem almost exciting. But of course one of his avowed aims had been to set the record straight on the preconciliar Church in order to give a more accurate presentation of the decades since 1965. He himself would have grown up in those times, of course, given his birth in 1949. Although the opening section was billed as a corrective of revisionist accounts, it had the same tone as the rest of the book—balanced, above the fray, intimate, and surprisingly artful. Was history supposed to be this interesting?

Janet liked the way he put the familiar and unfamiliar side by side.

Had there really been such a fight about contraceptives? Nineteen sixty-eight was a pivotal year in Morrow's account. That was when Pope Paul VI had written an encyclical reaffirming the Church's prohibition of all artificial means of contraception. Janet had never heard of the controversy it generated. Presumably a later Pope had taken it all back. As far as she knew, there was no objection to a Catholic's using the pill, for heaven's sake. The great opponents of the pill were the Greens, not the Catholics, except of course those Greens who happened to be Catholic too. The argument had to do with interfering with the ecology.

But Morrow wrote of it as an unresolved conflict, at least on the level of discussion. Janet's sense that most Catholics her age would be as surprised by this as she, was confirmed by the data given in the book. Imagine condemning contraception. It was like reading about Galileo.

Janet Fortin was a daughter of the East, but she had seen a lot of the country, particularly during the two Whitney campaigns, and she had marveled at the diversity and strangeness of the land: the backcountry of Louisiana, northern California, a little town like Helena, the largest in its state, although a city of any size is dwarfed by mountains—just look at Salt Lake. The Midwest was not only strange; it seemed like another country altogether, as alien as Canada just because on the surface it seemed so much the same. This sense returned as she drove south from Grand Rapids. Everything was all right until she left the main highway and headed west. The road rose and fell, following a serpentine course through hills just high enough to give an extended view of the countryside before the road dipped down again. In the middle of nowhere a car agency loomed, flags flying from dozens of poles, ablaze with lights, but no sign of life. Around another turn she came upon a cattle auction, the pens teeming with animals. Various rigs and trucks and pickups were parked, and there was a general air of slow-motion activity.

Many towns were explained by the lakes they had grown up around. The lakes themselves were ringed by cabins and cottages, like bathers' lockers on a European beach. Janet began to feel melancholy coming on. Would she find James Morrow in such a place?

His cottage was different because his lake was different. Janet could almost imagine herself in such a setting, maybe even enjoying it. The man coming toward her from the cottage had to be Morrow.

"Your daughter Mary introduced us once", she said, putting out her hand. "Janet Fortin."

"When would that have been?"

"At our graduation. You gave the commencement address."

"That's a long time ago."

"Thanks a lot."

His lips didn't part when he smiled, and his eyes were ironic as he studied her. Under this scrutiny she realized that she had developed a professional manner that was a combination of flirty and hands-off, the suggestion being that high times were to be had—but alas these were business hours. It was a manner she used even with Gene Wales, but of course that was different.

"Do you see Mary anymore?"

"No. I did call her before coming out here."

"Why?"

"I wanted to know the best way to approach you." She said it matter-of-factly, keeping the girlishness out of her tone, surprised that it took an effort. Had she become such a Washington girl after all, the kind Casey in the press room called DC/DC? Of course Morrow knew why she had come; he had been called by Lannan, but she did not want to start the discussion there in the driveway.

"What a nice place!"

He turned to look at the house and the lake beyond. "Come on. I'll show you around." He stopped. "Did you plan to stay?"

"Stay?"

"Over."

Like an idiot she did not understand at first, and when she did, she denied any intention of spending the night under the same roof with him; she realized that she was refusing what had never been even remotely intended.

"The reason I ask is that mornings here are best, particularly at this time of year. But then I've come to prefer autumn generally." He paused to see if she might say something. "I have the lake all to myself then."

Had he expected her to say something about his age? When he had first come out of the cottage and walked toward her car, moving slowly, leaning forward, the sweater seemed to hang loosely on him, and his graying hair looked as if he had spent the morning running his hands through it. He had not shaved, and the stubble on his face was white. She imagined him with a beard and decided he would look like a Spanish grandee by El Greco. His manner was professorial. He was wise rather than old, she thought, influenced by the passages from his book she had been reading. And he was still in his fifties.

They went around the cottage and down to the dock where a freezing Janet half-listened to Morrow talk about the lake, the neighbors, how long they'd had their place here, the changes they had seen. Finally they went inside where he had coffee on, thank God. She drank half a cup in a swallow, wanting the feel of its hot passage down her throat, and then sat back.

"I am here on behalf of the President. He instructs me to ask you if you would be interested in serving as our ambassador to the Vatican."

"I'm flattered."

"We think you are the perfect choice. Past appointees have been various, but at least one other was a professor."

"Tom Melady."

"Of course he had held another ambassadorial post before going to Rome."

"I have never been accused of being diplomatic."

"You are recognized as the leading historian of the Church in this country. And we're told that you have the respect of all factions."

He dipped his head as if to change the subject. "I am not a wealthy man."

"Doesn't matter. Unlike other posts, this one involves almost no personal expenditures on the part of the ambassador. The fact that you yourself are Catholic is a plus. Your predecessor was not. Perhaps he found it less interesting because of that. You've lived in Rome, haven't you?"

"On sabbatical, yes."

"And you know the city and the language."

"Latin?"

Janet liked his self-deprecating humor. And she had the impression that he wanted to prolong this exploratory part of the interview, treating her proposal as an amusing academic problem. Was he interested? She couldn't tell, but his willingness to talk about it suggested that he was. The fear that had brought her here, that Archbishop Lannan had committed the President without authorization and might even have floated the rumor of Morrow's nomination, faded.

The day had been cloudy, but now the overcast darkened, and evening came on rapidly. Asking if she meant to stay overnight had seemed merely polite, but now she wondered what time it would be when she got back to the airport at Grand Rapids. It was a two-stop flight to Washington no matter how she went, and from National it was at least half an hour to her apartment. Postponing the ordeal of that return trip had its attractions. Even if she didn't stay at Lake Powderhorn, she would doubtless have to spend the night in an airport motel in Grand Rapids.

"Will you need time to think it over?"

"No."

"Then you are willing?"

He shook his head. "No. Unwilling. Flattering as this is, I frankly cannot think of a single reason why the President should offer such a plum to me. And it is a plum. I could make a list of people who would love to have it."

"I have already stated the President's reason. He thinks you are the one for the post."

"He doesn't know me."

"His advisers do."

"You?"

"Yes. I am White House liaison with religious leaders. I pride myself that I am pretty well informed about the current state of the Church in this country."

"Tell me about it."

She turned her head and looked at him askance. "I don't pretend to know as much as you do. A good part of what I know I got from your book."

"I'm serious. Forget about my book. How would you describe the current state of the Church?"

Suddenly she felt as she had a week before graduation when she asked herself what she really knew after four long years of college. Her mind had seemed a moonscape across which vagrant winds had moved, uprooting anything remotely like an idea. Names, words, questions, authors—these had tumbled across the terrain, but they had not formed part of any whole that made up an understanding of herself and the world. Morrow's question conjured up that same moonscape.

"You think it's pretty bad", she said.

"It's not a matter of opinion. I put a good deal of work into giving an accurate factual account. It is simply a fact, an accumulation of facts, that the Church is only a shadow of what it was when I was young. You must have noticed a similar unraveling, young as you are."

"I am as old as Mary."

"As young as Mary."

This was not a discussion she welcomed. His daughter was married and a mother. If he wanted to talk about his specialty, fine; he was the authority and she was willing to listen, as long as a chance remained that she could return with his agreement to let his name go forward.

"Do you practice your faith?" he asked.

"How do you mean?"

"Do you go to Mass on Sunday, confess your sins regularly, accept Church teaching?"

"Wow."

"I developed the habit of asking direct questions while doing research for my book. Imagine that your answer to the question is no, in whole or in part. Once that would have called into question your right to call yourself a Catholic. But most Catholics would answer my question negatively now. That would have been unimaginable a half century ago. A Church made up of Catholics who do not accept Catholicism is, to put it mildly, in a state of decline. Imagine what it would be like if most members of the American Society of Chemists rejected the periodic table of elements."

"It is still the largest denomination in this country, unless we bunch all Protestants together."

"Most Catholics have become Protestants. I have tested this. If you ask Catholics their opinion of what Luther taught without identifying the source of the teachings, they accept it. A majority. Nonetheless, they would be startled to be told they had become Protestants."

"I don't think I'm a Protestant."

"Perhaps Pelagian would be more accurate. Of course I don't mean that anyone fervently accepts what Luther taught. It's just that they find it as attractive and plausible as any other description of what they believe. Luther himself would have been appalled by such closet Lutherans. For him it was a matter of life or death. Of eternal life. For the present generation, it is a matter of live and let live."

There was more. The primacy of conscience—"Christianity is whatever I say it is"—characterized Catholics of the day.

"Do you like risotto?" he asked suddenly.

"Who's he?"

He laughed. "I was referring to what I can offer you for supper. I learned to make it in Rome."

"Sounds wonderful. I'll help."

The invitation seemed to bode well so far as his decision went, no matter his earlier statement.

4

The Second Vatican Council ended in 1965, but even while it was still in session there had been a deemphasis of the Renaissance splendor that had surrounded the papacy. Pius XII had been carried into St. Peter's on a sedilia, swaying high about the adulating crowd. In one famous photograph, just after the war, with the basilica full of G.I.'s, he had stood as he was being carried in on the *sedia gestatoria,* arms spread wide, as if he were about to soar over their heads. John XXIII continued to appear in such style, wearing the massive triple crown.

After the Council, such pomp and circumstance were regarded as an insult to a world in which many were impoverished and starving. The usual suggestions that the contents of the Vatican museums be sold off and the money given to the poor had been made. Cardinals no longer received the traditional red hat, which in any case was never worn but hung high in the prelate's church after his death, there to rot away with time. *Sic transit gloria mundi*. The cardinal's regalia too was simplified, a biretta of appropriate color substituting for the red hat in the ceremony of installation. A small thing in itself, perhaps, but the liturgy too, even when correctly done, had been drained of mystery and had become a social occasion.

Thomas Lannan approved of all this; he had been convinced by liturgists who told him that the quality of worship had improved; he had learned to discount the claims of theologians, and their critics. Who was it that said that Christ did not become man in order that man might become a theologian? He smiled, until he realized he had read that in Jim Morrow's book. A quote from Ambrose? But he refused to be annoyed. He was seeking to enlist Jim Morrow in his campaign to get the red hat.

It was not the costume he hankered for but the status it signified. True enough, there was a partial and unheralded retention of some of the awe-inspiring aspects of the episcopal office. A pontifical Mass, with the archbishop with his crosier in hand, wearing a miter on his head and the pallium around his neck, was undeniably an impressive event, and the celebrant obviously something more than a simple priest. People, it turned out, liked it. They did not consider it undemocratic. And bishops loved it more than they would admit.

At Conference meetings, usually held in a posh hotel, bishops looked like any other group of conventioneers. Black business suits offset the Roman collars, and the chains of office were tucked half out of sight, the pectoral cross dropped into the inside pocket of the suit jacket. A group of managers discussing the state of the corporation. And upstairs afterward, in the hospitality rooms, good Scotch and better bourbon was drunk by men who had the capacity to hold their liquor. Oh, there was still the dwindling clique of conservatives as well as the little band of sanctimonious teetotalers who made a religion out of the environment. Twice they had come perilously close to pushing through a pastoral on ecology that had included a blast at artificial contraceptives.

"These are not the arguments of *Humanae vitae*", DeLucca had insisted, working his mouth. "It's not the same as pesticides." But people who hugged trees would not see the distinction. Who would understand Bernardin's allusion to a seamless garment?

"It will stir it all up again."

Over the years, practice and the quiet collusion of the clergy had made the official condemnation of contraception a dead letter, but enemies of the Church continued to raise the specter of overpopulation and tried to lay it at the Church's door. Senator DeWitt, a ferocious bigot, didn't help, quoting with obvious relish from magisterial documents declaring masturbation, fornication, and homosexuality abominations against the law of God. That was worse than having Crowe, an equally ferocious Catholic, answer probing questions with a simple yes, as when a reporter wanted to know if he accepted such condemnations. Just yes. After which the silence grew as the questioner let the answer comment on itself.

"The Church's moral teaching has not been rescinded", Fr. Leach said in his piping voice, squirming in his chair. "Except in seminaries, Catholic colleges, confessionals, and marriage preparation courses, that is."

"No need to taunt those outside the fold, Father."

"I was referring to misleading those within it."

Leach must have known that on such matters the Conference as well as the USCC had an impeccable record. Nothing taught by Rome had failed to be repeated or accepted in writing in Washington. It was a difference of styles. Rome spoke as if it were calling the world to order, a world which, like it or not, turned a deaf ear to the Holy See. Whatever rhetorical capital the present pontiff had inherited, he had squandered in endless travel and countless documents. The tarmac of too many airports had been kissed for anyone even to notice anymore, yet he had kept on going, dropping down out of the sky to smaller and smaller crowds. Except in Africa and Asia.

"How's young Leach doing?" Austin Fenny, bishop of Toledo, had asked Lannan.

"An amazing young man."

"Sound as a dollar."

"Are you taking him away from us?"

Fenny threw back his head and laughed. Of course. He had persuaded Lannan to bring Leach to Washington only to get him off his own back.

"What did he do in Toledo?"

"Caused a riot wherever he went. From the pulpit he assured the faithful that perhaps four-fifths of them were in a state of mortal sin. Because they use contraceptives. He did this in three parishes before I assigned him to the seminary."

"The seminary!"

"He needed an articulate as well as hostile audience."

Lannan nodded. Fenny had always stood firm whenever things got rough in the Conference.

"He has proved to be a moderating influence, Austin."

But nothing would remove the grin from Bishop Fenny's face.

A smile formed on Lannan's own face as he thought of the bishop of Toledo. How he envied the man's contentment with his minor diocese. Once he had marveled at the ease with which classmates had settled into parish work with the obvious intention of staying put for the rest of their lives. By contrast, he was a driven man. His manner did not show it; he was sure of that. He had cultivated an exterior that suggested that he would have been happy to be assigned to the faculty of the St. Paul Seminary, put in twenty years or so, to be rewarded with a debt-free parish, and the prospect of lots of golf and Florida in the winter. Once he would have imagined that being ordained bishop would have satisfied him, or archbishop. But now he was within reach of a red hat—it was owed to Washington if not to himself—and his heart would be restless until he had it.

And, as Maureen had the shrewdness to see, Jim Morrow could very well be the one to tip the scales in his favor. With such a protégé in Rome any remaining doubts about him should disappear.

5

The second artificial hip had taken Frank Bailey off the golf course for good. After years of playing with an 8 handicap, he had no intention to go out there and flail away like a duffer. For much the same reason, he had retired from teaching and wangled a sinecure as the archbishop's theologian. He lived in a condo overlooking an artificial lake, which, in Minnesota, was a species of perversion. He felt like a pagan Roman, exiled to his villa, alive only at the pleasure of the despot.

If you could call this living. Once his phone had rung off the hook whenever an encyclical or decree was issued by the Vatican, giving him the opportunity to address the faithful and cushion the blow of the latest outrage. The networks had wanted him seated next to their own anchor whenever the Pope came to the country. He grabbed the chance to put such visits into perspective. Someone had called him a self-appointed ombudsman—not a bad description. That had been Jim Morrow in his blankety-blank bestselling book.

When his phone rang this morning, it was his sister Maureen on the line.

"What time is it there?" he asked.

"I'm here."

"Here."

"In Minnetonka, with Jenny and her family. I saw the Most Reverend Archbishop Thomas Lannan when I came through Washington."

His sister's voice reminded him how remiss he was in keeping in touch with his nieces. Visiting them was far from a treat, of course; they and their husbands were neanderthal, both in politics and religion. The first time he had seen *Crisis* on a table he had been about to skewer it when Jenny began to babble about how much that magazine meant to her and Phil.

"It's very influential", he had said carefully.

"Why don't you ever write for it, Uncle Frank?"

She had been serious. Dear God.

"What did Tom have to say?" he asked Maureen now.

"That he hadn't talked to you for ages."

"He's got my number."

"In what sense?"

Bailey closed his eyes in pain. His own sister was as ultramontane as they come now, ever since her marriage to the Irish ambassador to the Vatican. No wonder her children were warped.

"We talked about Jim Morrow."

"He's written a book."

"Did you think I wouldn't know? I devoured it. In many ways it seems to be our story, doesn't it? Our generation's."

She went on, remembering how it had been when they were kids, when Frank was at Nazareth Hall and the front porch of their house was filled with his classmates during vacations.

"I think I was half in love with all of them."

They arranged to meet for dinner, just the two of them, no nieces or grandnieces, and he hung up, delighted at the prospect of seeing Mo but feeling too that his day was somehow ruined. It was Jim and that damned book. Frank Bailey would have called what he felt jealousy, if he had ever dreamt of writing such a book. The books he had written, indictments of the status quo, calls to action, had enjoyed a modest success, but his fame had resided on his reliability as a theological gadfly. Someone who had the guts to say it out loud and risk the consequences. He had learned very early that public dissent was the best insurance policy a theologian could take out. Any countermove would look like suppression, and there wasn't a bishop in the country willing to take a chance on being called a censor.

Morrow had eclipsed them all with a single book, and what a book. Eight hundred pages aimed at a restoration. It was a bitter pill to swallow. Harmon, Garelts, Quarles, and, from Rome, Iggie Wrenn, had called. It was like a roster of all those who had devoted the past thirty something years trying to nudge the Church in America into the twentieth century before the twenty-first arrived. They had borne the heat of the day, and now they had lost their audience to a book that was nothing less than an indictment of the bishops and the USCC. *The Decline and Fall* was all anyone had talked about for months. Bailey had reviewed it for the *Wall Street Journal*, but he might just as well have written it for *America* for all the attention it got.

"He is one of the de facto schism boys", Charlie Rankin had said, calling from New Mexico where he was in therapy.

"That's not Jim", Frank had corrected. "He was quoting the *Christian Century*." The Protestant publication had made the observation in 1968. It was important that criticism of Morrow be accurate. There was no need to invent reasons to resent what he had written.

"Morrow's up for some prize", Charlie had whispered.

"The Pulitzer? He's already won it."

"Something else. I've got sources."

They could be the voices Charlie heard when he was full of Scotch.

"How's the weather?"

"Don't ask."

"Sunny?"

Charlie did not like to be reminded of the great climate he enjoyed down there on the jag farm. Frank had the unsettling thought that too many of the aging corps of dissidents had gotten a free pass from the press, both secular and religious. Charlie's problem was at once something everyone knew about and a secret from the public. The shenanigans of others had also gone unmentioned. But Frank was prepared to excuse Charlie's drinking and Phipp's Franciscan mistress and all the rest of it. What else could you expect from men under the oppressive burden of celibacy in a Church whose notion of sexuality was medieval?

Maureen's call set Frank's mind going, and, with several hours to spare, he went impulsively out to his car with the intention of visiting Nazareth Hall. He drove out Snelling, and, after the state fairgrounds and the malls and the endless glitzy entrances to housing developments, real country began just before, off to the left, he saw the great square tower lift above the trees. He did not try to stop the pang of painful pleasure the sight of it gave him. He took the next exit and turned onto Juniper, following it beneath the freeway he had been on, a shaded tunnel on the other side of which, almost immediately, was the entrance gate. He turned in before he noticed the guard shack that now divided the road. He felt a sudden apprehension. Would he be prevented from entering? The place had long since passed into Protestant hands. He rolled down the window and smiled up at the old man seated in the shack.

"I used to go to school here."

"What?" The man wore the idiot frown of the hard of hearing.

"Long live the Pope", Frank said in a lower voice, gesturing ahead, easing his foot off the brake. The guard nodded and smiled and waved him on.

Long live the Pope? Where the hell had that remark come from? And at such a time. The evangelicals who had turned the former Nazareth Hall into a thriving Bible college were not likely to hire a guard who would think a cheer for the Pope was the password of the day. He himself was mystified that he had actually said that until he was on the branch of the road that would take him to the front of the school where it overlooked Lake Johanna. Then he had it. Chesterton had ended his letters to George Bernard Shaw with "Long live the Pope!" and Shaw had concluded his replies with, "To hell with the Pope!" Frank, whose sentiments were now closer to Shaw's than to GKC's, might more properly have quoted the playwright to the gate guard. It had been as a student here that he had read that correspondence, put on to it by Maisie Ward's biography of Chesterton—and by Morrow. They had been the closest of friends back then, Lannan, Morrow, Bailey. The triumvirate.

What had once been a dirt road through the woods was now blacktopped and lined with new buildings, alien structures that distorted Frank Bailey's memories. Even when he came in sight of the original building whose tower he had seen from the freeway—the only building when this place was the Hall—it was difficult to regain the pang of nostalgia he had felt at the sight of the tower. But once he had parked and got out of the car, with the Hall on his left and the lake on his right, he felt that he had been transported back into the land of his youth. *Introibo ad altare Dei; ad Deum qui laetificat iuventutem meam.*

The newer buildings were blocked from sight, the view

down the road toward the island was unchanged. The road circled the flagpole before continuing around the school in the direction of the power plant. The power plant and laundry. There had been more than one building, after all. And on the island was the chapel in which Archbishop Merritt was buried, enshrined on the site of the preparatory seminary he had caused to flourish.

The school had not been half a century old when they arrived, he and Morrow and Lannan, but to them at their age it had seemed hoary with tradition. And of course its presumed future had stretched into unending time. Like the Church itself, the seminary system of those days had seemed fixed, unchangeable, perfect.

The sound he made closing his car door echoed off the building. The main entrance was at the base of the tower, the chapel to the left of that, the school, all three floors, and various wings, stretched off to the right. An open, flagged patio led to the loggia that ran the width of the building, a columned arcade that had been an alternative to the inside hallway when they went from study hall to chapel for night prayers.

Frank began to walk toward the flagpole, drawn by memories that grew more intense and particular. It was eerily possible to believe that it was years ago and he was in his late teens, out for an evening walk with Morrow or Lannan. They had been inseparable, the stars of the class, Frank and Morrow intellectually, Lannan that and athletically besides.

From the flagpole, he looked down a sloping mall bordered by gravel paths to the bridge that led to the island. The bridge seemed unchanged. Then he noticed, beside the path, the plinth inscribed with "The Primrose Path of Dalliance" and beneath that, "Class of 1940". Frank Bailey stared at it. Why had the new owners left this standing? He descended to the wooden bridge, which, however much it seemed the same, must have been repaired, restained, rebuilt a number of times.

He was reminded of the boat in the story that was completely rebuilt as it crossed the ocean. Was it the same boat the passengers had boarded and later disembarked from? Even if no plank on the bridge was identical with the ones that had made it up when he was young, this was undeniably the same bridge. It had a high arch, so that boats could pass easily beneath. The pain in his artificial hips as he went over it reminded him that not all *his* parts were original either. They had crossed this bridge in the May procession, the whole school reciting the Rosary on the way, their goal the island chapel and Benediction of the Blessed Sacrament.

The statue of Mary still stood in the niche over the door of the chapel. What kind of evangelicals were these new owners? He stood with folded arms some yards from the chapel and closed his eyes and was enveloped in the time and space of long ago. My God. His breathing came in short gasps. He opened his eyes and shook his head. For crying out loud. He glared at the inscription on the great block of marble that served as threshold for the chapel. Most Rev. James Joseph Merritt, DD. 1889–1963. Merritt!

The archbishop who had built this chapel as a place for his future tomb had been posthumously exposed as a lifelong embezzler, squirrelling away money throughout his reign. It was stealing, and Furlong in his biography of the old crook had called it that. Of course Merritt had been corporation sole; he *was* the archdiocese, legally speaking, and there was no clear line between archdiocesan and personal funds. His estate had amounted to over two million in the market value of the securities he held; he had a cottage in northern Wisconsin and a condo in Tucson. Furlong had told Frank that he had evidence, though not enough to print the story, that Merritt had fathered a child by an Arizona waitress who thought he was just a businessman from up north, until she came upon his obituary and discovered who her lover had been.

"What does Furlong mean by insufficient proof?" Tom Lannan had asked.

"She kept no records."

"There's just her say-so?"

"Don't you think it's possible?"

"Where's the child?"

"She put it up for adoption."

"Did Furlong trace that?"

"The records down there are a mess. The courthouse had gone down in a big blow, and there were years of records missing."

"That sounds like insufficient proof, all right. Do you suppose the departed archbishop sent the storm that destroyed the records?"

"You're really a company man, aren't you?"

"Because I reject slander against a great churchman?"

"Great churchman!"

Tom had been serious. He might have told Frank that he was about to be named bishop, but he hadn't. It would have explained this unquestioning loyalty to other members of the guild.

Later that day he told his twice-widowed sister about Tom's defense of Merritt and got no satisfaction from her either. Maureen became thoughtful.

"Do you remember my friend Karen, Frank?"

The name meant nothing to him. "Why? Has she had an affair with a bishop?"

Her mouth dropped open at the question, and he quickly patted her arm in apology for scandalizing her.

"She's dead, Frank."

"I'll say Mass for her, in reparation."

6

Women undergraduates never aged beyond twenty-one; female graduate students were at most in their late twenties. The young woman from Washington, Janet Fortin, in her early thirties, seemed at once young and mature to Morrow. "I'm showing off", he thought. "I am trying to impress her."

This had less to do with the fact that she was an emissary from the President of the United States than because she was a friend of his daughter's. By making his book's case as he had, objectively, grounding it in an accumulation of statistics generated in part by the way people answered his questions, he had kept himself out of it. That is why he had cut Janet off when she suggested that his assessment was in some way an expression of antecedent commitments on his part.

He had developed his method after being frozen out at a number of meetings and campus lectures because he had been labeled a conservative. Members of theology departments, when they did not boycott his lectures, sat with knowing smiles while he talked. Even former students seemed concerned to distance themselves from him. But in those early days, he was emphasizing his personal judgment that the Church was going to hell in a hand basket. And he was accused of resisting change, of being fearful of the new church, of wanting to cling to authoritarian models—all the usual amateur psychologizing that substituted for discussion in the contemporary academy. Thus moral theologians began discussions of homosexuality by asking why perversion bothers us so. The issue ceased to be an objective one—is it morally right or not?—and became an analysis of a subjective reaction whose causes were presumed to be anything but the judgment that homosexuality was morally wrong. Even Mary and his other kids sometimes had seemed to have accepted the view that their father was some kind of throwback who wished he could put thumbscrews on everyone else. But once he had devised a set of questions whose answers would constitute what was to be discussed or appraised, he had been able to gain at least grudging consent that, on the basis of such data, it was difficult to say the Church was flourishing or that the much-touted *aggiornamento* had taken place.

"Let's talk about something else", he said, when at table Janet brought up his book again.

"First tell me what you think of celibacy."

"You mean for priests?"

She had a nice half-smile that both acknowledged his effort at humor and signaled that she herself was serious. He told her the reasons Paul VI had given for celibacy, which indeed were the traditional arguments for an unmarried clergy.

"It goes without saying that religious living in communities don't marry. The three vows—poverty, chastity, and obedience—are what make one a religious."

"What you usually hear is that by not having a family of his own a priest can devote himself wholeheartedly to others. But all kinds of married people do that, doctors, lawyers…"

"Professors."

"Right! Do you feel your family is an impediment when you deal with students?"

"That's not the essential argument for celibacy, Janet."

Speaking to her of the distinction between precepts and counsels and the nature of the priest as an *alter Christus*, he might have been verifying a fundamental claim of his book. Young Catholics knew next to nothing of their faith, of its lore and language and its embodiment in institutions. As a professor, he had watched it happen. Mention of sacraments, of grace, of original sin, brought baffled frowns from students whose entire education had been in the Catholic schools.

When Allan Bloom wrote in *The Closing of the American Mind* that his students at Cornell and Chicago no longer had in their imaginative repertoire the cadences of the Bible, he was speaking of kids who had come by and large from Christian and Jewish homes. Catholic kids were no better, perhaps they were worse.

Withers, a colleague in theology, had once voiced this complaint.

"Of course they're illiterate, Herbert", Morrow had agreed. "Before coming here they were taught by the students of your colleagues."

A cheap shot, of course. They were all to blame; the whole generation that had preened itself in the wake of the Council thought it was unlike those who had preceded it in the Church. They would throw open the windows to the modern world and let in the invigorating fresh air of the present. The windows had been opened, all right, but as much had flown out of them as had flown in, including, it sometimes seemed, the faith of our fathers.

"I just think it's sad that young men live alone the way priests do", Janet said. "It isn't natural."

The topic seemed of more than passing interest, although as far as he knew she was as unmarried as any priest. He assured her that priests have friends. "That is the central thing in a marriage, after a time, the friendship between husband and wife. Marriage is for the long haul."

"Mrs. Morrow is dead, isn't she?"

"Yes."

That was enough of that. He had no intention of making his personal sorrow a subject of chatter with this young woman.

"I should start for Grand Rapids."

"I'll give you directions to a better road."

"What message should I take back?"

He found that he did not want to repeat his earlier dismissal of the proposal. Her visit had been a welcome distraction. But not a distraction from work. Although he sat dutifully at his computer every day, he was not caught up in any compelling project. Suddenly the prospect of breaking out of the habits he had developed in order to write his book was welcome. The habits had become a pointless routine.

"What exactly does an ambassador to the Vatican do?"

7

Nate Patch was surprised to be the recipient of a scoop from the White House, chosen, he was told, as the appropriate representative of the religious press.

"Morrow!"

Janet Fortin was delighted by his reaction. The nomination was a promise that the President intended to recapture the innovative and surprising character of his first term. The handout stressed Morrow's academic credentials.

"We expect the hearings to go smoothly", Jane Fortin said, adding that they hoped the Catholic press would forego boasting of the appointment.

"What could go wrong?" Nate Patch asked. "Jim Morrow might be controversial among Catholics, but to the general public he's an obscure academic who struck oil with a book that is highly critical of his own Church."

"I hope you're right", she said.

Nate Patch was genuinely confused by the nomination of James Morrow.

"Did you run it by the NCCB?" he asked Janet Fortin.

She lowered her lids. "Have you ever heard of the separation of church and state?"

"You're going to be hearing a lot about it. Seriously, was Lannan asked?"

"No matter what I say it would be the wrong answer."

Patch thought about that. He decided she meant that Lannan had at least approved of Morrow. Leach, the anorexic ascetic on Lannan's staff, minced no words when Patch spoke to him.

"He is Lannan's candidate. The archbishop was asked to put forward a name and he named Morrow."

"I don't get it."

"That's because you share the general belief that Morrow is a conservative."

"Isn't he?"

Patch couldn't follow the Byzantine reasoning that Leach embarked upon. Morrow's book had not spared the official wire service of the Catholic Conference. He had begun with its budget, gone down the roster of the staff, not too subtly making the point that these people would have trouble getting a job in the secular world, dismissing the whole operation as beset by the same virus he had decided explained the wholesale decline of the Catholic Church in the country. Secularization.

His reference was to a letter issued by the American bishops before the Council. Patch found a copy of the thing. It was redolent of a Church familiar to Nate Patch only through the horror stories he had heard in college about the preconciliar Church. The bishops at the time had leveled an accusation at the whole country. It had been Morrow's inspiration to see that the charge of secularization now applied to the Church establishment as well.

Talking with Leach reminded Patch of the secret delight with which he himself had read Morrow's indictment of the Church. He felt as he had when Lorraine got going on his lousy job. She might have been voicing his unconscious thoughts. Leach was likening Morrow to the moles that had burrowed into the USCC and NCCB and, working from within, sapped the Church of her strength.

"People like you", Leach said, the tone of his voice not changing.

"Me?"

"You are a flak for the ecclesiastical establishment. A hired gun. You pump the official pap into the sclerotic system of Catholic journalism, corrupting the faithful..."

"It's terrible having my cover blown."

"May I ask you a direct question?"

"After all this indirection?"

"Are you a practicing Catholic? I ask out of mere curiosity. It has sometimes seemed to me that the only explanation of what comes out of this building, the Taj Mahal, is that it is manned by apostates."

Leach apparently did not need an answer to his question; in any case, he did not wait for one. He clearly regarded it as established fact that the bishop's bureaucrats were traitors to the faith.

"Are you saying that Morrow is an apostate?"

Leach laughed. "It would be so much simpler if he were."

"I don't understand."

"I'll go back to the beginning. You think Morrow is a conservative."

"It's not what I think. Everyone thinks so."

"But is he?"

"Read his book."

They were going in circles, but it was a way to pass the time until Monsignor Wales could see him. "I wonder where the idea of putting Morrow forward came from."

"From an old girl friend of the archbishop", Leach said, his eyes in the exact center of his round glasses.

"Are you serious?" A silly question. Of course Leach was serious. But was he crazy? "Who is she?"

Leach fell silent, studying Patch as he decided whether to say more. When he did speak, it was in riddles. "The clue will be found in the Vatican ambassador corps."

"I don't get it."

Leach thought again. "She is someone he knew as a young man."

He could get no more from him, but when Patch was finally talking to Monsignor Wales the secretary laughed at Leach's gossip.

"Fr. Leach is referring to Mrs. Maureen Kilmartin. Her husband was Ireland's ambassador to the Vatican. She is Fr. Frank Bailey's sister."

What a tight little circle it was. Patch had learned from Bailey of the long-ago friendship between Morrow and Lannan, between the three of them. Four apparently, if you included Bailey's sister. The information was a bit of a letdown. Leach had had him half-believing that Archbishop Lannan might figure in the article Lorraine was urging him to write about the misbehavior of the celibate clergy.

PART TWO

CHAPTER ONE

I

The announcement that the name of James Morrow had been sent to the Senate committee on foreign relations was news because of the continued high sales of his book. The White House spokesman mentioned the President's gratitude to Archbishop Lannan for his advice on the matter, with predictable results.

Lannan fought the impulse to skip out of his office so that Monsignor Wales could honestly say he wasn't in. But it could be risky to refuse a call from Frank Bailey.

"The general consensus is that you're out of your mind", Bailey said without fanfare.

"Who conducted the poll?"

"These were volunteers. I mean it, Tom, people are furious."

"About anything in particular?"

"Oh, come on."

Lannan took the phone away from his ear and smiled at Wales. They both could hear the distinct if profane voice of the infuriated theologian. Lannan returned the phone to his ear.

"The Vatican Embassy is not in my gift, Frank. Perhaps your friends should call the White House."

"You weren't consulted?"

Lannan's degree was in moral theology. A less sophisticated man might have felt pinned by Frank's question. It seemed he must either lie or tell Frank he had indeed called the right number to complain about James Morrow's being nominated American ambassador to the Vatican. Not at all. Obviously Lannan wanted the credit without taking any blame.

"Frank, if I had been consulted, it would be confidential, as I shouldn't have to tell you."

"The President expressed his thanks to you and the Conference!"

"Frank, say I was consulted."

"Then you're responsible."

Lannan laughed. "If only I had the power you imagine."

"If he wasn't your choice, you have to veto it. We can't have someone who has said what he has about you and the Conference and everybody else representing us in Rome."

"Veto it!"

"Tom, if the NCCB declares him unacceptable, the thing will be stopped in its tracks. It would be like senatorial privilege."

"Who've you been talking to?"

But abruptly, Frank changed topics. "I drove out to the Hall the other morning."

"You did!"

"You wouldn't recognize it."

"I doubt that." He swung away from his desk and looked through the window at the great blue dome of the National Shrine as Frank told him of going out to the island and up to the chapel where old Merritt was buried. Frank's tone altered as he spoke, softened. Had the memories gotten to him?

"I've never been back since they sold it, Frank. I wonder if Jim Morrow has."

They might have been reestablishing the Three Musketeers.

96

Except that Frank had called to oppose their mutual friend's appointment as ambassador to the Vatican.

"Did you read Jim's book?" Frank asked.

"I skipped around in it."

"Sure. I looked again at his chapter on seminaries. You can only understand it if you know how he felt about selling off the Hall."

"That was a stupid sale", Lannan agreed.

The buildings and land, with all that shoreline, had been sold for a million dollars, just to get rid of it. There had been agitation to turn it to some other use, a high school, a retreat house, a retirement home. Opus Dei had made a bid of four million, but the archbishop wouldn't even read the offer. Instead he called Gospel Ministries and told them they could have it all, nothing down, ten years to pay. Frank Bailey blamed Opus Dei for the archbishop's headstrong action. You could hardly blame Waters for not wanting an ultramontane establishment right under his nose. If the Evangelicals hadn't come along at the right moment, he might have turned it into a clerical retirement home.

A feature of Morrow's book had been a chapter devoted to the altered real estate holdings of the Church in America. From the mid-nineteenth century onward there had been an expansion explained by the influx of immigrants. By the turn of the century, the map was dotted from coast to coast with the land and buildings the Church had acquired to fulfill its mission. And so it had gone well past mid-century. In the sixties, the crest had been reached, and then, dramatically over a ten-year period, the phase of selling off Church property began. The preparatory seminaries were among the first to go, it being alleged that the conciliar spirit was against removing young men from their families at high school age. Dioceses, religious

97

orders, male and female, were soon divesting themselves of holdings at a breathtaking pace.

"For the first time I really feel that I've taken a vow of poverty", a young Franciscan cried ecstatically.

Morrow tracked her subsequent career. However it was with poverty, the vows of obedience and then chastity apparently weakened. When the young woman married, there was a photograph of her smiling defiantly into the camera, her somewhat sheepish, soon-to-be laicized, clerical husband on her arm.

"We have to get over our fear of the body", she said.

There were those who claimed Morrow manufactured the quotations if not the incidents he had taken to be emblematic of what had happened to the postconciliar Church. But Wales had done a check of a sufficient number of examples to convince the sceptics in the Conference that these were undoctored cases. Archbishop Lannan felt he remembered all of them, or at least other cases of the same sort. He could even remember a suppressed elation at the thinning of the ranks, a feeling he had scarcely been aware of before someone had noticed it in Fr. Giorgio, the spiritual director at the major seminary, who had been the counselor of so many priests and religious before they left. Giorgio seemed almost glad to see them go.

"'I alone have escaped to tell you'", Sweeney had murmured once, in comment.

"Watch those proof texts."

"Hey," Sweeney said, "I'm the biblicist."

The banter in the seminary dining room had gone off on a tangent, but that recurrent line assigned to the servants who return to tell Job that his flocks and fields and family have been systematically taken from him—*I alone have escaped to tell you*—seemed all too applicable to their situation. Sweeney reminded them that Job was being tested.

"And so are we. All the possessions, all the smug successes, as we thought them, are being taken away, disappearing before our eyes, almost overnight. We're being tested, and punished too."

"Punished for what?"

Sweeney's eyebrows looked false they were so full. He glared around the gathering.

"Complacency."

Of course Sweeney had once had a Dorothy Day phase and gone around the seminary wearing an altar boy cassock. From time to time he would comment on the well-tailored soutanes of others. "'Those who wear soft garments are found in the palaces of kings.'" Well on his way to becoming a biblicist even then.

Maybe there had been a sense of jettisoning excess baggage, in real estate and personnel, but undeniably there was a grim satisfaction in watching so many others desert their posts while standing firm oneself. That had been the intent of the remark about Giorgio. The old man did seem to take a ferocious satisfaction in advising men to leave. Maybe he thought that once they reached the point of raising the question they had already answered it in their hearts, whether they knew it or not. Maybe like Paul VI he felt that a point would be reached when all the fainthearted or discontented or misfits would be gone—laicized and sent into the world—and then the rest of the clergy could get to work implementing the documents of Vatican II.

"Bad psychology" was Morrow's answer to that. "Easy divorce increases the number of divorces."

"That's an analogy?" Frank commented.

"Think about it."

Lannan managed to end the conversation without having given Frank a straight answer. The fact was, he wanted to talk with Morrow before he made any comments. He had been told it was a risk to put forward the historian's name, something he had of course known. Would Morrow be at all mellowed by the nomination? Archbishop Lannan sighed. How he longed for the day when all the quarrels and divisions and animosities would be behind them. He smiled. He might have been thinking of those wonderfully complacent preconciliar days.

2

There was a buzz of angry excitement in the west wing, brought on by Willie Butterworth's reaction to the news of Morrow's appointment. As Janet Fortin went down the hallway to her office, the reverend's voice came to her in waves as she passed the open doors of offices where Butterworth's *Judeo-Christian Hour* was being replayed on VCRs.

"Did you hear it?"

"I don't have cable."

Casey Thomas looked at her as if she had said she relied on outdoor plumbing. "I'll put it on."

"I don't want to hear it." Janet got behind her desk, looked with dismay at the piles of work upon it, and then swung away to where the coffee pot—thank God—was aglow. She poured a cup before turning back to Casey.

"We expected a negative reaction from Butterworth. And from all the rest of them."

"He claims the President promised to eliminate the American embassy to the Vatican."

"When?"

"He played a tape."

Janet decided she had better listen to the program after all. Casey plucked the cassette from the desktop and put it into the

VCR. The TV, soundless, had already been on. In a moment, giant American flags, impossibly red and blue, began to unfurl on the screen, as organ music swelled to the tune of "God Bless America". Butterworth claimed he had twenty million viewers and reached at least that many more by radio, audio, and videotapes and a tireless lecture schedule. Butterworth was disarmingly worldly in appearance—handsome, well-groomed, expensively dressed—and he spoke in low, convincing tones. There had never been a whisper of adverse publicity about him. He had inherited wealth and for years had underwritten his effort with his own money, but now he prospered. His sad, sincere eyes lent plausibility to the most implausible and outrageous remarks. Janet sometimes wished they had a bishop or two like Butterworth.

"We used to", Wales had said. "His name was Fulton Sheen."

"Sheehan?"

"Sheen. You never heard of him?" Wales' expression was the pained one of a man made aware of the swift passage of time. "He was big on national television. I could get you a video..."

She discouraged that Who would want to watch Butterworth videos twenty years from now? On the screen, Butterworth was speculating on what the founding fathers would have thought of sending an ambassador to the Pope of their time. Even to ask the question was to know the answer. The First Amendment. The separation of church and state had stood the test of time; it was best for the country, and it was best for religion too. Was there a wistful tinge to this remark?

When she had talked with Morrow about the strong possibility that this doctrine would be invoked against him, he had gone on about it, scuffling through the fallen leaves as they walked the path around the lake.

"Protestants used that doctrine to keep Catholics on the

margin of public life. In those days, they rightly considered the state to be in their hands, dominated by their co-religionists. Do you know, when I was a kid we called the public school the Protestant school? Their playground was just across the street from ours and those kids were friends of mine, but the street between us has always been my image of the separation of church and state."

The President appeared on the screen, the clipping they were watching for.

"I'm not sure there's much point in it", he was saying in answer to a question put him during the campaign about the American ambassador to the Vatican. "Ronald Reagan introduced it. Before that, we kept in touch, of course. Nothing wrong with that. The Vatican is a great listening post, no doubt about it. But the fact is, my Catholic friends tell me it makes no-never-mind to them whether or not we have a Vatican ambassador. They don't want it."

He was asked what he would do about appointing someone to fill the vacancy.

The President smiled. "Is not doing something, doing something?"

He was assured it was.

"Then I promise to do something."

Laughter, applause, an exchange of glances in the press corps, and then Butterworth and his wife were back, telling their viewers they had just seen the President promise not to fill the vacancy.

Butterworth next showed footage of Senator Crowe attacking the President for promising to drop the Vatican embassy, and assured his viewers, all twenty million of them, that Crowe was not alone in thinking the President had made that promise. Well, he wasn't going to call the President of the United States a liar, but there was still time to withdraw that nomination and satisfy the President's Catholic friends who didn't want it and everybody else who cared about the separation of church and state.

A frantic search had begun through the video records of the campaign to see if there were any remarks that could be used to offset the damaging exchange Butterworth had shown.

"He promised to do nothing", Casey wailed. "That means he made no promise."

Janet looked at Casey. The press secretary's face was twisted in anguished loyalty. If their only defense was that the President was a slippery bastard who spoke with forked tongue, they would be in even deeper trouble.

So much of her job had become damage control, protecting the President from himself, from his earlier remarks, from his damnable tendency to trust the people he talked to and thus to make compromising remarks. Janet called Monsignor Gene Wales.

"Have you heard about Butterworth?"

"Yes."

"What do you think?"

"That his opposition is perfectly predictable. I would think less of him if he hadn't protested. After all, he's a Protestant."

"He claims the President promised not to appoint a new ambassador."

"Did he?"

"You didn't see the clip?"

"You mean the tricky answer."

"Butterworth took it as a promise. So did Crowe."

"More fools they."

"Tell me something. Is the embassy a big deal with the bishops?"

There was a long pause. "Why do you ask?"

"I'm just asking. And I'm the one who's asking, nobody else."

"Promise?"

She winced. Well, damn it, the President invited that kind of reaction. "Promise."

"I was kidding."

"I know."

"Let me put it this way. A week ago, the answer would have been different than it is today. You've talked to us; Lannan has consulted his colleagues; Morrow has been asked; the announcement has been made."

Well, at least she could say she had already floated the idea when someone else thought of it as the way to get the president off the hook. Within the hour that this suggestion was made—to have Morrow withdraw his name—Casey Thomas was sounding her out about the possibility.

"How would he take it?"

"How would you take it?"

Casey paused as if he were trying to dredge up a memory of integrity. "Wouldn't it be different if the post itself had ceased to be? That would cushion it."

"Only in billiards."

Casey held up his hands as if he were the muggee rather than the mugger. "I had to try it out."

In the days that followed, stories began to appear that the White House might not stand by its nominee for ambassador to the Vatican. Would it be withdrawn? Out of the cloud of words with which Casey responded to that question, Janet discerned the hope that the Senate would do the President's dirty work for him. James Morrow's name would be put forward, but as a gesture, no pressure would be exerted to gain support for the nomination. Other possible futures could be gathered from what Casey said, and they were featured in accounts of the briefing.

Janet wondered what James Morrow was making of all this, out there in his Michigan cottage? She couldn't remember seeing a television there. He had to have a radio, at least, so sooner or later he would become aware of this hullabaloo.

3

The days since Janet's visit had been the most delightful he had ever spent at the cottage, and the reason was not hard to find. He walked around with a valedictory air, certain he had made the mistake of his life in accepting nomination as American ambassador to the Vatican, determined to enjoy what might be the last time in a long while when he could just be here alone. Like Horace, he had put in a lifetime of scrounging and saving and working to buy this place. It was to provide his retirement haven; the essentials of his library had been gradually transported here; he had never liked the classroom and could depart it dry-eyed. He had the perfect retreat, everything but Horace's servant Lalage, and he had fallen for the first temptation to leave it.

His colleague in history, Pat Ryan, was already on his way north when he telephoned from his car.

"Jacques Maritain", he cried enigmatically.

After a moment, Morrow said, "You're dead."

"Ambassador to the Vatican."

"So was Shakespeare."

"Come on."

"Frank Shakespeare."

"Any relative?"

"Of Maritain's?"

"I'll be there in about two hours."

And he was, piling out of his huge Lincoln and hurrying

toward the cottage. When he saw Morrow he fell to his knees in mock adulation and brought his forehead to the ground.

Ryan's enthusiasm about the appointment increased Morrow's trepidation.

"I should have said no."

Ryan made a face, half smile, half frown, unable to comprehend the refusal of such an honor. Ryan had egged him into early retirement too, but that was because he had his eye on Morrow's campus office.

"I should stay here as I planned, writing."

"You can write in Rome."

Morrow looked around. "Just when I got this place the way I want it, this has to happen."

Ryan looked about with covetous approval.

"I hate the thought of locking it up, Pat."

"Don't."

And then it came. Ryan offered to buy or at least rent the cottage. "That way you wouldn't have to worry about it."

Morrow felt like a dog in the manger. He did not want Ryan enjoying the fruits of his years of planning. How could he explain that he would rather lock up the cottage, board up its windows, keep it *domus intacta* until he returned?

"My kids will use it."

"How long is an ambassador's appointment?"

"He serves at the pleasure of the President."

"He or she", Ryan primly corrected.

"Of course he can resign any time he wants."

"Rome", Ryan breathed, closing his eyes. He opened them again. "Do you have a staff?"

Aha. Morrow assured him that everyone else was career, only he would be the amateur. What did people who made a life of diplomacy think of political appointments? The thought was vaguely unsettling. It had not occurred to him that he might arrive in Rome to find hostility in the embassy.

106

He and Ryan went out to dinner, and it wasn't until they returned and were listening to the late-night news that they heard of the flap about the President's promise to shut down the embassy to the Vatican.

"That's a promise?" Ryan asked, when the clip from the reelection campaign was shown.

"Willie Butterworth thinks so."

It was worse than a promise; it was a deliberate effort to obfuscate the matter, to say yes and no at once. Morrow found himself sympathizing with Willie Butterworth, but at the same time he felt threatened. Just hours before he had been day-dreaming about withdrawing his name, but now he felt an impulse to fight for the job. Of course the President didn't give a damn about it one way or the other. Nor did Lannan. It was just a goodie Tom had extracted from the administration. The great mystery was that he had offered it to a man he should regard as a former friend if not an enemy. Maybe the whole thing was Lannan's way of getting even with him rather than doing him a favor.

"There's your chance if you want out", Ryan said.

Had Lannan expected this opposition from Willie and the Evangelicals? Morrow now sat in his Barcalounger as if it were a dentist's chair, apprehensive, waiting. It seemed paranoid to imagine that Lannan and his friends had seen this as a way to settle accounts with the historian who had depicted them as presiding over the demise of the Church in the United States.

What a damned fool he was. His children had been excited when he told them the news.

"Do you remember Janet Fortin?" he had asked Mary.

"Of course."

"She's the one who came to talk to me about it."

"She isn't married?"

"She works in the White House."

"The White House!"

"She says it sounds more impressive than it is."

"Well, I'm impressed. Of course, she always was a flaming liberal."

It had been pleasant to find how proud the nomination made his kids, and that increased his uneasiness when the Evangelical attack began and the responses from the White House became increasingly equivocal. Recalling his surprise that his name had come up, he wondered what sort of political game was being played.

He tried to find in the memory of his talk with Janet any sign that there was a hidden purpose in the nomination. If she hadn't been honest with him, he had lost all ability to judge character. He dismissed the idea of asking Mary what she really thought of Janet. But of course Janet and the administration could be the unwitting instrument of the public humiliation of James Morrow. How different the past few days seemed in the light of this new development. A panel of newsmen was discussing the Evangelical charge and the presidential promise.

Morrow's name was mentioned, but he was clearly just a pawn in whatever struggle was going on. Somewhere Lannan was enjoying this. What a circus the Senate hearings would be—if they even took place. Withdraw? The idea was repellent. If this was a ploy of Lannan's, he would be damned if he'd give him the satisfaction.

"It doesn't mean a thing", Janet assured him when she called after midnight.

"Just a quarrel between the preacher and the President?"

"Well, not quite. Some senators are getting into the act. Crowe is a member of the committee. He has offered to support the President—support his campaign promise, that is."

She wanted to know if the press had gotten to him. He was almost embarrassed to admit they hadn't.

"I don't seem to loom very large in all this."

"Monsignor Wales says, thank God it's you."

"Oh?"

"If we'd nominated a liberal, Willie could argue the nominee didn't even believe the same things as the Pope. This way, the quarrel is with the President."

4

Frank Partridge was halfway through his sixth term as United States senator from North Carolina, after moving over from the House according to the longstanding practice of his one-party state. The Senate was not quite one party, but until recently, Partridge's party had been in control throughout his tenure. He had watched with sadness the decline of a great institution. The gentleman's code that had governed senatorial conduct had withstood the election of several women. It was the new type of senator, male and female, that had put the body into steep decline.

Watergate had started it. The unstated rules had been violated in order to get Nixon. The poor bastard had been hounded for doing what every President since Roosevelt had done. His own party had deserted him and permitted the usurpation of power to take place, so that now there was bad blood between the parties. The bond of trust had been broken. An unpredictable righteousness and selective vengeance reigned. Men announced with seeming pride their sexual perversions and were seen in public with their catamites, while two senators had resigned under the pressure of unintelligible charges of sexual harassment. There was much confusion about money.

It was a longstanding tradition that men who arrived in the Senate poor retired as millionaires, a feat impossible to explain on the basis of salary. Billions were diverted every year to the pet projects of members with only routine complaint, but a vendetta was being waged against members of both houses who had carried on traditional practices that involved only a few thousand dollars.

Partridge was resigned to seeing the decline continue. He did not like the new breed of senator. He felt little fellowship even with members of his own party. His own position was unassailable, on the basis of current rules, but he had seen how easily rules can be changed. There were zealots all around, eager to destroy the traditions that had made the Senate great. Frank Partridge was sore at heart. His heart was divided too. Jackson, his aide, had given him a copy of James Morrow's book, and, with a contraband Cuban cigar and a generous Scotch and water, Partridge was turning over the pages.

He had never understood Catholicism. An aunt had told him that the Partridges had been Catholic through the war between the states, then drifted away.

"There weren't enough priests. They became Episcopalians."

He had convinced his aunt that it would do the family no good to publicize her genealogical findings.

"They'll think we're turncoats", she agreed.

Not precisely what Partridge had in mind, but her silence was welcome on any basis.

Jackson had provided the senator with a resumé of Morrow's book and that had sent him to the volume itself. He was fascinated by this dispassionate documented history of the dissolution of the Catholic Church in the United States. Partridge supposed he had heard of the ecumenical council referred to as Vatican II. He had been in the House while it was going on. But he had not taken much notice of the increasing independence from the old traditions that Morrow recorded. In his Protestant heart, Partridge took pleasure from this account of disappearing priests and departing nuns, of open defiance of the

Pope. An organization that had once been the marvel of its foes had disintegrated. The story was too much like the story of what had happened to politics during Partridge's lifetime for him to feel only pleasure. He never said it outright, but it was pretty clear Morrow deplored the story he was telling. Partridge had the absurd feeling that he would find a kindred soul in the President's nominee to the Vatican.

"This Mr. President's way of getting back at those bishops for all their complaints about a woman's right to choose?" Partridge pronounced the cant phrase in rich and sceptical Southern tones.

"How so?" Jackson asked. Jackson was a native of Massachusetts, a born scoundrel, but loyal to his senator.

"Morrow's history is the tale of those bishops failing to do what they were appointed to do. Who suggested Morrow to the President?"

"Archbishop Lannan."

"I find that hard to believe. Have you read the book?" Jackson wrinkled his nose. "I wrote the resumé."

"So you did. You still sure Archbishop Lannan suggested Morrow to the President?"

"The Vatican Embassy was what Lannan wanted in return for the help he gave during the campaign."

"What help?"

"Remember Justice Norman?"

"Ah, the lesbian. Of course."

"Lannan preached a sermon that got the administration off the hook. He was owed something."

"And that's all they asked for?"

"They probably feel the President pulled a fast one on them. Who's going to believe he didn't remember that campaign promise?"

"Promise? He made no promise."

"Tell that to Willie."

Willie Butterworth was a preacher after Senator Partridge's heart. He seldom missed watching the evangelist's nightly television show, and when he couldn't watch it live he made sure it was taped for him. Any real religion he had left was the kind Willie preached. Partridge despised the churches that put women in the pulpits, celebrated homosexuality, backed every whacko liberal program that furthered the moral ruin of the country, and, as far as Partridge could tell, no longer believed in sin or hell or punishment. It was doubtful they even believed in God, certainly not the God preached by Willie.

"They're trying to get rid of Professor Morrow. Send him out of the country at government expense." The explanation came to Partridge whole as he said it. He had no doubt it was true. Lannan and his liberal friends wanted to ship Morrow to what they probably regarded as Siberia.

"Willie has an appointment with you tomorrow morning, Senator."

The appointment had been made before the senator read Morrow's book. He wondered if he could succeed in convincing Willie that in Morrow they had an improbable ally. It was tempting to throw in with Willie, stop the nomination, and ruin Archbishop Lannan's desire to get an embarrassment out of the country. On the other hand, the prospect of prolonged hearings during which Morrow's account of his Church's decline could be given maximum publicity was even more tempting.

"I look forward to it."

Jackson smiled, certain he knew what that meant. It pleased Partridge to know that he could still surprise a man who had worked with him as long as Jackson had.

5

"It's an awful thing to happen to him", Janet said, but Monsignor Wales saw that she was fishing.

"Being nominated ambassador?"

"That damned preacher."

"Not that damned President?"

"Him too." But she looked over both shoulders first. "You know what he's like."

"Tell me."

Poor girl. How could she say something like that without just saying it? The President hoped Morrow would get the administration off the hook by withdrawing his name.

"Have you told Morrow?"

She dipped her head, then lifted her eyes. "I was hoping you would."

Wales put up a hand. He would give her no encouragement in this. He told Janet this was an insult to the NCCB as well as to a distinguished Catholic scholar.

"If the President wants to bow to Fundamentalist pressure, he can hardly expect us to make it easy for him. Is he accepting the charge that he promised to abolish the embassy to the Vatican?"

"It's not that simple."

Was the President really worse than other politicians, or just less adroit at concealing the fact that he believed in nothing, had lost all conception of the truth, and could be trusted only so long as loyalty served his purposes?

"I've heard you say as much of bishops."

"You have not!"

"Don't worry, it's not on tape."

Was she seriously suggesting an analogy between their jobs?

God knows what he might have said to Janet on those occasions when they had assumed cousinly confidentiality and told one another of their disillusionments. Cousins but not within the range of consanguinity. Was Lannan any more of a hero to him than the President was to Janet? The archbishop was smoother than the President, but then almost everyone was.

"The word out of Partridge's office is that Archbishop Lannan put Morrow forward just in order to get a pest out of the country."

"That's ridiculous."

"Is it? If it's even half-true, the President is going to wonder why he should do the NCCB's dirty work for them."

Wales did not have to be told that such remarks could be floated to the press so that what was currently an embarrassment to the President would soon become an embarrassment to Archbishop Lannan and the NCCB. It was his job to prevent that.

"Morrow doesn't really want that job, Gene", Janet went on. "When I was out there, it was touch and go. I actually expected to come back empty. He accepted the nomination, but I'll bet anything he's been having second thoughts ever since."

"Why don't you find out?"

She shook her head. "If it was just me, I would."

"Janet, this wouldn't be the first time a President withdrew a name under fire."

"It's not just the name."

The President now wanted to do what Willie had understood him to promise during the campaign. What in the larger order of things was an American ambassador to the Vatican? There already was an ambassador in Rome, as well as a consulate. It made as much sense as sending an ambassador to the Dalai Lama. Morrow's withdrawal would clear the way for getting rid of the post.

"He's in a dilemma. He owes you but Willie found that tape. He'll make it up to Lannan, you can count on that."

They sat for a moment in silence, letting the hollow words fade away. Janet wanted to know what she could report.

"I'll talk to Archbishop Lannan."

"Was that the idea, to get Morrow out of the country?"

Wales didn't answer the question. He no longer felt he knew the answer. Everyone had reacted to the naming of Morrow in the same way. Why was he being rewarded? Partridge's suspicion made sense, although Monsignor Wales could remember no flicker of a hint from the archbishop that he was really interested in deporting Morrow.

"No!" the archbishop said when Wales went to him with a report on Janet's unofficial visit. "Not on your life. No one is going to pull that kind of stunt on me or the Conference. A deal's a deal."

"They seem to think that Morrow will back out because of all this."

Lannan's hand went out for his telephone, then stopped. He sat for a full minute, thinking. Then he looked up at Wales.

"Monsignor, book a flight to Michigan. I wish I could go myself, but I can't. We want Jim Morrow to know that we are with him all the way on this."

CHAPTER TWO

I

Morrow had his pick of explanations, and none of them was flattering.

Had Lannan and his cohorts put forward his name in the full knowledge that Willie Butterworth would raise a stir about the campaign promise to close down the American Embassy to the Vatican? If so, a magnanimous gesture had been made at no cost. If the deal fell through, it would not be Morrow's sponsors who were at fault.

Or perhaps Lannan had been as surprised as the President when the filmed campaign promise came to light, and this dashed his plans to get a gadfly out of the country.

"It's a well-deserved reward for writing the definitive and fair history of what the Church has gone through in this country in the past quarter-century." The very confidence with which Pat Ryan spoke invited doubt.

Morrow knew what the NCCB thought of his history. They probably found it as fair as old Fr. Jordan had. Did fairness consist of pleasing no one? He had pleased Ryan, at least, who saw it as a sustained, documented account of the cowardice of a hierarchy that had permitted dissident theologians, neurotic nuns, and unruly universities to assert the right to decide for themselves what being Catholic meant.

What of the reason Lannan all but gave? It was simple ward politics, doling out benefits to friends, to a friend of his youth at least.

But if matters were Byzantine within the Church, they became more tangled as Morrow was drawn into the political arena. Neither Tom Lannan nor Janet Fortin suggested he withdraw, not in so many words, but their enthusiasm was under control. Stubbornly, Morrow responded to the committee's invitation and flew to Washington to meet with Senator Partridge, the chairman.

"Sir, I have read your book with profit and enjoyment. I congratulate you."

"Thank you, Senator."

Partridge's office looked like a trophy room: plaques adorned the walls in the space unoccupied by the dozens of photographs of Partridge beaming beside one celebrity or another. The room was heavy with smoke, and Partridge added to it without apology, puffing on a stubby cigar.

"Not many could be so honest about a beloved institution."

"I merely followed the historical method."

"That is what is so rare. If I were to write an account of this institution..." He made a large circle with his cigar. "I doubt that I could overcome the temptation to tilt the story in the Senate's favor."

"Have you thought of writing a history of the Senate?" Senator Broker asked.

As the senior senator from Morrow's state, she was escorting him on courtesy calls to members of the committee, and of course they had begun with Partridge. Broker was a fanatical anti-smoker, but there was no hint of that in her deferential manner. Do senators earn credits with one another when someone from their state is given a federal appointment? As far as Morrow knew, Broker had absolutely nothing to do with his nomination, nor was she on the relevant committee. Still he was grateful to her for taking him around. If Partridge ever let them go, that is.

The first fifteen minutes had been devoted to a tour of Partridge's trophies with appropriate anecdotes. Broker responded with shameless flattery. The discussion of Morrow's book was soon diverted into a discussion of a possible history of the Senate by Partridge, then regained the obviously familiar grooves of Partridge's decades in the upper house.

"I'm a Baptist", Partridge said, suddenly reversing field.

"Southern Baptist", Broker murmured, as if over a fine old breed. She herself was Unitarian, untrammeled by creed or cult.

"A strong case is being made by my co-religionists that the President promised them to abolish the post to which you have been named."

"Do you think that was a promise, Senator?" Broker asked, her tone sceptical.

"It's what Reverend Butterworth and the Baptists think, Margie. They might have opposed him openly except for what they took to be a promise."

"Are campaign promises binding?" Morrow asked, immediately regretting it. The question had been meant to comment on the President's penchant for making promises he did not keep, but it sounded cynical, as if he were so eager for the job he expected others to break their promises if necessary. Partridge's face lit up with a sly smile. He took a puff on his cigar and chuckled.

"I see what you mean."

"What does the President intend to do?"

"He doesn't confide in me. Things might go easier for him at times if he paid a little more attention to the cumulative experience of the Senate."

"He can't knuckle under to those preachers", Broker huffed.

"Knuckle under", Partridge repeated. "He knuckled under when he gave them his word."

Did Partridge think a promise had been made or didn't he? It was impossible to tell. He seemed well disposed toward Morrow, but on the matter of the putative promise he apparently sided with the preachers.

"He just wants to stick it to the President", Broker said when the interview was over and they were going down a wide, bright corridor. "And what a chance."

Either the President knuckled under to the preachers or he didn't. If he didn't, he incurred the opposition of those who, like the preachers, saw church and state as the paramount issue. As between allowing Baptist preachers to lead the President around by the nose and filling a post that, whatever one thought of it, had a track record and a tradition, there was but one choice. If on the other hand, he defied the preachers, he stood to lose the chance of beginning a second term without the open opposition of his co-religionists.

"But it is a second term."

Broker thought of that. The notion that one might do what one liked, even act on principle alone, with impunity, brought tears to her eyes.

"So how can Partridge hurt the President?"

"Oh, he has four lovely years to do that."

"Who would have thought there would be a commotion about this?"

"You're not wavering, are you?"

"No."

He had wavered before making this trip to Washington. Both the President through Janet and Lannan through Monsignor Wales had mentioned the view that withdrawing the nomination might be the only solution. Janet spoke ruminatively of some recent examples of nominees put through the wringer only to have their names withdrawn by the President.

"Is that what he's going to do?"

"No!"

"Is that what he wants me to do?"

With a spoon she moved ice cubes around in her glass, as if she were the Titanic trying to maneuver through. "I can't help thinking how reluctant you were when I put the idea before you."

"You were very persuasive."

"I think of that too."

He'd be damned if he'd help her. It was pretty clear that her mission was to get him to fall on his sword in order to take the President off the hook—to mix some metaphors.

"The more I think of Rome the more excited I get at the prospect of spending years there."

"Let's hope we can handle the Senate."

"Who's in charge of that?"

"Chase."

"He pretty good?"

"The best."

Wales was, if anything, more oblique. He invited Morrow to share the irony that the Vatican post seemed to mean a lot more to the Baptists than it did to Catholics. "I wonder what they think the ambassador does?"

"Kiss the Pope's ring?"

"You're right. We've lost the sense of ceremony."

"I suppose Archbishop Lannan is pretty angry about the administration's letting this controversy drag on."

"About the President's alleged promise?"

"Yes."

"Oh, we've heard from them. What they want is for you to withdraw."

"Janet Fortin was out here again."

"I know."

Silence enveloped them. Did Wales never weary of the job that was his? Was it for this that he had stayed the long seminary course and prepared himself for the priesthood? He now held the post that Lannan had once held, and his prospects were very likely the same. Did he want to be a bishop?

"Your job is more or less diplomacy, isn't it, Monsignor?"

"Not if a diplomat is one sent abroad to lie for his country."

"How long have you been in Washington?"

No point in telling young Wales that he had written a profile of him and melded it with others when he wrote his chapter on the bureaucratization of the Church. Bright young priests were put behind desks in a monstrous building in which many of the functions of the federal government were mimicked. They were a lobby and, like a lobby, thought in terms of parliamentary maneuvers, public relations, compromise. After years of such deadening labor, they were elevated to the episcopacy and developed a comparable bureaucracy in their dioceses, inspiring pastors to bureaucratize their parishes. In the end no one was responsible for anything anymore. Things were simply too diffuse for that. Superstition abounded, as if all these random activities somehow made collective sense.

"Providence", one bishop had explained.

"Leave God out of it."

Of course he hadn't said that aloud. He hadn't written it either. But he had come to think of the committees and bureaus of the bishops as populated with men who had lost their faith, who were simply doing a job, who in the still hours of the morning might whisper at the ceiling, "I do not believe in God."

2

"What faith are you?" Senator Partridge asked Jackson, knowing what was written in his aide's file.

"I was raised Protestant, Senator."

"Do you know how many kinds of Protestants there are?"

"As many as there are Protestants. Isn't that the idea?"

"Maybe you're right."

Not that Senator Partridge believed that for a minute. Things went hand in hand though, that was plain as a wart on woman's nose; now anything goes in religion and anything goes in politics. There had to be a right way. Even if you did not take it, there had to be a right way. Otherwise, everything was...

The thought drifted out of his mind and slipped across the room on the cigar smoke he exhaled.

"We were all papists once, I suppose."

Jackson stopped shuffling papers and stared at him.

"Before the Reformation, I mean."

"I never thought of that."

"Neither had I. Well, it's no wonder it fell apart then. It's falling apart again. That fellow Morrow is right."

"I've been answering inquiries about the hearings by saying of course we're going ahead."

"Who's been asking?"

"The press of course. Every member of the committee but one."

"Crowe?"

"How'd you guess?"

"He'd be afraid you'd tell him the nomination had been withdrawn."

"I called his office anyway."

"Was he in?"

"I didn't ask."

"See if he'd like to have lunch."

"Today?"

"Today."

Partridge needed a guide through the maze this Vatican appointment was becoming.

Crowe, tall, lean, ascetic, a fanatic jogger, slipped into the passenger seat with a neutral greeting. The man even smelled fresh and healthy.

"I thought we'd go over to Arlington; okay with you?"

"Is it about the Vatican appointment?"

"Yes."

"Arlington's fine."

"I'm going to have to rely on you pretty heavily on this one, Martin. There are pitfalls on this path I may not even recognize."

"Morrow's a good man."

"I had a fine talk with him earlier."

"How the Catholic bishops can read his history and not bow their heads in shame is beyond me."

"Talking to my aide Jackson just now, it came up that there was a time when we were all papists."

Crowe nodded with delight at this concession. "At least Luther and the others had the honesty to say they were breaking with Rome. Now we have anti-papists who want to go on calling themselves Catholic."

"Why haven't they been excommunicated?"

"Good question."

Liggio's in Arlington was jammed, but there was always a table for two United States senators. The buzz of recognition followed them through the room, and it acted on Partridge as a tonic. There was no life to compare to that of the public servant. He hoped that his having lunch with Senator Crowe would be an item on the evening news. That should send a chill through the White House. But the truth was that Partridge still had no idea which direction to take on the nomination.

"Morrow is too good a man to be used in this way." Crowe meant that Morrow was being used by the bishops, not the administration. "They neither know of him nor care. You know that. This was a payoff to the bishops for selling out during the campaign."

"In what way?"

"Justice Norman. Their obligation was to back up Cardinal Guevara of New York and say calmly and firmly what the Church's teaching on homosexuality is. Instead we got a sanctimonious sermon by Lannan that confused the issue entirely. The question is not whether sinners can be forgiven but whether there is a sin to be forgiven."

"The woman caught in adultery."

"The Lord told her to go and sin no more. He didn't say she was innocent because she had had a bunch of hypocritical accusers."

"I like a man who knows his Bible."

"You know what Belloc called it? Those few fragments of Jewish folklore that the Church chooses to regard as inspired."

"Who's Belloc?"

"He was a member of Parliament."

"After Churchill, the only one I ever trusted was Thatcher."

"I'm going to advise Morrow to withdraw his name."

"You're not!"

"I favor abolishing the American Embassy to the Vatican."

Partridge brought his gin and tonic quickly to his mouth. He was unprepared for this. Crowe was the most vocal Catholic in the Senate. There had never been another like him in Partridge's time. The public would be surprised how many senators at any given time were Roman Catholics, but by and large they had been like the Kennedys and Moynihans and

Mikulskis. It just didn't figure in their public life. Crowe flaunted his Catholicism, he seemed genuinely proud to be a Catholic, and he had an annoying way of suggesting that the country had better start taking its direction from the Catholic Church or it was all over. "I mean of course from the Vatican," he would say, "from the wonderful encyclicals of the Holy Father, from the great Catholic tradition of social and political thought." An amazing senator.

"Morrow is a good man," Crowe went on, "but he was put forward by Lannan and the crowd at the NCCB. The President has permitted them to think that the ambassadorship is their call. I hate to see the rug pulled out from under Morrow, but I'm for closing down the store entirely. We have to face up to the fact that this is a missionary country."

"Missionary?"

"Would you call it a Christian country?"

"I always have."

3

Antonio Vilani, hunched forward at the table, watched his guest eat his pasta, making Archbishop Lannan feel like the apostolic pronuncio's taster. Vilani himself ate nothing but fruit. His ulcer had flared up, and he was reduced to a vicarious enjoyment of the meal prepared by his cook, a widowed aunt from Padua.

"I imagine you had something to do with the nomination of Professor Morrow?"

"The President was good enough to consult me."

This casual way of putting it clearly impressed Vilani. Well, Lannan was impressed too. He was far from being jaded by the high position he held. There was still that final rung on the ladder, however, and keeping close to Vilani was part of the steady pressure. Well, not pressure. With this Pope, the surest way of *not* getting something was to ask for it. But he had to keep his name on the right lips.

"Morrow's account of the Holy Father in his recent book is very laudatory", he assured the nuncio.

"The book has been described as an attack on the American bishops."

"You must read it."

Of course Vilani would already have read it. He was a most conscientious representative of the Holy Father, and there would be little of relevance to the Church that would not find its way into his reports to the Vatican.

After the pasta came a saltimbocca that set off a variety of different yet complementary gustatory sensations before melting in Lannan's mouth.

"This is delicious."

"It is her specialty."

"Does she have any weak points?"

"She is lonesome for Italy."

"I don't blame her."

Vivian chuckled. "When were you last there?"

"I am sure Washington has a bad reputation in Italy."

"My aunt is paralyzed with fear. She never goes out."

No wonder she was lonesome. Lannan told Vilani that he had wanted someone as ambassador who saw eye to eye with the Holy Father.

"Surely that is true of any Catholic."

"Morrow's eyes are 20/20."

Antonio Vilani, good diplomat that he was, did not pursue the matter. He had never asked Lannan or any of his predecessors for an explanation when some scandal exploded in the press. He was simply a conduit, making sure that his superiors were well informed, leaving the judgments to them.

"There is nothing to the rumor that the President intends to withdraw the nomination?"

"Why would he do that?"

Vilani paused in slicing a banana. "It is not for me to tell you of the indignation of your Protestant countrymen."

"Willie Butterworth? A tempest in a teapot."

Vilani sat back. "I love that phrase."

"It captures Willie perfectly."

"I confess that American politics confound me. I had thought that the critics had a case when they claimed they were promised that your embassy to the Vatican would be abolished."

"Holding a politician responsible for everything he says during a campaign would be like holding a preacher to account for everything he says from the pulpit."

Vilani slid a slice of banana into his mouth and considered the comparison. He didn't seem to think much of it. Lannan wondered what Vilani's reports on him were like. He wondered how this luncheon would be described by the nuncio in his report.

"Cardinal Guevara also urged me to read Professor Morrow's book."

Was this a delicate reference to the different approaches he and Guevara had taken in the Justice Leslie Norman matter? Lannan longed to hear what Vilani knew of the Roman reaction to his sermon. Without independent corroboration, he found himself unwilling to be reassured by Ambrose Frawley's reports.

"It might be a good idea to have Morrow's book reviewed in *L'Osservatore Romano*", Archbishop Lannan said. Did Vilani remember that Lannan's sermon on Justice Norman had been reprinted in the Vatican newspaper?

"I am sure they would welcome one."

"Consider it done."

"You will write it?" The question suggested a welcome version of the current president of the National Conference of Catholic Bishops. A good administrator, zealous pastor to his flock, but for all that, keeping up the life of the mind. Of course he would review Morrow's book. Wales could rough up a draft, and Lannan would take it from there.

"We were in school together, Archbishop Vilani."

"You were!"

"A very long time ago. In the minor seminary."

"You mean Morrow thought of becoming a priest?"

"I wonder if he has ever stopped thinking of it."

"You make him sound like an extremely interesting man. He is unmarried?"

"His wife is dead."

"Ah."

"The review would be a good way of introducing the new American ambassador to the Vatican."

"You are that confident he will be appointed?"

Lannan smiled but said no more.

4

"Good for him", Janet Fortin said when Gene Wales telephoned to report on his visit to Morrow.

"I wonder."

"I meant *Bravo*."

"Would you have bet he would dig in his heels? I had the impression he was looking for a way out from the time you talked him into it."

"Maybe it's pride."

"Which goes before a fall."

"I meant dignity. Maybe he just doesn't want to play other people's games."

Didn't he feel a trifle unclean for the part he had played in the nomination? Janet certainly did. But then there were few moral triumphs in her job. What satisfaction can be derived from conning the media into running a story designed to mislead?

"What is our position on the Morrow nomination?" she asked her colleagues later. She was having a drink with Casey and Jaeger in an uncharacteristic moment of repose.

"Position? Supine." Casey waggled his brows. Why couldn't he grow old gracefully?

"Morrow's been nominated by the President. That's our position."

If they knew something she didn't, they had taken a blood oath to keep it from her. They were distracted by a pair of tumblers—the still-camera guys and gals who sprawl on the floor in front of the press room podium, snapping away during briefings; whenever the President showed up in the press room, they went crazy. Now, looking like aging college kids, they came noisily into the bar. Jaeger faced a woman wearing glove-tight jeans, an unbuttoned shirt, dyed hair hanging to her shoulders, and half-glasses. Janet, her drink undrunk, picked up her purse and left Casey and Jaeger to the strong possibility of a venereal evening. If casual sex was their idea of the good life, they were living in the right town.

There was a message from Morrow on her answering machine and a local callback number. Was he in town? She dialed it and was beginning to think she had missed him when he said hello.

"Janet Fortin."

"I'm in town."

"Where are you staying?" Why didn't she know this? He was at the Omni Shoreham. "Nothing too good for our nominees."

"It is a little effete."

"Big feet we put up elsewhere. Who's taking care of you?"

"Jaeger? He booked this room. I've been squired about by Broker most of the day."

"Are you going to dinner with her?"

"I'm on my own."

"Come on over, and I'll make risotto."

"I called to ask you out."

"That isn't how it works. You're the guest of the administration."

"Are they paying for the risotto?"

"Here's my address."

After she hung up, she turned and looked to where a fragmented night scene was admitted by the tilted blinds at her window. What was going on? Was she being punished for not convincing Morrow he should withdraw his name? Casey and Jaeger, when she thought about it, had been holding back. If she didn't know Morrow was in town, one or both of them had to. They all should know, for that matter, unless something funny was going on.

When Morrow buzzed, she released the door and was waiting by the elevator to meet him. He looked just as he had when she visited him in Michigan, which meant he was a fish out of water. How many ambassadorial nominees showed up in loafers, suntans, and a tweed jacket?

"It's good to get out of that suit. I seem to have put on weight."

"What'll you have?" she asked after she settled him in the living room.

"I thought you said risotto."

"To drink."

"You got coffee?"

"Hanging on to your north woods habits? I am going to have a margarita."

"*Olé.*"

"How did it go?"

He came with her into the kitchen and sipped his coffee while she made her drink. "Pretty well, I think. I want to ask you about Partridge."

Well, she wanted to ask him about Jaeger. Not that she would give him any indication that she had been cut out on the nomination. From Morrow's account it was difficult to know what tack Partridge was taking.

"Maybe he's responsible for the invitation", he said when they headed back to the living room.

"Visiting members of the committee is routine."

"I mean the call from the Reverend Butterworth."

"Call? Tell me!"

"It wasn't an hour ago. He called to ask me to appear on his program."

"Wow."

"Either a hookup from here or I could fly to Tulsa."

"Who have you talked with about this?"

He looked at her, and she realized she was treating him like a child.

"Have you talked with anyone since Willie called?"

"Well, I telephoned you."

She could have hugged him. That meant that Jaeger had no idea of this, and of course Morrow couldn't reach him now even if he had tried. Janet let tequila run over her tongue then swallowed it as if she really weren't swallowing. What advice should she give Morrow? By God, this would show them they couldn't play footsie with Janet Fortin. She had cultivated Morrow—twice she had gone on difficult missions to Michigan—and now they booked him into a hotel and let the visitation of members of the committee begin without even letting her know.

"What are you going to do?" Even as she asked, she was trying to think what decision of his would most upset her co-workers.

"I accepted."

"You did!"

"It seemed too good an opportunity to be missed. He has legitimate questions, and I'd like to answer them."

"On his show? With his audience? He'll murder you."

"We got along well enough on the phone."

"Have you ever watched his show?"

"Not lately. He did a series that interested me while I was writing my book. He seemed to think Vatican II had been a summit meeting aimed at the gradual takeover of the United States."

He grinned and drank his coffee, and Janet felt like crying. He was too nice a guy to have this happen to him. After several attempts by others to get him to withdraw, he had managed to arrange his own suicide on Willie Butterworth's show. And it had happened on Jaeger's watch. There was no way in the world he would be able to explain this. Her elation was short-lived. Who would care if Morrow was made an ass out of by Willie? That would do in his nomination, which was what the administration clearly wanted. If the preacher wiped up the floor with the professor, the administration's hands were clean. Janet almost groaned aloud as she imagined Jaeger taking credit for the outcome. The bastard. Even now he was probably tangling with that half-glassed monkey, unaware of what was happening.

She turned on the television to Willie's cable channel and left Morrow watching it while she went to the kitchen to try her hand at risotto. She was using minute rice and canned mushrooms, and the wine was a California red. But then he didn't drink wine. After tossing the salad, she made toast and sprinkled it with garlic salt. They would eat off trays in the living room. This was going to be a working dinner, after all. She would do what she could to hold down the damage Morrow would suffer on Willie's program.

"He's pretty smooth", Morrow said.

"Wise as a serpent and simple as a dove."

"The format does favor the host a bit, doesn't it?"

"Uh-huh. Usually that's just to make it clear he's the star of the show. You may be the first hostile guest he's ever had."

"Hostile?"

"He'll be a hostile host. Count on it. You're a minion of the Whore of Babylon."

"I wonder what he'll ask me."

"Let's think about that."

It was soon clear that he was far from being the babe in the woods his manner suggested. After all, the kind of questions Willie might ask were right down Morrow's alley, matters of history and theology.

By ten o'clock he was yawning. "It's been a long day."

"What's on tomorrow?"

"Tulsa."

"I thought you meant to go out there."

"My plane leaves Reagan National at 6:30."

"Tomorrow! You should have asked for several days!"

" 'If 'twere done 'twere well 'twere done quickly'."

"Who said that?"

"Mistress Quickly."

She shrugged and nodded when he laughed. She had missed some academic joke. "Don't try that with Butterworth."

133

5

The Senator Crowe file in Archbishop Lannan's office bulged with letters, Senate transcripts, newspaper clippings—a fairly comprehensive record of the discontent felt by the senator and those he presumed to speak for. The newest addition was a memo by Monsignor Wales on the conversation Crowe had had with Partridge about the Morrow nomination. The senator wanted the president of the NCCB to hear from the senator's own lips his decision to oppose the nomination of James Morrow and support a resolution that the American Embassy to the Vatican be abolished.

"Willie will love that."

"It won't be the first time Crowe has made common cause with the fundamentalists", Gene Wales said.

"Theirs is a common cause. But will it prevail?"

"Not if the administration pulls out all the stops and supports its nominee."

"You sound sceptical."

"They've had some of the same misgivings we have."

Lannan's jaw twitched at the ascription of responsibility to him. He had been a model of circumlocution when he instructed Wales prior to his trip to Michigan.

"Partridge and Crowe had lunch together rather conspicuously today."

"It looks bad for my old friend Jim Morrow, doesn't it? How I regret he is involved in this."

Was Lannan gifted with such self-delusion that he'd forgotten that it was at his initiative that Morrow's name had been put forward? It is not likely that the aide to a prominent man will hold him in awe, but when the actions of the great invite contempt, a point of danger has been reached. Wales was unwilling, even if he was capable, of joining Lannan in bemused reflection on the vagaries of Providence and the unpredictability of the works of man.

"It isn't the Senate that will do him in."

Lannan's patrician brows lifted. "The President?" He shook his head in cosmic disapproval. "A man to steer clear of."

Wales freshened Lannan's Scotch and then excused himself. His apartment was high up under the roof, luxurious, but diminutive. He was alternately ashamed and shamelessly proud of his quarters. Janet was one of the few non-clerics to have seen the place.

"The monk in his cell", she had murmured on her first visit.

"I am not a monk. Surely, I don't have to explain to you the difference between a diocesan priest and a religious."

"Just as surely, you are about to."

Why did the explanation seem to reduce to the fact that the diocesan priest could acquire wealth? The promise of celibacy was as practically confining as the vow of chastity, and a priest owed obedience to his bishop, vow or not. The religious stood out because of his vowed renunciation of personal property. Of course, in the event, this was more of a theoretical than a practical difference. There were few religious houses that had an air of austerity about them. The first time, some years before, that Wales had been a guest in the common room of a religious house, he had marveled at the leather chairs, the massive screen of the television set, and the varied contents of the liquor cabinet. Religious seemed to have assigned cars now, as once they had inscribed in books *Ad usum fratris Leonis,* though Brother Leo owned the book as much as any priest or layman owned his books.

"How can you acquire wealth on the salaries you're paid?"

"Some inherit it."

"That's not acquiring it."

"Of course most priests are poor, or of modest means."

Most but not all. There were those who had turned a small

sum into large thanks to years of following the market with prudence and caution and, from time to time, real daring.

Tonight Wales thanked God for his suite of rooms and drove away all thoughts of guilt for their comfort. From his miniature refrigerator he fished forth a beer, drank deeply, then picked up the phone and called Janet.

"What's going on?"

"In what respect?" Her tone was guarded.

"I see that Crowe and Partridge had lunch together."

"Morrow is making the rounds."

"He's in town?"

"I guess that means you didn't know either. I found out myself quite by accident. I feel like awful for my part in what's happening to him."

"Is the President dropping him?"

"I wish I knew."

"You don't know?"

"I seem to be out of the loop. Morrow was brought to town, put up in a hotel, and started to make the rounds of members of the committee, and I knew nothing about it. If he hadn't called, I might have read of it in the papers."

"He called you?"

There was a pause. "If you're decent you might come over and I'll tell you all about it."

"It's 11:45."

"I've got news."

He had slipped off his shoes but otherwise was still dressed. He told her he'd be there *quam primum*.

"When is that?"

"Right away."

He didn't wear a collar and pulled up the collar of his top coat, a silly precaution. Anyone who knew him would recognize him, and there was less possibility of raising eyebrows if he was in full clericals, but no matter.

136

"I still have some coffee", Janet announced.

"Coffee!"

"That's what he wanted."

"Well, I don't. Do you have beer?"

"Such a proletarian."

"I prefer it."

"To what?"

"Is that a margarita?"

"It was", she said and drained the glass. "Take a pew."

Within a minute she had given him the news. Morrow was off to Tulsa at the crack of dawn to appear on Willie's channel.

"My God, is he crazy?"

"He wants to disarm his critics."

"Willie?"

"We watched the channel while he was here; he hadn't seen it in a while, but he was unabashed. Maybe he can handle him."

"Sure."

"He's a very bright man."

"But is he shrewd?"

"If he were he would have sent me packing my first visit out there."

Janet was obviously filled with apprehension for Morrow. Tomorrow night at this time, Morrow could be dead as a dodo so far as a political appointment went, and public embarrassment would have its effect on his scholarly reputation. Millions watched Willie's channel, but millions more would see clips of any massacre that occurred.

"Willie just called him up out of the blue and asked him to appear on his television hour?" It was the fiction of Willie's channel that he himself broadcast live for only one hour each day, but at least a third of the daily programming featured the taped founder, owner, and pastor of what Butterworth called the Cable Church.

"It seems to have been more like a challenge."

"I wonder if someone put the idea in Willie's head. Senator Partridge?"

"When all the dust settles I want to sit down with Morrow and tell him just what happened and who made it happen."

Janet paused. "He's not naive. What really bothers Morrow is that someone—Willie, anyone—should think that his religious faith somehow disqualifies him for office in this country."

"A man of principle."

He might have been noting that neither of them worked for a man of principle. There were ways of describing the mode of operating of those in positions of power in church and state that were not damning. Politics is, after all, the art of compromise. To fail to recognize this, was to become a progressively less audible trumpet. The need to reconcile opposites often made the reconciler seem duplicitous, not speaking quite the same way to rival camps, never expressing his own full unvarnished thoughts on anything. But the skills of the ruler soon became the vices of the manipulator. When someone like Morrow came among such old hands at forever avoiding the full truth, he was a novelty and, inevitably, a victim.

Wales drove home wishing that he had been able to speak with Morrow before he went off for his Tulsa ordeal. At the same time he was glad he hadn't had the opportunity. What could he have possibly said that would be helpful?

6

A stretch limousine with tinted windows, opaque to outsiders, picked up Morrow at the Tulsa airport. The driver was accompanied by a man of indeterminate age who seemed to be wearing make-up. It turned out that he was.

"Sheller", he said in tones of self-deprecation. "I came right from the set. Reverend Willie welcomes you to Tulsa and to the Cable Church."

Tom Sheller, it emerged, was the anchor of "News and Good News" as well as host of "This is The Day the Lord Has Made", a morning show that mimicked the morning shows of the secular networks.

"We operate as an alternative to the networks, not just on their edges. Our viewers stick with us all day."

The makeup, doubtless meant to smooth over Sheller's pocked skin, had dried into a problem of its own. When they were on their way, Sheller said, "I thought you might bring someone with you."

"Oh?"

"Advisors, that sort of thing. Frankly, Willie was surprised you accepted his invitation."

"I thought it was kind of him to ask me."

Sheller glanced at him. "He thought the administration would prevent it."

"Well, here I am."

"Did the administration try to prevent your coming?"

"I didn't ask their permission."

They came to a stop at an intersection, and, looking out at the pedestrians, some of whom were regarding the car with something other than delight, Morrow realized that they could not see into the car. It was unsettling to look at people only a few feet away and be utterly invisible to them. The car started forward, and was followed on its way by hostile glares.

The Cable Church looked like a college campus, and that in a sense is what it was, although the Bible formed the single subject matter of the curriculum. The studio was a church, a great glass structure whose steel steeple reached like a stalagmite into the Oklahoma sky. The limousine was waved through the gate, circled the church, and disappeared into an underground garage from which they were whooshed by elevator to the office of the Reverend Willie.

The evangelist, seen so often on television, seemed an old acquaintance, if not a friend. His hand was soft and warm.

"I'll just say hello and welcome you, Professor Morrow. You have approximately an hour before we go on the air. The Reverend Sheller will take you where you can be alone. I find that interviews go best if the participants are kept apart until the broadcast. That way everything is fresh."

"In my case, stale, I'm afraid."

"Oh, I doubt that, Professor. Anything you need, just ask for it."

"At my age my first request is always the location of the restroom."

Willie laughed too heartily. He seemed displeased by reference to bodily functions. Ah well, it was a foolish thing to say, however true.

During the next hour it occurred to Morrow that leaving him alone was part of a practiced device to gain psychological advantage. The room he had been taken to looked like a movie set, and he was almost surprised to find that the books in the shelves flanking the little electric fireplace were genuine. Some Readers Digest condensed books, but for the most part publications of the Cable Church and several other religious publishing houses.

He sat in a straight-backed chair, folded his arms, and closed his eyes. The best preparation would be to keep his mind a blank. He had no idea what he had let himself in for. Should he be worried? Janet Fortin had regarded him as she might a lamb on its way to slaughter, but of course, like the others, her interest was appearance rather than reality. What a way to spend one's life, trying to make events appear favorable to one's cause, whatever it was. Janet and her colleagues cared less about what might actually happen in an exchange with Willie than what they could persuade people had happened. He moved his head slowly from side to side. This was no way not to think of what lay ahead. He called up the image of Lake Powderhorn as seen from the porch of his cottage, and he could almost feel the wicker chair beneath him. Peace descended upon him, and in moments he was asleep, but the image of the lake and the sense of being at his Michigan cottage came with him into sleep.

He came awake at the urgent sound of Sheller.

"Are you all right?"

Sheller had washed off his makeup. Only gradually did anxiety give way to relief.

"I fell asleep."

"When I came in I thought at first…"

"That I was dead?"

Sheller was embarrassed. "I didn't expect to find you asleep."

"I got up very early."

"I'll take you to the set."

Sheller led him along a cluttered corridor between props and various electrical gadgetry. They came out into the open, and at the far end of a vast area, an illumined set was visible. Permanent seats rose in semicircles from floor level, filled with men and women, most of late middle age, waiting patiently. Sheller led him onto the set and placed him in a chair. From behind, a lavaliere microphone was slipped around his neck, and before he could prevent it, a soft brush moved rapidly over his face. Sheller turned and without a word went away. The brushing was completed, and Morrow was alone. He became aware of dozens of pairs of eyes fixed on him, curious, wary, some frowning. Heads leaned toward one another, and the sound of whispers filled the studio.

Suddenly there was a great burst of applause, organ music swelled, and Butterworth swept onto the stage and took his seat, a chair elevated somewhat above Morrow's. The evangelist beamed at his audience, blessed, and greeted them all and then, having paused, told them who his special guest was. His look was stern when he addressed Morrow.

"Professor Morrow, you have been nominated to be Vatican ambassador. Why should the United States recognize a religious leader?"

"The Pope? He is also the ruler of Vatican City."

"An area smaller than that of the Cable Church. You don't seriously mean that the Pope is a government leader like our President."

"It's not a question of what I mean. It's simply a fact."

"Do we have an ambassador to the Dalai Lama?"

"We have embassies in Iran and Israel and a number of countries where our distinction between church and state does not apply. The Queen is head of the Church of England, of course, and we have an ambassador to the Court of St. James."

"Foreign countries. The question is, does it apply here!" Willie looked triumphantly toward his audience and was rewarded with an approving murmur. He let it go on for a moment before lifting his hand. "Do you believe in the separation of church and state?"

"I don't consider it a matter of belief. Particularly when it means so many different things to different people."

"What does it mean to the Supreme Court?"

"Reverend Butterworth, neither you nor I are likely to permit the Supreme Court to determine our beliefs."

Butterworth's adamant opposition to *Roe v. Wade* had made him a stalwart of the prolife movement.

"I applaud your refusal to let the court override common sense on the matter of abortion", Morrow went on. "Most people know that an expectant mother is expecting a child."

This slogan of Butterworth's anti-abortion campaign brought an approving reaction from the audience.

"Now let's not confuse the issue, Professor. If you were the U.S. ambassador to the Vatican, who would have your first loyalty, the Pope or your country?"

"As ambassador?"

"What if the Pope commanded you to sabotage American participation in population control programs in Italy?"

"Population control?"

"The distribution of contraceptives to the poor and needy."

"In Vatican City? If I find any poor and needy there, apart from Franciscans, I will recommend that we send food and clothing, not contraceptives."

"Is your primary loyalty to the Pope or to your country?"

"Didn't Christ give us the answer to that? I render to Caesar the things that are Caesar's and to God the things that are God's."

Willie threw himself back in his seat. "Do you confuse the Pope and God?"

"No more than the Pope does."

The audience had grown restive, and Morrow sensed anxiety that their hero was not doing as well as they expected.

"Reverend Butterworth, isn't your fundamental concern that the U.S. ambassador to the Vatican gives Catholics an unfair advantage over Protestants?"

"No! I don't want any advantage. I am not interested in confusing my religion and my citizenship."

"That's an odd disinterest."

"Odd! That's what this country is based on."

"I have to disagree with you there, Reverend. For most of our history, religion was looked upon, quite rightly, as the chief influence on the public life of citizens and the bulwark of society. I can't imagine Abraham Lincoln making a secret of his religious beliefs. It's only in very recent times that a dogma has been created by the courts, a so-called wall of separation, that has the end effect of treating religious faith as a menace. They'll permit us to believe in God so long as it makes no difference in how we live and act. That's not my idea of what it means to be a Christian. And I don't think it's yours either. I have always admired the courage with which you make your beliefs known in the public forum. This country owes you a tremendous debt, Reverend Butterwoth."

The applause seemed to relieve the tension in the studio. Morrow joined in, applauding his host.

"You have written a book about your Church, haven't you, Professor?"

"Yes, I have."

"I understand that you think things have been going badly for Catholics?"

"Indeed I do, and in many ways. And they are self-inflicted wounds, the worst kind. We've been the victims of some very strange interpretations of Vatican II, the great ecumenical council held in the early 1960s."

Butterworth seemed to have read the book, but what interested him most was the controversy over birth control. "Why do you make such a fuss over it?"

"For the same reason we make a fuss over abortion. Of course it is not *our* fuss, as if it were a rule of the club. It is God's law. Some Catholics seem to think the Pope can change God's law, but of course that's nonsense."

"But the Pope is infallible."

"Only as an interpreter of God's revelation. His power is delegated. It is the power Christ delegated to Peter. No more than Peter does he have the power to teach anything that conflicts with Christian revelation."

"But he can add to it?"

"Yes. But only in the sense that you do when you preach the Gospel, telling us what it means, not just reading it. You have told millions how that Book speaks to our times."

The audience liked that too, of course, and let Butterworth and the television audience know they did.

"I don't think anyone ever compared me to the Pope before", Butterworth said; but he said it with a laugh.

"You have a lot in common. Above all, a rock-solid faith in the truth of divine revelation."

The interview continued, going off in various directions, with Butterworth obviously less and less intent on putting Morrow on the spot. And then, soon as it seemed, the hour neared its end.

"Professor, I want to thank you for coming all the way out here to Tulsa, and on such short notice. You are obviously a man of great integrity."

"Although Catholic?"

Butterworth roared with laughter, the audience joined in, and moments later as the program ended Butterworth heaved from his chair and took Morrow by the hand. On a monitor Morrow caught a glimpse of their handshake behind the rolling credits.

"I wish there were more Catholics like you, Professor."

"I wish there were more Protestants like you."

It ended in a love fest. Butterworth lifted their clasped hands high, and the audience gave them a standing ovation.

An hour later Morrow was headed back to the airport.

7

Archbishop Lannan sent Gene Wales out to National to intercept Jim Morrow when he returned and to bring him to his residence. The feeling of dread with which he had watched the

Butterworth Show had quickly given way to admiration at the way Jim had handled himself. A certain disaster had been turned into a surprising triumph. The sight of the two men standing with raised clasped hands on the familiar set of the Cable Church was an image that would sweep away all opposition to the nomination. Lannan realized that he had written off Jim's nomination as a lost cause. Now it seemed a certainty.

"Our man in Rome", Lannan said, turning to beam at Gene Wales.

The monsignor nodded, brows lifted, but said nothing.

"Imagine what they're thinking over at the White House, Gene."

"Pretty much what we are, I suppose."

Lannan laughed. The administration's treachery had failed to sink Jim Morrow. He would owe his appointment far more to himself than to the President. Only after Gene had gone back to his own office did another less-welcome interpretation of his secretary's remark occur. Had Gene meant that they had acted in the same way at the NCCB as they had at the White House? He dismissed the thought. It simply wasn't true. Hadn't he called Jim to assure him of his wholehearted support when things began to go sour? Jim Morrow would remember that, even if Gene Wales had forgotten.

The corridors buzzed with the excited reaction to Morrow's appearance on the Butterworth channel. "Professor Pacifies Preacher" was the headline on Compuserve, and the story told of the victory of reason over bigotry. Lannan was not surprised to hear an hour later, when Fr. Leach looked in to tell him, that Morrow's arrival was being carried on television.

"Live?"

"C-SPAN."

Even so. Lannan followed Leach into an office where several staffers stood around a television set.

Once more, Jim came across impressively. Lannan had never

thought of his old friend as photogenic or as adroit as he had proved himself in Tulsa. He felt a twinge of envy until Cathy Hammersmith, a Dominican nun, gave him a toothy smile.

"Your choice is vindicated, Archbishop."

On the screen, a reporter was suggesting to Jim that he had skillfully manipulated the evangelist, beating him on his own turf. Jim looked at the woman.

"I'm sorry you got that impression. Reverend Butterworth and I had a useful exchange of views. I wish there were more of that going on. He is a wonderful man, with the concerns of his faith and his country at heart. If I was able to allay any fears he had about the good citizenship of Catholics, I am glad. I wonder how many Catholic bishops would have acted as manfully as Reverend Butterworth did."

"What do you mean?"

"Well, I've heard him dismissed as a fundamentalist, an extremist. But any Catholic has essentially the same faith as Reverend Butterworth. After all, there is only one baptism."

"Is it true that they put you in solitary before the program began?"

"They provided a quiet place for me to take a nap. I got up very early this morning."

"What was that you said about the Catholic bishops, Professor?"

Lannan went back to his office with the sinking feeling that Jim Morrow's triumph was not going to trickle down to him. Jim did not sound like a man who would be grateful to his old friend for putting his name forward as ambassador. Would Jim do him harm in Rome? His phone rang, and he picked it up himself.

"Tom? Maureen. Wasn't he wonderful?" She just assumed he would know she meant Jim Morrow.

"I hope he knows it was your suggestion that I send his name to the White House."

"I'll never let him forget it."

"You also said his appointment would be helpful to me in Rome."

"It will be, Tom. I promise you."

Just like that his good spirits were back. His euphoria lasted until Gene Wales returned empty-handed. He had been beaten to the punch.

"The White House?"

He hesitated. "Janet Fortin."

The committee hearings went smoothly, and two weeks later his nomination was confirmed by the full Senate. James Morrow was the new United States ambassador to the Vatican.

PART THREE

CHAPTER ONE

I

Mrs. Christiansen lived in a residence on south Lyndale, a block from the Crosstown, filed away with others her age, awaiting with wary eye the common fate. Maureen parked her car and walked slowly toward the entrance. A melancholy gloom seemed to advance to meet and envelop her. Inside the street door, an inner door slid open, and she became aware of three women parked in wheelchairs aimed at the door. They looked as if they were contemplating an escape.

"Margie?" the chubby receptionist said, when Maureen asked for Mrs. Christiansen. "How nice. Please sign in."

As she did so, Maureen heard a whirring sound. The three motorized wheelchairs drew near.

"Are you her daughter?" the receptionist asked.

"A friend of her daughter."

"Thank God." The woman stepped back from the counter and brought fat little hands together, eclipsing her nameplate on which "Norma" was stamped. Patty cake.

"Why do you say that?"

"She's always talking about her daughter, but we've never seen her." She leaned toward Maureen and whispered across the counter. "They make things up."

Maureen felt no impulse to tell Norma that Karen was dead.

"Suite 45."

That seemed as distant as "sweet 16" here. Maureen was given directions. She hadn't expected to be given the run of the place. The three wheelchairs turned slowly clockwise as she passed. The corridors ran beneath low ceilings, the walls were papered colorfully, the floor was carpeted. The whole place looked clean and comfortable, but there was the pervasive air of a mortuary viewing-room and the faint smell of urine.

At the end of a hallway, she turned right and came upon another set of double doors. Through them was a parlor with numbered doors indicating the suites. At 45, only the bottom half of a dutch door was closed. Maureen looked over it into the room.

The old woman sat immobile, staring straight ahead, as if at a television screen, but there was no television in her line of sight. Sun played on the curtained window; a low bed was the most prominent object of furniture. Maureen saw that there was a television with a darkened screen in the corner.

"Mrs. Christiansen?"

There was no reaction. The old woman continued to stare ahead. Knocking had no effect either. Maureen opened the dutch door and stepped inside. She was two feet from Mrs. Christiansen before the old woman noticed, but when she looked up her expression did not change.

"I'm Maureen. Maureen Bailey? Karen's friend."

The old woman leaned forward as Maureen spoke, then put her fingers in her ears. Maureen realized that she was doing something to her hearing aids.

"What?"

"Maureen Bailey. I knew Karen."

The mouth dropped open, but then she shook her head slightly. "Again."

In the end, Mrs. Christiansen handed Maureen a pad, and she wrote down the message.

"For heaven's sake!"

"I got your letter."

"My letter."

"You wrote me in Rome." Maureen wrote this down for her too. The old woman considered the page.

"In Rome?"

"I live in Rome." She printed out the words now, telling Mrs. Christiansen what she had said. Indirection and diplomacy seemed out of place. "Did Karen have a child?"

The old woman nodded. And began to talk. It was better then, just listening, even though Karen's mother said she did not recognize Maureen.

"I'm older."

"What?"

She waved it away. Words had to be used economically here, no subtleties or jokes.

Karen's little girl Peggy had lived with Mrs. Christiansen, even when Karen did not. The old woman said that she had raised her granddaughter just as she had her own daughter. Not that she was complaining. Peggy was a wonderful girl. A hoarse whisper. "Not half so wild as her mother."

"Peggy."

"Named for me."

There was a cedar chest against the wall, and Mrs. Christiansen instructed Maureen to open it. She wanted one of the dozen photograph albums in the chest. Maureen was shown picture after picture. She easily recognized Karen, and the pictures of her daughter brought back memories of that summer at the Catholic Youth Center. The girl had the same provocative good looks her mother had had at that age, and in every picture she flirted with the camera.

"The father?" Maureen asked, not looking at the old woman.

No response. Apparently she hadn't heard. Maureen wrote

out the question: Do you have any pictures of the father?

The old eyes narrowed, and she began to rock slightly back and forth. Her mouth trembled.

"You told me in your letter", Maureen said, to relieve the old woman's distress, but she was not heard.

"A priest", Mrs. Christiansen said finally, the word whistling through her dentures. "That's why they never married."

Maureen sat back and closed her eyes. Dear God. Any hope that the old woman had forgotten her accusation was gone. She had specifically named Tom Lannan. But that made no sense. If Tom Lannan was supposed to have fathered Peggy the summer they all worked at the CYO, he was not yet a priest then. If he had not married Karen, holy orders were not the impediment. But perhaps he had not been given the choice. In her letter, Mrs. Christiansen had not said that the father knew of the child.

"How old is Peggy?"

She wrote the question; the old woman thought, but she could not come up with an answer. Not to remember something that important would have seemed encouraging if Mrs. Christiansen were not so old. Was there anything in the cedar chest that might say? Maureen studied the photographs for a date or some indication of when they were taken. Perhaps that could be determined from things in the background of the picture, but she found no clue.

The longer she spoke with Mrs. Christiansen, the less sense the old woman made. It was difficult to know what to make of her story.

"Have you told people?"

A shocked look, as if this was a dark family secret. But then why did she discuss it so freely with a stranger she did not recognize as her daughter's friend? The suggestion was that no one else knew.

"Where did you get my address in Rome?"

"From the priest."

"Here?"

"Fr. Szabo."

Mrs. Christiansen rose when Maureen said she must go. She positioned herself behind a walker and started toward the door. Apparently she meant to show her guest out. It became clear that she wanted others to see that she had had a visitor. There were more old people gathered by the door of what turned out to be the dining room. It was four-thirty in the afternoon. Early birds. Maureen stood there for several minutes, on display, and before leaving, bent to kiss the dry wrinkled cheek offered her. The others witnessed this affectionate farewell with different reactions.

"I'll be back", she said brightly.

Several pairs of milky eyes looked resentfully at her. But then their attention, including Mrs. Christiansen's, was drawn to the just-opened doors of the dining room, and they moved at what speed they could command to their tables.

Maureen stopped at the counter and asked the receptionist where she might find Fr. Szabo. Norma thought she was inquiring about another resident. Maureen explained that he was a priest who visited Mrs. Christiansen.

"I don't know any Fr. Szabo."

"Isn't there a chaplain here?"

"Ministers stop by."

She called Frank to see if he knew such a priest.

"Chet Szabo? Sure. He was pastor of St. Charles in Mendota."

"Where is he now?"

"Dead."

"When did he die?"

Frank rubbed his chin and looked about on the ceiling. "Five years ago? Maybe ten."

"Hmmm." Maureen looked at the phone, wondering

155

whether she should tell Frank more, not that she would have done so over the telephone.

"Why do you ask?"

"I visited the mother of an old friend of mine today, and she mentioned him."

"When are you going back?"

"Next Monday." She would fly out of Minneapolis then, but she intended to stop in Washington. Like it or not, she meant to tell Tom Lannan about Mrs. Christiansen's story.

That afternoon, she drove alone to Excelsior where she parked and then walked along the shore, looking out at the little bay. Minnetonka was made up of bays that had the shape of pieces from a jigsaw puzzle. Once there had been an amusement park here, a great attraction to the youth of Minneapolis. She had come here once with Karen, and it had been like a vacation from her real self. Karen encouraged two boys who talked to them, and they spent hours together, on the ferris wheel, on the merry-go-round; and Maureen let the boy, a perfect stranger, kiss her. That was all, but Maureen had felt awful. Karen never alluded to it afterward, thank God, and there had never been a repetition. But then Karen and Tom started doing things together.

They couldn't be called dates, exactly, not at first. Remembering Excelsior, Maureen had wanted to say something to Tom, or at least to Frank, so he could ask his roommate what he was up to. In those days, a seminarian who dated was subject to expulsion. But it was Fr. Parente who spoke to Tom. Maureen learned of this because of the version of the scolding she got via Frank. It was pretty obvious that Tom had depicted Fr. Parente as a suspicious man with an overly active imagination. A week after Fr. Parente called him in, Tom took another job, in the bottling plant at Grain Belt Beer in Minneapolis.

It occurred to Maureen now that Fr. Parente might have

clearer memories than Mrs. Christiansen. The youthful foibles of the current archbishop of Washington were very likely to stick in the priest's mind.

2

Monsignor Gene Wales went back to his desk in the outer office after he had taken Mrs. Kilmartin into the archbishop's office, leaving the door open. He was busy at his computer when he heard the door of the Archbishop Lannan's office close. As if on signal, Leach stepped in from the hallway.

"Who's the lady?"

"Which lady?"

"Come on."

Wales just looked at the cadaverous cleric from Toledo. Ever since Leach had suggested that James Morrow was a crypto liberal and that his lengthy and detailed account of what he regarded as the crumbling of the Catholic Church in the United States in the decades since the Council was actually an endorsement of all the changes he criticized, Wales had decided that civil distance was the best stance to take with the staffer who had been wished upon them by Bishop Fenny.

"It's Mrs. Kilmartin. Just answer yes or no", Leach demanded.

"Yes or no."

Leach's face twisted in a smile. "A disinterested observer would say that you are protecting your boss from suspicion."

"What would an interested observer say?"

"Actually, I know it's Mrs. Kilmartin. I had a little chat with her driver downstairs."

"Does she have a driver?"

"From the Irish Embassy. Pretty nice. I understand that she and the archbishop go back a long way, to when they were youngsters in Minneapolis."

"Is that right?"

Undaunted, Leach took a chair and put a thin, brown paper cigarette in his mouth. "Mind?"

"Matter?"

"That is very witty. An epistemological joke." He lit the cigarette. "Nate Patch told me all about it."

"Epistemology?"

Smoke rolled from Leach's mouth as if it were his departing soul. He decided that monologue was preferable to dialogue and began to discourse on the time when Archbishop Lannan, James Morrow, and Frank Bailey were classmates in the minor seminary of the archdiocese of St. Paul.

"They were known as the Three Musketeers. Predictable seminary humor. And not understood, at that. The man who told me thought the description might have been based on a Steve Martin movie made a quarter of a century after the fact. I pointed this out to him. That was my mistake; he clammed up. Fortunately, I could rely on what Patch had learned. Our very own Clark Kent actually flew out there. But only as fast as the speeding plane that bore him. One would not have thought of him as an investigative reporter. He has spent his life slightly revising official handouts and putting them on the wire. Anyway, the widow Kilmartin, also the widow of one Raymond Barrett, was born Maureen Bailey. The stormy petrel's sister! Now you know as well as I do that it was after a chummy little lunch in Arlington that his excellency had the brilliant idea of sending James Morrow's name over to the White House. Why do you suppose Lannan would propose his presumed enemy? Because he is an old friend, that's why. One of his oldest. Do you know that he flew out to Notre Dame to officiate at the funeral of the late Mrs. Morrow?"

It was painful to listen to Leach tell him things he already knew—Wales had accompanied the archbishop on the trip to South Bend—but he was also hearing things he had not known. Whether or not it was sinister, a gossip like Leach could make the fact that the archbishop and Mrs. Kilmartin had known one another since they were kids, plus the fact that she was the sister of the leading dissenter among American theologians, look extremely curious. Who would listen to Leach? It appeared that he had gotten most of his information from Nathaniel Patch. It was hearing of Patch's visit to Minneapolis that hit Wales. Not that he gave any indication of this. Leach babbled on, indifferent to the fact that Wales had turned back to his computer.

Should he inform Lannan of what Leach was saying? One of his unstated functions was to prevent the archbishop from being blindsided. There was something to be said for making a little announcement about the longstanding relationship of the three musketeers, including a mention of the sister of Frank Bailey. If anything, this would win back credit to Lannan for the appointment. Or blame. And wouldn't Frank Bailey be disarmed by being made to seem one of the inner circle?

The archbishop buzzed. Leach sprang from his chair.

"Stick around, I'll introduce you."

"Another time."

And Leach scampered off down the hallway. Wales went into the inner office where Mrs. Kilmartin turned an apologetic smile on him. Lannan hunched forward behind his desk.

"Gene, Mrs. Kilmartin came here in an Irish Embassy car that's waiting downstairs. Would you mind telling the driver he needn't wait?"

"Please?" Mrs. Kilmartin added. At the moment, Monsignor Wales thought there was little he would not do for this gracious lady. He felt a surge of anger at Leach's malicious speculations. Mrs. Kilmartin was on her way back to Rome and had stopped to say good-bye. That was what he had decided not to tell Leach.

"Of course."

"Mrs. Kilmartin and I will be leaving, Gene. We might be gone when you come back."

This brought her to her feet. She extended a gloved hand, and Wales took it. "If I can ever run an errand for you, Monsignor, let me know. This was his idea."

"I don't seem to have a key to the car", Lannan said, emptying the contents of his pockets on the desk.

Wales took his from his key ring, put it on the desk, and left, still aglow from the brief encounter with Mrs. Kilmartin.

It was a shame there was no Mrs. Morrow to reign in Rome as Mrs. Kilmartin had when her husband represented Ireland at the Vatican.

3

Mentioning Leach's enigmatic remark to Lorraine had been unwise: ever since, she had been after Nate Patch to pursue that spoor.

"Pursue it where?"

She brought her chin chestward and looked at him over her glasses.

"Lorraine, this is a woman he knew a long time ago. Not even Leach thinks they have seen one another in years."

"Didn't he say she put the bug in his ear about Morrow."

"Maybe she's got something going with Morrow."

Lorraine took this under advisement. Patch found the topic unsavory. Whatever criticisms there might be of the journalism he practiced, it steered clear of character assassination or even the milder forms of prurience. Lorraine took a different tack. "Nate, it doesn't have to be hanky pank. Think of it in terms of melancholy regret. The fifty-year-old man gets together with an old flame and is beset by thoughts of what might have been."

"There isn't any evidence that she proposed Morrow, let alone that she is an old flame. That's just Leach's inflamed imagination."

"Is that right?"

Lorraine, it seemed, had been doing a little digging on her own. A waitress at the restaurant in Arlington where the two lunched had given her a word picture of the clearly intimate tête-à-tête between the archbishop and the impressively handsome woman with a sort of Irish accent.

"He was wearing clericals."

"Some rendezvous."

"She came for him. She just dropped by."

"Have you been talking with Leach too?"

"Nate, we'll write it together." She put her hand on his as she said this, and his stomach did a slow revolution at this reminder of a lost intimacy.

Was she saying that going after Archbishop Lannan could bring them back together again? He put the question to her.

"I don't think of this as going after him. This is a story about the tragedy of celibacy. The loneliness as the shadows grow longer. The impulse to see again the missed possibilities of youth."

"Have you written this already?"

"Just the frame. We need anecdotes, instances, cases."

"How about Fr. Leach?"

Lorraine shuddered. "Sympathetic cases."

"You want me to fly out to Minneapolis?"

"Do we have a deal?" The pressure of her hand on his increased. He felt that he was being seduced. At least he hoped he was.

They went back to the apartment they had shared as if everything was as it had been. The divorce did not of course dissolve their marriage. Not in the eyes of the Church. Even so, there was a zesty element of the illicit as they slid between the sheets. His side of the bed dipped under his weight, and she rolled into his arms.

Later that evening she called her agent and told her about the proposed article. The agent would get right to work on it in the morning.

"She suggested we think book."

Was there any need or interest in yet another account of the travails of the celibate? It seemed to Patch that this was overworked territory, but Lorraine persuasively argued otherwise.

"It's all in the approach. Our tone will be more in sadness than in anger. The human side of it, the personal touch."

Lorraine made a pile of tapes interviewing the wives of laicizied priests. These often choppy unions were meant to illustrate how years of enforced celibacy made a man unfit for marriage.

"Enforced?"

"How many would make a promise of celibacy or take the vow of chastity if it weren't a condition for ordination to the priesthood?"

"How many men would get married if it entailed monogamy?"

"Huh?"

"Think about it."

"I'd rather not."

He placated her. He wanted to get her back to the uneven playing field of the matrimonial bed. Abstinence had made him raunchy. He said as much, and as they went back down the

162

hall to the bedroom she worked the thought into their projected article.

"Have you been faithful?" she purred when they were once more entwined beneath the covers.

"In thought and deed."

More purring. A thought teased his mind.

"Have you?"

"Oh, Nate."

Later, lying awake, it occurred to him that that was not a direct answer to his question. A cloud of anger formed and then dispersed. He lay a claiming hand on the rounded thigh of his sacramental if not legal wife and drifted into sleep.

Before flying to Minneapolis, he put one of the tapes Lorraine had made into his walkman and listened to the interviews with the wives of priests. A common thread in their complaints was the unrealistic expectations of the celibate when he took a bride.

"A honeymoon, okay, but sooner or later things have to settle down. I mean, every night? He had no notion at all of how a woman feels."

Nate Patch would not have claimed such knowledge for himself. Had he been demanding of Lorraine? The question seemed to presuppose that she would simply accede to his demands. But the rhythm of a marriage is established mutually. It occurred to him that these complaining women had still accorded clerical status to their mates and deferred to them accordingly. Many had ended up in the divorce courts anyway. The ex-priest, ex-husband, almost invariably had married again within a year. Lorraine had less luck interviewing these second wives.

"They don't think of them as former priests. They never knew them as priests. The first wives usually did. In fact, the affair started before he decided to leave."

Somewhat to his surprise, Nate found that Janet Fortin had strong views on the subject of celibacy.

"Just try to get a clear explanation of it", she said. "Priests don't seem to know the reason why they can't marry."

"You mean, apart from their promise not to?"

"They don't know the reason for the promise."

"How do you know all this?"

She looked at him in silence for a moment. "I have a relative who's a priest."

4

Let bygones be bygones, Janet had agreed with Casey after the great James Morrow contretemps. They had tried to pull a fast one on her, and it hadn't worked, but she wasn't going to get mad about. But she would get even, first chance she had.

It helped to have someone like Casey to despise. He marked a level to which she had yet to sink, and that provided some consolation. Gene Wales, on the other hand, had been guilty of no treachery to the now-confirmed ambassador to the Vatican, but he had come away from the experience with an altered view of his boss.

"His excuse was that he thought the President had been using him."

"And vice versa."

"Maybe they were both right too."

So what did that make them? Janet had not gone into politics with the idea that it would be an edifying occupation. She had been prepared to fend off predatory males, and it was a good thing; some men seemed to think they had seignorial rights over any female they outranked. The politician himself of course presumed a divine right to bed whom he pleased. There were girls who counted scalps, as it were, happy to have provided sexual solace to the great man. Casey, her ostensible boss, was persistent, even after rebuffs, and Janet felt certain that that had been behind his attempt to bypass her on the Morrow nomination. The triumph in Tulsa, as it came to be called, was one he shared with her, even though, before the outcome, he had blamed her for Morrow's idiotic acceptance of Butterworth's invitation. The surprising result lifted all boats, and they were pals again.

"Let bygones be bygones", he said.

"Right", she said, punching his upper arm. It was tempting to direct her fist at his goateed chin.

It was different with Gene Wales. He had known she was out of the loop before Tulsa; it was sheer accident that Morrow had decided to call her. But she had acquiesced in the nominee's going to Oklahoma, assuming the sure debacle would be laid at Casey's door. She was no better than Casey really and that hurt. What she could not understand was why Wales thought he had been a traitor. It turned out that he felt tainted by what Lannan had been willing to do.

"Have he and Morrow gotten together since the confirmation?"

"Tomorrow night. The three of them."

Mrs. Kilmartin was the third. That was nice, Janet thought; the old friends being brought together after so many years of separation. Maureen Kilmartin was a pleasant surprise. Having been told by Gene Wales that her brother was Frank Bailey, Janet had been prepared for the worst. But the patrician, almost foreign lady, who so visibly enjoyed being with Archbishop Lannan, had captivated Janet. And set her mind going on the sad practice of enforced celibacy in the Catholic priesthood.

"Don't be misled by the disgruntled, Janet. No one can go through the seminary without being acutely aware that that is part of the deal. For most of us, it is the single biggest thing we come to terms with."

"Gene, wouldn't you rather be both, a priest and married?"

He wrinkled his nose. "I don't know. I've learned to think of them as alternatives."

"That's sad."

"How many married people do you know who are jumping with joy?"

He had a point and didn't let it go. The point was not whether life had its difficulties, but whether one stuck to his promises. Too many people were willing to walk away from their obligations when the going got rough, even though everyone was told beforehand it would be rough as well as smooth. Priests were influenced by that. How could they not be? It was as close as he had ever come to letting her know what it was like inside the psyche of Eugene Wales.

"Is there a Maureen somewhere in your past?"

Of course he didn't answer. She would have been frightened if he had. She realized that she wanted him to be a man of steel, steadfast, without doubt. When she left, she put her hand on his arm and got on tiptoe to kiss his cheek.

"Monsignor Icicle", she whispered.

"Good-bye, cousin."

5

"Is she ga ga?" Tom Lannan asked, when Maureen told him of her visit to Mrs. Christiansen.

"She is very old. I saw some photographs of Karen's daughter."

166

"You didn't meet her?"

"No. She lives in San Diego."

They were seated at an outdoor table of an eatery situated not a hundred yards from the runway, on which planes descended into Reagan National. It was an off-time, however, and air traffic was not what it would be in an hour or two. Lannan imagined himself landing and catching a glimpse of himself, seated here with Maureen, listening to a story that brought weakness to the back of his legs and emptiness to his stomach. But his smile did not waver as he listened to what he wanted to regard as a story of senile inventiveness.

"Do you remember her now?"

"Now?"

"When I mentioned her to you before, you weren't sure you did remember her."

He looked thoughtful as he nodded. "A mousy blonde girl, wasn't she?"

"Not mousy, no."

"But blonde?"

"Yes."

Maureen had handed him the letter she had received in Rome, but he had not taken it from its envelope, concentrating on what she had to say about her visit to the retirement home in south Minneapolis. He did not want to read the letter. He did not want to talk about this. But above all he did not want Maureen to think that he was really disturbed by what she was saying. He looked at the envelope.

"Are you sure she wrote it?"

It had never occurred to her to doubt it.

"Where did she get your address, Maureen?"

"She said from a Fr. Szabo."

"Wasn't that true?"

"Frank said he's been dead for at least five years."

My God, had she talked about this with Frank? He looked beyond her at the water, at the parking lot, at the people there to watch the planes come and go.

"What did Frank make of her story?"

"Oh, I didn't tell him. Tom, you do realize that some people would eagerly believe such a story."

"You mean Frank?"

"Not likely. You know what I mean?"

"Jim Morrow?"

He had shocked her, and the best way to quell the anger that rose in him as a result was to suggest he get them another beer.

"Not for me."

"I'll be right back. I want to hear all about this."

The restaurant was a low-frame building, weather-beaten, but surrounded by scrubby trees whose colorful leaves gave the place a fleeting charm. It was silly to resent Maureen's obvious admiration for Jim. She would not have come to him with old Mrs. Christiansen's story if she did not think it incredible. It had been an act of friendship to bring him this potentially dangerous news. He had no doubt that she would guard it from anyone else. She had not told Frank. She would not tell Jim.

"What should I do?" he asked, when he was once more seated across the table from her.

Her eyes looked into his for a long moment, and he had the unnerving feeling that she could see right into his soul.

"Nothing. Karen is dead, and this is just a story she told her mother, picking you for some reason of her own. Tom, I know what she was like. It doesn't surprise me at all that she got into trouble. She was a girl who was on a collision course. Tom, she might not even have known who the father was."

"How well did you know her?"

"Well enough."

Maureen seemed to be feeling the uneasiness that should be his; now she was the one who had enough of the subject.

"The letter alarmed me. I admit that. But now that I have talked with Mrs. Christiansen, that isn't my reaction any more. There is almost no chance that she would mention it to anyone else. I got the impression that they had kept the paternity of Karen's baby a deep family secret."

"I wonder why she wrote to you?"

"If she got my address from Fr. Szabo, she waited a long time to make use of it."

"Were you and Karen close friends?"

He sensed her uneasiness once more. "We were friends, yes."

That would explain perhaps why the deep family secret had been divulged to Maureen.

"I wonder if she told her granddaughter."

"Tom, let's not talk about it anymore. I just wanted you to be forewarned, in the remote possibility..." But she made a gesture, as if to wave off even the remote possibility that he might fall victim of such a scandal.

Would the daughter, he wondered, resemble her mother?

CHAPTER TWO

I

Jim Morrow flew business class. First class on transatlantic
flights did not attract him: behind the curtain of privilege
were wide leather seats facing a blank wall. One could work
in business class, and there wasn't the crush there was in
tourist. It was an odd thought that he was going abroad to
represent his country. He had spent several weeks saying
good-bye, concentrating on friends at the dangerous end of
the actuarial table.

"Italy is no better than here", Hershey had said. "Maybe
worse."

"Half the politicians are in jail."

"I take it back."

Hershey, a Notre Dame colleague, had suffered a stroke a
year ago and was strapped uncomfortably in a wheelchair. He
had always taken the keenest pleasure in finding dark clouds.
Their friendship had deepened while Morrow was at work on
his book; Hershey seemed to think that Morrow aspired to be
the Oswald Spengler of the Catholic Church in the United
States. But if he had formed any theory about the decline, it
would have been closer to Gibbon than Spengler. Closer still
to Toynbee—there is hope in cycles. Hershey had no interest
in hope.

"Politicians have always been hyenas. Do you know those

lines of e.e.cummings: 'A politician is an arse on which everything has sat except a man'?" Hershey's laugh was a snort.

But it was the wider social scene that fed Hershey's sense that the West was in steep decline. The random murders that had begun a decade before on the freeways of southern California, had spread to the inner cities, then on to the tourist industry of Florida, and now menaced affluent suburbs.

"There are no safe places left", Hershey said with satisfaction.

"All men are mortal."

"That refers to natural death."

From violence to sins of the flesh, reversing the order of the *Inferno,* favorite reading of Hershey's. ("I always read up on a place before going on a trip.") But it was this world he groused about.

"Everyone's screwing but no one's having babies."

He had the statistics, of course: the three million abortions a year and a population ten degrees below zero growth. Male homosexuals died by the thousands, cursing the government whose billions had failed to find a cure for their disease.

"They are the victims of the sexual revolution."

"No one can be his own victim."

"They were told that sex was whatever they wanted it to be, life an endless orgy with no punitive sanctions. They have a right to complain."

"Not to me."

Getting away from Hershey made him feel like Dante escaping from hell. But Hershey's hell, like Dante's, was a spectator's hell, to be enjoyed and talked about, lessons drawn from it too, perhaps, though one of Hershey's points was that they were beyond lessons.

Were things really so bad? At an altitude of nearly forty thousand feet above the Atlantic, the cabin aroar with the air through which they slipped at God knows what velocity, Morrow did not dispute Hershey's view of the modern world. He shared the description if not the attitude toward what was described.

Hershey derived from his gloomy view only misanthropy. Human beings were a sorry lot, on their way to destroying themselves and their world. But what did it all mean? When Morrow had written his history, he had fought against the negative exaggerations of Hershey's outlook, but still things looked unprecedently bad. One almost longed for the cleansing threat of a nuclear enemy. Wallowing in peace, though involved in half a dozen minor wars under United Nations command, his country did indeed seem to be on a path of self-destruction. Concern with the wider social context was necessary to his history of the Catholic Church—one of his themes was that Catholics had adopted the outlook of the secular world and imposed it on their supposed leaders—but faith should provide another interpretation of what was happening. Eschatology, the end times, the end of the world.

"I hope you won't be foolish enough to predict that", Monsignor Ramos of The Catholic University once said. Ramos had written on Sepulveda and Bernal Diaz. His face looked as if it might have been carved on the bowl of his pipe.

"I suppose it's because these are our times that they look to be the worst."

"History is meant to provide the perspective that corrects for closeness."

"That's why I say there've been times at least as bad as these."

"Such as?"

"I mean of course bad for the Church."

"Name a worse time."

"The fourth century."

Ramos pondered this, but of course he must have thought of it himself. Arianism had seemed to swamp the Church despite Athanasius. A majority of bishops had wavered and accepted Arius' view that Christ was not the God Man, thus repudiating the central claim of Christianity.

"Worse than the Reformation?"

"Before or during?"

"How ecumenical you young men are." But Ramos laughed, or tried to. "I think you are right about the fourth century though. I reread Newman last year. Was Newman an historian? I don't know. He is one of those geniuses, or saints, impossible to classify."

"I once thought of writing a history of all the people who were convinced they lived at the end of the world."

"Beginning with the evangelists?"

"Every age is the end times for those living in it, even if their end is not an absolute ending. I suppose death is end enough. What could the end of the world add to that?"

"The final judgment."

"In the political order, the party out of power is certain their opponents are presiding over the ruination of the country. Quite apart from that, serious questions have been raised whether the United States can survive much more freedom without a shared conviction on what the good is. If the good is whatever's chosen, the result is chaos."

"The Church is not a country."

No, it wasn't, and bad times for the Church had a significance far beyond the fate of this country or that, or of this civilization or that. The Church was moving toward a culminating time when time would be no more.

The plane shuddered as it passed through banks of clouds, and Morrow could sense the fear, the repressed terror, that was suddenly another presence in the plane. He realized he was gripping the arms of his seat. End times, indeed. He might go out at thirty-nine thousand feet if the plane were torn apart by turbulence.

Some saint had said, when asked what he would do if told the world would end in half an hour, that he would go on doing what he was doing. He was playing billiards when the question was put to him. His seemed as good an answer as any. If the world were coming to an end, and he knew it, Morrow would still be on his way to Rome where he would present his credentials to the Vatican secretary of state and have a private audience with His Holiness.

2

The drive from Dennis McHugh's apartment to the embassy offices on the Via Aurelia was five kilometers, measured from point to point. The time it took McHugh to cover that distance varied from day to day. But it was neither the distance nor the time it took to traverse it that characterized his morning drive; rather it was how long it took before the imbecilic behavior of other drivers turned him into a raving maniac.

McHugh had the face of a parrot: black, unblinking eyes, straight hair that shot back over his head, a beak of a nose more Roman than any native's. Where had he gotten it? There was not another like it in the family. His mother's explanation was that he had been delivered by Caesarean section. Her lips rolled back from her great teeth when she smiled. McHugh had been in Rome almost ten years, rising to the rank of first secretary. At the beginning he had told himself that he would get used to driving in Rome, that Italian drivers would cease to terrorize and aggravate him. Each day, he left home a rational animal and arrived at the embassy a madman, shouting aloud to himself, cursing the cars around him. Once settled behind his desk, he was once more the suave, sane diplomat, and no one, he was certain, could have guessed the ordeal he had just been through. He might have been leading a double life.

Today he would meet James Morrow at the airport, being taken there in the ambassadorial Mercedes, a prospect almost pleasing if it were not for the enforced company of Luigi the driver. Luigi no longer thought of himself as an employee. His putative employers came and went—some in a few years, others lasting only slightly longer—but he remained, a version of *Roma eterna*. His manner was not so much arrogant as insufficiently attentive, but then his lascivious, fifty-eight-year-old eyes were always on the alert for a female body to ogle. Breasts, a bottom, legs, so long as they were a woman's, egged him into a poetry of sorts. He was a generalist; he loved the short and the fat and the tall, the old and the young, almost anything so long as it was of the opposite sex. All talk? That was one theory, but McHugh had surprised Luigi and a cleaning lady in a closet off the kitchen and knew otherwise.

"You know this new guy?" Luigi asked, when he pulled out of the embassy gate and onto the Aurelia, tipping his crushed cap forward.

"Only by reputation."

But Luigi had already been distracted. My God, what an animal. The driver was singing the praises of a woman of whom he had caught but a fleeting glance.

"He is a famous historian."

"Who's that?"

"The new ambassador."

The new ambassador. McHugh had read Morrow's history of the Church in America and was struck by the persistent note of involvement. Was it possible that Morrow was still...

The car swerved to avoid a truck backing into the avenue, bounced off one of the curbed islands set randomly in the path of traffic, and continued on, Luigi consigning the trucker to the lower depths of hell.

His heart in his mouth, McHugh realized that he had been on the verge of prayer. But his faith was gone, no need to try to deceive himself, so gone that he hardly missed it. Rome had been the final blow. In the States, McHugh had been caught up briefly in the protracted battle between progressives and conservatives and had felt more affinity with the latter. If he had believed as little as dissenters did, he would have dropped the thing then and there. Still, he was careful not to join a side.

His degree was from Princeton, art history, but he had emerged from there into a job situation that made a mockery of all his years of study. Before receiving his degree, he had refused to worry about the gloomy job reports, assuming that none of that applied to himself. How could he fail to find a position in some marvelous little college with a lovely campus, small enrollment, high salaries, bright, inquisitive students? Easily, as it turned out. He found himself lusting after jobs in urban colleges that would never have met the standards of his graduate school fantasies—and failing to get them. A remark at a party led him to take the State Department exam, and the rest, one might say, was history.

"Morrow!" Fr. Hill, one of the Paulists at Santa Susanna, the American church in Rome, had squealed. "Morrow!"

"At least he's a Catholic."

"At most he's a Catholic."

Fr. Hill's eyebrows grew luxuriantly in all directions. He was an exaggerated example of what can happen to the cleric who lives in too close proximity to the Vatican. Awe gives way to familiarity, and familiarity soon produces its fated offspring. Unshaven monsignori, traces of last week's pasta on a cassock, the glacial insolence of bureaucracies the world over, had turned Anselm Hill into an anti-papist on the order of a Jehovah's Witness.

"American Catholic", he would boast. "American, not Roman."

"You sound like Dante on his Florentine origins."

"Ah, Dante." And Hill was off on the number of popes Dante had put in the inferno. Hill had gotten along fine with Carver, the retired ambassador, a Mormon who had his doubts about Joseph Smith. The two men had often sat into the late hours trading negative remarks on their respective faiths.

Was Hill's description of Morrow as an ultramontane exact? That he recorded the travails of the Church in the sad tones one would use in telling of family misfortunes was true, but one did not have to take sides to agree that the Church had been in decline for more than a quarter of a century.

"That's bosh", Hill retorted. "What do you miss from the old Church?"

Hill was unmoved by statistics indicating a precipitous decline in Mass attendance, plummeting financial support, increase of divorce and remarriage, the incessant quarreling among factions, the frightening drop in the number of priests and nuns, the devastating punitive damages exacted by the courts when clerics were found guilty of corrupting youth. Hill waved it all away.

"We've been on a shakedown cruise. There are casualties, sure, and many jump ship. We're getting down to the real Catholics, McHugh, and they've always been a small number."

It was the kind of discussion McHugh had religiously avoided with Carver. Perhaps with a Catholic ambassador the subject of religion could be even more easily avoided.

Luigi had reached the Grande Riccordo Anulare, one of the belt lines encircling Rome, and increased speed. There were cars in all three south bound lanes as close as those in a train, each moving at 120 KMP. An image of the Gadarene swine leapt to McHugh's mind as his heart leapt to his throat. One slight mistake by one driver and there would be a pileup of hundreds of cars. Was he destined to meet death in an automobile? His hands gripped the seat. The small pain he felt in his right hand was caused by a hairpin. Did Luigi use the ambassadorial car for assignations? Why should he be surprised? The maniac would mate at a bus stop if given the chance.

After a harrowing ten minutes they turned off the Grande Anulare and were rocketing toward the sea and Fiumicino. McHugh's lips formed the once familiar words, *In manus tuas, domine, commendo spiritum meum.*

3

The plane descended slowly into Leonardo da Vinci airport, and Morrow looked down at the cypresses, ocher buildings, and clumpy Italian fields. He felt as if this were a homecoming, which was not entirely ridiculous. He had been in Rome perhaps half-a-dozen times in the course of his career, but twice for extended periods of research in the Vatican Library. During his second stay, he had availed himself of the library at the American Academy as well. How almost sensuously attractive the scholarly life could be, nestled in some corner of a library, making notes as one read, the slow accumulation of data, longing for and at the same time dreading the time when the work would be done, the book written. A woman must feel such emptiness after giving birth, but she can hold the baby to her breast and begin another and long association with her child. A book when done is gone definitively. The only solution is a new project.

After his history of the Church in America, the first book of his to cause a stir outside the sedate corridors of academe, he felt no desire to take up the task again. He would not have said he was too old, but he had done what he was likely to do as a scholar and would only repeat himself, using the same capital over and over, working variations on the book that had brought him fame. The totally unexpected nomination to the American Embassy to the Vatican had rescued him—from a retirement he did not yet want, from scholarship of which he had had enough.

The plane touched down, the engines reversed, and through the roar came the applause of the passengers. This was a custom Morrow had never understood. Were the passengers surprised that the pilot had managed to find the Rome airport and bring them safely down? Was it out of a similar relief that the Pope had kissed the tarmac when he visited and revisited and visited yet again the countries of the world?

His diplomatic passport startled the immigration officer, and Morrow was told he should not have waited in line; he should have come directly to the counter.

"*Non importa.*"

It was his first sentence in the language he was determined to master. He read Italian with ease; he had made do ungrammatically and awkwardly in restaurants and shops and libraries when he had been here before, but now he intended to speak Italian like—well, like a diplomat.

"Do you know the Italian language, sir?" Senator Partridge had asked at the hearings.

"Yes, Senator."

"And Latin as well?"

Partridge was determined by that point to show his good will toward this papist appointee of the President. Rev. Willie Butterworth himself had endorsed Morrow.

"I began the study of Latin at thirteen."

Ohs and ahs. He felt ridiculous stating such tidbits of autobiography as if they had significance. But the hearings were a ritual, the condition of confirmation and the sinecure in Rome. After being sworn in at the State Department, he'd had two minutes with the President, just time enough for a handshake and photograph. Any self-importance the hearings had brought on was swept away by the almost hustling farewell from the man whose representative he would be.

Convoyed by several *carabinieri*, he was hurried through to where McHugh was waiting for him. Morrow noted the facility with which the first secretary handled the situation.

"How long have you been here?"

"Eight years."

Morrow nodded. It would have been silly to congratulate McHugh on his Italian. The driver Luigi was dispatched for the ambassador's luggage while Morrow and McHugh waited in the car.

"You had a good flight?"

"It was uneventful."

"You'll be able to take a nap if you'd like. You can meet the staff tomorrow."

That was a relief. Once seated in the comfortable Mercedes, Morrow felt tiredness settle over him like a blanket. He was certain that if he closed his eyes he would fall immediately asleep. He actually did nod off on the drive into the city despite the half-suppressed yelps with which McHugh reacted to the driving of Luigi.

"He's crazy", McHugh said when Morrow was shaken awake.

Morrow glanced at the driver, wondering what his reaction would be, but McHugh assured him Luigi knew almost no English.

"I have uncle in Chicago", Luigi cried, aware at least that they were talking about him.

"Bear or cub?" McHugh asked with a smile. "Never trust him", he added, turning to Morrow.

He had no choice whether or not to trust McHugh. The man was efficient, whatever his other eccentricities. His manner was one of general not quite resigned exasperation. He obviously needed a vacation, but Morrow could not spare him, perhaps not for months.

"What does an ambassador do?" an interviewer had asked him.

"I'll let you know."

With such quips he had disguised the fact that he had little idea what his duties would be. Paul Claudel had continued to write poems and plays; Jacques Maritain had been French ambassador to the Vatican, and nothing Morrow read of that period suggested that Maritain had been weighed down with work. Morrow's model would be Hawthorne and Howells, temporary expatriates subsidized by their governments.

His apartment was on the top floor of the building that housed the embassy. If he had imagined settling within the walls of Vatican City itself, with bishops and cardinals forever in the vicinity, he would have been disappointed. The embassy was several miles from the Vatican; there was a staff of six, including Luigi, and it soon became clear that his functions were indeed minimal.

"Basically, the job is ceremonial."

McHugh meant that his schedule would consist of as many receptions and dinners and banquets as he could tolerate.

"You yourself give two receptions a year: one for the other ambassadors to the Vatican, the other in conjunction with our ambassador to Italy for the whole diplomatic corps."

Passages from Claudel's journal came to him—the tedium of dining out, the need for a limitless supply of small talk, conversations in which nothing of substance was said.

"I'm not much for ceremony."

"That's up to you, of course. There are many Americans living in Rome."

Pests, in a word, McHugh explained, retirees, employees of American companies, some writers and journalists, to a man or woman convinced that the diplomatic corps' main function was to serve them.

"In what way?"

"Papal audiences, Masses in the Pope's private chapel. We have had two claims to private revelations—women who wished to tell the Pope what the Blessed Virgin had confided to them."

McHugh did not mean the recent events at Viterbo where Caterina, a young woman in her twenties, had been in danger of enforced psychiatric treatment until she reluctantly claimed to be having visitations from the Virgin. What was the message? She was not authorized by the Blessed Mother to say. But her doleful expression when she said this, so reminiscent of Our Lady of Sorrows, indicated the news was not good. Morrow had been briefed on the matter in case it came up in the Senate hearings. There had been speculation in the Italian press that the message concerned the United States. Any references to Italian piety during the hearings were to be deflected. Above all he was to avoid discussion of Caterina, the seer of Viterbo.

The staff was there to greet him when they arrived at the embassy. Morrow shook their hands, bowed, accepted their welcome, glanced at his office, and then went upstairs. He lay down on the bed fully dressed and before falling asleep realized that he did not remember a single name of those he had just met. Thank God for McHugh.

4

Monsignor Ambrose Frawley called for Morrow on the Via Aurelia in a little car that he had maneuvered onto the sidewalk, no other parking spot being available. He wore a three-piece, black suit and a Roman collar that seemed to tilt his fat, pink face upward.

"Do not think of me as a scofflaw, Professor Morrow. It is the Roman way. Both *via* and *modo*", he added, but his sly smile negated the pedantry.

Morrow had been in Rome a week, two days of which had been spent in protracted sleeping and napping. He had never before been so affected by jet lag, if that is what it was. Perhaps for the first time in his life he was relaxing. Not even the Michigan cabin had induced such lethargy. Frawley's invitation had been made with gentle insistence.

"It will be good for you to know him", McHugh observed, rocking back and forth as he said it.

Morrow had the sense that if he did not accept the invitation he might go into hibernation. Whatever his task in Rome was, it was not catching up on his sleep.

"You must bring me up on all the news from home", Frawley said expansively. "How is our mutual friend in Washington?"

"Archbishop Lannan commissioned me to send you his best."

"We are in constant communication. As you can imagine."

"Oh?"

Frawley cast him a smile that dimpled his cheeks. "Already a diplomat. Thomas Lannan lusts to be made a cardinal. And with good reason, of course. For the archbishop of Washington, the capital of the most powerful nation on earth, not to be a cardinal, well..."

"What are his prospects?"

"Excellent. But not in this papacy."

No need to prime this pump. For the rest of the drive, over their magnificent meal in Raymond's off the Via Veneto, while having drinks in Frawley's rooms afterward, then on the drive back to the embassy, Frawley held forth tirelessly. All Morrow had to do was look receptive and from time to time make a perfunctory interjection, and the narrative flowed.

Frawley's dark hair was brushed back over his head, unparted. He had a meaty nose and bright brown eyes that shone as he drew on his bottomless fund of ecclesiastical gossip.

"Have you met Cardinal Benedetto yet?"

"I am scheduled to present my credentials to him next week."

"Insist on seeing the Holy Father. That will set a good precedent. You mustn't let them treat you like the Bolivian ambassador."

Benedetto, as Frawley described him, was a man of holiness, of learning, and of Borgia-like cunning besides.

"His ambition is selfless. I am sure he would be content to be a simple priest, but he cannot keep his hands from the levers of power."

Power seemed to mean ecclesiastical appointments that could be of interest only to clerical careerists. Did Frawley sense his reaction?

"The Curia is not the Knights of Columbus, Professor. These titles and prefectships have meaning. One needs constantly to remind oneself that the shop is really run by the Holy Spirit."

No sarcasm, no ironic tone, matter of fact. Frawley redeemed himself in Morrow's eyes, and the endless flow of gossip became almost interesting. Particularly as it bore on the Church in America.

"His Holiness wrote us off years ago, of course. He found

some heartening things on his visits, but basically he saw a church in an advanced state of decay. He has read your book, by the way."

"Has he?"

"I am sure he will mention it when you see him. You will have confirmed his own judgment. People forget that he visited the States before his election. Then he moved around almost anonymously, meeting with people like Jude Dougherty in Washington and the Hitchcocks in St. Louis. No one dreamt then that he would become Pope. I am told that he already saw the Church in America as almost beyond hope."

"Dissent?"

"That, of course. But imagine how sensate our culture must have seemed to him, coming out of Eastern Europe. How decadent. Of course the flood of laicizations was in full tide, nuns had already freaked out, the marriage tribunals were annulling marriages right and left. Nothing that has happened since has surprised him."

The delay, if delay it was, in Lannan's elevation to cardinal began to make sense. Frawley nodded when he voiced the connection.

"Lannan has been careful, but he is no O'Connor, not even a Law or Hickey. Waffling does not sit well with His Holiness. Oh, how I wish I could put this as plainly to dear Thomas, but one has to be so careful of archiepiscopal edginess. It does not please him that his fate rests to the degree that it does in my poor hands. But I cannot eradicate his record. He has not stood tall with the Holy Father, and the cardinalate is uniquely in the Pope's gift."

"But is it purely personal?"

"Like Newman or de Lubac? No. We are after all talking of the archbishop of Washington."

Frawley had ordered for them both without apology, selecting the wines and sending the waiter, the wine steward and the owner, Raymond, himself into raptures with the choices he made. Morrow was beginning to feel a bit like a country bumpkin.

"What is your diocese, Monsignor?"

"Rapid City."

"South Dakota!" He could not keep incredulity from his voice.

"Can any good come out of Rapid City? as the Gospel does not ask. How did a boy from the Black Hills of Dakota end up in a cushy post in Rome? Providence and luck and some pretty heavy scheming. I was sent to the Angelicum for theology and knew I never wanted to go home. I have been here ever since, man and boy."

Later, in Frawley's suite at the North American College, with a lovely view of the illumined dome of St. Peter's at the window, they sipped brandy, and Morrow brought the voluble monsignor back to Archbishop Lannan.

"There is no chance of more cardinals being named soon?"

"It would have to be soon."

"How is the Pope's health?"

Frawley shrugged. "There are always rumors. Even so, at his age." He sipped and then enjoyed the taste of the brandy before swallowing. "The College of Cardinals is at its lowest number in twenty years. He could make twenty-five or thirty appointments if he chose."

"If he did, he could scarcely overlook Lannan."

"That's where you come in, of course."

"I?"

"The Holy Father is aware that it was Thomas Lannan who proposed your name to the President. The Holy Father likes your book. Lannan played you like a card."

The joker? Morrow resented this interpretation of his nomination. But Frawley was not through.

"Your coup with the fundamentalists gained you independence of course. With one stroke, you became your own man, beholden neither to President nor to sponsor. You saved your own nomination. Butterworth's interview has even been shown several times on RAI. You can be sure that the Holy Father has either seen it or has been thoroughly briefed on your performance."

"I might have made a damned fool of myself."

"No doubt. I am sure most thought you would. But you did not. Instead you triumphed."

"Did you see the program?"

Frawley lowered his head and looked at Morrow through his brows. "I have it on videocassette. I could put it on."

"Dear God, no."

The evening with Frawley gave him much to think about. He was at once repelled and fascinated by the unrelenting clericalism of the man. Frawley ate, drank, and breathed the Church. Little else other than food seemed to interest him. Lying awake, unable to fall asleep, Morrow looked back on Frawley's performance as obeying all the canons of classical drama. Suspense, high points, low points, and finally his apparently sincere praise of Morrow's handling of the Protestant opposition to his appointment. The image of himself as adroitly dialectical, bearding the fundamentalist lion in his den, emerging as hero, was headier than the wine. Morrow sat up. Frawley said that Lannan had sought to play him like a card. But the monsignor had played him like a musical instrument, winning him with the most corrupting weapon of all, flattery.

Morrow threw back the covers and sat on the edge of his bed. He had a vision of himself, a man in late middle age, overweight, in a new and exciting setting, all too vulnerable to temptations that in his native habitat had lost their power over him. With Frawley he had felt a growing sense of being near the center of things, of having other people's destinies some-

how in his control, of being one of the wise and great. Ronald
Knox had had another view. When asked why he never went
to Rome, he replied, "On the voyage of the spiritual life, I
tend to avoid visiting the boiler room."

Dear God. He crossed the room, sat in a chair, and looked
at the dim light admitted by his windows. To be told that the
Pope had read his book had filled him with a pride that had
seemed justified. Vanity of vanities. What would come next,
avarice? It was humbling to be reminded of how fragile he was.

He stood, paused, and then lowered himself to his knees.
"There is only one tragedy: not to be a saint." How he loved,
and trembled at, that line of Leon Bloy's. At all costs, he must
avoid becoming a tragic figure in that sense.

5

Luigi swung through Porta Sant'Anna, showed the Swiss guard
the diplomatic decal, and was waved through with a salute.
Not even Luigi would drive more than 20 KPH in the diminutive papal city state. They passed the Church of St. Anne, the
commissary, and the Vatican press and went through another
gate into the Court of San Damasus, now a great cobblestone
parking lot. McHugh exited on one side of the car, Morrow
on the other, both men in formal attire. James Morrow was
about to present his credentials as American ambassador to
Cardinal Benedetto, Vatican secretary of state.

Morrow had no desire to be blasé on this occasion. He
savored the pomp and circumstance as they went down the
wide, high-ceilinged hall and then up the grand staircase. The
paintings, the statues and vases, the authoritative sound of

marble beneath his new shoes, the sense of a tradition—it all stretched back through the centuries to connect finally with the tomb of St. Peter beneath the great basilica. It might not be the official view of the American government, but Morrow was credentialed to the vicar of Christ on earth.

At the end of a series of antechambers, Benedetto rose from behind a desk that seemed miniature in the vast office. Behind him windows opened onto balconies, and their hangings drifted ghostlike in the slight breeze. Benedetto came around the desk and approached Morrow, arms extended, a smile on his face. To Morrow's surprise, the cardinal embraced him, then stepped back, and looking up at him, gave his outer arms two reassuring taps.

McHugh stepped to Morrow's side and gave him the leather-bound documents. Benedetto took them, lifted the cover, and glanced at the contents. He handed the closed case to a cleric who skated forward to take it.

"Welcome to the Holy See, Mr. Ambassador."

"The President asked me to bring his personal good wishes to you, Your Eminence, as well as to His Holiness."

"Who awaits you, Mr. Ambassador. But first I want a few minutes with you myself."

Taking Morrow by the elbow, he directed him toward brocade chairs that encircled an inlaid table.

"You have written a very interesting history, Professor."

Morrow nodded, and Benedetto proceeded to give a summary of *The Decline and Fall of the Catholic Church in the United States*. Clearly he had done more than page through the book.

"Alas, a similar book could be written about every country in which the Church once flourished. The whole center of gravity has shifted eastward and southward to Africa and Asia."

"*Sicut erat in principio*", Morrow said, and then had a swift image of Partridge.

"As it was in the beginning", Benedetto murmured in accented English, nodding. "Just so. Africa apart, we seem to be returning to the churches Paul knew."

If Benedetto was depressed by this prospect, he gave no sign of it.

"I was particularly struck by your judgment that the second extraordinary synod of 1985 marked the end of a process."

"Thanks to the *Ratzinger Report* that appeared just months before the synod."

Benedetto dipped toward his steepled fingers, kissing their tips. "The *Panzerkardinal*."

The enormous good will that the Pope had at first enjoyed extended to his prefect of the Congregation for the Doctrine of the Faith, and when sentiment turned, it was Cardinal Ratzinger who had been the first to be openly vilified. In 1985, an extended interview with the journalist Vittorio Messori appeared, and soon it was translated into a dozen languages. For the first time, there was official acknowledgment that there had been a twenty-year-long effort to pervert the meaning of Vatican II. The directness and frankness of the German cardinal were a welcome change from cautious circumlocution.

"The only thing I regretted about the *Rapporto* was his mention of the third secret of Fatima." Benedetto shook his head and raised his hand to his brow.

"And announcing that it would not be made public?"

"People have an inordinate curiosity about private revelations, particularly secrets."

"Have you read the third secret?"

Benedetto pursed his lips, then nodded. "And now people want to know the secret of Viterbo."

The conversation had taken a turn Morrow would never have expected. There had been only a brief account of the Holy See's diplomatic initiatives. Was this only the small talk that is the stuff of diplomatic life? But it had started with his account of the decline of the Church in the United States. "If there is no secret, a secret will be invented."

Benedetto placed his palms flat on the carved arms of his chair and levered himself forward. "But come. The Holy Father will be expecting us."

The man he had seen only from a distance—a small figure in white all but lost in the crowds that attended his appearances—seemed mythical when confronted man to man. The Pope waited for him, hands clasped to control the tremor, stooped, his Slavic face a map of weariness and tragedy. The burden of leading the Church in these strange times struck Morrow, and his heart went out to this man whose gentleness belied a rocklike adherence to the faith that had been entrusted to his care.

"For Partridge and the President", Morrow thought, as he bent to kiss the papal ring.

The Pope took Morrow's hand in both of his, and his eyes were lively. "Sia lodato Gesù Cristo."

"Amen." Morrow said it in his twangiest American voice, afraid that the Pope intended to speak in Italian.

"I am glad that your country has sent you here, Professor. And at this time." He nodded, and then the eyes twinkled. "Will you write a book about the decline and fall of the Vatican?"

"God forbid."

"The book or the fall?"

"The one depends upon the other."

Benedetto seemed to be enjoying this exchange. McHugh handed Morrow the gift for the Pope, his history in white leather binding.

"Thank you, thank you. This copy will go to the Vatican library."

"I have spent many hours there."

"Perhaps you can continue your studies, despite your duties."

"If I find a subject."

"We must talk about that, Professor."

The Pope said a few words to McHugh, and then Benedetto led them away. The secretary of state was beaming.

"I think you will be invited back often, Mr. Ambassador." Outside, as they walked to the car, McHugh's manner had changed. Morrow no longer felt like the new boy who needed to be guided about. At the car, McHugh barked at Luigi, and the driver slouched around the car to open the door for the ambassador. The visit seemed to have been an all-round success.

6

A month later, Senator Partridge showed up with his wife, in Rome on some trip connected with official business.

"The FAO, Mr. Ambassador." Partridge pronounced the acronym sounding like a golfer giving a warning. He referred to the U.N. agency, the Food and Agricultural Organization.

Waldo Blintz, the ambassador to Italy, was down with sciatica, so they had been joined for dinner by the Consul Joseph Coyne and his enormous wife.

"How long have you been a widower?" Ella Partridge asked Morrow in motherly tones. Her expression grew tragic when he told her. "And you are faithful to her memory?"

"A man should never make the same mistake twice", Partridge said, leaning forward.

"Oh, Frank", she cried, lashing his arm with her napkin.

"Your husband is just quoting Heraclitus."

"Who is he?"

Partridge answered. "A confirmed bachelor."

But Ella had more important things to talk about. Was it true that she should dress all in black and wear a mantilla when she was presented to the Holy Father?

"It's the custom. But you need not."

"Oh, but I want to. I found the most beautiful dress down there by the Spanish Steps."

"You'll look like a nun", Partridge said.

"That would be good enough for you."

"For not sticking to my guns? Morrow, it was my intention to join forces with Willie and abolish this post. You cut me off by that performance on the television, but I could have gone on alone."

"And lost", Ella said.

Mrs. Coyne offered advice on the proper etiquette for ladies in the presence of the Pope.

Small talk at table—what Morrow had dreaded—yet here he was, babbling away, catering to the politician on his way through, passing the time in essentially pointless activity—when he wasn't working on his new project.

It had been, in the phrase, an offer he couldn't refuse. A week after he had paid his formal call on Benedetto and the Holy Father, a Vatican car had come for him and whisked him up into the Alban Hills to Castel Gandolfo where the Pope awaited him. They dined with only an Irish priest at table with them, the Pope's secretary, there to smooth over any linguistic difficulties. The Pope ate with great gusto, putting away soup and pasta and a glass of wine. There was no conversation while they ate. That began only after the dishes were taken away.

"Cardinal Benedetto tells me you spoke with him of the *Ratzinger Report*." The sentence came out in slow deliberation.

"We had been talking of the second extraordinary synod of 1985. In my book I assumed that the interview published as the *Rapporto* was a prelude to the synod."

The Pope neither agreed nor disagreed. "An extraordinary man, a holy man, Joseph." The Pope drank off what was left of his second glass of wine. "He spoke to the reporter of the apparitions of Our Lady as signs of the times. They had begun to be reported everywhere."

"Cardinal Benedetto and I spoke of the third secret of Fatima."

"Yes." The Pope turned the gold ring on his right hand. "I want you to read it, Professor."

CHAPTER THREE

I

In 1917, in a small Portuguese village, three illiterate children were tending sheep. Lucy, the oldest, was 10; her cousins Jacinta and Francisco were several years younger. They were devout children who would often pray the Rosary together. On the thirteenth day of six successive months, the Blessed Virgin appeared to these children, enjoining them to secrecy about most of what she told them. Jacinta and Francisco died within a few years of the apparitions, but Lucy lived into an extended old age, as a nun.

Lucy received another visit from the Blessed Virgin in her convent chapel and eventually wrote down what she and her two cousins had been told in 1917. This account was given to the local bishop and much later found its way to Rome, where Pius XII decided not to open the envelope sealed with wax. John XXIII, in the presence of his confessor and several cardinals, had the secret opened. His only comment was that it did not concern the years of his pontificate. When Paul VI read it, he immediately flew on pilgrimage to Fatima. John Paul II apparently read it; it is certain that Cardinal Joseph Ratzinger did. The matter came up in Vittorio Messori's famous interview with the prefect for the Congregation of the Faith.

"Cardinal Ratzinger, have you read the so-called third secret of Fatima?"

The reply is immediate and dry: "Yes, I have read it."

Why had not the contents of this secret been made public? Is it to hide something horrible?

"If that were so," he replies, avoiding going further, "that would only confirm the part of the message of Fatima already known. A stern warning has been launched from that place that is directed against the prevailing frivolity... It is that which Jesus himself recalls very frequently, 'Unless you repent you will all perish.' "

Thus Cardinal Ratzinger indicated that there was no warning in the message of Fatima that was not already known from Scripture. It adds nothing to what a Christian already knows from revelation. That is why the Pope saw no reason to reveal the secret. But his further explanation for not publishing the secret suggested that the secret was not merely a repetition.

"To publish the 'third secret' would mean exposing the Church to the danger of sensationalism, exploitation of that content", Ratzinger added.

No wonder this had fueled apocalyptic speculation. Scholars drew attention to the point at which the public message was cut off: "In Portugal, the dogmas of the faith will never be lost..." It seemed a fair conjecture that the faith would be lost in other countries and that dreadful things lay ahead for the Church and the papacy.

It was this secret that Morrow read in the office provided him just down the corridor from the secretary of state. Curious clerics had looked in at him when they went by; but while he read the secret, Benedetto had the door closed and seemed to be standing guard as Morrow sat at the desk.

It was a single page, written in the careful hand of Sister

Lucy, and its contents made it clear why the Pope would not wish to publicize the message.

When he had finished reading, Morrow looked up at Benedetto, but the cardinal secretary of state said nothing and his face was expressionless.

"I can't take notes?"

"No."

"Let me read it again."

He did, slowly, reading the simple Portuguese as scholars had read before the invention of printing, reading as if this might be the only time he would see the text before him, which doubtless in this case was correct.

The handwriting was that which he had seen reproduced in books on Fatima, the accounts Sister Lucy had written in later years at the request of one superior or another, this one at the request of the Blessed Virgin herself—if the apparitions were authentic. The Pope and Benedetto had not said so in words, but their actions, as indeed the actions of previous popes, suggested that the apparitions and attendant revelations were presumed to be the real thing.

Morrow merely registered the contents of the handwritten page, not wanting to appraise, assess, or react to them in any way. A few minutes later, he pushed back from the desk. He waited, but Benedetto said nothing.

"Thank you, Eminence."

"His Holiness wanted you to see that."

"Yes."

The page was taken away. An hour later, Morrow was once more in the presence of the Pope.

"You have read the message?"

"Yes, Holy Father."

"A prophecy half-fulfilled commands attention."

Morrow nodded. Half the message he had read was a

description of the late twentieth-century Church, but it was based on an apparition of more than three-quarters of a century before. Was the Holy Father assuming that the rest of the dreadful secret would also come true?

"I have a request, Professor."

The Pope wanted a memorandum, an annotated version of the secret that would match actual occurrences with what had been predicted.

"I did not take notes."

"Have you forgotten the contents?"

"Of course not."

"Whenever you want, you can consult the manuscript again."

But it had impressed itself on his memory, and he could call it up as if from a hard disk, the way he had brought up chapters of his history on the computer.

"The woman from Viterbo is coming to see me", the Pope remarked.

That was all.

That afternoon, Morrow drove himself to Civitavecchia and then followed the coastal road to where a Norman castle had been turned into a hotel restaurant. He sat on the open terrace, where the sea breeze worried the awnings and threatened to blow away the tablecloths, and ordered a pot of tea. It came with several molasses cookies wrapped in cellophane. St. Augustine had come along this coast with his companions and his mother. Monica had died not far away, at Ostia. One could imagine out there Phoenician craft, Roman triremes, the boat in which Aquinas had sailed from Leghorn to southern France on his way to Paris; one could imagine ships of the Third Reich and then of the Sixth Fleet. Even looking out to sea, the Campagna had a way of making all periods of history contemporary.

It was not a historian's habit to think of that sequence of events as coming to an absolute end.

2

"My spies tell me you have become a confidant of the Holy Father", Frawley said merrily, as if Morrow would welcome an opportunity to knock down the rumor.

"We've become inseparable", Morrow replied in a jocular tone.

Frawley smiled and reconsidered his approach. "Not many people realize that Benedetto is a classicist. He taught in Milan, actually wrote an introductory grammar, and published a collection of Latin aphorisms."

"I own it. I mean the collection of aphorisms."

Was this Frawley's way of hinting that he had discovered the source of the Latin quotes that had prefaced the chapters of Morrow's history?

"My edition of the text of Propertius, with translation, proved to be an open sesame with Benedetto", Frawley said, in a rare allusion to his scholarly activity.

"He has been very gracious to me. I mean, of course, to the United States."

"He might show his graciousness by seeing our mutual friend elevated to the cardinalate."

"I couldn't bring up such a topic."

"Why not?"

Did he have to explain to Frawley that he was not at the Vatican as the representative of the NCCB or USCC?

Frawley went on. "Turn about is fair play."

It was an odd notion of *quid pro quo*, the contemporary

equivalent of the red hat for the American ambassadorship to the Vatican. But his position had not been a gift of Lannan. Given the turn that events had taken once his name had been put forward, it was difficult to think of Lannan as even a remote cause of what had happened. After all, he had sent Wales to Michigan to suggest that Morrow withdraw his name.

"Why can't you press the matter with Benedetto, Monsignor?"

"My dear fellow, if I bring it up yet again he will think of me as Johnny one note. A word from you would carry more weight than the umpteenth repetition from me."

Morrow promised nothing. Perks and honors and elevations over one's fellows more than ever seemed meaningless. Half the time he wished he had not been shown that communication from Sister Lucy; the other half he was fascinated by the uncanny correlation between prediction and what had actually happened in Europe since. It was the remaining, unfulfilled prophecy that gave him a sense of vertigo.

There are certain beliefs that have become so familiar their reality escapes us. All men are mortal. The odd mad scientist aside, no one disputed this as an eternal truth. What human being could doubt that one day he would die and be no more? Yet how many really believed it, lived their lives in the light of that sobering truth? If the prospect of hanging concentrates the mind, it is only when it is an immediate prospect. The criminal running the remote risk of execution is not deterred. How different the fact of mortality must look to the moribund. It is not that they have learned something new; they realize as they never have before the truth of what they have always known.

He did broach the subject of Lannan's becoming a cardinal with Benedetto.

They were seated in the brocade chairs in the secretary of

state's office. The prelate fingered his pectoral cross and then ran his hand over the sleeve of his cassock.

"Professor, there are days when I miss the simple black I put on when I entered the seminary. Ratzinger always wore a black soutane, you know, with pectoral cross and scarlet zucchetto. The bishop longs to be a simple priest. The Holy Father, perhaps, remembers with regret when he was but a bishop. It is easy to mock the ambitions of others, but when one's own become hollow—is that wisdom or some rare vice?"

"The question is rhetorical, as addressed to me."

"The College is considerably diminished. Cardinal del Acebo died in Buenos Aires yesterday."

"Will there be a new list?"

"There *is* a new list. It has been ready for... When the Holy Father wishes, I shall make recommendations." He leaned toward Morrow. "I tell you absolutely *sub secreto*. Archbishop Lannan's name is on it."

"Why is the Holy Father delaying?"

"Delaying?" Benedetto smiled sweetly. "Here we think in centuries, Professor. Millennia." The smile went. "It is in God's hands."

Morrow would have preferred not to have been told this. Getting the information but being bound to secrecy was worse than not knowing at all—or than relying on gossip and guesses.

"He is on the list", Frawley confided. "I have it on the highest authority."

Had Benedetto told Monsignor Frawley in the same way he had told Morrow? A secret twice told is as good as a public announcement. But Frawley's sources proved to be somewhat removed from the highest authority.

"Then Lannan can relax."

201

"Relax! The Pope is in his eighties. He could go any minute."

That simple truth suddenly had a significance for Morrow it would have lacked a month or two before. As soon as a Pope died, a conclave of the cardinals was called to elect his successor, mourning mingling with the need to carry on. If Lannan were made cardinal before that, he would take part in the election of the new pope. If not, well, who knew what the future might bring?

"Actually, apart from missing the conclave, his chances would increase."

"How so?"

Frawley's eyes went in search of a way to put this. "Ever since the Council the Church has been trying to hold itself together, resisting the need for radical change. All to good purpose, mind; to have let the winds loose right away would have blown the Church away. But the time for easing up has more than come. The next papacy will be, in the terminology of the media, a liberal one."

"Pavese?"

There had been yet another article, this time in *Le Monde*, saying much the same thing Frawley was saying and pointing to Cardinal Ettore Pavese of Milan as the obvious man to loosen the Church's identification with a fixed and inflexible morality, permitting, without of course endorsing, a freer stance in the area of sexual morality. Procreation is a wonderful thing, but is it the purpose of life? Thus asked the French journalist. Frawley would doubtless put it a good deal more delicately. And then *30 Giorni* ran a piece in which the possible inclinations of the cardinals eligible to vote—those eighty and younger—were calculated. Cardinal Pavese's prospects were rosy.

3

In the rolling Kentucky horse country east of Louisville, approached by a lesser road that runs through villages and towns and mobile homes mounted on concrete blocks, mobile no more, lies the monastery of Gethsemani. The spire of the abbey church rose above the leafless trees, fallen leaves swirled on the narrow road, and Thomas Lannan, at the wheel of a car he had rented at the Lexington airport, was almost disappointed by the familiarity of the scene. In Washington, the idea of coming here had had the allure of a retreat on the far side of the moon, but half-forgotten previous visits had filled his subconscious with images that emerged to match their originals.

The abbey had become famous during what Morrow insisted on calling the golden age of American Catholicism, bounded by the end of World War II and the closing of the Council, twenty years which, in the historian's account, saw a surge in Catholic culture, Catholic spirituality, and Catholic influence on the country. President Kennedy, Fulton Sheen, and J. F. Powers figured in this account, but also looming large was the monk of Gethsemani, Fr. Louis, known to the world as Thomas Merton. Kennedy had been assassinated; after a stellar television career, Sheen became bishop of Rochester; the Council was convened; and Thomas Merton, that oddest of figures, the famous hermit, began the intellectual unraveling that would be completed by the Vietnam War and his panmonastic view of religion.

Merton's 1948 autobiography *Seven Storey Mountain* had touched the imagination of young men back from the war. There was a sudden dramatic rise in contemplative vocations; new Trappist abbeys sprang up across the United States in a way reminiscent of the great Cistercian revival of the twelfth century (Morrow's analogy). Merton's books flowed from the presses—meditations, spirituality, lives of saints, poems—seemingly in any genre that could be put to the purpose of reminding mankind that we have here no lasting city. Morrow, relying on Michael Mott's life of Merton, painted the tragic figure of a man who, having preached to others, himself succumbed to the allure of a nurse in a Louisville hospital to which an illness took him. He had been saved from making a complete fool of himself by the young woman, who saw more clearly than the monk who had spent decades in the contemplative life the folly of his proposal. In Morrow's history, the trajectory of Merton's life functioned as a great metaphor of what would become the postconciliar collapse.

Evelyn Waugh had been impressed by Merton's conversion, if not his prose. The English author had carefully edited the British version of the autobiography. Waugh also wrote for *Life* an essay, "American Century in the Catholic Church", in which he professed to see signs that America, of all places, would be the place where the Church would next flourish. Morrow had used this essay to great ironic effect. The fundamental question was: How had a church, seemingly so vigorous in the period before the Council, fallen so precipitously in so short a time in the wake of the Council? In a matter of a few years, crowded seminaries and convents, three and more priests in every parish, faithful observance of Church law, and divorce, unheard of among Catholics, had given way to bare ruined choirs (Gary Wills had applied the Shakespearian phrase to the demise of the Jesuits); nuns metamorphosing into bachelor gals, counselors, or fashion plates; a steep decline in Mass attendance; the desertion of their posts by thousands of priests; annulments becoming laughingly easy to obtain. Why? How?

However blandly they might be described, Morrow's facts were simply facts, and only a different interpretation of them could counter his. There were not wanting those who read success where Morrow saw failure. An extrinsic devotion, rote-like abiding by rules and observances, flight from the stern tasks of the world for spiritual self-indulgence had given way to service, to concern for peace and justice, rather than the morbid calibrating of one's inner life.

On the whole, Lannan was attracted by Morrow's account. Of course one did not announce such things. A bishop must take care not to side with one part of his flock against the other, despite the incessant pressure to enlist him to crush the opposition. Two days before, at his prie-dieu after Mass in his private chapel, Lannan had found himself praying fervently that the Pope would name him cardinal.

"You're on the list", Frawley had insisted on the transatlantic phone.

"There are lists and lists." Hit lists, shit lists, laundry lists, imaginary lists...

"I have it on the highest authority."

"Benedetto?"

"If I had not been told in confidence, I could confide in you", Frawley said, chortling smugly. Lannan made a note to tell Frawley no secrets. But Frawley was already privy to his anxiety over the red hat.

It was then that Lannan lifted his face from his hands and looked at the beautifully ornate tabernacle on the altar before him. Jesus his Lord, sacramentally present, Body, Blood, soul, and divinity, was there with him. The mother of the sons of Zebedee had come to Jesus asking that James and John be accorded first rank, one seated on his right hand, the other on his left. And Jesus replied that she did not know what she asked. Promotion amounted to demotion as she would understand it. Her sons would suffer as Jesus suffered. Lannan was filled with shame at his raw ambition. What on earth difference did it make whether or not he was cardinal? Answers to that crowded in on him—the coming conclave, the honor to his diocese, the whispers among his brother bishops if he were passed over—but he pushed them aside. O Lord, have mercy on me a sinner. He had to get away, to go on at least a brief retreat, and regain peace of soul.

He had made the arrangements himself. No one but Wales need know about this. There had been too much publicity about prelates going off to find themselves, leaves of absence, forays into mission activity on a temporary basis, ambiguous furloughs that suggested drying out or psychiatric care. Lannan had no intention of starting rumors suggestive of instability or, worse, that he was in the grips of unwonted religious fervor. Imagine the headline "Washington Archbishop Retreats to Trappist Abbey". That could be interpreted in so many ways, none of them helpful to his career.

There it was again, striking him almost with surprise. I am an ambitious man, he told himself. I have put myself in the power of others by wanting things that only they can confer. My center of gravity is no longer within but shifts from power source to power source, wherever the next prize or honor or promotion will come from. Not a welcome line of thought, not least because he had systematically avoided it for years. To withdraw for a time and pursue that unflattering interpretation of his clerical career took on the nature of an almost sensuous attraction. He would go off into the woods and look unflinchingly into his soul, certain that what he would find there would cause him great pain.

Arrived at his destination, he brought his car to a stop in the second parking lot but left his bag on the back seat when he went to the gate and rang the bell. It was a grey midafternoon, the air was chill, but it was the silence he was aware of. A natural silence that accommodated the raucous sound of a crow as a Japanese garden needs contrast to its overwhelming order. Already he felt a further silence, the Trappist silence, not so stringent as it once had been—*aggiornamento* had struck everywhere, save, he was told, the Carthusian hermits—but it remained nonetheless a radical difference from the incessant chatter of the world.

The gatekeeper, when he came, was deferential, but Lannan thought it a generic deference, to be shown to beggar and archbishop alike. The guestmaster, Br. Patrick, remembered Lannan from his previous visits.

"It has been years", Lannan said, and it came out as an apology.

"That long?" Patrick, once a whiz of Wall Street, was no longer governed by ordinary time.

"My bag is still in the car."

"I will get it."

Lannan went for it himself, but Patrick came along, remarking that he had never before seen the model of Mercedes that Lannan had rented. A flicker of curiosity? Lannan felt an absurd impulse to chide the monk, warn him against worldliness. It was a sharp reminder of what demands the mediocre make on those who strive for something more. We have need of sanctity, at least in others.

"Fr. Abbot is away. Perhaps he will return before you leave."

"I would like to stay three days."

"Then you will see him. I will put you in the bishop's suite."

"No." Lannan hesitated. How to put this? "Any room in the guest house will be fine."

If he expected an argument from Patrick, he was disappointed. Without comment or visible reaction, Patrick took him to the guest house and to a room on the second floor.

"I am usually to be found downstairs. If there is anything…"

"Everything is fine."

And the door closed on the narrow room. The bed was

narrow too, but it occupied half the width of the room. A small table was wedged between it and the wall, and on it was a small Big Ben alarm clock of a kind Lannan had not seen in years. On his previous visits he had accepted the bishop's suite—no lap of luxury, but palatial compared to these quarters. Patrick had put his bag on the bed. There was a coat hanger in a corner but no closet. The room obviously did not encourage extended visits.

Lannan sat on the bed, picked up the clock, put it down. Someone had set it for 1:45 A.M. Vigils in the chapel. There was a schedule on the table. He picked that up, then put it down again as well. He could reach out and crank the window further open. He closed his eyes and let the silence and, he hoped, peace descend upon him. He lay back and fell immediately asleep.

Two hours later he was wakened by a bell, not the church bell, but one that was being rung below. Disoriented for a moment, he located himself and felt a shiver pass over him. He might have been embarked on some illicit adventure. Wales could hint to the curious that he had gone for a few days to the archdiocesan camp in Virginia, though if anyone telephoned he would not get an answer. It was voluptuous to be so out of contact. He went downstairs in jeans and sweatshirt, leaving his ring in the room. Patrick was unlikely to make a fuss over him if there were other guests, and Lannan wanted to be simply a man among men.

During the guest house meal, an audio cassette of Basil Pennington at his most ethereal failed to destroy Lannan's mood. There were four other guests: a bearded fellow from the Notre Dame publicity department, a priest from Akron whose breath suggested that he had fortified himself before coming to table, and two Calvinists whose interest in medieval studies had brought them to Gethsemani. Backless benches, no cloth on the wooden table, hot thick stew, and bread that lent credence to the notion that it was the staff of life. Had he even tasted bread for years?

After a walk in the main quad of the abbey, he got his breviary from his room and went into the visitors' loft of the church to read the office of the day. He would recite vespers and compline so that he could fully attend to the chant when the office was sung in half an hour. He read slowly, which made him realize how mechanically he rattled off the psalms on an ordinary day. In this atmosphere his ordinary life seemed one of total superficiality. Even so there was a fifteen-minute interval after he finished during which the monks began to appear in the choir below, arriving one or two at a time, suddenly there, leafing through the great psalters propped before them. The abbey church was high and narrow, like Lannan's room. The windows had planes of glass of various shades of gray, like the graphics on Wales' laptop computer. Lannan had moved to the front row of the loft so that he had an unobstructed view of the choir below and the far-off sanctuary. It looked like a set for a movie involving Beckett. No wonder those medievalists had come here. They sat round-eyed across the aisle from Lannan. Did they perhaps imagine themselves down there, robed, cowled, adding their voices to the reedy recitation of the psalms, choir answering to choir? *Nox nocti indicat scientiam.* The Latin of the nineteenth psalm which was being sung came to him, and he was back in the major seminary, chanting vespers, his whole life still before him.

He thought of his possible self down there in choir. A resigned archbishop, somewhat in the manner of Cardinal Leger of Montreal, in the monastery after an active ecclesiastical life to end his days in the demanding round of monastic life. The fantasy stayed with him throughout his retreat.

On a street corner in Viterbo, north of Rome, there is a pulpit from which Thomas Aquinas is alleged to have preached. Morrow went to the old papal residence, where the Curia would have stopped briefly in its constant progression through the papal states in Thomas' time. Here was the chapel in which a papal conclave had been prolonged for six months until French forces burst in, arrested two Orsini cardinals, and prompted the swift election of Martin IV. High on Morrow's reading list since arriving in Rome was Pastor's lives of the popes, a topic on which Monsignor Frawley had made himself expert.

But it was Benedetto, all but unrecognizable in street clothes, who had brought Morrow to this town north of Rome. If the cardinal meant to travel incognito, the Vatican City plates would have given them away. The visionary had sought refuge in a convent, and it was there that Benedetto had arranged to meet her. Morrow would have pleaded his imperfect Italian as an obstacle to going, but curiosity overcame him. Word had come to the Vatican that the Viterbo visionary had something to communicate to the Holy Father. It was Benedetto's assumption that she would confide in him.

They were taken to a parlor that might have been furnished with the discarded tables and chairs and gewgaws of the families of the nuns. When Benedetto sat, his feet did not quite reach the floor; but he lay his own arms on the plump arms of the chair, ready for the woman to be shown to him. Nuns had fluttered about them from the moment they opened the door to the cardinal, and Benedetto waved away their attentions with a practiced gesture that seemed both to acknowledge the fittingness of their subservience and dismiss it as a bother. Did he imagine the visionary would behave similarly?

She was a tall, olive-skinned woman in her mid-twenties,

clad in a longish but stylish skirt and a sweater, with a black shawl over her shoulders. She stood before Benedetto with her arms at her sides, ignoring the presence of James Morrow.

"You wish to see the Holy Father?"

"I have a message for him."

"A message."

"From Our Blessed Mother."

She said this matter-of-factly but reverently as well. This was the woman allegedly visited by Mary over a period of some months. She was a midwife, intelligent but without education, a woman of great dignity. When Benedetto held out his hand, she did not hesitate, but genuflected and kissed his ring.

"I have come from the Holy Father, Caterina. I will take your message to him."

"No."

Benedetto affected surprise. "My dear woman, I am the secretary of state, the confidant of His Holiness; I am here at his request."

"I am instructed to speak to him directly."

A lifetime of diplomacy proved of little avail. Half an hour later, they were where they had begun, with Benedetto offering to take her message, she insisting she must give it directly to the Holy Father.

"Is it a secret?"

"That is not for me to say."

"If it isn't a secret, you can trust me with it."

"I trust you, of course. But the Virgin told me to give her message directly to the Holy Father."

Benedetto kissed the fingertips of his joined hands. Then he had it.

"You can write out your message, and I will deliver it unread to the Holy Father."

"I cannot write."

Was it possible that intelligent human beings at the end of the twentieth century in a civilized country were illiterate? Caterina was.

"Someone else can write it for you."

"I cannot tell it to anyone but the Holy Father."

Benedetto's impatience was not feigned. "Are you ready to go immediately?"

"Yes."

"I have a car outside. We can start at once."

She stood and started for the door, calling Benedetto's bluff. The mother superior was furious and scolded Caterina for her impudence. The woman listened to the rebuke, without protest, but it was fully clear she would do only what she thought the Blessed Virgin had instructed her to do, and that was to speak directly to the Pope.

Caterina was put in front, next to the driver, who, after a tentative ogle, kept his eye on the road. The presence of the woman in the enclosed car was palpable. Benedetto attempted conversation, but then he fell silent. Morrow had read of the odor of sanctity. Was holiness palpable as well, sensed like another ingredient in the atmosphere? Caterina sat motionless on the short ride to Rome. On the Anulare, they passed a prostitute, discretely displaying herself at the side of the road. Her eyes met Caterina's as they swept by, and Morrow saw the expression on the prostitute's face change. When he looked back, she was standing, looking after the car.

In Benedetto's office, there was a reenactment of the dialogue in Viterbo. The cardinal seemed to think that being inside the Vatican, in the vicinity of the Pope, surrounded by pomp and power, Caterina would consent to let the secretary of state take down her message.

"I must see the Holy Father."

"Do you imagine that anyone can just break in on the Pope?"

"It is not I who have come. The Blessed Lady has sent me to speak for her."

It was a dilemma, but one Benedetto had faced when he made the decision to go to Viterbo. The mother superior had been sending him urgent messages. To visit Caterina already gave some patina of approval to her claim to be visited by the Virgin, as if the Church accepted it. Bringing her to the Vatican may have seemed less ambiguous, since it clearly indicated that the Vatican took the woman seriously. But to present her to the Holy Father would elevate her to the status of Sister Lucy, the seer of Fatima, whom Paul VI had received. This was not a decision Benedetto could make.

He picked up his phone, dialed 1, and sat back in his chair. It was said that during the reign of Pius XII, staff knelt when they spoke to him on the phone. Benedetto gave a crisp account of the visit to Viterbo and of Caterina's demand. He fell silent as he listened.

"Yes, Holiness."

He nodded, again listening. His eyes flicked to Caterina, then to Morrow, then upward to the ceiling, as if he were appealing to a yet higher authority. He hung up the phone and stood.

"Come", he said to Caterina. "I will take you to the Holy Father."

Benedetto was back, alone, in five minutes, frowning. Caterina had asked to be alone with the Pope.

"This is all wrong", he said. "All wrong. Professor, you have witnessed an experienced diplomat make a major mistake."

"What else could you have done?"

Benedetto considered that. He took comfort from it.

"You are right. The Holy Father was more than willing to see her. You would have thought he had sent me to Viterbo to fetch her."

5

Abbot John returned, and Archbishop Lannan paid his respects.

"You must move to the bishop's suite, Your Excellency."

"I am comfortable where I am."

"Comfortable?" The abbot smiled. "We are to make guests welcome, not comfortable."

"It was good of you to make room for me on such short notice."

The abbot was more tolerant of small talk than Patrick, but Lannan realized that he was speaking needlessly.

"Come see me again", the abbot said.

Later, fantasizing about resigning his see and entering Gethsemani, he wondered if Abbot John's remark had a providential ring to it, meaning more than he could have known. When he wasn't walking through the fields of the monastery, Lannan sat in the loft of the monastic church or downstairs in the pews behind the choir stalls. He formed an image of himself, head completely shaved, down to 170 pounds, lean and spiritual in his Cistercian habit, free at last of all the petty distractions of this vale of tears.

By the third day, the persistence of this fantasy gave him serious pause. Had he been led here by the Spirit and offered a choice on which depended the fate of his immortal soul? He reviewed the antecedents of his decision to come away to Kentucky. He had been prompted by the sense that his life was being frittered away in trivia, "measured out in coffee spoons", in T. S. Eliot's phrase. Suddenly he was furious with himself for footnoting his own thoughts. He longed for simplicity, for yes meaning yes and no meaning no. Had he been led here to Gethsemani, seemingly acting on the spur of the moment, to face a crossroads of his eternal life?

"If one of my priests sought entry here, what would the procedure be, Fr. Abbot?"

"Is this just a hypothetical question?"

"No. He has made me aware of his desires, and they may be serious; it is difficult to say."

"And you are concerned about losing one of your priests?"

"If he had a genuine vocation, I would not stand in his way."

"I have just returned from France where a retired archbishop entered one of our communities."

"I almost envy him."

"Just almost?"

Lannan was on the verge of saying, I am the man, I am the priest who seeks entry, what must I do to be saved? But something stopped him. The two men sat in silence until the abbot said, "I am always here if you wish to see me."

When he closed the door behind him, Lannan broke into a sweat, as if he had just made a narrow escape. Well, he had. He went outside and strode off briskly through the pasture, his foot skidding on sheep droppings when he forgot to keep alert. His mind was blessedly empty; he seemed to be responding to the great globe itself, enveloped in its atmosphere, a denizen of the biosphere, one of billions of human beings.

"Congratulations", Patrick said, when they sat at table.

The medievalists had gone and only the priest with whiskey on his breath remained. Lannan looked at Patrick. He realized that the audio was not turned on. Patrick handed him the Louisville paper.

A consistory had been held. "Pope Names Twenty New Cardinals."

His own face looked out at him from a picture the size of a postage stamp.

PART FOUR

CHAPTER ONE

I

James Morrow picked up a book from a table in Monsignor Frawley's sitting room.

"Who's Anthony Kenny?"

Frawley in the next room needed the question repeated. "A Brit."

On the cover of the paperback book a black-and-white photograph of a young man, smiling from ear to ear, wearing cassock and collar and large brimmed hat, St. Peter's in the background, was balanced by a color picture of the boy grown old, gnomelike in academic garb. *The Path from Rome.*

"He was master of Balliol; now he lives in Rhodes House. He's a philosopher."

Morrow studied the cover. If the publisher had intended the effect Maritain had when he included a series of pictures of Luther in *Three Reformers,* it seemed unkind to its author. Not many flown priests in the States had written a book on their loss of faith, thank God. The few books that had appeared were an embarrassment in several senses.

Morrow had come to the North American College to dine with the faculty; afterward he would speak to the assembled students.

"Your book", Frawley answered, when Morrow asked for guidance on a topic. He forbore mentioning that he had written several books. Whether he liked it or not—and he was not objecting—he was now identified with his history of the Church in the United States. But then, as he wrote it, he had meant for it to be his *magnum opus*.

Frawley was done up in the full panoply of his monsignorial office for the occasion, looking like the colonel everyone knew would be a general before any of his classmates. Apparently he had postponed the process himself.

"One must never divulge such matters, of course, but take a case. To fly off quite young to the dubious distinction of being Angel of the Church of Boise, say, or remain in the Holy City as the eyes and ears of the American bishops, close to the pulse of things—well, what kind of choice is that?"

"So you think Rome is the pulse?"

Frawley tucked in his chin. "Of course."

"That is not the line one hears at home."

"Don't you believe it. It is not Rome, but the present Pope they profess to disdain. You quoted that awful remark, 'A puff of white smoke and everything will be different.' Just wait until the need for a conclave comes. They will be here in force to make sure things turn out right this time."

"And Thomas Lannan will be one of the electors?"

Frawley rolled his eyes. "Thank God. He's been like a woman having her first child."

"With you as midwife."

"Best not pursue it. Offhand similes are not my forte."

"When's the big day?"

It would be another month before the new cardinals were solemnly inducted into the College in St. Peter's. Frawley found it amusing that in number the group would rival Lannan's ordination class. Nonetheless Thomas Lannan, as cardinal, would be one of slightly over a hundred men drawn from the world over, and it was the cardinals under eighty who would elect the next pope.

"And from among their number." The monsignorial brows lifted, the Irish eyes twinkled. "Thomas Lannan, the first American pope?"

"You mean of the Roman Catholic Church, of course."

"Ho ho."

They went into a refectory filled with young men impatient for their dinner. Frawley led Morrow to a raised table under a massive and busy painting, put his guest at his right hand, then looked out over the refectory until he was rewarded with silence. He signed himself with the cross. "*Benedicite.*"

"*Benedicite*", roared the young men in response.

He continued. "*Benedic, Domine, nos et haec tua dona quae de tua largitate sumus sumpturi, per Christum dominum nostrum.*"

"*Amen!*" roared back the young men as chairs were pulled out noisily, then sat upon, and hundreds of conversations began. This was neither the time nor the place to continue even the bantering exchange begun in Frawley's suite. The rector looked out over his wards, monitored the way they were served, then fell to with gusto.

The young clerics in this room, if the future was like the past, would return to the United States to assignments that put them on a path leading to ecclesiastical preferment. Here were the future bishops and archbishops, cardinals too; here were the chancellors and rectors of the next generation. In his history, Morrow had pointed out that many of those who, in 1968, had defied the papal judgment that the traditional ban on artificial contraception still stood in the age of the pill, had studied in Rome; and a majority of those had been in Rome during the Council. The dominant figures of the hierarchy at that time had also been, to a notable degree, products of a Roman education. This was still largely true. The bishops who had permitted if not covertly encouraged an independent and critical attitude toward the Magisterium were beneficiaries of a Roman education, either prior to or after ordination. What to make of this?

Morrow despised polls and certainly did not consider the random interviews he himself had conducted as anything more than sufficient basis for his own reflections on the matter, take them or leave them. Had too-close proximity to what Frawley called the pulse of power induced contempt? Morrow had never been happy with the secular parallel that occurred to him, Fitzgerald's *The Last Tycoon*, in which a legendary producer shows a young lady the back lots and sets of Hollywood, effectively puncturing the great illusion of the screen. A reviewer in *Newsweek* suggested another: the great Oz, when the curtain is pulled away and Dorothy and her friends see how the awesome illusion is created.

Later, when he gave his lecture, Morrow felt somewhat accustomed to his audience, and they had been able to get used to the sight of him at table with the rector. Frawley delivered an unctuous introduction, tolerable only because of his jovial, semi-facetious manner. The young men attended to Frawley carefully, obviously delighting in the orotund style and the surprising turns of phrase.

"Our destiny is in our names, needless to say, which is why our speaker tonight was fated to spend his life looking toward yesterday. Raised now to diplomatic eminence, he has agreed to give the lessons of history to those who would otherwise be doomed to repeat them. How to address him is a problem. He comes to us wearing two hats, that of ambassador as well as that of professor. It is not true, as his admirers say, that he has two heads. Or is it his detractors who say that? In any case, with enormous pleasure, and anticipating along with you an enlightening evening, I turn the lectern over to the United States Ambassador to the Holy See, the Honorable Professor James Morrow."

History is gossip, finally. Morrow organized his presentation around three anecdotes: the Charles Curran flap at Catholic University and its resolution in the courts twenty years later;

The New Nun, a book written in the early seventies that predicted a renaissance in religious orders that would follow on dropping the traditional habit, and the precipitous decline ever since in religious vocations; and the sit-in strike to save a historic Chicago church scheduled to be closed because of declining parishioners. In peripheral vision he saw Frawley lean forward when he recited the much-cited lines of the Shakespeare sonnet:

Upon these boughs which shake against the cold,
Bare ruin'd choirs, where late the sweetbirds sang.

Of course he did not leave it there. The signs of hope were not welcomed by all, but there they were: Opus Dei, The Legionaries of Christ, Cardinal O'Connor's Sisters of Life, the flourishing of such dioceses as Peoria, Lincoln, LaCrosse, and Arlington.

Perhaps twenty minutes were devoted to questions from the floor, most of them indicating that these young men had a very imperfect understanding of what the Church in the United States had been like during the period 1945–1960. Without that understanding, the postconciliar Church could scarcely be seen for the debacle it was.

"You make it sound like a golden age", a prematurely bald young fellow said to Morrow when they were having sherry in the recreation room afterward.

"There were lots of good things going on."

"But wasn't it all superficial and rote? Were people's hearts in it?"

"Like now?"

But the questioner was not to be put off. After all, Vatican II was called to renew the Church. If everything was fine, what was the need for a council?

"I suppose renewal is a perpetual necessity. But it is important to know what John XXIII meant by it."

It was a stimulating evening; and, in a way that surprised him, Morrow realized that he missed teaching, missed being with the young, missed that combination of deference and defiance that characterized the bright student.

"A pretty impressive bunch of young men", he said to Frawley afterward.

"Did you think so?"

"Aren't they?"

"If they impress they are impressive. But James, they know so little. You heard the questions. There is a great chasm separating them even from people my age." He paused. "Imagine what it must be like if the only Church you had known was that of the past twenty years or so."

Back in his apartment he enjoyed the afterglow of the evening. He missed the classroom more than he had realized; it was undeniably pleasant to have an audience of bright young people. He thought of all the classes he had faced over the years, growing old himself while his audience seemed caught in a time warp, forever young. Still it had been on the margin of the life he and Mabel had shared, the life that had included the children. Wife and children are the true measure of one's passage through time. Now Mabel was gone, his children grown, and here he was on the far side of the world beginning a new life.

But the presence of Maureen Kilmartin, as she now was, seemed to carry him back to the time before teaching and Mabel and all the rest.

"You were my idea, you know."

He waited, welcoming the opportunity to look at her in silence. He was not going to respond to enigmatic remarks. There was something of the girl he had known long ago in the handsome woman Maureen had become, veteran of two marriages, twice widowed. "I'm bad luck", she had said earlier, and then let it go. It was not a topic he wanted to pursue, not least because he felt himself drawn to her.

"You do realize that it was my suggestion that Tom Lannan propose your name to the President."

"Then I will blame you if things turn out badly for me here."

"Oh, no. You will have only yourself to blame. Your great coup on the evangelists' home turf landed you the job."

"Well, it will give me a chance to get to know you again."

"That's what I had in mind."

2

Rafael Trujillo, dean of the Vatican Diplomatic Corps, gave a dinner of welcome for Morrow, to which the physician of the Holy Father was also invited, and inevitably the topic of the Pope's health came up. Mondini, a brilliant diagnostician and legendary gossip, prefaced his every remark with the proviso that he was speaking *entre nous*.

"Is it serious?" Maureen asked. She was there as the widow of the Irish ambassador, and Morrow found her almost a stranger in this setting, a stately woman with her high-bridged nose and the marvelously graying hair that had fascinated Morrow from the moment he saw her.

Mondini cast his eyes toward the ceiling. "At his age, a cold can be serious."

"He has a cold?"

Maureen's question cast something of a pall over Mondini's performance; but he was Italian, and she was taken to be from what Joyce had called an afterthought of Europe.

"But a warm heart, madam. A strong heart. And in many ways of course a broken heart."

Murmurs of sympathy went round the table, and Mondini had his audience back again. Speaking around the waiter who was serving him, keeping eye contact despite elbows and serving dishes and his own interest in what was being put on his plate, he answered affirmatively when asked if the Holy Father still did his daily exercises.

"Religiously." His brittle mustache twitched, but he went on. "For fifteen minutes beginning at five."

Morrow glanced at his watch. Was the man whose exercises would begin in 7 hours already in bed? He put the question to Mondini. Suddenly the table was aroar with authoritative voices. The schedule of the Pope was a matter of detailed knowledge, or claims to knowledge, in the diplomatic corps. The trouble was that the claims were conflicting. The German ambassador's assertion that the Holy Father did not even go to his bedroom before midnight was countered by the apodictic affirmation that, true as that once had been, it was true no more.

"He tires more easily now", Mondini said, unwilling to concede the chair.

It was clear that for these people the Pope was a mythical creature: his habits, his health, his everything, was fascinating to them, yet they seemed scarcely more informed than other citizens of the Holy City whose work brought them into contact with the Vatican. Most of them, he was to learn, saw the Pope only on ceremonial occasions. He had been granted extraordinary access, something it seemed best not to make known, though he did feel a competitive impulse to say how hale the Holy Father had seemed to him when they chatted the other day. To have given in to that impulse, would have been to cross the line separating integrity and the world of diplomacy.

That wasn't fair. He did not feel at ease with this group, though why he should question their obvious contentment with their assignments was unclear. Good for them, when he thought of it. But more and more he began to doubt Claudel's frankness when the great poet wrote of the reluctant if punctilious performance of his ambassadorial duties.

Over coffee in the library he spoke with Maureen. She gave him her complete attention: great green eyes looking directly into his, intent on his every word. It turned out that her hearing was somewhat impaired and such attention was necessary.

"Why did you stay on here in Rome?"

"My home is here now." Her mouth closed on the possibility that she might tell him the story he had already heard from others. Her husband's car had been bombed one morning, horrible tragedy enough, but three years later when a reformed member of the gang gave testimony, it turned out that the bombing had been a mistake. The intended target had been the Venezuelan ambassador.

"Do you go to Ireland often?"

"Seldom. Everything has changed. Of course I feel the same way about the States. Don't you?"

"That it's changed?"

"I meant rather your feeling about it. I have read your book, Jim. I can't find my copy, though, and I want to read it again, now that you're here."

"I'll send you a copy."

"Nonsense. I'll buy one."

Morrow resolved to have one sent to her in the morning. For this he needed her address. The tips of her teeth were visible for a moment, but again she pressed her lips tight and drew an elaborate printed card from her handbag. He remarked on her having kept up her old diplomatic friendships.

"Oh, none of these people were here when my husband was ambassador. Except Trujillo of course." She glanced at her host. It occurred to Morrow that Trujillo had been the intended target of the bomb that had killed Sean Kilmartin.

227

Whatever Latin American quarrel might have been invoked to justify that had long since been settled. "I do see them from time to time. The individuals change, but the group does not, if that makes any sense."

"What doesn't change?"

"The gossip. Item number one is always the health of the Pope."

"There seemed to be a division of opinion."

"They really know very little. As for Mondini..." She smiled at the physician who stood with a balloon glass in his little hands, holding forth on something inaudible to them. "Don't fall ill in Rome."

3

Three days later he received a note from her saying that she had read his book again and hoped that she would soon have an opportunity to discuss it with him. He was about to ask McHugh to invite her to lunch in his dining room on the Aurelia, then decided to make the call himself. He did not want to confuse seeing Maureen with his official duties.

"Wonderful", she said, when he suggested lunch. "I hope you mean today."

"You pick the place."

"Do you know Alla Rampa?"

He said that he looked forward to getting to know it. To avoid difficulties, she suggested they meet first somewhere he did know; and he found her, as she had promised, waiting for him in the Caffe Greco where Byron and other British had whiled away the idle hours. Fellow tourists, earlier strangers, come to Rome, as everyone does eventually, as to some primordial home town.

"Rome has always been full of foreigners."

"Like us?"

Her smile involved her entire face, and Morrow felt drawn into its benevolence.

Alla Rampa was located below Trinità dei Monti, its tables spilling out into the little plaza from which the eponymous ramp gave oblique entree to the Spanish Steps. The house in which Keats had died was a few feet away.

"I have been collecting Roman travel books", he told her. "Goethe, Stendahl, Hawthorne, Howells, James. It's almost a genre unto itself."

"Will you write your own?"

They had been taken to a table against a wall; bread had been put before them, wine was on its way; the place was vibrant with a pleasant constant noise to which their table, like the others, added its own contribution.

"I'm more likely to write about the ones I read."

"That could be a delightful book."

"You sound like an editor, spurring an author on."

"I found your book so sad."

"How so?"

Her smile had faded. "It is like reading about the end of the world."

"It is the end of *a* world, certainly. The Church in America will never again be what it was."

"It is not just America. Within a few decades, Ireland has got well on its way toward being a post-Christian country. And as for Italy, well, look around you. More and more, the faith is seen as an impediment to progress."

"Not impediment enough."

Progress meant divorce, abortion, sexual freedom, the great

false promises of the age, which too quickly led to smashed homes, alienated children, disease, and pornography. She conjured up a celtic twilight as she spoke. Morrow knew these things, in the way the reader of newspapers knows things, but Maureen Kilmartin spoke of them as one would of a death in the family.

"In Ireland, the Church and society were so unified that they unravel together."

"Surely the Irish hierarchy is as solid as it ever was."

"Oh?" She almost whispered the name of a bishop whose illegitmate son had emerged from the past with a great deal of fanfare.

"Surely that was unique."

"Dear God, I hope so. It's a dreadful thought that even one more should turn out to have fathered a child now grown to manhood and been cavorting with the mother off and on ever since."

There was that added edge to her voice, the female's penchant to see her sister Eve as at the bottom of such things.

"Ireland is ripe for such a book as yours."

He was about to launch into what would have been a standard spiel about the historian's subject, that which has passed away and is no more, but they both knew they were talking about something very specific, the alarming alterations in their Church.

"The smoke of Satan", she said, citing Pope Paul VI's stunning remark that the hand of the Evil One was discernible in the distortion of the Second Vatican Council.

It was a relief to order, a process that transformed Maureen. Preoccupied sadness was gone like a morning mist, and her marvelous smile returned as she consulted with the waiter and with Jim and gave her full attention to ordering their meal. Why did she seem so different from Monsignor Frawley as she did this? Perhaps he considered fussing about the details of food a woman's work, not a man's. Her task accomplished, she put her arms on the table and leaned toward him.

"So who will be the next pope?" she asked.

"The next pope!"

"It sounds morbid, I know, but the Holy Father is now by any standards an old man. He could go any moment."

"But so could anyone. People my age keel over all the time."

"Your age." She sat back and narrowed her eyes as she studied him. "You and Frank and Tom Lannan are all the same age."

"And you're what, five–six years younger?"

"Do you guess weights as well?"

"Am I close."

"I am fifty-three. And what I didn't know about you I read in the press coverage during the fuss over your nomination."

His academic colleague Ryan had written to assure Morrow that he was still busy gathering the print coverage of those days into scrapbooks. Perhaps when his time as ambassador was over, he could read those stories and news reports with enjoyment. Ryan painted a word picture of him lolling in his chair beside the fire in his Michigan cottage, the murmur of the lake outside, leaves drifting slowly down. It was the current season Ryan was describing, and it was a clear bid for the use of the cottage; and for a moment Jim almost relented, but he thought better of the impulse. If Ryan ever got the freedom of the cottage, it would be no easy matter to get him out again.

"You are a Pisces." Maureen confided.

"Surely you don't take that sort of thing seriously."

"I am a Libra."

"What does that mean?"

"You really don't know?"

"No."

She had been born at the end of the September, Morrow in

231

February. "If we were young and I were flirty, I would point out that that is a very good match."

He would have guessed her to be fifty. But there was no need to guess. He had already learned her age from McHugh.

It was well for her to joke about this quasi-date, neutralizing its romantic significance. They were two lonely people, both of an age, who were much affected by the loss of a beloved spouse. The Roman setting exercised an influence on him that would not have been present if they had come together only in the States. When Tom Lannan had brought her along to lunch in Washington, identifying her as Frank Bailey's sister, she had been only a pleasant, scarcely remembered person from the past. But his emphatically bachelor digs in Rome, a setting in which Mabel had never figured, the undeniable status his ceremonial post conferred on him, and Maureen's handsome attractiveness made the desire to get to know her better in this unlooked-for present, not searching for her in time and memory, both intense and welcome.

4

Monsignor Wales had collected data for Archbishop Lannan on the average age at which men are raised to the College of Cardinals, and, a few Borgias aside, Thomas Lannan felt that he was doing pretty well to be named at the age of fifty-five. Even so, it was sobering to realize that he had only twenty-five years as a potential elector of popes and of active priestly life. Paul VI had ruled that the holders of sees had to relinquish them at eighty. None too soon in some cases, but awfully early in others. Thomas Lannan did not even want to admit the concept of retirement into his mind. Like the upsetting conversation he had had with Maureen about the letter she had received from Mrs. Christiansen, there were things he did not wish to think of at all.

The Holy Father was in his eighties; he would have to live a very long time in order for Lannan's eligibility as an active participant in a conclave called to fill the empty throne of Peter to run out. That he would cast one of the hundred or so votes that selected the Pope's successor was certain. The uncertainty lay in how soon this might happen.

"I am praying for his good health", Wales had said, with odd emphasis.

"Of course." However perfunctorily, every priest the world over said a special prayer for the Holy Father at each Mass.

"Until you're invested, in any case."

This note of uncertainty did not endear Monsignor Wales to Lannan. Wales was the most dutiful of aides—prompt, reliable, respectful—though still after five years, aloof. Lannan sensed that deep in his heart, Monsignor Wales did not approve of him. And now, just back from his unscheduled retreat at the Trappist abbey at Gethsemani, despite the scarcely repressible elation at being named cardinal, Thomas Lannan understood.

In rural Kentucky, caught up temporarily in the ordered life of the monks of the monastery, he had seen himself and his clerical ambitions in a cold, unflattering light. Abbot John had been shrewd enough to realize that Lannan was inquiring about himself when he asked about the procedure for a diocesan priest to enter the monastery. The attraction of that plain, regulated life had been almost concupiscent. The attraction had intensified rather than diminished, so much so that when Brother Joachim congratulated him and showed him the newspaper, Lannan's first thought was that he was being torn from this safe harbor and forced out into the terrible sea again.

The thought, feeling rather, had been crowded out by an enormous sense of relief and gratitude.

"*Te Deum laudamus*", he managed to say.

Ten minutes later, on his knees in the abbey church, saying prayers of thanksgiving, he imagined a future biographer interviewing Joachim. "How did he take the news, Brother?" "His first words were the opening of that age-old hymn of thanks, *Te deum laudamus.*" "How would you translate that?" "We praise thee, God..." Imagining this, Lannan felt a twinge of regret that he had not quoted a psalm instead. *Non nobis, domine, non nobis, sed nomini tuo da gloriam.* Not that it mattered. By the time any biography of him appeared, no one would know any Latin at all, and the psalms would have been subjected to yet another barbarization into basic English, nullifying any resonance they might have in the minds of future readers.

Lannan smiled. It was a thought worthy of Morrow. He frowned. Had he read that in Morrow's book?

Wales had provided him with another memo, listing the heroic and saintly cardinals of more or less recent times: Cajetan, Bonaventure, Borromeo, Bellarmine, Manning, Newman. The list went on: Mindzenty, Wolensky, Stepinac... How sweet to call the roll of such names. Lannan was resolved to earn a place on that short list. The first thing he would do in Rome would be to have a long talk with Jim Morrow, the kind of talk they had not had for years. There was a role awaiting the cardinal archbishop of Washington in the history of the Church in America, and Lannan had the feeling that Jim could help him define it. In his new status, Thomas Lannan could afford to manifest the courage he had, for better or worse, been keeping under wraps too long.

Frawley had sent on clippings from Italian papers about the visionary of Viterbo, who had allegedly had a private audience with the Holy Father. Lannan pieced together the story, checking it with the English edition of *L'Osservatore Romano.*

234

"Did he see her?" he asked Frawley, telephoning him before noon so he would catch the rector of the North American College before his evening began. Frawley was a legendary trencherman and a regular at fashionable Roman tables.

"I verified it with Benedetto."

"What does he make of it?"

"He is all three monkeys rolled into one. He wouldn't be secretary of state otherwise."

"Thank God, the story wasn't picked up here. Can you imagine what the media would make of it?"

"I remember the fuss in the press about recent consultations by First Ladies with astrologers."

"Exactly!"

"Morrow reminded me of Ratzinger's reference to the secret of Fatima in the famous *Report*."

Lannan emitted the obligatory groan at the mention of the former prefect of the Sacred Congregation for the Doctrine of the Faith, and then remembered that Ratzinger was a heroic figure in Morrow's history.

"Publicity apart, what do you make of the Pope consulting women who claim to have had private revelations?"

"Well, he didn't ask my advice", Frawley said fruitily. "Don't imagine that the Italian press thinks the woman is the witch of Endor. She's become a sympathetic public figure by desperately trying to avoid that role."

"He'd do better consulting with Benedetto."

Frawley was oddly reluctant to pursue the topic, but surely he must see that taking seriously women who claimed to have received heavenly visitors, no matter how momentarily popular, was wildly unwise. Imagine the popes of the time consulting Bernadette or the seers of Fatima. The Holy Father had kept the traditional distance from Medjugorje, despite its global fame.

"Morrow and Benedetto went to Viterbo to fetch her."

What could he say to that? Jim Morrow seemed to have

235

gotten very tight with the Vatican in short order. But of course he was here as ambassador to the Holy See.

The ceremony at which Thomas Lannan would be officially inducted into the College of Cardinals was January 21, the Feast of Saint Agnes. Five weeks away.

Wales prayed for the health of the Pope, lest he should be called to his eternal reward before that January date. Lannan would have liked to inquire about his status in the interim. One might be nominated bishop, but of course until the consecration one was not yet a bishop. Surely that did not apply here. Cardinal is an honor, not an order in the Church. The ceremony was merely a confirmation of an appointment already made.

He was sure of that. But not sure enough to put the question to anyone whose answer might disturb his certainty.

5

In the new calendar year, Jim Morrow drove to Viterbo again with Maureen, this time as a pilgrim. They joined the crowds who waited patiently to get into the cathedral and file with glacial slowness past the statue before which the woman allegedly received messages from the Mother of God.

"Allegedly?" Maureen said, taking him up on the qualification. She wore a silk dress with a full skirt, beautifully patterned, and a large-brimmed, black hat that made her hair look silver. She had gone with him to the Villa d'Este on condition that he would take her to Viterbo.

"One mustn't anticipate the judgment of the Church."

"Oh, pooh. If she's good enough for the Holy Father, she's good enough for me."

"You don't know what the Pope thinks of her."

"He received her in audience."

"Would you like a list of the dubious characters he has accorded a similar courtesy?"

"This was private and by invitation."

"Who's your source?"

"Everybody knows it."

It seemed that everybody in Italy did know it, as well as many from abroad. This made his own keeping of the confidence seem slightly absurd, but maybe Benedetto thought he was one of the sources of the rumor. He could hardly seek an audience to assure the secretary of state that he was no gossip. In any case, Viterbo bulged with pilgrims; there wasn't a hotel room to be had, nor a seat at a restaurant. As had happened again and again in other places, there were many for whom an apparition meant prosperity, and Viterbo was proving to be no exception. The local bishop all but forbade people to come; the visionary herself was kept incommunicado; but there was a brisk business in photocopied sheets that purported to be the transcript of the seer's talk with the Pope.

"That's nonsense", Morrow snorted. "They were alone together."

"How do you know that?"

He shut up. Maureen bought a photocopied sheet, giving ten thousand lire for it, but they did not read it while they were in the line that inched slowly up a side aisle of the cathedral to a statue of Our Lady that looked like a million others the world over. Well, what did he expect?

They had only seconds for a swift prayer when they reached the side altar, and then they were urged on their way to let the line advance. An unshaven man in cassock and surplice, presumably the sacristan, extended a collection bag, jingling its contents. Maureen dropped in a handful of notes, and Morrow did the same.

"I thought you were withholding judgment?"

"That will go to the cathedral."

They stopped at a country restaurant on the way back to Rome, taking an outside table, to enjoy the unseasonably sunny afternoon. Maureen read to him from the photocopied sheet, and the awful threats of coming woe clashed with the scenery, the restaurant, and the delight that he felt in her company. More than once he caught himself about to formulate the thought that Mabel would have liked her.

"My God, I hope this isn't true", Maureen said, stopping her reading of the sheet that fluttered in the slight breeze as she held them. They told of even more turmoil in the Church, a swift succession of popes, schism.

"Prophecies tend to be pretty grim."

"Were there prophecies at Lourdes?"

The spate of apparitions had begun with La Sallette and reached a peak with Fatima. In recent weeks, Morrow had come to know a good deal about Fatima, the better to situate the secret he had been asked by the Pope to read. He had been particularly struck by how unintelligible its forecast would have seemed to anyone at the time, let alone the children to whom Mary had appeared. That could not be said of what the woman of Viterbo had come to tell the Pope.

"More of the same", he had suggested to Benedetto when the cardinal gave him a summary of the summary he himself had been given by the Pope.

"Oh, worse", the older man had said. "Far worse."

The Secret of Fatima had told of the sufferings of the Pope and the defections of many clergy, priests and even bishops among them.

"It seems to speak of him", Morrow had said, when he had talked with Benedetto about it. "*Lui*" here was always the Pope.

"Yes."

"Does he think so?"

"It is not a question I would ask him."

The woman of Viterbo was predicting far worse troubles ahead for the Pope's successor.

Not a question I would ask him. . . . Benedetto's answers often politely avoided the question. Or was this simply diplomatic obfuscation? When you are not speaking simply for yourself, what you say must be circumspect. The Circumlocution Office? Only in part. Not everyone is owed an answer to any question he might choose to ask.

His visits to Benedetto had given Morrow a basis for imagining how the Pope spent his day. Much of it was ceremonial, appearances, statements, receptions, saying pontifical masses in St. Peter's. But on an ordinary day the public duties came in the morning.

"What does he do in the afternoon?"

"Sometimes he receives new ambassadors." Benedetto smiled. "There are private audiences."

"Does he have any time to himself?"

"Oh, yes."

There was a Ugandan as well as an Irish secretary, but Benedetto was as close to the Pope as anyone else. Morrow formed the impression of a reasonably secluded papal existence: time for prayer, for reading—Morrow's own book would have occupied many hours—for writing, as the Holy Father still did, most of the documents that went out over his name. It seemed an enviably sequestered life in Benedetto's account of it. More than enough time to factor into his thinking the significance of such documents as the Secret of Fatima. Had the old man hoped that its predictions were now fulfilled and there might be something like tranquillity ahead? It was not completely fanciful to think that, Portugal apart, the faith had indeed been lost in France and Spain and even Italy.

"The collapse of the Soviet Union, so unexpected, so impossible to explain on any merely natural basis, almost seemed to herald the fulfillment of the promise of Fatima."

"The conversion of Russia."

"Yes. That was to be the reward for heeding Mary's wishes: prayer and fasting, true conversion of heart." Benedetto shifted his weight in his brocade chair. "But has such conversion taken place?"

"Wouldn't one just man have saved Sodom?"

Benedetto laughed. "You have been reading the Holy Father's mind."

"But Russia is not converted."

Benedetto shrugged.

When Morrow was taking his leave, Mondini came bustling in, looking about importantly. He bowed to Morrow and then waddled toward Benedetto. The two men were leaving Benedetto's office by the door leading to the papal apartments, when Morrow headed for the exit.

It seemed natural to tell Maureen these things. But it was pleasant to put such thoughts away and simply to enjoy their leisurely lunch.

CHAPTER TWO

Janet Fortin was at the ceremony in the oval office when the President, surrounded by the congressmen and senators who had shepherded it through the upper and lower houses, signed what its critics called the Death Bill, making assisted suicide a right not to be interfered with. Justice Norman had personally stayed a lower court's decision that opponents of euthanasia could impede non-physicians from helping people kill themselves on any basis that physician and patient found compelling. The bill had sailed through on the wave of indignation created by the judgment, which, to the public's satisfaction, she had reversed.

"This is a historic day for freedom", the President said. It was also the anniversary of *Roe v. Wade*, the Supreme Court decision that ushered in the age of abortion.

The President used enough pens to distribute them to each of the sponsors. Behind the signing party, Casey was visible, smiling into history. The President schmoozed the press afterward, reluctant to let them go. He did not want it overlooked that he was a man who delivered on his campaign promises.

"How about the Vatican Embassy?" Horvath, columnist, scourge of the talk shows, growled, but he was shouldered aside by his euphoric fellows in the media.

Janet cut across to the gate leading to the executive office building. Once outside, she looked up at the magnificent building, glanced toward the street, and then started walking, wanting to get away. She skipped through traffic to Lafayette Park, where she sat on a bench, pulled her coat tightly about her, against the January chill, and looked at the White House. Horvath's fruitless reminder of the storm over the apparent campaign promise to shut down the Vatican Embassy in turn reminded Janet of James Morrow. A day like this brought back her visit to his cottage on Lake Powderhorn in Michigan. Did he miss it now, she wondered, surrounded by the baroque and renaissance architecture of Rome?

Others might sit here and look with awe across Pennsylvania Avenue to the legendary White House, curious about all the wonderful goings-on within, but Janet was tired of it all. The bill that had just been signed, redescribe it as they tried, was what its critics said it was, a message that when people were used up or a nuisance or ill, in the minds of others or in their own, they could simply be destroyed and gotten out of the way. It no longer made any difference whether it was the person himself who, under the stress of dreadful pain or misfortune, was tempted to think of himself as just a thing to be done away with. Now as was increasingly the largely unreported case, the old and the ill and otherwise inconvenient were being put out of their misery by relatives who felt the misery even more, for whatever reason. Had any society since the Third Reich treated people like Kleenex, to be used and disposed of? What kind of dignity was there in being thought of, particularly by oneself, as something to go out with the trash?

Janet wandered on to a bookstore a block away and browsed along its shelves. Again, she had a powerful desire to be just a woman from a nearby office, aware of politics only via the news, not implicated in the schemes and dubious policies of this administration.

On the sidewalk outside, a public telephone was enclosed in a plastic bubble. From it she called her "cousin" Monsignor Eugene Wales. (He had traced the connection, and it was remote and non-consanguineous, but she liked to think of them as being relatives.)

"It sounds awful."

"It means we could marry. There's no impediment."

"Not much", she had said, flicking his collar.

"Hi", she said now. The street looked surreal through the scratched discolored plastic that enveloped her. "Got a minute?"

"Sure."

"He just signed the Death Bill."

There was a silence, and then, "This should mean war."

"Should?"

"Where you calling from?"

"Can we get together?"

They could. She suggested a drink, but he didn't want to go into a bar wearing his collar. So they agreed to meet at his apartment.

Forty-five minutes later, shoes off, drinking beer from the can, she spoke to him as to a priest as much as to a more or less imaginary cousin.

"I feel implicated, Gene. Morally corrupted. If I help out on such a bill, smooth its passage, how can I say I disagree with it? If only that damned Leslie Norman hadn't overturned the lower court decision, we'd still be debating the bill."

"It would have passed eventually."

"Have you people given up too?"

"It isn't giving up to recognize that you are a minority. In the society, maybe in the Church too."

From retirement, the one-time archbishop of a large Midwestern city observed that God had placed the earth and its inhabitants in man's care, and man himself was an inhabitant of the earth. The implication was clear, but he drew it anyway. "It is a supreme act of our freedom to decide that the time has come when God is calling us home." He wasn't making a personal announcement, as it turned out, but an instant poll had convinced a wire service that most Catholics believed as the retired archbishop did.

243

"This is some war if we keep losing all the battles."

"Headlines are not reports from the only front that matters."

"Whistling past the graveyard", she suggested.

The bill was not just a removal of impediments to euthanasia, but also a commencement of active government involvement in it. It was now an item of health care!

"You feel you've colluded in this? It requires all of us to approve and finance acts we know to be intrinsically evil. This is a moral Armageddon."

She had a vague notion that Armageddon was associated with disaster, so she let him develop the thought. The war he had in mind was a taxpayers' revolt, a refusal to take part in homicidal activity.

"William Bentley Ball, the feisty constitutional lawyer, and others have been working on ways and means of enabling those who see the evil of this to withhold their taxes in protest."

"That's good!" She said it with enthusiasm because of her ambiguous feelings when the bill was rushed through Congress.

"Petitions are already coming in for a special meeting of the executive council of the NCCB."

"You don't sound too pleased."

"Oh, I *want* war. We've sat still for too long: compromised, accommodated, made mental reservations. We've been on steady retreat for years."

"So what's the problem?"

"Archbishop Lannan wants to wait and see. 'Let's not lose our calm.'" Gene seemed to be imitating the archbishop. "He doesn't want to rock the boat before he goes off to be made a cardinal."

2

Fr. Dooley, an assistant pastor at Santa Susanna, asked Frawley what was going on between the new ambassador and Maureen Kilmartin.

"New? Blintz has been here nearly two years."

"To the Vatican, Monsignor. To the Vatican. James Morrow."

"What was the question again?"

"Of course, if this is a confidential matter…"

Dooley, a Paulist, always had a chip on his shoulder. He was known to explain elaborately to the Americans in Rome whose pastor he was, that priests who were members of orders were not given ecclesiastical honors, like canon or monsignor and the like.

"We have set our face against such worldly things", he was wont to say, somewhat wistfully Frawley believed. He in turn, when Dooley tried that stuff on him, made a point of mentioning to Dooley all the members of religious orders who were being named bishop.

"It looks like a trend, Jack."

"Thank God I'm too old", Dooley said, after a minute.

"Jack, they picked an auxiliary in Indiana the other day who is ten years older than you are."

This was petty and mean, however much fun, and Frawley cut it out after getting a particularly severe Capuchin when he went to confession on the Via Veneto.

"You priest?"

"Yes, Father." Of course he had stated this at the outset.

"What kind?"

"Diocesan."

"*Ché?*"

"I am not a member of a religious order."

"Ah." He seemed relieved. "*Seculare?*"

"Yes, Father."

"Even so, you must be good. Charity", he intoned, and went on for ten minutes practicing his English while Frawley strove for patience on the other side of the grille. He had gone by his usual confessor's box because there was a line of penitents waiting. The imagined alternative was a fast recital to a stranger and then be on his way. Ha! He gritted his teeth and closed his eyes and took it like a man. His penance was to say a fifteen-decade Rosary every day for a week.

Later, kneeling in the airless church, recovering from the ordeal, he began to see it in a new light. Had he come to expect congratulations from confessors because of the blandness of what he had to tell them? Obviously this was because his conscience was not as sensitive as it should be. God knows, he ran no risk of scrupulosity. And then he thought of the way he had been teasing Jack Dooley and felt an impulse to go back into the box and tell the Capuchin about that. Of course he didn't. But he had resolved to treat the Paulist differently in the future.

"It's all new to me, Jack. What have you heard?" he said now.

"Oh, it's probably nothing at all."

"Tell me."

They were standing in the Santa Susanna lending library where Dooley had come upon Frawley seeking anything by J. F. Powers, an author Morrow had recommended extravagantly. He had just taken *Morte d'Urban* from the shelf when Dooley tapped on his shoulder and flashed his dentures in a smile. He should have gone home for dental work.

Dooley had been told by several ladies in the parish that Maureen Kilmartin and James Morrow had been seen lunching together several times.

"They even went to Viterbo together."

"Have you been there yet, Jack?"

"Have you?"

"Of course."

"On pilgrimage?"

"Just covering my bets."

Dooley stepped back, to see if Frawley was serious. "I never even went to see Padre Pio."

"There's not much to see in Viterbo anyway."

Dooley, with typical Irish contrariness, disagreed. For someone who professed disinterest, Jack Dooley knew all about the visionary, the statue of the Virgin, the average time it took to get to it once you were inside the church.

"It doesn't weep or anything like that. The woman herself is not on display. All people come away with are accounts of her messages, which have been disavowed."

"What's the message, Jack?"

Dooley shrugged. "Fortune cookies always give a flattering description or a vague promise of good things in store. These private revelations are just the opposite. The times are bad, and all hell lies just around the corner."

"Have you read her message?"

"Parishioners bring me things." It turned out to be a copy of an alleged message to the visionary of Viterbo.

"Still got it?"

Dooley went through the motions of seeking to remember. "It could be downstairs in my office."

"I'd like to see it."

"Tell you what. I'll make a photocopy and send it to you."

Frawley tucked in his chin and looked at Dooley over his glasses. He knew a run-around when he saw one.

"Okay, now. I've got a photocopier. Come on."

First, Frawley checked out the Powers' novel. Dooley had a copy of the Viterbo revelation ready for him when he looked in the office.

"I've got some Cutty Sark", the Paulist whispered, looking naughty.

"Ah hah."

Frawley had come to prefer wine and brandy to hard liquor, but taking a seat and having a glass of Scotch seemed part of the penance the Capuchin would have given him if he had confessed to uncharitably twitting Jack Dooley.

3

He became so much at ease with Maureen Kilmartin that he almost confided in her that he was writing a memo for Benedetto, destined for the Holy Father, giving an assessment of the Church in America in the light of the secret of Fatima and the Viterbo message.

"I suppose you get regular reports from the nuncio?" Morrow said to Benedetto. Bureaucracies were famous for redundant activities.

"Archbishop Vilani has not been to Viterbo. Besides, you are an expert on the Church in your country."

Morrow felt as he had the first time he was asked to write an article for an encyclopedia. That something coming out of his typewriter would have the authoritative aura of a standard reference had been less flattering than he would have thought. For such a task, one had to abandon all personal style, and he found himself composing paragraph after paragraph as if he were omniscient. It was the most difficult writing he had ever done, and he declined all such invitations ever since. Writing a report for the Pope was painfully like that.

"Hasn't the woman disavowed this?" Morrow had passed on

to Benedetto the photocopied sheet Maureen had bought in the streets of Viterbo.

"She says, quite truly, that she did not make the message public. The bishop confirms that this is indeed what she dictated in response to his request after she had reported to the Holy Father. How it got into circulation he does not know."

"At least the Holy Father needn't worry whether or not it's true. It won't affect his papacy."

"He is in considerable pain now."

"I noticed Dr. Mondini visited him the other day."

"He comes every day. There's not much good that medicine can do now. Or much harm, I suppose."

"He's that ill?"

Benedetto, overweight, gaudy in his robes, turned the ring on his right hand as if it were a symbol of the vanity of this world. "All men are mortal."

Benedetto changed the topic then, but this unsettling exchange lent new urgency to Morrow's task although, on the other hand, it seemed odd to be preparing doomsday information for a man whose days apparently were numbered.

Like that of most public figures, the medical history of the Pope was common knowledge. He had been a robust athletic man when he was elected, and his first years had been whirlwinds of activity, jetting about the globe, kissing the ground in country after country upon landing in a gesture that was to become his signature. Then there was the shooting in St. Peter's Square, more serious than had at first appeared, requiring a number of operations. Since then a series of ailments, each more serious than the last, and still he went on, growing old in office, then older, until he became so venerable it was imaginable that he would go on forever.

Frawley had picked up the news from Mondini. "But I suppose you know all about it."

"Mondini doesn't confide in me."

"Mondini confides in everyone. I sometimes think that's why he was chosen as papal physician. He makes press releases unnecessary."

"He says the Pope is ill."

"Not just ill."

"Ah, well. He's eighty-four, after all."

"Lannan telephones almost every day."

The investiture was two weeks off, and there seemed reason to doubt that the Pope could preside. On the other hand, he continued with his Wednesday audiences and Angelus appearances on Sunday noon, a reassuringly familiar figure appearing high above the crowd. His voice, amplified through the great square, seemed strong, still pronouncing the Italian with great deliberation.

A week later, Archbishop Thomas Lannan arrived in Rome and was whisked to the Villa Stritch, the retreat for visiting American bishops, from which he telephoned Monsignor Frawley, who telephoned James Morrow.

"I have been summoned to the Villa Stritch by our mutual friend. He asked me to bring you along."

"When are you going?"

"This is ridiculous, I know. He asked to see me immediately. His wish of course is my command. What excuse should I give him to explain your absence?"

"Oh, I'll come along."

His ready acceptance would invite the notion that his day was an undemanding one, as indeed it was. But Frawley already knew that, if anyone did.

The night before, Morrow had completed his analysis of the alleged revelation of the woman from Viterbo. On the basis of the knowledge he had acquired in writing his history of the Church in the United States, he advised that there was little likelihood of the predictions in the message coming true and that the relation of what she said to the secret of Fatima was tenuous at best. But of course the message concerned more than the U.S. He had just returned from delivering his more or less reassuring memorandum to Benedetto. He and the cardinal had sat in facing brocade chairs, as Benedetto read what Morrow had written. When he had finished, he looked slyly at Morrow.

"Would you have written with similar certainty of a prediction of the breakup of the Soviet Union a year before it happened?"

"I am not an expert on the Soviet Union."

Benedetto acknowledged the point. Morrow waited, assuming that he would now deliver the report directly to the Holy Father, but that was not to be.

"He is indisposed today. But who knows, your report may restore his strength."

Morrow had returned to the Via Aurelia somewhat deflated. He had anticipated discussing what he had written with the Pope himself, answering objections, making it clear that his were the conjectural judgments of a historian. Not that he really doubted that the Viterbo visionary's predictions showed little or no knowledge of the United States. Her references to it might have been to a country on the moon.

But Benedetto's reminder that the fall of the Soviet Union had taken everyone by surprise, including the experts, gave Morrow pause. He thought too of the mystifying obscurity of the 1917 Fatima revelations about Russia and its conversion. The children could not possibly have understood what that reference meant. No more did the woman of Viterbo pose as an expert on what might happen in America or in Europe. Her claim was that she was simply delivering a message that was not her own.

Morrow had gone to the Vatican with the thought that he had fulfilled the Holy Father's assignment and that now he

could turn his mind to less depressing things than private revelations. But he had returned still haunted by the message of
Viterbo. No wonder he was eager to be diverted by Frawley's
invitation to visit with Lannan at the Villa Stritch.

Lannan was with a tailor, being fitted for his new cardinal-
atial robes. He had assumed a new dignity and importance of
which he seemed unaware.

"How is he?"

Frawley looked to Morrow.

"How is who?"

"The Holy Father", Lannan said in a strangled whisper,
glancing at the tailor who was fussing with the hem of his
cassock.

"Ill", Frawley said, resignation in his voice.

"How ill?"

"He spoke at the Angelus on Sunday."

"I know that. Is there any later word?" Suddenly he caught
himself, as if realizing how unseemly his concern for the Pope's
health must seem in the circumstances. He smiled, held out his
arms as if to display his palms. "I had a dream on the flight over
that the Pope had died and that I would be given the news as
soon as I landed."

"The Pope is alive", Morrow assured him.

"Has Monsignor Frawley told you of the question that has
been raised about the status of those who have been named
cardinal if the Pope who names them dies before they are officially inducted into the sacred college?"

"What is their status?"

Frawley said in a drawling voice, "There are, predictably,
two schools of thought."

The tailor helped Lannan out of the robes, bunched them
in his arms, and smiled, the pins in his mouth suggestive of
acupuncture. In trousers and shirt sleeves, Lannan was a far less

imposing figure. Well, what would the Pope look like if he were seen not wearing his familiar white cassock?

"Let me take you two out to dinner", Lannan suggested, after donning rabat and suit jacket. The thick gold chain of his pectoral cross lay diagonally across his chest, the cross tucked out of sight.

"Are you sure you don't want to get some sleep?"

"How can I sleep at a time like this?"

It was an evening of reminiscing—Lannan's reminiscing. He recalled for his guests the retreat he had made prior to being ordained auxiliary bishop, the anxiety he had felt when Washington fell open and a rival gained surprising support.

"I had convinced myself that it did not matter, other opportunities would come, it did not have to be Washington. And then the appointment was made."

"I did not sleep for two days before my ordination", Monsignor Frawley said.

"Don't get me started on ordination", Lannan said.

"What about ordination, Tom?"

"After all those years of preparation, looking forward to the great day, it should have been joyful. I was terrified. Subdeacon, deacon, neither gave me pause, but the priesthood! What if I betrayed my vocation, what if I lost my faith, what if I had been deluding myself that God wanted me to be a priest?"

"Scrupulosity", Frawley said. He had the look of a man who had been robbed of his subject.

"Exactly. I fought it and won, and thank God I did."

Lannan's worry about his status should the Pope die seemed paranoid rather than scrupulous. His nomination and that of nineteen others was known throughout the world. Even if the Pope died, his successor would surely renew the nominations. That would be a magnanimous initial act of a new pontiff.

"Have you met Pavese?" Frawley asked.

"I've arranged to meet with him in Milan day after tomorrow."
Before the ceremony in St. Peter's. Thomas Lannan seemed
to be covering every contingency.

Morrow had seen colleagues maneuver for promotion and
academic preference; he had watched the obsequiousness of
the untenured turn to easy arrogance once job security was
theirs. And he had observed the sycophancy of administrators
toward the faculty, and vice versa. So why was he faintly scandalized by Tom Lannan's undisguised ambition for this honor
whose one significance was that it would make him a papal
elector, a function scarcely to be exercised more than once?

If Frawley were similarly driven, he did not show it.

4

Basil Trenton, a very generous Knight of Columbus, offered
the services of the executive jet his company kept in Europe,
but Thomas Lannan had to share the plane with a thin young
man with a very full mustache and a manner that was an odd
blend of confidence and uncertainty.

"When I have an interpreter with me, the meetings tend to
be in English, but when I travel alone I find myself dealing
with monoglots", said his young companion.

"How is your Italian?"

"Not as good as it will be. I decided to do without an interpreter this time." He grinned. "Sink or swim."

"How long have you been with Unitel?"

"In Europe? Not quite six months."

His name was Smote, Gillian Smote, and while he was an
American citizen he had been raised and schooled in various
far-flung places to which his father had taken his family.

"But never Italy. So of course I was assigned here."

Lannan welcomed distraction from his own thoughts and was happy to hear from Smote the difficulties of raising a family as an employee of an international company.

"Knowing what it did to me as a kid, you'd think I would have avoided it like the plague. But I would have died of boredom in Chicago or Denver."

"So you have a family."

"One girl. We're expecting another."

The problem of schooling lay in the future, and his wife had domestic help of a kind she would never have had in the States. They were beginning their descent into Malpensa when it occurred to Smote to ask Lannan why he was going to Milan.

"On pilgrimage, in a way."

Smote feigned understanding, but the time for conversation was over. The young man was making a last-minute check of the contents of his briefcase, anticipating the coming appointment, eager to confront any linguistic challenge.

Lannan had been assured that Cardinal Pavese's English was more than adequate.

"Better than the Pope's", Frawley had assured him.

Unlike young Smote, Lannan would prefer not putting his Italian to the test. A world-class genius could sound like an idiot speaking a language he only imperfectly understood. Lannan had been struck by an old newsreel in which the legendary Einstein sounded like any other immigrant. He had come to Milan to cement his relations with Pavese. Just in case...

No one awaited him in the terminal for private planes. Smote waved as he was whisked away by an earnest man who had awaited their entry, holding a sign reading MOTES. Lannan was glad to see go out of sight a possible witness of the fact that Cardinal Pavese had not sent a car for him. Not that he had told Smote why he had come.

When he asked about cabs, he was told a bus was about to leave for the city, and he was immediately taken by the image of himself arriving in the humblest conveyance for his interview with the cardinal archbishop of Milan. But once under way, staring from his window as country gave way to urban sprawl, it occurred to him that Pavese might take amiss a display of humility. Perhaps once he was definitively within the city, he should get off the bus and take a taxi to the archbishop's palace.

No. It was not Pavese who had let him down, but Frawley. The rector of the North American College had agreed to convey to the cardinal's office the exact time of arrival of Cardinal-designate Thomas Lannan. Had Frawley failed to make clear that he would be coming by Intertel executive jet? The contrast between arriving by private plane and setting off for the city in a bus that seemed designed for discomfort, lurching and swaying, taking every bump with a maximum of unabsorbed shock, might have been amusing if he were sure that his arrival was awaited in the great house on the cathedral square, opposite the Galleria.

The day was overcast, no sun to alleviate what weather and pollution had done to the stone of the buildings lining the street they came along. On right and left, the first floors of the buildings seemed to form a single store, but of course these were small and independent enterprises, their windows bright with wares—men's and women's clothing, shoes, bags, cameras—with pharmacies and restaurants and bakeries and *alimentari* regularly represented. They passed a church, and Lannan touched his pectoral cross and murmured a prayer.

The bus stopped at a hotel that seemed to be the end of the line.

"*Dov'è il duomo, per favore?*"

The passenger he asked looked at him as if he were speaking a foreign language.

"Duomo", he repeated. *"Catedrale."*

A woman overheard and said, *"Guardi. Il duomo è la."*

He followed her pointing finger and caught a glimpse of the cathedral square down a narrow street.

"Grazie", he said and set off, switching his overnight bag to his right hand.

Despite a construction fence and a flock of pigeons that rose like a storm cloud from the pavement of the square, his first view in years of what he remembered as the most beautiful of Italian cathedrals was breathtaking. Until it reminded him of the Mormon temple on the outskirts of the District of Columbia. But there was no golden statue of the angel Moroni topping this structure; instead its dozens of upthrusting white stone stalagmites created a light ethereal effect.

Despite the hour, the signs were already lighted, because of the dullness of the day. "Martini" glowed in red neon above the palace occupied by the archbishop. Lannan became aware of bells tolling, those of the cathedral and others; suddenly it seemed as if the bells of every church in Milan were adding their sound to the mournful din. Lannan was puzzled. Was there some local holiday he had not been told of?

At newspaper kiosks he searched the headlines for a clue, but found none. He would have asked the leathery face that peered from among the glossy magazines, fluttering lottery tickets and newspapers, but he was deterred by the oddity of a man in a Roman collar asking why church bells were ringing. He was deterred as well by the bare, mammoth breasts thrusting from the shiny covers of the magazines.

He was admitted to the archbishop's palace and put into a room, and five minutes passed before a young priest with a tragic countenance came for him.

They went Indian file down a long hallway, entered an elevator the size of a phone booth, and began a long, silent ascent. Had Paul VI used this elevator when he was archbishop of Milan? Lannan was still formulating the question in Italian when the elevator came to a preliminary halt, then jerked upward several inches more. The young priest stepped out and held the door for him.

Pavese's study was on the top floor; a wall of windows overlooking the square and providing a good view of the facade of the cathedral. The cardinal rose and came to meet him, but his expression was almost as dour as the young priest's. Nonetheless, there was an energy and authority about the man. Pavese was the odds on favorite to be elected pope at the next consistory, the candidate of the secular press as well as much of the religious.

"Terrible, terrible news", Pavese said.

Lannan stared at him. "Why are the bells ringing?"

Pavese peered at him. "You haven't heard?"

Lannan shook his head, but something in Pavese's eyes prepared him for the news.

"The Holy Father is dead. He died this morning."

5

The great piebald trunks of plane trees along the Tiber, the walk matted with their fallen leaves, the sound of a dredge in the river—its rusted barge half-filled with muck—engaged on the endless task of keeping the channel open competed with the roar and whine of the endless flow of traffic along the river road, a mad acceleration of motorized lemmings dashing toward the next red light; it was a scene of peace and chaos all at once.

Maureen stopped and laid a gloved hand on the wall that ran along the walk. Morrow put his bare hand over hers. She was looking back up the river, past the Castel Sant'Angelo, to where the great vaulted dome of St. Peter's rose timelessly above the river, the traffic, the lesser roofs. They had just come from the place where her husband had been killed by terrorists ten years before. The death of the Pope had fallen on the anniversary of her husband's assassination. It was a season of endings.

"The city is the same as it was when we came, yet how different it seems."

Birds fluttered down, strutted importantly about, flew off. Thus their ancestors had gone about their birdlike lives when Morrow first visited Rome. It occurred to him that the whole bird population of Rome might have been replaced since then, yet somehow these birds were the same.

Maureen nodded when he expressed this thought, feeling as he did so like an adolescent philosopher.

"Of course the same could be said of the cars."

"Fiat voluntas tua." She turned and looked up at him with the oddest smile, and there were tears in her eyes. "That was Sean's repeated phrase in traffic, spoken with great exasperation."

She searched his face through her tears, and then she was in his arms, refuge against her grief, comfort in the realization that time flowed as inexorably as the river—her husband was gone, the Pope had died, she grew older. She tried to move away, but he held her, and when she looked up he lowered his lips to her forehead.

They stood there, a man and woman in mid-life who had known one another less than two months, with decades of unshared memories, but at this moment as close as lovers.

Silently they drew apart and, hand in hand, continued along the Lungotevere, the leaves beneath their feet audible, but what she said was eclipsed by a blatting horn.

"What?"

"All the cardinals are different too."

"Pigeons, starlings, cardinals..."

The unstated somber truth was that each of them, Maureen, himself, would soon be gone, and others would walk these streets and enact the same old drama, ever different. He stopped and filled his lungs with air, not thinking of what noxious fumes he might be introducing into his lungs.

"He was an old man", he said.

"And now where the body is, the birds must gather."

"Cardinals."

McHugh had brought him the news of the Holy Father's death, and then they had listened to radio and television, but there was little more than the simple message, repeated over and over. The Pope had died in his sleep, toward morning, and had been found dead by his Ugandan secretary at six o'clock when he checked to see why the Pope had not appeared in the chapel to say his Mass. On Vatican Radio there was a short interview with the reluctant secretary. The death had apparently been peaceful. There was a rosary in the pontiff's hands.

"The bedside light was on."

The reporter pursued this as of great significance. He could not have fallen asleep while reading if he had been saying the Rosary. What had he been reading? There was a Testament, the odes of Claudel... (A week later they would learn there was also a copy of Waugh's *Sword of Honor* and a paperback western, *Valdez Is Coming,* by Elmore Leonard. The last was a book Morrow had mentioned to the Pope. The bedside lamp became in the more imaginative accounts of Italian newspapers a dying man's protest against the dark into which he was going.)

Earlier, when Morrow was told Mrs. Kilmartin had come, he went immediately downstairs. She was in her car at the curb, and he slipped into the passenger seat.

"I tried to telephone."

"I'm glad you came."

"Can you come with me? I can't keep blocking your driveway like this."

"Where are we going?"

"For a drive."

She might have meant a drive in the country, something relaxing, distracting, but she stayed in the city, so attuned to the madness of traffic that it no longer seemed to bother her. Of course she had a destination. On the street where the body of Aldo Moro had been found in a parked car, there was a kind of civic shrine, with fresh flowers brought there each day by anonymous citizens. But there were no commemorative wreaths where Sean Kilmartin had been blown to pieces, along with his car, the assassination a case of mistaken identity—who would want to blow the Irish ambassador to the Vatican to kingdom come? Maureen doubleparked and pointed out the place, and then wasn't sure she had it exactly. Horns of the cars whose passage she was impeding started up as, biting her lower lip, she hesitated between a spot where a small delivery truck was parked and another where a diminutive Fiat was nosed into the curb.

"There", she decided, pointing toward the truck, and then her car began to move forward.

Mabel had died in the hospital in postoperative care, but he felt they had already parted at home, weeks earlier, when it was clear that there was no cure for what she had. His only regret was agreeing to that final pointless operation, a decision Mabel had left to him. By then he could already see in her eyes a posthumous look.

Maureen had driven here and parked beside the Tiber, wanting to see St. Peter's but not to join the throngs who moved dreamlike over the bridges and up the Via della Conciliazione toward the great square, the vigil already beginning. Morrow was glad he had gotten away before Frawley or Lannan called. He could not at the moment bear to hear Church politics discussed, chatter about the coming conclave and the successor to the Pope. Far better to be with Maureen and mourn the passing of a good old man and taste again their private sorrows.

6

Maureen had still been holding the letter from Minneapolis telling of Mrs. Christiansen's death when she heard on the news about the list of new cardinals. Had Tom's name been mentioned, or was he simply in her mind because of the letter? There were many people she could have asked if the archbishop of Washington's name was indeed on the list, but it was Jim Morrow she called.

"His eminence, Thomas Cardinal Lannan" was his response.

"Thank God."

"You sound more relieved than grateful."

"He had been dangling for so long, Jim."

"Three years?"

"That's a dangle. Have you talked with him?"

"No."

"I think I'll give him a call."

"He's not in Washington."

"Oh?"

"His secretary said he had gone on retreat. He wouldn't say where."

A little silence. Did they both doubt that Tom had gone off somewhere to examine his soul?

"Well, it worked. Maybe he should have tried prayer earlier," Jim remarked.

"Do people pray to become cardinals?"

"Of course. Some pray to become pope."

"Not Tom, I hope."

In the event Archbishop Lannan surfaced, in the inevitable journalistic verb, at the Trappist abbey in Kentucky. To his credit, he tried to get back to Washington without saying where he had been, but some of the questions put him suggested it might be wise to identify his refuge. The press conference swerved away from the tempting topic of ordinaries of dioceses who burned out and took leave to study the piano or fulfill other strange ambitions that had been strangled by their ecclesiastical duties. The cynical interpretation of the media, only hinted at in print, thank God, was that they needed drying out or counseling. Maureen found the image of a bishop being counseled by a therapist rather than his confessor a comic one.

"You think priests have their psyche removed at ordination?" Frank had growled when she expressed this to her brother.

"Frank, I don't think they have anything removed. I thought they received something."

"Sure. A license to be roughed up by Church bureaucrats every time they try to put the Council into effect."

"Wasn't the Council a bureaucratic achievement?"

Frank was devoid of all sense of humor where his own self-image was concerned, and he saw himself as a Lone Ranger seeking to restore justice and renewal in the Church after the Council had been hijacked by John Paul II. After all these years, the role was getting bedraggled, even if you conceded Frank all the assumptions it required. Another thing she had learned not to bring up was the way he and the other Lone Rangers always seemed to be trimming things down so that being a Catholic lost its distinctive meaning. Divorce, contraception, acceptance of the so-called sexual revolution ("It sounds like a brothel trick", Sean had said of that phrase), abortion, and now euthanasia. All this had been done with a maximum of gobbledegook and flattery. Modern Catholics no longer wanted their life micromanaged by a bunch of celibates who had no idea what the real world was like. That real world seemed to be lived in suburban affluence the way Frank described it, another irony, since he had visibly winced at the location of Teresa's house.

"How much is he making, Mo?"

"Plenty."

"They can afford kids", he said after a moment.

But it was people who could afford them who had maybe just two kids and called it a day, devoting themselves tirelessly to chauffeuring them from soccer field to music lessons to art classes, on and on. Of course Teresa did that with hers, but now she was expecting another.

"The kids are more excited than I am, Mom."

"Oh, I doubt that." She added, after a pause that neutralized it, "They can't be more excited than I am."

Excitement was not what she herself had felt when she had learned she was pregnant with Teresa. Unconsciously she had realized that a new baby tied her ever more irrevocably to life with Ray. Maureen had felt apprehension bringing her own children into the world, but the cause of her apprehension had been within the family, Ray's unpredictable character—a mixture of an almost adolescent irresponsibility with a business shrewdness that must have been more effective because of his seeming naïveté. But now the difficulties for families seemed to come from everywhere outside so that if there were any internal weakness collapse was all but inevitable. When she considered what one had become used to on television, on billboards and newsstands, things that would have caused shock but a few years ago, even the immediate future seemed menacing. There were those who thought that license given its head would weary and bore and fade away. That had been an excuse for permitting pornography. Patrons would grow jaded and turn to more meaningful entertainment. There was no basis for the prediction at the time, and of course it had been disproved by events, but it is in the nature of things that such experiments cannot be undone once they have been permitted.

"You have never known war", Mariska Cioran would say, nodding her head and letting her blue eyelids close over her enormous brown eyes. Mariska had survived occupation and concentration camp. The frivolity of Americans was a favorite subject of hers at ambassadorial get-togethers. She would search Maureen out and relay to her some outrage she had heard of in the United States.

"You have to know more Americans to understand us", Maureen had said loyally. It was best not to dispute Mariska's story; as often as not she had a newspaper clipping in her bag, usually in a language Maureen could not read, but it had the look of evidence all the same.

"You have never known suffering."

But war and suffering had not prevented Europe from leading the way to neopaganism; Mariska herself was gone to God now and thus could not be bothered by the spectacle of her own native land becoming a consumer society that was almost a caricature of the West. The workers' states were no more, but all their citizens longed to wear the denim that had once clothed laborers before it became the very quintessence of chic.

It wasn't softness or escape from war but original sin, the tendency built into human beings to do the wrong thing. Maureen prayed that Teresa would have the wisdom and luck to bring her children up well in these crazy times. Maureen herself had already left Ray when he died in the accident; mere waiting would have brought escape if she had trusted to dumb luck only a little while longer. The letter she had received from Minneapolis meant that the threat to Tom Lannan's reputation was gone. He had been right to let the story run its course. Mrs. Christiansen, Maureen read, had died peacefully in her sleep two weeks before.

PART FIVE

CHAPTER ONE

I

When Peggy told Julian O'Keefe that her grandmother had died, he felt like God or her guardian angel, hearing something he already knew.

"Didn't you say she raised you?"

Ever since that day in Thousand Oaks, Julian got unsettling reminders of her mother whenever he looked at Peggy. Her expression now was the puzzled one her mother had worn when she came upon him rummaging through her souvenirs in her bedroom, just before anger took over. But then he had had the same feeling when he faced Mrs. Christiansen.

Genetics is a mysterious thing—producing three generations of women whose appearance seemed to owe nothing to the male chromosomes necessary for their conception. But what was mysterious to him was doubtless understood by geneticists, or would be. The great alternative story to Christianity had won the field long since—cosmic events proceeding with law-like inevitability from a chance cast of the dice—so long ago the words invented to express it were as opaque as their meanings. Once under the tutelage of Fr. Leach, Julian would have scoffed at the naturalist account, observing that it required a faith every bit as blind as religious faith. Can any good come out of chance? And whence came the factors or elements or whatever that had chanced to enter into such fateful relations eons ago? All this struck him as mere cavilling now. One had to postulate something, and bits of matter had the advantage over God in being things we could know directly. At the beginning of Peggy's life had been her grandmother, and now she was gone. Her mother's death had not affected her this much, as Julian observed.

"You had to see her apartment up there, a thousand religious reminders in Thousand Oaks. It was all so obvious, bargaining with God because of the life she had led."

"Having you?"

"That's exactly it. I represented her big sin that she had to make up for—after a slew of lesser ones of course."

"Was your grandmother religious?"

"She was Catholic."

Julian did not ask if Peggy was making a subtle distinction. His role at the moment was to provide sympathy and support. It was clear that he did not represent for Peggy any sin, big or little. She had a very meager fund of theological lore, most of it confused. The rule she lived by was that love excuses everything.

"*Amor vincit omnia.*"

She waited with a little half smile.

"Love conquers all."

She took this as an overture and stepped into his arms. Their affair seemed a matter of ballroom dancing as much as anything. She was forever stepping dramatically into his arms, and his first impulse was to take a turn or two with her; one, two three, one, two, three. Did he love her at all, he wondered, but then there was need for some standard against which to measure what he felt, and he had none. He responded to her expectations and that seemed to suffice. Her cinematic imagination made up for whatever was wanting in him as a lover.

"Will there be a funeral?"

"I talked with the director, who said he would talk to a priest. They handle everything; that's part of the arrangement." This meant she would not fly to Minneapolis. If the thought of that old woman leaving the world unescorted bothered Peggy, she did not show it. Julian was almost disappointed. He had needed no excuse to avoid her mother's funeral in Thousand Oaks, but he had willingly gone. His presence seemed to cancel his earlier visit, though the second would have been unnecessary without the first. Going to Minneapolis would have had a different meaning, and if the nurses and attendants recognized him from the visit in which he had persuaded the old lady to write the letter to Maureen Bailey Kilmartin, questions might have been asked that could only disturb Peggy.

It was Leach who had told him of Frank Bailey's sister and the connection of both to Thomas Lannan, the information just flotsam on his flow of gossip, the teller unaware of how important this was. His old mentor had been surprised and delighted to hear from Julian.

"I am sometimes tempted to blame myself for what happened to you."

"You mustn't do that."

"I don't. I resisted the temptation. The onus remains on those who treated you unjustly. I comfort myself that I was not guilty of that."

"And how is Washington?"

"Compared to what? I am an Israelite in Egyptian exile. All this was depressing enough when seen from afar, but experience from within it will, I pray, shorten my time in Purgatory. I retain my sanity by pretending that I am employed by a very large advertising agency."

Leach proceeded to recount anecdote after anecdote about his work with Archbishop Thomas Lannan. Julian had called in the hope that some way of using the information he had discovered would emerge from talking with Fr. Leach. And so it had when Leach got onto Lannan's tireless efforts to align himself with both sides in any dispute.

"It is why he tolerates me here, my dear fellow, make no mistake about it. And on the other hand there is his longtime friendship with that stormy petrel par excellence, Frank Bailey."

Bailey, Lannan, and James Morrow too, the author of the account of the disintegration of the Church in the United States.

"It tells you how superficial the usual sortings out are, Julian. Bailey's sister lives in Rome, a widow, and a papist to the soles of her feet, or so one hears."

Maureen Bailey Kilmartin would be his means of conveying obliquely to Thomas Lannan that at any moment he could become the object of a fatal news story. Through Leach he was able to monitor the effect of the letter. The lady had come to Washington; she went on to Minneapolis; she returned to Washington.

"They were hatching the Morrow nomination, you can be sure."

A conversation with Leach amounted to patient listening. The priest went on and on about the Morrow appointment as if it had been a closely kept secret that would not have spread to the West Coast. It became clear to Julian that a letter addressed to Maureen Kilmartin at the Irish Embassy at the Holy See would reach her.

In the wake of Mrs. Christiansen's death, all that seemed to be for nothing. If Lannan had been warned by Maureen, and there was every indication that he had, the archbishop must be feeling only relief now. And it coincided neatly with his nomination as cardinal. There were moments when Julian believed that there was a Providence and that it was working against him. Until he reminded himself that Peggy still existed. If she had been her mother's big sin, she was also Thomas Lannan's.

He would almost certainly think of her that way. And now, as cardinal, his exposure would be even more devastating.

And then the old Pope died.

"We are going to Rome", he told Peggy.

Her pretty face became even prettier when she was surprised.

"We are going to make a film of the papal election."

2

From the North American College, St. Peter's and the Vatican can be reached in a matter of minutes, or could be if the intersecting traffic did not have the pace of a demolition derby. In their first years, students were drawn to the great basilica as to a magnet; and who could cross the great square without casting a glance at the windows of the papal apartments from which on Sundays at noon, at the Angelus, the old Pope had continued to address the crowd below? His raspy, unmistakable voice was amplified, and it was possible to remember the first years of his pontificate when he had been vigorous and athletic in manner as well as in deed. But now that activity had stopped forever.

Ambrose Frawley put himself at the disposal of the house, so to speak, appearing in the library, the recreation room, just strolling about, a kindly father ready to console those in his care. If not many availed themselves of this, it mattered little. Like the Sixth Fleet, he was showing the flag. Predictably Wilber of Davenport stopped him to frown over the theological question.

"At this time there is no pope, right, Monsignor?"

Frawley nodded, sensing deep thought on the horizon.

"And the cardinals will get together and elect another in a couple of days."

"I hope it doesn't take them so long."

But Wilber did not swerve. "However long, there is some time when the succession is broken."

"Things are in good hands, Charlie; never fear." The monsignorial shoulders went back and the red line of his buttons bowed out to meet the storm.

"How can men who aren't popes make a pope?"

There it was, the episodic theory of the papacy as Frawley thought of it. We speak of the unbroken line since St. Peter, but it is a broken line, cut each time a pontiff died and it was necessary to replace him.

"Have you read Ignatius Wynn?"

Wilber of Davenport had not read Wynn. The rector urged him to do so, as Wynn addressed the concerns he had expressed and others besides. This enabled him to disengage without the sense of having failed.

Wynn, reflecting on how the successor to Peter had been named, cited several sources to the effect that the choice had not been confined to the apostles, as had been the case in the selection of Matthias to replace Judas Iscariot and keep the number to twelve. The faithful generally had been in on the selection. And so it had gone for some centuries, Wynn and his authorities suggested, so that quite apart from multiple popes and antipopes and the usual elements of argument about the Petrine succession, the great point to be drawn was that the pope was the delegate of the people. Note that until quite recently there had been no requirement that a cardinal be a priest let alone a bishop, so that the latter-day method of electing a pope in the College of Cardinals actually supported rather than weakened the case Wynn was intent on making. Oh, he was willing to concede that when the people chose a bishop, as Augustine had been chosen bishop of Hippo, the laying on of hands by other bishops, assuring the apostolic succession, was required. But there is no ordination of a pope. The man chosen by a two-thirds vote in the conclave of cardinals is by that very fact pope.

"It is a profoundly significant fact, then, that at the very apex of the pyramid of the hierarchical church we have one who is the choice of the faithful at large, through delegates perhaps, but among those delegates the laity have been and can be represented. The pope is the spokesman of the people within the Church because of the character of his election and must accordingly see his role as mediator between the various elements in the Church."

The legalistic argument went on and on, but its practical meaning was clear. Wynn wanted a bottoms-up church, as Frank Bailey had put it, rather than a top-down. Jim Morrow had called these two models, citing unnamed sources, the Topless and Can Can models. What would Wilber make of it all? Ambrose Frawley wasn't sure what he himself made of it, as a theological argument, but as a *prise de position* in current disputes its meaning was clear. There were many who longed to be out from under the constant micromanaging of the Vatican. By and large these were bureaucrats complaining about other bureaucrats. There was a delphic endorsement of Wynn's book by Cardinal Pavese to the effect that now more than ever it was wise and needful to return to the very sources of our faith.... He might have been talking of any book.

Back in his rooms, Frawley poured a splash of cognac and, going to the window from which he could see the dome of St. Peter's, lifted his glass in tribute to the dead Pope. But before bringing it to his lips, he murmured a prayer for the repose of his soul. The dollop of liquor seemed somehow irreverent— the "Bottom's Up Church"?—and he put down his glass undrunk. An empty throne stirs sentiments of unease in even the most democratic breast. Had not last November's presidential election evinced the usual spate of rededication to the democratic faith? The people had spoken, reelecting a man almost universally considered the most unprincipled president in the history of the nation, but what mattered was their choice. Such effusions went beyond the mere legal fact that a majority rules to the implicit assumption that what they do is right. Few now invoked the theological justification, that God invests power in the people and that they then delegate it to others. *Vox populi, vox Dei.* It was rather couched in an act of faith in the democratic system, the American experiment. But the Holy Spirit guided the Church; without that it would just be another organization in which people constantly jockeyed for positions with power its own justification.

The telephone rescued Frawley from the labyrinth of thought. It was Maureen Kilmartin.

"May he rest in peace", she said without preamble.

"Amen."

"I suppose you're a Pavese man?"

"Whatever I am will not have any effect on the election."

"What does this mean for Archbishop Lannan?"

Ah. That was the question. Around the world there would be others like the archbishop of Washington who had longed for the red hat and had finally made the list—but now their patron was dead; what would their status be? Here was an ecclesiological problem to which Wynn had not turned his subtle mind.

"I know of no precedent, Mrs. Kilmartin."

"Cardinal Pavese says that he considers them colleagues in the sacred college."

"Oh?"

"To do otherwise would be to thwart the wishes of the late beloved Pope."

Pavese's chances of election had looked good but of course not certain. The addition of a new cadre of grateful electors could only strengthen his position.

"Well, his opinion is certainly more important than mine."
His tone suggested that the concession covered the present
point and was not to be generalized. Frawley had carefully
cultivated his reputation as the American *éminence grise* at the
Vatican, allowing bishops in whose appointment he had played
no role to think that it was his nod that had been decisive.
Archbishop Lannan had become restive and doubtful of Frawley's power. Still his reputation stood, and he did not want it
weakened with such old Romans as Mrs. Kilmartin.

"He is on his way to Rome from Milan now."

"Cardinal Pavese?"

She laughed. If she could bottle that lovely music she could
brighten the world and make a fortune. "Tom!"

"You are a veritable font of information, Mrs. Kilmartin."

"Jim Morrow told me."

This was bad. It would not do to be in the position of one
receiving rather than dispensing inside information. No one
seeing the serene expression on Monsignor Frawley's face and
the solid dignity with which he held the phone to his ear and
with closed eyes attended to his caller would have suspected
that he was reeling within.

"Naughty, naughty", he chuckled. "Ambassadors are supposed to keep secrets."

He took the initiative then and told her that he had not
undertaken lightly the long work of keeping Lannan's name on
that list against the objections of those who had deplored a
number of his public actions and thought he should be punished.

"Your suggestion that he promote Jim Morrow was essential. With one fell blow he took care of his enemies. Cardinal
Pavese is right. The late Holy Father gave considerable thought
to these nominees. They cannot be considered anything less
than members of the College."

She took obvious comfort from this, and Monsignor Frawley rose to eloquence in conveying how he, and of course others, had championed the cause of Archbishop Lannan, and there was little danger that they would desert him now. But after he hung up, it was less the echo of his own unctuous reassurance than her obvious pleasure in being reassured that stayed with him. The rumors that floated about like gnats, surrounding any figure in the Church, had of course swirled around Thomas Lannan as well. Of late there had been enigmatic murmurs of some past liaison. In Frawley's experience, such rumors almost invariably turned out to be false. He himself had been described as a trifle too fey and showing suspicious favoritism toward students in the house. Nonsense, of course. The world had ceased understanding the nature of manly friendships. Thus he was inclined to dismiss the thought that occurred, that perhaps Maureen Kilmartin, the sister of Frank Bailey, and thus acquainted with Tom Lannan from his youth, might be...

But he shook the thought away, even as he filed it deep in his memory.

3

All she had to do was say no, she wasn't going, she didn't want to go to Rome, no that wasn't it, not entirely but she had broken up with a boy once, the first boy she had really loved when he said, just telling her, surprise, surprise, you're going to love this, we're going to Europe, he already had tickets on Icelandic Airlines, won from someone as a bet so they would be flying under other names and that was supposed to make it even more irresistible, anonymous airlines, he said and grinned, he loved loving himself and usually she couldn't blame him, she felt the same way, and it was pretty good, anonymous airlines, but she had felt revulsion from the first mention and tried finally to tell him Europe was old and dirty and what wasn't was a stupid imitation of us so why go, and where did she get to be such an authority he wanted to know and partly it was what her grandmother had said but reenforced every time anything about Europe came up, creepy old buildings, shades of gray, stone twisted and carved and dirty with age and smog and the people skinny and pop eyed and all smoking like chimneys but basically she was scared, being uprooted and torn out of everything you know into languages you didn't speak only they all spoke English now, Eric was an authority too and she had thought of all the foreigners speaking broken English, her grandmother in a way, there was a strange Minnesota cadence to her speech that Peggy had picked up and after all it was Julian who had noticed it and coached her until she spoken basic southern Californian, you could hear it in old films with Ingrid Bergman and Sophia Loren and even when you thought they hid it they had to hide it and that was another thing and Julian agreed, all this being gaga for foreign actors was nuts, Emma Thompson was a one-man hit squad on all the progress that had been made in movies and it was good enough for her that that swishy actor she got work for ended up getting arrested with a whore in his car on Wilshire Boulevard doing to him what Emma Thompson never would and Peggy had no desire to play Jane Austen or Shakespeare with dresses choking her throat and two hours of nothing happening that made any sense to anyone in the audience, will he or won't he get enough money to do nothing the rest of his life like a gentleman so she can cling to his arm with adoring looks and have babies until she's blue in the face, Peggy wanted to be a star in the American manner, a Marilyn Monroe, Julian didn't laugh when she said it and gave her the Mailer book which she hated it and so did Julian as it turned out, Mailer wanting to be Afro-

American all his life, so he could know what it was like to be an underdog and Mailer already a Jew and Julian laughed until there were tears in his eyes, she owed him so much, she did, using him, learning everything she could, but wasn't he using her, the way he directed her she could tell that she was his goldmine and together they had done so well and the agent she had that Julian didn't know about was shopping around the infomercials sure he could get some enthusiastic responses, not with the studios, the studios are dead, he had ideas, just trust him, and in the meantime there was no need to tell Julian, what if nothing came of it and he might see it as ingratitude but so did she that's why she hadn't told him and what did a film about the Pope have to do with her career, well, nothing, he admitted as much, she wouldn't even be in it, she would be there as his righthand man, he depended on her, she should know that now, close against her, holding her upper arms, talking soft and warm in the way that scared her, he was dangerous, she would not want to have him against her but that had never seemed anything to worry about because her career was his career, he did not intend to have infomericials as the top of his game, that was the point of the film in Rome, he tried to describe to her what he had in mind, a documentary, yes, but breaking through the genre the way infomercials broke through the barriers of the commercial, he tried to explain it to her but she didn't follow him, he was brilliant, she sensed that, and she had no idea he knew so much about the Catholic Church she wondered if telling him that about her father being a priest had made more of an impression on him than he had let on and she was sure that beneath the cool he didn't like the way she reacted or didn't react to her grandmother's death although he had seemed to approve of her control at her mother's wake and funeral but that was easy Karen was a stranger who the last time they had talked had given her some beads, a rosary, and tried to make her promise she would say it every day and she didn't even know how but wouldn't say so because then her mother would have taught her, maybe they would have gone through it together, her mother said it every day, the whole thing, fifteen times ten, and Peggy had been almost caught, anything with numbers fascinated her, she might have told her mother how the number 24 always showed up when anything good happened to her and she put the rosary in her purse and several times when she was nervous she put her hand in her purse and ran the beads through her fingers and wished she knew the prayers you were supposed to say her mother thought she knew all kinds of things she didn't and so had her grandmother as if you inherited religion the way you did looks and they all did look alike, it was really odd as if she could see herself as she would be when old or middle-aged only she would never be like her grandmother who was the saint her mother wished she was but there was too much water over the dam for that and the agent had just given her the fish eye when she asked him to look out for Julian too, he would be the man's agent only if the man asked, maybe, but look, kid, I thought you wanted to make a break so go ahead she told him, yes I do, but it has to be a secret and that is why in the end she said well yes of course I'll go to Rome what would I do without you, too much, he didn't say anything, but she could feel him thinking, wondering why she had added anything as obvious as that.

4

"Tell them they either send you to Rome or you're through", Lorraine advised, and her advice carried weight because she herself had thrown off the yoke of security and routine and had embarked on a new path.

"We have a man and a half in Rome already."

"Who's the half?"

"Sissy Fuss."

Lorraine laughed. Sylvester Roche had already been a figure of fun when he and Lorraine joined Catholic News Service, and since then he had only been confirmed in that role. It was when he threatened to become an Anglican if the Pope didn't cut it out that he was assigned to the Vatican. Had they hoped he would quit? Not a chance. When he left, his excuse was that now he was going to dig up the real dirt. He had become a screaming papist within three months and recently had been initiated into the Knights of St. Gregory with much pomp and ceremony. Among the congratulatory wires was one that asked if he didn't consider his new dignity a conflict of interest. How could he expose the machinations of the Vatican while accepting such an honor? Sissy wrote a column arguing that there could never be a conflict of interest between a Catholic journalist's professional duties and his faith.

"What about our book?" Nate asked.

"We'll write a book about the election, about the late papacy, whatever. This is an opportunity you can't miss."

"I'd miss you." Whenever his interests flagged in the book on women who had married priests, Lorraine would respond with the blandishments of the marital couch. She was acting like a woman who had married a priest.

"I'm coming with you, dummy."

He didn't have to threaten to resign. He didn't even have to request the assignment. A conference was held, and it was common consent that Nate Patch was the man for this job. "Not to take anything away from McDonald. Or from Sissy for that matter. But we need an eye that is both experienced and fresh to insure that our coverage will be the best." It was the kind of remark people in his dreams addressed to him. Patch's abiding impression was that his colleagues thought him dull and predictable. But he was experienced, God knows. He was the senior man in the Washington office now, and it was pleasant to think that the others looked up to him as a man of wisdom and talent.

"I'll take my wife with me."

Quigley fell back, a look of horror on his face. "You've married?"

Patch nodded. Quigley sat forward.

"Did you get an annulment first?"

"Lorraine and I are back together."

Relief all around. An irregular marriage was not the credential they wanted for their special correspondent for the papal election.

It seemed that everyone he met in the next few days was going to Rome. Except for Leach. He lifted his eyes piously at the question.

"I am saying a novena of Masses for the repose of the soul of the late Holy Father. One can only hope that he escaped the fate Dante reserved for those who betray their office."

Patch just stared. This was a remark he would never have expected from a priest of Leach's orthodox pretensions. But then Leach thought that James Morrow was a secret liberal.

"He was a great Pope", Patch said. "One of the greatest. I hope to live long enough to read all he wrote."

"Commendable, commendable."

Wales had already left for Rome, to join the archbishop, and Leach was eager to explain the urgency of the trip. The official mourning period would last three days.

"The opening of the conclave is still days away. The question has arisen as to who is eligible to sit as elector. Will the putative Cardinal Lannan be inside when the doors are sealed shut or will he, like the rest of us, wait outside?"

It was not the first thing that occurred to Patch nor, he now noticed, to anyone else at the service, but clearly the death of the Pope who had appointed him cardinal affected Thomas Lannan's status. Was he or was he not a cardinal?

"There were monsignors, as you doubtless know, whose dignity lasted only for the length of the pope's reign who appointed them. That is not the problem here. The question that arises is, what precisely makes one a cardinal: being publicly named one by the Holy Father or being formally inducted into the sacred college?"

"What's the answer?"

"Ah, Nathaniel, your question conjures up a pleasant assumption, that what Fr. Leach thinks interests anyone in the Church save as an indication of madness. After a time, one ceases to form opinions, they carry so little weight. Thomas Lannan is or is not a cardinal independently of my considered view that he is not."

"Not."

"Certainly not. I will explain."

Patch felt that he was escaping the Oldest Member in a P.G. Wodehouse golf story when he pried himself loose from the cadaverous Cassandra of the USCC. Skipping down the steps of the Taj Mahal he found that he was eager to be off to Rome. Everything in the Washington headquarters had a tentative air.

The thought that struck him on the bottom step made him pause and then shamble thoughtfully to the traffic light where he waited to cross to the National Shrine. In the lower church, with penitents whispering in the confessionals all around him, he sat and stared sightlessly at the altar, thinking of the old woman in Minneapolis and the archbishop of Washington.

The letter he had received was of the kind usually disposed of in the wastebasket: anonymous, insinuating great scandal—in this case, involving Thomas Lannan and suggesting that he visit a Mrs. Christiansen in a Minneapolis rest home. The reporter that started taking such letters seriously was heading for professional ruin. But when the book project took him to Minneapolis to interview a woman who had married two priests, not just one, he went around to the rest home.

He was shown into a room where an elderly woman with a lovely smile was listening to the television with the volume turned so loud that the walls seemed to reverberate.

"Is that a favorite program?"

Her smile wavered but returned.

"Do you mind if I turn it down?"

She thought a bit, lifted her eyebrows, and smiled even more brightly. He turned down the set. She seemed surprised by his action.

"I'll turn it up again in a moment."

"I can't hear a word you are saying." She thrust a pad at him, and he printed out his name and that he was a reporter.

"It's Agnes who's 103. I'm just in my 90s."

How could he take seriously a letter telling him that this woman had information about a child born out of wedlock to Thomas Lannan when he was a young man? When Lannan was named cardinal, Nate had not thought of that visit to the Minneapolis rest home, but now after his talk with Leach, always a depressing experience, it appeared as a potential threat, not only to Lannan but to the Church. The thought crossed his mind that he could ask Leach what he thought of it, but he did not need any special grace to know that that was a bad idea. He sat on for half an hour. Was he praying? He said no prayers in the usual sense, but he had an unusual sense of Christ sacramentally present on the altar, continuing to exercise his ministry in all those whispering confessionals. The sharing by men in the life of God, that was what the Church was, and he felt sick at the thought that more scandals could distract believers and nonbelievers from that fundamental fact.

Before flying off to Rome, he called the rest home in Minneapolis and was in the course of explaining who he was and why he wished to ask about Mrs. Christiansen.

"Margie? Oh, she's no longer with us. Margie passed away."

He hung up the phone with the unsettling thought that a prayer had been answered.

5

The Catholic Church was once again, if only momentarily, the darling of the media. Programs were devoted to the intricacies of the papal succession, to the minutiae of conclaves, to the significance of white smoke and black. The pageantry of Rome, of the Vatican, the music and liturgy, the architecture, the art—who could resist it? It was so much more pleasant to highlight than the doctrines that went against the modern mentality. Julian O'Keefe noticed all this and smiled.

"What did you say?" Peggy asked. She was over her terror at being forty thousand feet in the air. She wrapped herself up in a blanket and clamped on a headset. Individual monitors were installed in the seatback before one so that passengers could select their own entertainment. Julian felt that he was on a kind of vacation and had no desire to look at the films of others.

"Lilies that fester smell worse than weeds."

"Is that from a song?"

"Elizabethan." He could tell her anything.

She was off on the House of Windsor and the latest newsworthy antic of wayward royalty. It had become a tired subject. The same was true of the faults and foibles of the clergy. Elmer Gantry might be a skunk, but he had his lovable side.

Still, the higher they are, the greater the fall. The more beautiful the flower, the more odorous its corruption. He had set out to bag an archbishop and now had a cardinal in his sights.

Or an almost cardinal. Leach had been unhelpful: "Julian, I completely debriefed myself to a journalist not an hour ago. You could call him. No, don't. He would bore you to death. He and his wife are actually doing yet another book about priests who stray."

"Nathaniel Patch."

"You've heard of him?"

"Well, of his wife."

"For heaven's sake. Did you tell him we are friends?"

Friends? Perhaps they were.

"The reason I ask, is don't. But I need not warn you of the danger of being associated with a pariah."

Leach had mentioned Mrs. Patch before, and checking her out, Julian had learned of the book project and of her obese husband Nathaniel. Was it foolishness or a species of insurance that had induced him to send the letter about Mrs. Christiansen to Patch? The remote hope had been that Patch would mention it to Leach, and the story would come back to Julian, perhaps with additional useful information. In any case, he could not have Leach associating Julian O'Keefe with Thomas Lannan. The plummeting prelate would give far more satisfaction to Julian if no one knew who had engineered his fall.

CHAPTER TWO

I

Old Roman hand though he was, Ambrose Frawley had never before been in the city when a pope died and another was to be elected: the events were like two ends of the same thought. It had never occurred to Frank Bailey that Frawley would have been a schoolboy when two papal elections had followed so quickly on one another that both popes chose the same name, a name never before taken by any pope, at least not in combination. John Paul I and John Paul II, the picks meant as a tribute to the popes of the ecumenical council Vatican II.

"He was the death of the Council", Frank growled.

Although Bailey had arrived in Rome unannounced, he asked for and received accommodations at the college. Of course Frawley put him up; the rector tried never to take sides and sought to be everyone's friend. Sort of. The students appeared to be excited to have Bailey in residence, and Bailey was delighted to find that he could hold their attention with his feigned indifference. He was here, he told them, in his capacity as journalist.

"What paper?" a callow young man from Nevada inquired.

"Sic transit trolley car", Bailey groaned. "Has it come to this?"

"Fr. Bailey is a syndicated columnist", Frawley explained, and none too soon. He seemed to be enjoying the fact that some of these young men knew little about Bailey and the protests he had organized.

"This should give the column a boost", Bailey said, then dropped the subject. Once he had been carried in seventy-five diocesan papers and two secular papers, enabling him to boast that he had more direct access to the faithful than the Vatican. "And I understand them better too", he used to add.

Those had been the golden years. Of late, Bailey had withdrawn in bitterness, to tend the garden of his tell-all memoirs. The prospect of that volume made many jittery, both his friends and his adversaries. He had overheard the nervous reaction to the prospect of a book that, truth to tell, existed only in scattered notes. The two-thousand-word article had become his basic creative burst. The stormy petrel, it was whispered, carried a grudge to abnormal lengths and, in the saying, never forgave a favor or gave quarter to a foe.

He spent his first day at the Vatican press room on the Via della Conciliazione, renewing old alliances, catching up on the gossip. He was astounded to see Ignatius Wynn there, his weak eyes glittering with the prospect of combat, getting about in a wheelchair, one arm still in a sling...

"*Arma virumque cano*", Frank greeted the improbable Aeneas.

If Frank Bailey was a legend, Ignatius Wynn was a myth. His multivolume distortion of the sessions of Vatican II had set a standard for the years since. Press releases from the Vatican were now treated with the same routine scepticism as those from secular governments; the basest of motives were assumed to lie behind decisions, appointments, documents; the Vatican press corps was soon indistinguishable from the gangs of semi-sober scribes and tough broads in whose hands the reputations of worldly leaders reposed.

Frank wheeled Wynn up the street to an outdoor table where they were joined by Ben Trovato, Rome correspondent for the *New York Times*, a retired Catholic, as the Australians say, wearing chips like epaulets, delighted to find such kindred souls as Wynn and Bailey. His eyes burned through the thatch of his bushy brows.

"You survived the accident."

"I'm retired in our generalate here", Wynn explained, a little edgy at the realization that Trovato had thought him dead.

"How can you stand it?" Frank asked.

"I'm well looked after. I like it. There are one or two young men here pursuing their studies."

"One or two?"

"For several years we had none." Wynn pulled at his lower lip. "The scandal."

"Are you an Appenine?" Trovato asked, stopping his glass midway to his mouth. The Appenines had been rocked by a financial scandal, involving the two top men in the order. Swiss bank accounts had drained away the money sent in by the faithful to further the good works of the order.

"He's a Thaddeist", Frank said impatiently, whether at the thought of all these penny ante orders still clinging to life or at Trovato's ignorance, it would have been difficult to say. In any case, he succeeded in annoying both of his companions.

Pederasty had decimated the ranks of the Thaddeists. When the scandal broke, their three remaining seminaries had been shut down, and it was nip and tuck whether the order would be suppressed. The father general and his catamite went off to Nepal, purportedly to become monks of an eastern sort, but they were of course refused. Tales of their excesses in the fleshpots of the Far East soon lost their news value, at least for the secular press, but the clerical grapevine hummed with them. By the time the Augean stables had been cleansed, there were forty members left. The head of the order in the States was 37, a former Carthusian; and the superior general lived in Rome with the remnant Wynn had mentioned.

"You were lucky to be away, Iggie."

"I suspected those guys from the first time I saw them."

"You should have said something."

"I did. How could I know I was complaining to one who sympathized with their weakness? I was rebuked for homophobia."

"I remember, I remember", Frank said, and he did. Wynn had done a crisp little piece on "heterophobia" that had found a home in the pages of *Crisis* under a pseudonym that fooled no one.

"They edited out my conclusion that unless celibacy is dropped we'll have nothing but Oscar Wildes in the priesthood."

"Who's it gonna be?" Trovato asked, steering the conversation toward more newsworthy clerical gossip.

"Pavese", Wynn said.

"If we're lucky", Frank might have been crossing his fingers.

"He the only candidate?"

"Oh, there's Benedetto, of course. He's mentioned if only as a courtesy."

"Be-ne-det-to", Trovato repeated, as if he were learning the language. He hated Italians unless they were from Philadelphia or related to him.

"The secretary of state."

"I know who he is. I'm trying to visualize him in white."

"Don't bother." Bailey sat forward. "We've waited for years to undo the damage done by the dear departed. It's a chance we can't afford to lose. Benedetto would be more of the same, and that would be fatal."

"Why an Italian?"

"After what we've been through, an Italian looks good. Besides they've been in exile in their own country, watching the internationalization of the Curia, the dispersal of power and influence. They're ripe for a restoration. We can deal with Italians."

Trovato looked at Bailey with grudging admiration. "You're really ready for this, aren't you?"

"I've been dreaming about it for years."

"And talking in your sleep", Iggie said.

Bailey gave a half-playful push at Wynn's wheelchair, and the Thaddeist rolled toward the curb, gathering speed. Trovato nearly upset the table getting to him, but he saved him from pitching headfirst into traffic.

2

Lannan had returned from Milan by train, calling Frawley from Stazione Termini and asking how he could get to the Villa Stritch by public transportation.

"You can't. I'll come get you."

"Oh, would you?" His voice was almost plaintive.

"Of course. In fifteen minutes or so; keep a lookout for me."

"I'll have a coffee in the restaurant here."

"Good."

"Fifteen minutes?"

"At the most."

This was far from Lannan's usual telephone manner, let alone that of a prince of the Church. Why on earth had he come by train? He had flown off in a private jet, on just the sort of visit he should be making at such a time. Of course when he left, the Pope was still alive. Had the news affected Lannan so much?

The traffic was terrible, and twenty minutes had passed before Frawley made the turn in front of St. Mary Major and approached the Termini on the east side. A figure in black, gripping an overnight bag with both hands, stood, almost on the curb, looking frantically at the passing cars. Frawley bulled his way to the curb and hit the horn. Lannan jumped back as if he were about to be run over. Frawley opened his door and got his head and shoulders out so Lannan could see who it was, earning for this courtesy a cacophonous concert from the drivers he was momentarily inconveniencing. Lannan scooted to the car and into the passenger seat where he sat, still gripping his bag.

"You can throw that in back."

Frawley did it for him. Lannan seemed almost in a state of shock. He spoke of it on the way to the Villa Stritch: the crowded compartment on the train, the woman whose purse had been stolen and who had screamed and wept for hours. Lannan's ecclesiastical rank meant nothing in such a situation, and he found himself unable to do anything helpful.

"The conductor was useless. Apparently this happens all the time."

"I didn't think it necessary to warn you about trains."

"What a country."

"Why did you take the train?"

"I thought it would give me time to think."

He told Frawley how he had gotten the news of the Pope's death. "They were the first words out of Pavese's mouth."

"He's the front runner in the press."

Lannan nodded. "He's obviously given it a great deal of thought."

"The books are a pretty sure sign."

Over the past four years, Pavese had published several volumes of sermons and another of occasional pieces having to do with the ups and downs in the Church since the Council. He had also published an appreciation of Manzoni, which particularly endeared him to the Milanese. And there was a book of meditations.

"He gave me a copy of that."

"It's really quite good." Frawley added, "Some men at the college have used it."

Calling it a campaign would be unkind, but Pavese had displayed his versatility, and his spirituality. The theme the secular papers took up was Pavese's suggestion that there had been perhaps an overemphasis on sexual morality. He didn't suggest any change of doctrine, just a wider context.

"He's accused of holding a fundamental option view."

The idea behind "fundamental option", more or less, was to assess moral deeds, not as isolated occurrences, but as part of a life's plan. A whole orientation is not destroyed by one or two acts that don't quite fit it—such was the theory.

Lannan nodded. "That sounds reasonable enough."

"Leave it to Janet Smith to point out that Paul VI explicitly rejected it in *Humanae vitae*."

"Did he?"

"*In verbis*. And of course so does *Veritatis splendor*."

Lannan had the look of a man who was not a close student of papal encyclicals.

The Villa Stritch had a tonic effect on Lannan, and he was able to joke about his arrival at Malpensa and the bus ride into Milan. A bracing drink had him commenting on his impressions of Pavese from a more worldly point of view than he had displayed on the drive from the Termini.

"I've heard the Holy Father on *ad limina* visits, but I've never had a real conversation with him. He talks, you listen. Pavese is a listener. Bernardin once said that's how we've learned to put together pastoral letters, by listening. Wouldn't it be something if the whole Church were run that way?"

"Morrow doesn't think so."

"Morrow?"

"Chapter fourteen on pastoral letters."

"He seems happy enough here, doesn't he?"

"Very. And it isn't entirely due to Mrs. Kilmartin."

Here Maureen was known as the widow of the Irish ambassador to the Vatican, Sean Kilmartin. Lannan winced at the reminder of the husband blown to pieces too small to bury in a car bombing. He should have said more to Maureen about that in Washington. He wasn't surprised to hear that she and Jim Morrow were often seen together.

"I suppose he might marry again", Lannan mused.

"I don't say it's come to that, or anywhere near it. They enjoy one another's company."

"We can't have our ambassador to the Vatican inviting speculation about his personal life." Lannan was being facetious.

"The two of them are above reproach." But even as he said it, Frawley wondered whence his certainty came.

"Mrs. Ambassador" was McHugh's way of referring to the now omnipresent Maureen Kilmartin, but then she had eclipsed McHugh with the ambassador, and he felt there were confidences Morrow shared with her and not with him. What dark secrets there could be, Frawley would have been incapable of saying.

Despite all the hullabaloo stateside, Monsignor Frawley could see no particular value in having a special ambassador to the Vatican. Our Italian ambassador was often of Italian lineage, usually a Catholic, he could do double duty, as indeed he had before Franklin Roosevelt sent Myron Taylor as a personal envoy.

"What did Jim Morrow say about pastoral letters?"

"In a nutshell, that bishops are masters of the faith and appointed to teach the faithful, not repeat back to them what they already hold. There are five pages devoted to a meeting at Notre Dame with the committee that wrote the economics pastoral, bishops scribbling like schoolboys while experts enunciated incompatible expert opinions."

"Are we supposed to be economists?"

"That was his point. Bishops should be bishops, not retailers of economic theories."

Lannan shook his head, as if to rid it of this thought. "I guess I didn't read that chapter. Bernardin was right, the pastorals represent a new departure in teaching."

"Being taught?"

Lannan looked at him, unsure whether the monsignor was voicing his own opinion or reporting on Morrow's.

"Tell me more about Pavese", Frawley suggested.

Lannan drew on his cigar. "The most important thing he said was that he intended to insist, as a sign of continuity, that the twenty of us who were named cardinals take part in the election."

3

To James Morrow's surprise, Janet Fortin looked into his office and said, "Hi", for all the world as if he should have expected her.

He rose to greet her, came round his desk, and received a second surprise when she gave him a big hug and touched his cheek with her lips.

"Now the other", he said. "In the French manner."

"Hey, that wasn't a French kiss."

She strolled around the office, shaking her head and making a wet disapproving noise. "Wait until Senator Partridge hears about this Renaissance splendor."

"He's already been here."

"That's right."

"Besides, the building went up in the year seven."

"Is it that old?"

"The seventh year of Mussolini's reign. The Thousand Year Reich was a modest claim next to his."

"You're supposed to ask me what I'm doing in Rome."

"What are you doing in Rome?"

"I bummed a ride on Air Force Two. The Vice President is here for the funeral. Well, not here. He's spending some time in Naples so I came up from there."

"By train?"

"By naval bus." She made a face. "Sounds worse than a French kiss."

"Where are you staying?"

"The consulate made arrangements. Of course I called from Air Force Two, so what could they do?"

"So this is just a visit?"

"My cousin's here."

"Your cousin lives here?"

"Monsignor Wales."

"I didn't know you were cousins."

"Third or fourth. Non-consanguineous. He can explain it, I can't."

"How long will you be here?"

"Well, the Vice President's here for the funeral. He will return afterward, and I can bum a ride back. Gene's staying for the whole thing, funeral and election."

Gene was Monsignor Wales, who would have a ringside seat during the coming historic events and be as involved in a papal election as a non-cardinal could be. Each elector had a chaplain who, while excluded from the actual proceedings, could count on confidential asides from his cardinal, and Wales had worked for Lannan a long time.

"I'd like to take the two of you to dinner. Or lunch."

"Today?"

Morrow laughed. "Why not?"

"I meant lunch."

It was eleven thirty. "Let me make a call?"

Maureen suggested a restaurant in the Borgo Pio, just outside the Vatican. "Afterward I want to say a Rosary for the Pope in St. Peter's. In the eucharistic chapel. Who is this couple?" asked Maureen.

"She's right at my elbow, or I would tell you all about her." Janet punched at him, and he turned away with a laugh.

"She sounds playful", Maureen said.

"She greeted me with a French kiss." Again he was punched.

"Maybe you two would like to be alone."

"Oh, there'll be four of us. 12:45?"

"Make it one."

Despite the fact that it was January and even *sede vacante,* the Vatican still seemed to draw as many visitors as when there was a pope to be glimpsed or heard. The restaurant Maureen had chosen was on a very narrow street, but there was a covered courtyard with a fountain and an overflow of tables. The proprietor recognized Maureen, and within five minutes they were seated and Morrow could make proper introductions. Janet first, then Wales, who was in civvies.

"Oh, Monsignor Wales and I have met. When he was on duty", said Maureen.

"And in uniform." He seemed uneasy out of his clericals.

"They're cousins", Morrow remarked.

"Relatively speaking", Janet said.

"You know that Mrs. Kilmartin's husband was the Irish ambassador to the Vatican?"

"Was?"

"He's dead."

"And you stayed on." Janet, unaware that her question had touched on tragedy, looked around with a radiant smile and sighed. Following her gaze, Morrow felt the scene grow quaint and attractive. Even the cats slithering about seemed animals one might grow to love.

"Viterbo", Maureen said firmly when asked where the two young people might visit.

"I meant in Rome."

"You'll see plenty of Rome. But go to Viterbo."

"What's the attraction?"

Maureen looked at Morrow. "Well," he said, "for one thing, a papal election was held there."

"That's not the reason."

"You tell them", Morrow said.

"There is a woman there who has visions. The late Pope took her quite seriously, as our mutual friend can attest."

"Private revelations?" Wales' expression was pleasant, but his voice was heavy with disapproval.

"She has been remarkably accurate thus far."

"In what way?"

"She predicted the death of the Pope."

"I could have done that", Janet said.

Morrow did not want to discuss the Viterbo visionary. It was one thing to talk about her with Maureen, but he sensed the scepticism in Janet and Wales. He certainly did not want the report he had written for the late Pope to become a topic at this festive table. A carafe of wine had arrived, red, and he poured it elaborately, diverting the others to the more immediate matter of food and drink.

The woman in Viterbo had predicted more than the death of the Pope, which as Janet said, was a fairly safe bet. The other things, the things that had weighed on the Pope even after Morrow had produced his analysis suggesting that her forecast was not credible, given her remarks about the United States, required revelation. Or an unusual imagination.

"Now if she predicted something like the collapse of the Soviet Union and peace between the Arabs and Jews..."

"You can't predict the past."

"I said like."

"Would you care to go there?"

Janet looked at Wales. "To have my future told?"

He seemed embarrassed by her retort, but she was distracted by the sensation of a cat moving between her ankles. She yelped, looked, and tried to gather in the cat, but it sprang away and took up its station on the water fountain.

"Look at all the cats."

"Don't order canneloni", Maureen suggested, but it was their joke, and the others did not understand.

"Tell us about flying with the Vice President", Morrow suggested.

And Janet regaled them with the account, they were told of her ride from Naples in the naval bus, and then she went on to White House gossip. Maureen was fascinated, and Janet was in better form than Morrow had ever seen her. What an attractive young woman she was. That is what he said to Maureen when lunch was done and Janet and Wales had gone off down the narrow street to the car he had rented.

"A woman in love", Maureen replied.

"In love?"

"Of course. They make a nice couple."

"Don't be silly. He's a monsignor. Besides, they're cousins."

Maureen just looked at him. "Relatively speaking."

4

Cardinal Pavese went more or less unnoticed on his passage from his archiepiscopal palace to the Biblioteca e Pinocateca Ambrosiana to visit with his old professor, mentor, and friend,

Angelo Forlani. To enter the Ambrosiana was to reenter the world of his youth: hours and days and months spent turning the pages of Muratori, consulting the fourteenth-century manuscripts that had gone into the slow composition of his esteemed scholarly work, *Nominalism in Lombardy*.

Having entered the reading room, he caught the doors in their swinging and eased them to a stop as he looked at the rows of desks reserved for fellows and toward the slightly more prominent desk of the director. Elsewhere in the world, directors of institutes and museums and libraries might be little more than administrators, but the tradition of the Ambrosiana was that the director was engaged in scholarship like the other fellows, as Forlani had been before being named director. Such administrative tasks as the post entailed were reluctantly and with much grumbling attended to. Forlani was the acknowledged expert on St. Ambrose's years in Milan—his monograph on the baptistery discovered after World War II, published in only 1,500 copies, now fetched upwards of three thousand dollars from collectors intent on holding it until its value climbed yet higher.

Forlani sat hunched over his work, shading his eyes against the already shaded lamp on his desk, more surely present in the past of which he read than the bright January day that had brought Pavese the half-mile from his residence. Forlani's grizzled fringe of hair had been combed by distracted fingers into a wild halo, his jowls were unshaven, and the collar that peeped above the turtleneck sweater he wore as vest was not an example of impeccable linen. Pavese did not disapprove. A well-groomed Forlani would have been a contradiction in terms.

Forlani stirred as he read, becoming aware of the figure standing beside him, being drawn slowly from his absorption in a better time to the nuisance of some silly request or another. When he turned to see the cardinal archbishop, the annoyance in his eye did not alter to obsequiousness as it would in a lesser man. But perhaps he saw beside him, not a prelate, but the boy he had schooled in Latin years ago.

"May I have a word with you, *Direttore?*"

Forlani bowed, looked wistfully at the work spread on his desk, summoned a menial, and gave him stern instructions to pay special attention to the director's desk in his absence.

"What is that manuscript?" Pavese asked.

If any patron of the library had picked up the manuscript as casually as Forlani did, he would have been in danger of having his hands chopped off, metaphorically. "It is a holograph of Aquinas."

"May I?"

Forlani hesitated, then retaining the manuscript, held it for the cardinal to see. Pavese had done a little work on the *litera inintelligibilis* of St. Thomas, and he recognized this manuscript whose unreadable hand he had toiled over.

"The *Summa contra gentiles?*"

"A quire of Book Three."

Pavese murmured appreciatively. Forlani laid the manuscript on his desk, glared meaningfully at the attendant, and led the way to the director's office. It was there, in secure cabinets, that some of the most precious manuscripts in the collection were kept. It was in this room that a predecessor of Forlani's had sat, eventually to be catapulted into the See of Peter as Pius XI. And it was here that Pavese wished to discuss his own prospects at the coming conclave.

"It is all over", Forlani said with the flicker of a smile. "Don't you read the newspapers? *Il Messagero* is even speculating on the name you will select."

"Ambrose perhaps", Pavese murmured but with a smile.

"Is it true?"

"You know that such stories are woven out of thin air. You are the first one I will speak to seriously about these rumors."

As they spoke of his prospects for the papacy, Pavese was reminded of another conversation some years before, when he had come to Forlani with the letter appointing him auxiliary bishop of Pavia. Acceptance meant turning away from the scholarly path on which he had just begun to win renown.

"You will never read a serious book again", Forlani had predicted, and he hadn't been far wrong. "You will gain thirty pounds within a year." That too had come about. "You will ascend higher and higher." The old priest's hand had lifted as he spoke and then it waved, bidding adieu to the life of learning.

"Then I should refuse?"

Forlani looked at him in silence. "You have already decided. You want my blessing."

"Do I have it?"

Forlani had given it, but not until he had spelled out again the choice the younger priest was making. The cardinal had sent Forlani the books he had published in recent years, but the director could not be expected to take such productions seriously. One of them had indeed been little more than a popularization of a long out-of-print Forlani work on Augustine.

"Newspapers aside, what are your chances?"

Pious words began to form in Pavese's mind, but he had the good sense not to bother Forlani with pro forma declarations of submission to the will of God. "I am told the College is evenly split between Benedetto and myself."

"Are the votes firm?"

"That is what I am told."

"Then it will be a third."

Pavese could not prevent a pained expression from rippling across his face. "There is another possibility."

"Oh?"

"As you know, His Holiness, shortly before his death,

named twenty new members of the College. If they were admitted as electors, my chances would improve."

"But they have not been given the red hat."

"Some canonists assure me that nomination is tantamount to creation. It is not like being named bishop, where, prior to consecration, one is simply a priest and that is that."

Forlani's lower lip puffed out, and he scratched at his unshaven face with a card picked up from his table.

"And other canonists say otherwise."

"There is no unanimous opinion", Pavese conceded.

"Who decides?"

"The conclave."

"And won't the division be the same?"

"As between Benedetto and the forces of progress?"

"Between Benedetto and yourself", Forlani said, rejecting the slogan.

"I think they will be seated."

Forlani did not like it, that was clear. The old head hummed with memories of past conclaves, earlier efforts to secure a certain result prior to the time when the electors were locked in. Pavese could almost hear the old man give the etymology of *conclavium,* with spring sweet at the windows of the classroom, chalk dusting his soutane, his gold-rimmed glasses awry on his head as he endeavored to see over and through them for different purposes.

"I will follow the proceedings with interest."

"You do not wish me well?"

"I wish you what God wishes, *Eminenza.*"

So it was with neither blessing nor curse that Pavese left, seen off at the door of the Ambrosiana by Forlani, who blinked against the unaccustomed sun, peered curiously at passersby, as if he were surprised there were still some among the living, not yet reduced to dusty records.

"*Arrivederci, Direttore.*"

"Next time in Rome?"

"As God wills."

He tried to mean that too as he slipped through the Galleria and several steps beyond before a murmur of recognition began. Pigeons rose like a scruffy pentecost as he crossed the square, but his mind was again full of calculations, appraisals, guesses, anxieties. Inside his residence, in the elevator, he thought of the American who had come to see him a few days before: Archbishop of Washington, the capitol of the free world, the one remaining superpower. The media clichés clanged like implications of the city's name, but it had not been lost on Pavese that Thomas Lannan had come to him in deference, mindful that, however badly Italians had been treated during the recent papacy, they still dominated the Church. Obviously, the American looked forward to the day when an Italian would once more occupy the See of Peter. Another reason to insist that those who had been named cardinals by the late Pope should be seated in the conclave. Clearly it had been with that in view that their names had been announced. And the current rules for papal elections were clear on the matter.

5

The chapel in the Villa Stritch did not do full credit to the Chicago cardinal after whom this retreat for the American hierarchy just outside of Rome had been named. Lannan, kneeling in thanksgiving after saying Mass, chin propped on his fist, followed the elegant tracery of the white marble phoenix laid on a bed of gold. The baldachino seemed too much in so small a chapel and in any case had been designed to cover an altar stuck to the far wall. That altar had become an altar of repose, and a chaste slab covered with snow-white and heavily starched linen stood before it, an altar at which in the modern mode the celebrant faced the people. Or an empty chapel, as had been the case for Lannan's Mass. He moved his cuff. It was not yet six o'clock. After a sleepless night, he had decided to give up all hope of rest and begin the new day.

The dead Pope now lay in state on a great bier before the doors of St. Peter's Basilica, and for three days, morning, afternoon, and throughout the night, the faithful had passed by the body—vested, mitred, gloved, the ring missing from his hand, having been broken by the camerlingo immediately after his declaration that the pontiff was indeed dead. Some professed to be surprised by the crowds, it having become received opinion that the Church yearned for a new leader, that the simple faithful were tired of their pastor and desired a new one who would attend more to their needs and discontents.

"Let *aggiornamento* begin at last", Bailey cried at table in the North American College and again on a visit to the Villa Stritch, where he was greeted with false affability and palpable wariness of this public scold who had made life more difficult for the prelates during the years since the Council. He proclaimed the same to his fellows in the press room on the Via della Conciliazione and over drinks with the correspondents for *Newsweek, Time,* and the *New Yorker.* He was made the subject of a little sketch in *Catholic World Report* for his pains, entitled "Rancorous Lazarus Resurrected: By This Time He Stinketh". Bailey loved it; once more he was the eye of the storm, an *enfant terrible* of pushing sixty.

"What's wrong with *aggiornamento*?" an elderly archbishop asked, twisting his hearing aid in the dim hope that he could pick up the table talk at the Villa.

"'Let it begin', he says. "As if it hadn't."

"As if we haven't had more than thirty years of it", Bishop

Mankowicz of Syracuse added, and his tone suggested that that was more than enough.

"He's for Pavese."

"Everyone's for Pavese."

"Not those who are for Benedetto."

A moment of silence followed during which all seemed to agree that the discussion ought not to go farther here. After all, there were some at table who would be discussing such matters in earnest all too shortly. Thomas Lannan still did not know whether he would be among them.

"Of course you will", Boston assured him.

"We will vote you in", agreed New York.

"If it is canonically legitimate", San Francisco purred.

"Then of course you can count on me."

Los Angeles hoped the conclave would not get bogged down in credential fights. The remark, recalling political conventions, brought frowns to those who had pledged Lannan support.

"The nation's capitol should be represented."

"Baltimore won't be", the deaf archbishop observed. Baltimore, the primatial see, had not had a cardinal since an archbishop in the nineties. His successor had espoused every whacko notion put forward by dissident theologians. From the pulpit he had expressed the hope that females would soon stand beside him at the altar.

"They already are", groused Monsignor George Kelly when he got in to see the nuncio on the matter.

It was these remembered conversations that had kept sleep from Thomas Lannan, and even now as he tried to pray he found himself reviewing what had been said and by whom and with what intonation. If reassurance was to be had, it came from recalling his visit to Pavese, and the reason was clear. Pavese needed him, something that was not true of his tablemates at the Villa Stritch. Lannan of course knew all too well how the public promise faded when serious discussion began behind closed doors.

A surprised Wales looked into the chapel. "When you didn't answer my knock, I checked your room. When did you get· up?"

"I've already said Mass."

Wales eyes widened further. "You should take a pill."

It had become a world of pills—pills against pain, against stress, against conception, to induce abortion, to lift or lower the spirits.

"Let me have the keys of the car."

"I'll drive you."

"No, I just want to drive."

Wales looked as if he might refuse his boss the keys to the rented car. "How long has it been since you drove in Rome?"

"Perhaps you should give me absolution first."

In the car, studying the dashboard before starting the engine, he told himself that he must not joke about sacred things. The greatest danger for the priest was to get too used to the office he held, the acts he performed, the graces he dispensed. Faith slipped away under too much familiarity.

Wales, apparently assuming that he himself would bear the expense of the car, had rented the smallest of Fiats, one whose gearshift presented difficulties for Lannan, particularly getting it into reverse, and until and unless he mastered that, he must remain in the parking lot staring at a bush whose leaves reminded him of a magnolia's. On the knob of the shift was engraved a diagram showing him where the various gears could be located, but whenever he put it at reverse he was rewarded only with a metallic complaint.

There was a tap at the window. Lannan cranked it down. Wales told him he must first push the shift stick down and then move the knob. Several tries at this finally brought success, and Lannan lurched away from the bush while Wales danced out of harm's way. He waved at Wales without daring to take his eyes from his task and moved more or less smoothly out of the parking lot onto the winding road that would bring him to the highway into Rome. Here, despite the hour, each time he readied himself to enter the highway, an automobile would appear out of nowhere and go past in a roar of sound that filled him with terror. What if he had driven onto the highway, What if, as happened twice while he awaited a propitious moment, the motor died when he did? The speed of the miraculously materializing cars was such that they could never stop in time. A crash at that speed would send him on to where the late Pope now was.

His intention was to visit anonymously the Pope's bier and offer a prayer for him along with the rest of the faithful who were paying their respects to their lost spiritual leader. He finally dared to pull onto the highway, crouched over the wheel, the hair on his neck tingling as he saw in the rearview mirror a car swell into visibility. It went past with a rush of wind and a blare of horn, but now Lannan had claim to the inside slow lane, and he had no intention of leaving it. Let the other maniacal motorists exceed the 120 KPH speed limit, he would settle for 50 which, if Wales' system of calculation was correct, was equivalent to 30 MPH.

He got hopelessly lost twice, once he entered the city, swept along by traffic in a panic, certain he was getting farther and farther from St. Peter's. When for the second time he approached the Ponte Milvio, he had acquired the requisite callousness to ignore the protests from other drivers and cut across three lanes into a gas station where he asked directions. Before he escaped, a three-man seminar had formed to discuss the issue: the man he had first asked, a woman who wiped his windshield while the debate went on, and an empty-eyed youth who stood shaking his head and pointing. Lannan took the direction of the pointing finger and discovered that he had passed within a block of the Vatican several times.

Parking was forbidden where he left the car, but the signs had not prevented dozens of others from lining the curb. He followed the wall to the corner and turned to pass eventually the Porta Sant'Anna, then entered the Bernini colonnade and joined the line moving across the piazza toward the bier of the deceased Pope.

All over the world, uncomplicated sadness was felt at the passing of a man who had become a familiar figure in all but a few countries on the globe. He had been lionized at first, setting records with the crowds he drew—records that were later used as measures of his alleged decline in popularity; but the crowds remained huge by any standards other than his own. Lannan became aware that some in the line were weeping, moving beads through their fingers. These mourners contrasted strikingly with little groups enjoying the occasion as if it were festive. For the most part, however, the people were silent and serious, determined to express their love for the departed Pope.

Lannan permitted simple sorrow to fill his own breast. This was the Pope who, on the advice of the papal nuncio, advised in turn by American prelates, had raised Thomas Lannan to the dignity of the episcopate. This was the Pope who in one of his last acts had named Thomas Lannan cardinal. In this crowd, considering the infinitesimally small number of princes of the Church compared with the throngs of the faithful, he might have been appreciating for the first time the enormous honor the late Pope had done him.

And what other motive could he have had if not to name more electors of his successor? It seemed a matter of simple justice that the late Pope's choices should take their seats with other members of the College when the conclave began. Lannan was sure that if these mourners were polled they would agree in overwhelming numbers. Perhaps a poll ought to be taken, to shore up Pavese's intention to make seating the twenty the first order of business. Maybe Frank Bailey could be induced to see that such a poll was taken.

But all such thoughts left him when for a moment he stood looking up at the tilted bier where the body of the Pope lay. *Requiescat in pace,* he prayed. *Fidelium animae per misericordiam Dei, requiescant in pace.*

And then he was pushed along. It seemed so small a thing to do after the harrowing drive from the Villa Stritch. Would he ever be able to find his way back?

6

Giancarlo Benedetto lay on a narrow bed in his quarters, his hands folded on his considerable stomach, his eyes closed and teeth gritted, waiting for the anti-acid pills to work. Imagine an Italian whose stomach now rebelled at the dishes on which he had been raised in Palermo so many years ago. Thoughts of his parents, of the Sicilian countryside, of the little place his brother had purchased for him near Trapani, brought on another sweeter pain. Dear God, how he longed to return to the scenes of his youth, to retire, tend his own vines, prepare for death. Several times he had discussed it with the Holy Father and been refused.

"Not yet, Gianni, not yet."

"I am old, Holiness. I have grown stale in my work. You need someone wiser and more vigorous."

"I need you. Besides, you are younger than I am." A Slavic smile. "Almost everyone is."

Among the most welcome visitors to the late Pope had been the retired cardinals, four of whom were his seniors and like himself had taken part in Vatican II. To Benedetto he said, "It is a frightening thing to be of the oldest generation. But it would be far worse to be the only survivor."

Such visits were never as lengthy as the Pope would have wished. His guests were not up to prolonged sessions, but while they lasted they covered the gamut from sadness to thin old laughter. Benedetto smiled at the memory of those sounds that had drifted to him from the Pope's sitting room. At the same time he realized that his gastric pains had subsided. For a minute more he remained there, enjoying the absence of pain, then swung his legs over the side of the bed, and sought his shoes with his feet. He pushed himself away from the bed and stood, five feet five inches high, two hundred and forty pounds, rotund, unprepossessing, beset by the dream of a holiness that had escaped him over the long years of his priesthood. He had tried to use that argument with the Pope when he pleaded to retire.

"Do you think all the simple priests of Sicily are saints?"

"I am concerned about my own soul."

"If you thought you were holy, I would let you go."

"My soul is dry. I am tempted by despair."

"Your soul is no cause for despair."

"But the state of the Church!"

"Now you are coming to my faults. When I think of what has transpired while I have sat here, despite my efforts..." There was no longer the playful expression with which the Pope discussed Benedetto's dream of retirement.

"It is not your fault. You have done all that you could do—the visits, the encyclicals, the extraordinary synods, the catechizing, the audiences, the Angelus talks, the fall of communism..."

The Pope had clamped his hands over his ears. An image came to Benedetto of his father listening to the radio with earphones to make up for his defective hearing. Did he think that if he went home he would find it as he left it, his parents once more alive, nieces and nephews young, he himself thin and able to eat all the pasta his mother served him?

His parents were dead, and now the Pope was dead, and there was nothing to prevent his returning to Sicily again. All this talk about Benedetto as *papabile*. What nonsense. Let Pavese have the job. The cardinal archbishop of Milan had no idea what it was like to sit on the throne of Peter. The late Pope had likened it to an electric chair, with a very weak current.

"And I oppose capital punishment!"

By all reports, Pavese yearned to be pope. Well, he was welcome to it. Benedetto was determined to remove his name from consideration as soon as anyone put it forward. There would be nothing magnanimous in the gesture. He did not want the job. He had seen what it had done to the man who had created him cardinal and named him secretary of state. Benedetto had tasted enough of honor and renown to know how empty they were, how dissatisfying, how far from compensation for the grueling schedule. The next pope would have to travel because his predecessor had traveled. Benedetto had long been excused from the papal travel party. The Pope's absences had been a foretaste of the present, except that then there was the certainty that in a week or so he would be back. And there had been the television coverage, making him seem near when he was far off.

Adjusting his pectoral cross, Benedetto paused. Where was the Holy Father now? Where was his soul? A wave of doubt washed over him at the familiar belief that somewhere the soul of the pontiff continued to exist, that he was, if anyone deserved to be, enjoying the vision of his Creator. Suddenly it all seemed make-believe, a story to assuage the fear of death, pure fantasy.

Benedetto was standing before his dresser, and his eyes met the reflected eyes of a man who for the first time in his life was experiencing doubts against his faith. He dropped to his knees and lay his head against the edge of the dresser, closed his eyes. At prayer, at meditation, shutting out the world had always brought into play the images that summed up his creed like the stations of the cross, the mysteries of the Rosary. But now there was only darkness.

"My God", he cried aloud. "I believe. Help thou my unbelief."

Perspiration stood on his forehead like untold beads of mysteries he had never before encountered. And then as quickly as they had come, his doubts were gone. But the experience had been sufficient to remind him what a thread of grace our certainties hang from.

CHAPTER THREE

I

Ignatius Wynn in his wheelchair had worn thin so far as Frank Bailey was concerned. The proliferation of amenities for the handicapped—parking places, entry ramps, special elevators—created the impression that the halt and the lame made up half the human race. Wynn of course insisted on being rolled to the front of the room for briefings and invariably asked the first question, for all the world as if he were the dean of the Vatican press corps, despite his decades-long hiatus.

"Who's the old bastard?" a lad with indecisive down on his upper lip and a deep crease over his nose asked Frank in the coffee bar next door.

"Which one?"

"The one in the wheelchair?"

Frank regarded his questioner. Was he being baited? He had been unable to control his muttering in the just-ended briefing, which Wynn had dominated with his obsequious questioning.

"What paper you with?" he asked.

"I'm electronic media." The youngster named a lesser cable network.

"The old guy's a plant."

"A plant!"

"He's some cardinal's nephew. More likely his son on the wrong side of the blanket."

"Who does he write for?"

"He says he's writing his memoirs."

"What's his name?"

"Uccello."

The young man was stunned at the thought of such manipulation. Frank let it go then, having cast bread upon the waters. There were other oddities in the press corps. Nathaniel Patch was okay on domestic stuff, but what did he know of Rome? And there was a slinky Californian film producer with a blonde in tow. *O tempora, o mores.*

"What?" The young man wrinkled his nose. Frank Bailey realized he had spoken aloud. He bought the young man a glass of sweet vermouth.

"Is this alcoholic?"

"It better be."

"But I don't drink before dark."

"Try it."

The boy sipped at it, tasted, widened his eyes, and tasted again. "It sure doesn't taste like wine. I hate wine."

The briefing had been unimportant, an identification of the notables who had come for the last obsequies of the late Pope that morning. James Morrow had accompanied the Vice President; the house of Windsor had come up with a second cousin whose life had been untouched by public scandal. Wynn lapped it all up, and his interest proved contagious. Bailey had fled for the bar. Priming the electronic journalist was a bonus.

Ben Trovato joined them, and after a time Frank went out onto one of the pedestrian islands in the Via della Conciliazione and stared toward St. Peter's. Workmen would be busy in the Sistine Chapel, transforming it for the conclave. The restored Last Judgment would brood over the proceedings in all its original splendor, and from the ceiling prophets and sibyls and the depiction of the creation of Adam would look down at an election that would define the Church's third millennium.

"You in or out?" he'd asked Lannan on the phone.

"It has to be voted on."

Frank scowled at the phone. He already knew that. "What's the guess on how it will go?"

"Pavese is optimistic."

"If he carries this, he's a shoo-in."

Lannan was not in a talkative mood. Frank could hardly blame him. Despite a lifetime of debunking and demythologizing the hierarchical Church—which persisted in ignoring its replacement by the people's church that had been Bailey's dominant theme for decades—the aging dissident was not immune to the awful power of that relative handful of old men. Once, enraged at the late pontiff, he had remarked that a puff of white smoke was all that was needed to bring about the change the Council had intended. Well, there would be a puff of white smoke soon. If Bailey had retained the habit of making novenas, he would have begun one on behalf of Pavese's candidacy.

He had moved to a single in the Hotel Columbus across the street, to be closer to the action. He crossed with agility through the traffic and took a high stool at the hotel bar. The woman who came to take his order looked, from a distance, like a cross between a Leonardo Madonna and a survivor of *la dolce vita*. Close up, behind the bar, with the rows of bottles as backdrop, she was not served well by the ray of sunlight that found its way in through the lunette topping a tall window. She was excited because she had seen the prince of Monaco, the crown prince of Liechtenstein, the Windsor cousin, and the Vice President of the United States.

"The man with him is our ambassador to the Vatican."

"He is so handsome."

"The ambassador?"

She gave him a look. "The Vice President. I didn't see any ambassador."

"If you saw one you saw the other."

It annoyed him that she thus denied him the opportunity to mention that he and James Morrow had been classmates. What is more, one of the new cardinals who would surely sit in the conclave, was also a classmate. Perhaps he was lucky to have been spared telling her all that. He might also have told her that he had once interviewed the prince of Liechtenstein in order to write a scathing article on the bogus remnants of once-important Catholic lines. But that had been this young man's father. So many of his stories were old ones, dated, no longer of interest. It was painful to think that Lannan and Morrow were at the start of new careers while he was trying to reactivate an old one.

"Another?" Her brows rose fetchingly; her smile revealed an edge of gold on an eye tooth. She might have been a mother urging nutritious food on her child. Bailey was notorious for his crusade against celibacy as a cruel exactment from men who wished to do something special for God. His solutions had been two. Either let priests marry or make the priesthood temporary so that a man could retire into domestic bliss. He himself had never been tempted by the matrimonial state, as Flo could attest. There had been another episode during the steamy late sixties of which he preferred not to think, except occasionally to ponder how close he had come to ruining his life with a neurotic ex-nun whose baptismal name was Maris Stella. She spelled shipwreck, and he was glad he had seen it in time. Since then, he had behaved warily with women, preferring to be the champion of the sexually active from the sidelines, so to speak. Even in the privacy of his own mind he managed not to think of Flo. She was as humdrum as a wife.

The woman behind the bar, employing her wiles to get him to order another drink, repelled him. He declined, fitted himself into the tiny elevator, rose to his single room where he had a good belt from the bottle of Scotch he kept there, and then, arranging himself on the bed as the Pope had lain on his bier, drifted into a restless sleep. In his disconnected mind, the events of the day played on, and he imagined himself in the Sistine Chapel, lecturing the cardinals on the state of the Church and their manifest duty to elect someone who would acknowledge the long struggle people like himself had carried on for the real Vatican II.

2

James Morrow returned to the embassy on the Via Aurelia after the funeral, the Vice President having gone immediately to the airport.

"A sad thing", the Vice President had said on parting, shaking Morrow's hand.

"He was an old man."

"It will be hard to get used to the idea of a new pope."

Was he thinking of the next American election? Most likely, he was simply uttering another of the ceremonial remarks that appeared to make up his life. He shook McHugh's hand too and then was driven away in an unobtrusive car. Morrow thought of Maureen's husband. Public life was a constant hazard. Of course he did not think of himself as a public figure. No more, he supposed, had Sean Kilmartin.

McHugh said, "I wonder how long it will take them to elect a new pope? In recent years, they've made up their minds fairly quickly."

"Even before the conclave", Morrow remarked. "I wonder what Pavese will be like."

McHugh had made himself knowledgeable about the cardinal archbishop of Milan, preparing a succinct and informative memo for Morrow. The medievalist background surprised Morrow; he wasn't sure why. Even the denizens of the Vatican prefectures came from interesting backgrounds, by and large. Some had had preclerical careers in banking, the military, as entrepreneurs. But most were the products of a clerical education and had no life outside of it. In Pavese's case, his scholarly activities must have seemed a natural prolongation of his clerical studies.

"What is nominalism in Lombardy?" McHugh wondered.

Morrow suspected that Pavese himself might have difficulty answering that question now, so long ago was his involvement in such research. His more recent publications had been the object of scrutiny in the press, particularly his *Reflections on Gaudium et Spes*, which, retitled *Whatever Happened to Vatican II?* had sold well in the States. It had been translated into a dozen other languages as well and was widely taken to be the cardinal's program for his possible future papacy. Administratively he was for more decentralization; pastorally he was portrayed in the secular press as prepared to accept the widespread practical rejection of the Church's moral doctrine. Widespread, that is, in Western Europe and the United States. In Latin America too, where the austerities of liberation theology had given way to sexual liberation of the yankee sort.

"Is Janet Fortin here as liaison with the White House?"

"How do you mean?"

"I wondered why she stayed on."

"She's still in Rome?"

McHugh nodded, seemingly torn between delight at knowing something Morrow did not and wondering whether it was welcome news.

"Maybe she's taking some leave."

McHugh dismissed this possible reference to his own unwillingness to take a vacation. "I keep running into her and her cousin."

"Eugene Wales?"

"I didn't recognize him at first, without his clerical clothes."

"I hope he wasn't nude."

"Ho ho."

He mentioned it to Maureen, offhandedly, and her brows arched above her glasses. "The kissing cousins?"

"It's an American custom." He leaned toward her and kissed her cheek.

"I'm not your cousin."

"I noticed that."

"I suppose you'd be more affectionate if I were, in the American way."

"Monsignor Wales is a mature, prudent man. He's not Tom Lannan's right-hand man because he raises eyebrows, even eyebrows as lovely as yours."

"Caesar and Caesar's wife?"

"Whoa."

"I meant that both must be beyond reproach."

Jim Morrow wondered if his strong defense of Tom Lannan was his response to the stupid call he had received the day before. "Did you know that Archbishop Lannan's daughter is in Rome?" a man asked.

Click. An American voice. The call had its effect. He sat stunned, unable to rid his mind of the question that repeated itself in his head. Given recent events, it was possible that someone might publicly accuse Tom Lannan, and in the nature of such accusations only someone as adroit with the media as Cardinal Bernardin was likely to come out of it a winner. He had resolved to tell Maureen about it but on reflection thought he would then just be playing the caller's game.

"Well, soon they'll be locked up in the Sistine Chapel."

But this was not yet settled. The undisputed electors had not yet been inclaustrated and thus had not faced the issue of seating the twenty men the late Pope had nominated though not formally installed as cardinals. If he had lived to do so, of course they would participate in the election, new as they were to the College, but the sitting cardinals were going to have to listen to conflicting interpretations of their status, and then decide.

The debate would turn on the meaning of canon 351, paragraph 2: "Cardinals are created by decree of the Roman Pontiff, which in fact is published in the presence of the College of Cardinals. From the moment of publication, they are bound by the obligations and they enjoy the rights defined in the law." Those words seemed obviously to settle the matter for those in favor of seating the Twenty. But if laws applied themselves there would be no need of lawyers. Strict constructionists pointed out that the late Holy Father had not published the decree in the presence of the College of Cardinals. The opponents conceded this, in a narrow sense, but argued that in an age of instant electronic communication, such publishing did not require that the addressees be present in the same room. They were virtually present, in cyberspace. Smiles formed as this argument was made, and the debate went on. Moreover the rules published in February of 1996 were crystal clear on the matter. Paragraph 36 read: "A Cardinal of the Holy Roman Church who has been created and published before the College of Cardinals thereby has the right to elect the Pope...even if he has not yet received the red hat or the ring, or sworn the oath." But what does "published before the College of Cardinals" mean?

Benedetto had been interviewed by *Civiltà Cattolica* and shown himself decidedly ambiguous on the subject. He was not yet clear, he said, about what was being proposed. If it was thought that the cardinals could by voting add to the number of electors, he was sure this was not the case. But this is what they might be construed to be doing if they voted to seat the twenty. The interviewer suggested that the vote would simply recognize what the late Pope had done.

"Or been about to do", said the secretary of state.

Frawley had given a dinner for Lannan, Morrow, and Bailey in his private dining room at the North American College. The idea was to bring the three musketeers together on the eve of the conclave.

"If Benedetto opposes us, we will not be seated", Lannan said in a voice seemed meant to exclude all emotion from it.

"But Pavese is for you", Frank Bailey insisted.

"Conclaves make strange bedfellows", Frawley said, wiping wine from his lips.

"Let's not get into that", Bailey said, then clearly wished he hadn't. "The point is a good one. Alliances are formed, past agreements forgotten, friends betrayed."

"Remember Greeley's famous tapes?" Morrow asked.

The Chicago novelist had included, in the materials he bequeathed to the Rosary College archives, audiocassettes he had recorded while in Rome, sketching the scenario for a conclave that would put on the throne of Peter someone worthy of Andrew's respect. He had been enormously embarrassed when they were made public, insisting such materials were meant to be embargoed. Be that as it may, perhaps because of a fulsome dinner, Greeley had written with a novelist's flair of a conclave that had many of the aspects of Chicago politics. Indeed it was Cardinal Bernardin, momentarily in Greeley's good graces, who was to be the recipient of the manipulations Greeley imagined.

"Greeley!" Bailey dismissed the man as an irrelevancy.

"What was interesting about it was his assumption that it would be people outside the conclave who would exercise decisive influence on it."

"Bosh."

"I don't remember it that well, Jim", Bailey said.

"Neither do I."

"It was eminently forgettable. His friends said he was drunk."

"What did his enemies say?"

"What his friends said. Only they didn't think it excused him."

Morrow wished he hadn't brought it up. But Bailey's attitude toward the conclave was far more cynical than what he could remember of the Greeley tapes. In any case, Bernardin had not become pope, and the clerical novelist was a third of the way into a solo voyage around the world in his thirty-foot sailboat, scheduled to take five years. A month before Benedetto had shown Morrow a Palermo newspaper that had a photograph of the bald but bearded round-the-world voyager at Pantaleria, where he had put in for a few days of repairs.

"What will you do on Thursday?"

"Attend the high Mass in St. Peter's. Pavese wants us in the procession to the Sistine Chapel. He thinks it will have a beneficial effect if we are waiting outside the doors for our fate to be decided."

Bailey approved of that. "You ought to march right in with them."

Frawley got off on some of the more historic conclaves, mentioning inevitably the one held in Viterbo.

"Pavese means to blow the roof off the Sistine Chapel", Bailey said.

"We'll see."

Lannan's tone was the wary one of a man who has known the ups and downs of church politics. The equivalent of the fat lady singing was the puff of white smoke rising from the chimney of the Sistine Chapel. Anything might happen between now and then, and any understandings Lannan had could be affected if ignoring them could influence in a decisive way the selection of the new pope.

"Will Monsignor Wales be with you in the conclave?"

Lannan nodded.

"Cleanse my lips, O Lord, and purify my heart." Reading by bedside lamp, gray dawn at the windows, Thomas Lannan lifted his eyes and looked across the room to the great crucifix above the prie-dieu. If he had more devotion, he would get out of bed and kneel while he prayed.

But it was the recurrence of biblical verses rebuking his ambition that had stopped him, not the fact that he was warm in his bed as he lifted his mind and heart to God. He thought of Gethsemani and the feeling that had possessed him there. If this were a monk's cell he would not be saying his morning prayer solitary in bed. He would be standing in his stall in the unheated chapel, watching his breath form before his face, as if he were encoding the psalms.

Last night he had sat in an armchair in this room, lights off, his mind at once a riot of disconnected images and a blank slate, as if he were incapable of forming the images into a pattern. If that had been his life passing before his eyes, he did not recognize it. What came to him were not the cherished images of the past but others he had suppressed and forgotten that had somehow gotten loose and were determined to destroy his self-esteem. At the Hall, despite his string of triumphs, he remembered a time in his second year when he had in desperation cheated on a Latin exam. He had led the class in Latin, but when an exam loomed for which he was unprepared, he created a crib and used it; and no one ever suspected him of cheating. The performance was just the one he would have brought off if he had indeed studied.

When he was seventeen, out on a walk once with Morrow and Bailey, they stopped at a miserable gas station in the middle of nowhere, at an intersection where few cars passed. The driveway was packed dirt lined by dirty weeds, the single pump even then was ancient, and the building under the dilapidated overhang seemed deserted. They stopped because Frank needed to find a bathroom. Otherwise he threatened to do it in the middle of the road. They had approached the station laughing, mocking their friend, yet sympathizing with him. Frank pushed on the door of the station, and it opened to the frantic, feeble barking of a dog, but before he could pull it shut, a human voice was heard, shushing the dog and telling them to come on in.

Inside dust danced in sunlight weak from forcing its way through dirty windows. A woman was enthroned in a broken-down easy chair, one leg in a cast and propped up before her, her dress riding up her legs in an immodest way of which she was seemingly unaware.

Her name was Agnes, the mangy dog was Billy, her livelihood was this gas station, and she was delighted to have company. They told her they were from the Hall.

"The place across the lake?" One hand hung over her chair and stroked Billy's head as she looked up at them.

"Yes."

"What kind of school is it?"

"A seminary."

"Catholic, ain't it?"

"Yes. Do you have a restroom?"

"Use mine."

The office seemed to be her home as well. There was a hot plate with a battered pan on it. Bailey stepped carefully toward the back.

"Through the bedroom", Agnes said.

"What happened to your leg?"

"Oh, my God, that leg. I broke it, and they took off the cast, and I went and broke it again."

There was a crutch for her to get around on, but she seemed

not to have moved from her chair. Lannan realized that she was wearing a light blue nightie. Was she all alone?

"There's Billy."

There was a cloudy glass case that contained candy bars and cigarettes and cracker jacks, stacked like archeological finds. When Frank came out, they bought some bars and then left.

"God, what a place", Bailey said, looking back. "The toilet didn't flush."

They observed a minute of silence, realizing what he meant. Lannan was surprised at the cruelty with which the three of them had spoken of that woman, seated with a broken leg and an old dog in a gas station that looked abandoned and probably didn't have two customers a day. Later in chapel Lannan accused himself of heartless lack of charity for his feeling toward Agnes. That night in bed, he had an image of her nightie and remembered the glimpse he had bad of her blue-veined inner thighs.

He went back alone, telling himself the good deed meant even more because she was such an unattractive woman, pathetic, repellent, sitting with her dirty dog in the squalor of that station. His knock was not answered immediately. He heard a toilet flush inside. He knocked, and she shouted come in.

She was propped on her crutch, with a pail in her hand, by the door to her bedroom.

"It's you. I wondered why Billy didn't bark. Which one are you?"

"Tom."

"Give me a hand." She held out hers as she maneuvered backward toward her chair, then lowered herself into it. "How about getting that hassock under my leg?"

He lifted her leg and could not keep his eyes from the hem of her nightie. His eyes lifted and met hers.

He did not know how to describe what then happened when he knelt in the confessional the following morning, but he knew he had sinned gravely. Whatever had happened had been Agnes' doing, he should never have let her do such a thing to him. But he couldn't tell the priest he was sorry for what someone else had done. The grate slid open and the profile of Fr. Gersh, who had been a Navy chaplain, came into view. Lannan could have cheered.

"I committed an impure act."

"Once?"

"It was with someone else."

Silence on the other side of the grill. Then, "Another student?"

Lannan did not understand the question. "Agnes."

"I don't want to know her name."

In a rush, Lannan began to tell the priest everything that had happened; it seemed important that he understand, but Gersh stopped him.

"You're sorry?"

"Yes, Father."

"You going to see this girl again?"

"She's a woman."

"Say five Hail Mary's and make a good act of contrition."

Gersh began to recite the formula of absolution, made the sign of the cross, and pushed the grill shut. The penance was no heavier than the usual one Lannan received for peccadillos. He rose from his knees and felt that he was floating when he crossed the crypt and hurried upstairs to the chapel where the morning Mass was already under way.

Why had such a memory come to him now? Had he ever recalled that event before? He did not think so. Yet it had emerged from the past as he sat in Rome waiting to see if he would be acknowledged to be a prince of the Catholic Church and thus one of the electors of the new pope.

He had never again been tempted to sins against the flesh until the blonde Parente got into such a state about. Until then, Agnes had fulfilled the moral role of making even the thought of sex repugnant to him. He associated it with that dreadful woman and her arthritic old dog, sitting in squalor like a spider in its web, waiting for a victim to arrive. The memory came again in the gray dawn. He offered a prayer for Agnes, presumably now among the dead if not the faithful departed, but his heart was not in it. She had become a symbol of wickedness, of evil, one of the grotesque figures that had challenged Virgil and Dante as they went down into hell. Agnes represented the perpetual possibility of the deed done wholly out of character, in circumstances so surprising, one's guard was down. There could be no other Agnes in his life, but he could fall from grace in a moment without the help of God. Was that the meaning of the memory? At the moment it drove out thoughts of Karen, dead now, and her mother too whose letter had brought Maureen to his office.

He reviewed his conduct since receiving the news of his nomination from Fr. Joachim at Gethsemani. Those weeks had been a time of raw ambition, of wanting something desperately, out of motives he did not even want to scrutinize, only to realize that it might be taken from him. Or be postponed until there was a new pope. But a new pope might decide to make a new list. If the conclave that elected him failed to seat the twenty nominees for cardinal, it would be because their nominations had been rendered void because the Pope who made them but had not had time to raise them to their new dignity. The thought that this prize might be snatched from him roused in him a spirit that rejected even the possibility of that happening. He would not let it happen. He would... Thomas Lannan realized that he was possessed of the spirit that permitted crimes to be committed. He could believe that he would harm greatly, even kill, anyone who deprived him of this one crowning honor of his clerical life.

His eyes had been fixed on the figure of the crucified Christ but had lost their focus. Now the bowed, crowned head, the cruelly extended arms, the nails driven through palms and joined feet, pierced his soul. He felt the defiant mood depart. He threw back the covers and crossed to the prie-dieu and knelt. *Domine non sum dignus*, he prayed, and he meant it. He was not worthy to be a Christian let alone a priest. But he was an archbishop who had come to regard his office as an achievement, as a deserved reward, as his due. *Lord have mercy on me a sinner.*

He might have been whispering the words through a grill into the ear of Fr. Gersh.

4

Gene leaned toward her and said in a rehearsed tone, "I love you."

Janet couldn't believe it and didn't know what to reply. She loved him too, in a way. He was fun to be with, and these days in Rome had been great, but he had taken off his glasses and was staring at her with large unfocused eyes.

"Of course you do."

"Janet, I'm serious."

"I demand no less of cousins who tell me they love me."

He looked away and scraped his lower lip with his teeth. "We've had so much fun here in Rome."

"And the best is yet to be."

He turned to her, eyes moist and eager.

"Tomorrow you march into the Vatican with Archbishop Lannan and get to be one of a handful of witnesses to the election of a new pope."

"Do you think I care?"

"I do. Everybody does. Well, nearly everybody. Has Lannan's status as an elector been settled?"

"He still doesn't know whether or not he's a cardinal."

"What do you think?"

He put on his glasses. "I'm not sure. Both sides have very persuasive arguments. The negative argument looks stronger, but maybe because it threatens us."

Us. Him and the archbishop. Janet felt that she was going to escape this amazing turn of events after all.

"Even to be there when the squabble goes on will be exciting."

"Actually I can live with either verdict. But being shut out would destroy Tommy's self-esteem. He left home a cardinal-designate, and if he has to return an also-ran, well..." Gene smiled slightly at the prospect of his boss' embarrassment. It was what had drawn the two of them together: a contempt for their bosses that they had not had to express.

He took her hand. "Janet."

She put her free hand over his and gave it a pat. "You've been a sweetheart, showing me around, neglecting your duties, but now it's back to work for both of us."

"Is that all it meant to you?"

"It meant more to me than it did to you."

"I doubt that."

" 'Doubt that the stars are fire, doubt truth to be a liar, but never doubt I love.' "

He was confused, as she meant him to be. Was she encouraging him or giving him the kebosh?

"You know what I like to think, my darling Monsignor?"

"What?"

"That our common relatives are amused that we have come to know one another and get along so well together."

And so it went for half an hour more, as she weaned him from the mood that had prompted his declaration of love. Janet realized that she had encouraged his feelings, largely because she felt safe in trying to. Surely a priest, a monsignor, her cousin at whatever remove, would not succumb to the blandishments of a hardened political gofer. The perspective of Rome had enabled her to see what her status was. She was little more than one of the eager college kids who volunteer and are given all the menial tasks in a campaign, loving every minute of it. But after the campaign, they return to real life, whereas she had hung on and at 31 was doing essentially what she had done at twenty-four. And how expendable she was. Any cutie just out of college could move into her office and do what she did. Would she even be missed? To ask the question was to know the sad answer.

So these days in Rome had been a harmless testing of an alternative. She would put herself in harm's way, get serious about a man, think of marriage and a normal life. That would involve what she and Wales had done, running about a romantic locale, attending the art fair in the Via Marguta, spending an afternoon in the Baths of Caracalla and a whole wonderful day at Tivoli. And food food food. She had never eaten so much in her life. And she had flirted with Wales as the stand-in for her imaginary lover. She had given him two choices. To slap her or to fall in love. He had fallen in love so now she had to slap him. It was no part of her plans to enter into a quasi-incestuous clerical romance.

"I told myself I would leave the priesthood, and we would stay right here..."

He looked at her with what she would have described as cow eyes, except for the gender confusion.

"But the priesthood wouldn't leave you, would it?"

He turned away. "No."

"So this is all off the record, okay?"

She let him take her hand. "Aren't you going to kiss me?"

She tilted her face to his lips, then turned the other cheek

332

like a good Christian. In her room, with the door locked, she threw herself on the bed, not knowing whether to laugh or cry. In the end she cried.

5

During the last conclave, Pavese had been chaplain to his predecessor as cardinal archbishop of Milan. Now he was here in his own right, as an elector, as one who had widely been described as *papabile.* But such speculation was carried on in the secular press. Now they were together in the Sistine Chapel, temporarily remodeled for the purpose. Worldly calculations had been left outside; here it was the Spirit who would move among them and illumine them as to the choice they would make. Pavese, seated in the third throne from the front, in the row that stretched from the gospel side of the altar, lifted his eyes to Michelangelo's Last Judgment, which would witness the judgments they would make here.

On the earlier occasion, at this point, Pavese had withdrawn to leave the cardinals to their awesome task. He had begun his vigil by reciting the full fifteen decades of the Rosary. His piety, despite his Lombard origins, had been southern in its need for emotion. The Ignatian Spiritual Exercises had never appealed to him, no matter the urging of his predecessor, a Jesuit. Pavese found the Exercises too cerebral, too finely calibrated, lacking in spontaneity. He responded to the style of St. Grignion Marie de Montfort, whose doctrine of true devotion to the Blessed Virgin had risen in favor with the simple faithful as it fell off the radar screen of intellectuals, but Marian devotion in general had suffered in recent years. Pavese thought of himself as a chevalier in Our Lady's service, her knight errant, burning with a true and chaste love.

333

Had high office changed him? He could not deny it. An archbishop has less control over his life than the lowliest curate. Most of his time was spoken for without consultation. What would have been the point in consulting him? He had to confirm, meet with his priests, visit the parishes of the diocese, oversee the many and varied works under his jurisdiction. And raise money. There was little time left for himself. He felt cast in a huge ceremonial pageant, the chief figure as often as not, performing a function as archbishop, not personally, but just as his predecessors had and as his successors would.

If a diocese made so total a claim upon one, what must be said of the Holy See? The popes had been called prisoners of the Vatican since Pius IX shut out the new Italian state that had treated the Church so badly. That political isolation was long a thing of the past, but still the pope was a prisoner. Global travel only underscored the rigid routine of the papal day when he was in the Vatican or at Castel Gandolpho, ostensibly on vacation. The audiences went on, the *ad limina* visits, the reports from the prefects of the various congregations, memos from the secretary of state. Yet the Pope was reputed to be a saint, ever recollected, even in the center of vast crowds. Pavese had studied films of the Pope saying Mass in various stadiums and basilicas and sports parks around the world, and it seemed clear that no Curé d'Ars saying a solitary Mass at five in the morning could concentrate more on the sacred deed he was performing.

Cardinal Pavese closed his eyes, but before he could pray a hand was laid on his arm. It was Cardinal Seidl.

"I will introduce the resolution immediately after the opening prayer."

Pavese nodded but said nothing. He was conscious that everything he said or did now could become a matter of history.

"It may be a tie."

Pavese widened his eyes. "Then what?"

"I would argue that there is no majority against and that should suffice..."

Cardinal Seidl appeared to have convinced himself of this. Pavese was far more interested in the principal vote for which they had gathered.

"How do things look after that?"

Seidl squeezed his arm. "Not everyone opposed to the Twenty is for Benedetto."

Pavese cut him off with a smile. Seidl was too indiscreet to be a comfortable ally.

Old Llano, dean of the College of Cardinals, created Cardinal by Paul VI, one of only three here who had been Fathers of the Second Vatican Council, rose slowly to his feet; and then the chapel filled with the noise of nearly a hundred cardinals following suit.

"*In nomine patris et filii et spiritus sancti.*"

"*Amen.*"

"*Veni creator spiritus...*", Llano intoned in an unsure voice, and then the chapel filled with the recitation of the hymn to the Holy Spirit, asking his guidance of their doings. Llano was too old to vote, of course, but all cardinals were welcome to the conclave, and several other ancient men were among them. Llano's visage had grown more and more birdlike with the years. Perhaps that was an appropriate metamorphosis for a cardinal.

There was a rustling noise as they sat after the opening prayer. Seidl remained on his feet. "*Volo quandam quaestionem ponere, fratres dilectisimi in Christo.*"

More than a quarter reached for headsets, unable to follow Seidl's Latin—or anyone else's, for that matter. There had been bishops at Vatican II who had a *peritus* to translate for them, and this all but reduced them to kibitzers rather than participants. No wonder the *periti* had come to think of the Council as theirs. One of the *mots* in Morrow's history was that the *experiti* had become the postconciliar *experts* on what the Council really meant.

Seidl's motion to his beloved brothers in Christ was that they seat as electors in this conclave the twenty cardinals named by the late Holy Father.

The debate that followed was conducted with such unction and tact—the assembly addressed as brothers in Christ, dearest ones, excellent and eminent fathers, etc.—that an observer might have missed the underlying inflexibility of the two sides. Two-and-a-half hours went by before Pavese asked to speak.

"I shall vote against the proposal of our esteemed and beloved brother, Cardinal Seidl. The situation, as has been said many times, is without precedent. None of the superb and subtle arguments on its behalf seems to justify our setting a precedent in so important a matter. I know Cardinal Seidl will understand how, quite independently of the merits of his proposal and the many persuasive arguments that have been made on its behalf, one may still vote no."

He resumed his seat again with dignity, and he could feel the response of the others. His allies had expected this announcement; his enemies were surprised and suddenly drained of animosity.

The vote was taken in a way that was a rehearsal for those to come. One at a time, they approached the altar, genuflected, and mounted the steps to the altar on which a golden chalice awaited the card on which they had written *placet* or *non placet*. The cardinal dean then took the chalice to a table placed midway between the rows of thrones and counted the ballots with great deliberation. By a two-thirds vote it was decided not to include the Twenty in the proceedings of the conclave.

There followed a recess during which aging bladders were drained, espresso drunk, and, in the case of Llano, a nap taken.

But then he had fallen asleep twice during the debate over the Twenty.

When Pavese emerged from the *gabinetto*, Benedetto about to enter, stepped aside to let him pass. Pavese bowed to the cardinal secretary of state.

"A noble speech", Benedetto murmured.

"I hope the late Holy Father will think we did the right thing."

"We had no choice", Benedetto said. He added in a purring tone, "As you so eloquently put it."

It was of course foolish to think that so obvious a ruse could have caught Cardinal Benedetto by surprise. But Pavese had put himself on the successful side of the vote and earned, he was sure, credit with many who might hitherto have regarded him as too much the candidate of the secular media. Benedetto might pardonably think that the papacy was owed him. He had labored in the Vatican for two popes, had been as close a confidant as the late Pope had, his Irish secretary aside. Riley was fluent in Polish and could talk with the Pope without fear of being overheard. Indeed, the Irish monsignor adopted the gestures and facial expressions of the pontiff as he spoke his language and there were times when he seemed to be a mimic even when in conversation with the Holy Father. Riley had gone into deep and genuine mourning on the death of the Pope, refusing to talk to the journalists eager to get a word picture of the Pope's last hours. The Irishman was too wise to succumb to that, even if he were not so truly weighed down by the death of a man he had admired and loved. The sensational stories about the death of John Paul I made it clear that there was nothing the secular media would stop at now. Speculation about poisoning had been engaged in almost matter-of-factly, with no thought to the reputations of those involved.

The smell of cooking veal met Cardinal Pavese as he returned down the great, wide corridor toward the chapel. He was starved, hungry without having realized it. A salad, some pasta, a *coteletto milanese*, with a good red wine, seemed the definition of contentment now. He stopped, arrested by the thought that one among them would have his meals in the Vatican for the rest of his life, would never return whence he had come, leaving all unfinished business to the one who would come after him. But so the Holy Father had left things for his successor, things that Benedetto at least would be well aware of.

The first act of the new pope should be to induct the excluded twenty into the College of Cardinals. Any discontent at being excluded from the conclave would thus be wiped away with a single gesture. How pleasant it would be to be the one who made that gesture.

After they reconvened, Llano, refreshed from his nap, began an endless talk on the solemn obligation that sat on the shoulders of the College.

"I myself will not vote. Therefore I know my words will be taken as wholly disinterested. Many Italians have found these last years difficult. They have felt that something that was theirs by right had been taken from them, that it was temporarily in alien hands. I confess that I myself often felt the same way. How wrong we were. The late Holy Father has exhibited to the world that the papacy as well as the Church is international, global. Like Peter himself, he came to Rome from a far place, and it was here that he died. We have been freed once and for all from the belief that the pope must be an Italian."

There was restless stirring among the Italians. Llano might say that he shared their feelings, but how could he? More mystifying still was the present point of his remarks. No non-Italian was being taken seriously by anyone as a candidate. Benedetto and Pavese were by common consent the only serious possibilities. But Llano was far from through.

"One thing however has not changed, and that is the wisdom of choosing someone whose experience has been close to the throne of Peter, one for whom the path ahead will be familiar. Many will remember the difficulty the late Pope had in fitting into the Vatican. Those difficult first months were the basis for the feeling among Italians I have already mentioned."

Pavese's backers began to murmur at this obvious plea for Benedetto, but it was Benedetto who begged to interrupt the esteemed and excellent Cardinal Llano.

"I feel it only just to say that stories of the late Pope's difficulties in accustoming himself to his duties have been largely due to the imagination of secular journalists, spurred perhaps by some discontented lower-level employees among whom a rumor had spread that the Holy Father intended to shut down the commissary, thus forcing them to shop in the city and pay full price for their purchases. There was no truth to that, of course, but to the best of my knowledge that is the only basis in fact for the discontent mentioned. I may add that a case could be made that experience here may make a man less likely to look at the Church with fresh eyes. There are many, as we know, who have spent the years of this papacy in all but open dissent. However ungrounded their dissent is, it would perhaps continue into the next papacy if the impression were created that no real change at all had taken place."

The chapel erupted into babel as a dozen began to speak at once. Pavese sat back in his throne, wondering what the real point of Benedetto's words had been. He had galvanized his supporters, all of whom wanted recognition so that they could refute what their champion had said. Seidl, seated across the aisle, caught Pavese's eye and shrugged. Pavese did not acknowledge him. In the great mural over the altar, Satan and his minions were spearing the damned into the flames. Pavese's hopes seemed similarly doomed by Benedetto's speech. A candidate who exhibited reluctance to be elected, who seemed actively to be promoting his rival's cause, would exercise a powerful fascination on the electors. Thus it was that in religious orders the one who shunned office, who sought obscurity as a roue pursues pleasure, was thrust into office as prior, abbot, superior general. The same rule applied here. He who showed signs of wanting to be pope would die a cardinal.

The animated reaction to what Benedetto had said went on, while Pavese pondered what response it might require of him. It was imperative that he speak before they adjourned for the day. To let the sun go down on Benedetto's apparent self-sacrifice would make any response in the morning seem the product of night-long pondering. This time he caught Seidl's eye and nodded. The voices continued around him, but cardinals had turned from their microphones and spoke without benefit of amplification. Pavese rose and stepped close to his microphone.

"Dearest brothers in Jesus Christ", he said, and his voice came back to him from the walls and ceiling of the chapel. "Dearest brothers in Jesus Christ."

The voices began to die away, unable to compete with his, however deliberately and calmly he spoke.

"Brothers, we have had a long day. We have already made one momentous decision; we have listened to wise words. But we have not come here to debate or to spend time on lesser matters. We are here to select the next Vicar of Christ on earth. Let us not have prolonged and unnecessarily wearying sessions. It is with that in mind that I put before you as our next Holy Father the secretary of state, Cardinal Giancarlo Benedetto, and ask that voting begin immediately."

Silence. Utter silence. And then pandemonium. Out of the chaos emerged a consensus. They would adjourn for the day and begin in the morning in a more orderly way.

"The first order of business", Cardinal Llano announced,

"will be the selection of a cardinal secretary of the conclave. We must proceed in order."

The discussion and vote on the twenty had got them off on the wrong procedural foot. They had neglected the traditions of the past, though they were free to follow them or not. Until Benedetto had spoken, and then Pavese, ordinary deference and civility had sufficed, but now, the proceedings having been thoroughly confused by the two leading candidates, it seemed best to retire for dinner and begin anew in the morning.

After Benediction of the Blessed Sacrament, they filed out of the chapel. Outside the doors, they broke up and milled around. Cardinal Benedetto smiled enigmatically at Cardinal Pavese and gave him a little bow. After a second, Pavese lifted a hand, but held it motionless. He had thought better of giving his brother cardinal a blessing, fearful that it might be taken as a tad too papal.

6

When Bailey heard that the Twenty had been excluded from the conclave he couldn't believe it. And he couldn't believe Lannan was taking it as philosophically as he pretended.

"What reason did they give you?"

"Reason? None."

"And you're just taking it? Good God, Tom, you're as much of a cardinal as any of them."

Lannan just looked at him.

"I mean it. You're Thomas Cardinal Lannan, damn it, and they can't undo that."

"There are perfectly good reasons against including the Twenty."

"What? That it never happened before?"

"That's part of it, of course. It's a legal matter, Frank; you know that. Lawyers don't deal with the unique. Everything has to fall under a category."

"So you're on the outside looking in."

"Like you."

"Have you talked to any others of the Twenty?"

"I don't know any of them. It's unclear how many are actually in Rome. Only seven showed up for the Mass in St. Peter's."

Frank took out a box of cigarettes and flipped open the lid. He inspected its contents before extracting a filtered cigarette. After an unsuccessful search of his pockets, he asked Lannan if there was anything like a match in the Villa Stritch. Lannan had been watching his friend with fascination.

"I thought everyone had quit smoking."

"I have taken it up again. When in Rome, and all that. Cigarettes are inexpensive here, not being taxed to finance their cure, and I breathe secondary smoke in the press room anyway. Care for one?"

"I don't even remember enjoying them."

Frank shrugged. He had found a packet of cerini, miniature waxed matches, that flared into flame like fire hazards. Soon he was smoking contentedly.

"Pavese must have lost the first round. Unless of course he's playing another game."

"Such things never go as planned. They're not the result of planning."

Frank was delighted to find that blowing smoke rings was a skill that, like riding a bicycle, simply awaited reactivation. "*Ubi vult spirat?*" he asked, releasing an unringed stream of smoke.

Lannan nodded. It was convenient to invoke the Holy Spirit when things were going your way; when they were not, it was best to lend God a hand. Frank spoke the same language and thought the same thoughts as Lannan, but for Frank they had become merely the lingo of believers. Did he still literally believe that a Mighty Being underwrote the universe and brooded over the megabillion happenings in the world of nature as well as the countless comings and goings of each and every human being on earth, a speck in a galaxy lost among who knew how many galaxies in a universe exploding outward toward some cosmic Armageddon? It was best to think of the patois of his faith as a *façon de parler.* It need not be literally true in order to play its useful and consoling functions. Once Frank would have called his present state a loss of faith. Now he thought of it as a mature and critical way of going on being a Christian in a world where even the memory of it would be lost before long.

Why did he continue to be caught up in the inner workings of a Church defined by what he knew to be a dying belief? To dig he was not able, to beg he was ashamed. He had been at it too long to set it aside, and for what? Becoming a stock broker? An insurance salesman? A counselor? How many former priests had made careers guiding the harried and neurotic, fitting them for this world, rather than preparing them for the next?

"Did you ever think of leaving, Tom?"

"Did you?"

"Never. It would have been like conceding the whole thing to my enemies."

"Enemies like me?"

Frank managed not to laugh, but released a stream of smoke. They sat on the veranda in dying winter sunlight, the leaves above them rattling in the wind. Blowing smoke rings lost its interest when they were so quickly dissipated. Did Tom Lannan fancy that he was one of the stalwarts, a member of the late Pope's legions, intent on clamping down on every effort to open things up and make the Church what John XXIII had envisaged? Lannan was what the Marxists used to call a useful idiot, aiding the revolution without quite realizing it. As president of the NCCB, Lannan like his predecessors had put distance between himself and conservatives. It would have been worth his career to be praised in the *Wanderer* or have it known that he subscribed to *Catholic Dossier* or read with pleasure the *Fellowship of Catholic Scholars Quarterly*. Did Lannan know that the Fellowship at a recent meeting had given him their Nicodemus Award, reserved for bishops who whispered their support while keeping Monsignor Kelly's army defanged and without influence in the NCCB and USCC?

Over the years, it had been Charlie Curran, Richard McBrien, and Dick McCormick who had been invited to speak at bishops' meetings, while Grisez and Finnis and Fessio and the now Most Reverend Bill Smith had not gotten the time of day. Lannan had continued this tradition as president of the NCCB. It was what gave Frank hope that, as cardinal, better still as elector of the next pope, Lannan could be trusted. Yet here he sat on a Roman evening being philosophical about the fact that Pavese had given him the shaft and not gone to the wall to insure that the Twenty would be seated in the conclave. That did not bode well for the outcome, but if Lannan was concerned he sure as hell didn't show it.

"Why would he betray me, Frank?"

"To further his own chances."

"So what's your complaint? If I was kept out of the conclave in order to insure that Pavese would be elected, the desired result is had, and you should rejoice."

Good point. And self-effacingly made. Frank thought about it. He liked it. It made sense, political sense. It was the kind of maneuvering that the Holy Spirit needed in order to do his stuff. So let Pavese wheel and deal and end up as pope and then they could begin.

"Maybe I will have one of those", Lannan said and reached for the box of cigarettes. Bailey leaned forward and lit it for him. A puff of white smoke rose gently but then was blown away by the wind. "Have you seen Maureen much while you've been here?"

Frank frowned. "I've been meaning to call her."

"Why don't we call her?"

"Now?"

"We're both free if she is, right?"

But Maureen had already gone out for the evening. Irrationally, Thomas Lannan felt twice rejected.

7

A thin spiral of smoke began to appear from the chimney emerging from the Sistine Chapel, and a murmur went up from the waiting crowd as the smoke thickened and its color became unmistakable.

"*Bianco! Bianco!*" cried the crowd. "*Abbiamo un Papa!*"

In the tradition of conclaves, the ballots were burned in the little stove from which the great chimney rose toward the ceiling: wet straw was added to produce dark smoke, to signify an inconclusive result of a vote; white smoke announced that an election had indeed taken place. And it was indeed white smoke that now lifted into the Roman air. A new Pope had been chosen. Shortly he would appear on the balcony overlooking the square, vested as the pontiff, and offer his first blessing *urbi et orbi* to the ecstatic crowd filling the square.

The crowd grew as the news spread. Ben Trovato had called Bailey at the number he had left with him and now, with the Timesman, was shouldering his way through the mob, following his photographer, who used his equipment as a battering ram to clear their passage. Trovato's eyes were raised to the balcony as they pressed toward it. These were moments not to be missed. This was why he had spent these weeks in Rome. No wonder Bailey had unceremoniously slammed down the phone as soon as he heard the news. It should not take him long to get here from the Columbus Hotel. If the grumpy cleric missed any of this, he would probably blame his fellow journalists.

Fellow journalists. An odd way to think of Frank Bailey, but then he was an odd priest. You could talk with him man to man, but if Trovato was lucky enough to have a priest at his bedside when he died, he sure as hell wouldn't want it to be Bailey. Frank's attitude toward the Vatican and the election was the most cynical in the press room. Trovato had seen the surprise in the Timesman.

"Is he still a priest?"

"As far as I know."

"He certainly doesn't sound like one."

"He tries not to."

"Why?"

"Good question."

The Timesman was caught up in the enthusiasm of the crowd they elbowed through. Trovato heard the name of Pavese and turned to see who had spoken the name of the cardinal archbishop of Milan. Part of the excitement was that they would not know who the Pope was until he appeared on that balcony. Would it be Pavese? Trovato realized that the excitement would diminish once they knew, the suspense would be gone, and they would all be guessing what the new man would do.

Trovato had two different stories 95 percent written: one swung around Benedetto, the other around Pavese. They were already faxed off to New York, and his additions would go off minutes after the new Pope had made his appearance. The computer swinging over Trovato's shoulder had a cellular phone fax, and he could communicate with New York instantaneously. It was an odd contrast, that electronic immediacy and a puff of smoke as signal.

"This is fine", Trovato shouted, stopping the photographer.

"Aren't we going inside?"

"No, no. He'll come out up there." He showed Norm the balcony. Good God, if they hadn't stuck together Norman would have been inside the basilica and missed the whole thing.

Now the waiting began, but a different kind of waiting than had characterized the past weeks and then the past days when the cardinals were in conclave. In ten minutes, twenty, a halfhour, hardly more, the new Pope would be presented to the world. An expectancy came over the crowd that did not silence it but altered the sound arising from it.

"Who'll it be?" the Timesman asked, his eyes darting from Trovato to the balcony and back again.

"People are saying Pavese."

"From Milan?"

"From Milan."

"Do they know?"

"They know what we know. Nothing. They're guessing. What has anyone been doing since the old guy died but guessing who would be next?" Trovato spoke with impatience. There was something ghoulish in the immediate shift of attention to the late Pope's successor.

Trovato had found in the Pope a resemblance to his father, who had been pushing fifty when Ben was born and lived to an old age, as old as other kids' grandfathers. Every time he saw the Pope, Ben thought of his father and what his father would think of what he had become: divorced from Bernice, remarried to Judy whose career kept them apart so much that they

347

got together as furtive lovers rather than husband and wife. Of course, in his heart of hearts, Ben did not think of them as husband and wife. His father wouldn't have. And neither would the dead Pope. Would the new Pope be someone who would say, "What the hell, let bygones be bygones. You got tired of Bernice. It happens. Now you got Judy. Enjoy, for God's sake. Tomorrow we're dead." It was not a judgment Ben expected. It was not one he wanted either. The trouble with guys like Bailey was they didn't understand how important the rocklike Church was even to those who bitched about it all the time.

Something rippled through the crowd, and there was a great intake of breath. On the balcony above, several men had appeared, to drape a banner over the rail. Another man brought out an old-fashioned microphone on its stand and placed it close to the railing. Again the balcony was empty. An impatience began to move across the great piazza like wind through a field, and then a cry went up, tentative and expectant at first. A prelate had appeared and then another, cardinals, and one of them flicked the microphone and roared into it.

"*Annuntio vobis gaudium magnum. Habemus papam! Habemus papam!*"

The roar that went up lifted the hair on Trovato's head, and he saw that Norm was hollering as loud as anyone. The kid was a Southern Baptist, and here he was cheering a new pope.

And then a figure in a white cassock stepped to the microphone, his arms outspread, and the volume of the cheering went up several notches.

"Who is it?" the Timesman cried. "Which one is it?"

But the answer was to be heard all around them. Giancarlo. Giancarlo.

"Benedetto. They've elected Benedetto."

PART SIX

CHAPTER ONE

I

The day after the election, the Honorable James Morrow went down to his waiting car, accompanied by Dennis McHugh, who has having trouble retaining his usual aplomb. From other embassies other ambassadors would be starting out on the same official visit. Did his counterparts feel a similar sense of being involved in an event of historic moment? What they had gossiped about for years had happened, and now there would be a new pope to talk about.

"This is a great thing to have happen on your watch, sir", he had said earlier.

And on McHugh's, of course. His aide had never been in Rome for such a dramatic event in the history of the Church. The line of popes stretching back to St. Peter numbered 270 in an unbroken line, though there have been moments when all seemed confusion and it was unclear who precisely, among several claimants and rival popes, the successor of St. Peter was.

But out of confusion had always come clarity as to who was the Vicar of Christ on earth.

And now there was Giancarlo Benedetto, native of Sicily, who had taken the name John Paul III. The choice of title was widely understood as being prompted by gratitude and admiration for his two predecessors, but some saw sinister implications. McHugh had secured a video of the interview with Frank Bailey in Rome but broadcast in New York.

"A clear victory for the old guard", Frank pontificated. "Nothing will change. That's the message of this managed election of John Paul III." Frank pronounced the title almost angrily, through gritted teeth.

"What changes won't come about?"

Frank rattled off what had long been his standard account of the post-Vatican II Church, a suite of clichés all too familiar to Morrow, who had given this viewpoint more than its due in *The Decline and Fall of the Catholic Church in the United States*. Hennessy and Dolan had adopted that viewpoint with more and less subtlety, while Gleason and O'Connell strove for historical objectivity. Morrow had given equal space to those who gloried in the title of traditional and orthodox, if not always in the label conservative. His professional colleagues and friends would know where his own choice lay, but he had set out to write a fair and evenhanded book and prided himself that he had accomplished it. The initial criticism from both sides had been brisk, but it was followed in the end by the grudging concession that he had indeed provided a balanced picture even if what the events pictured tilted now toward one side now toward the other.

Jim Morrow understood what Frank Bailey was saying, and it gave him satisfaction to know that it was true. Pavese had encouraged the belief that with him as their pope those who had felt they were wandering in the wilderness during the previous papacy would finally come into their own. No longer would the Church's moral teachings stand athwart the spirit of the times. The Church must be in dialogue with the contemporary mind, which was the product of so many new developments, many of them having occurred since Vatican II, in the various cultures, in science and technology, in the exploration of space; and the Church must learn as well as guide. Was it really possible, he asked rhetorically, that so many, both inside and outside the Church, were wrong in questioning a moral teaching whose reiteration in recent years had caused so much pain?

By such remarks Pavese had given it to be understood that a new day was dawning. As pope, he would be reasonable. He would take seriously the practices of contemporary society and attend to the pain of those who did not want their rejection of a few moral rules to exclude them from communion with the Church. Benedetto, on the other hand, never passed up a chance to praise *Veritatis splendor*, the book-length encyclical in which the Pope had laid out the moral vision of Christianity, had weighed and found wanting the methods employed by moral theologians who rejected Church teaching, and restated the essential connection between professing to be Catholic and living a Catholic life. Christian morality was not negotiable.

"Why is it always about sex, Jim?" Frank Bailey had asked during an interview with Morrow in preparation for the book.

"It?"

"Magisterial documents."

"They're not."

"That isn't the impression people have."

"Frank, there are two connected reasons for that. Our age is obsessed with sex, so of course papal statements drawing attention to the chaos and despair this obsession brings about are taken to be the only important ones. It's not as if the Pope had come out against all the fun we're supposedly having. The results are anything but fun."

"He should talk more about love."

"I can just see the headline: 'Pope Loves Love'."

"I'm serious."

"I can tell by your laughter."

The second reason was that dissenters like Bailey had set the tone for the secular press' view of the Vatican. Between the end of the Council in 1965 and 1968, when *Humanae vitae* appeared, contraception had been portrayed as the guarantee of a happy marriage. Reports of the papal committee studying the matter gave credence to the view that contraception would be judged moral. When Paul VI repeated the age-old ban on contraception, people like Bailey were out on a limb. They had staked their reputations on a change that did not happen. Rather than crawl back, they had sawed away at the limb, and when they fell, they accused the Pope of not being part of the tree. The slogan that the Pope was obsessed with sex originated with them, and they had taken comfort from Pavese's delphic remarks.

Benedetto on the other hand promised continuity, no rocking of the barque of Peter, staying the course that had been set by the previous pontiff, his dear friend.

Morrow looked up. Luigi had taken a road that swept behind the Vatican and turned into a street that brought them to the entrance to the museums. On an ordinary day, long lines of tourists would be streaming in and out these doors, but today they gave entree only to the diplomats assigned to the Vatican. In the initial ceremonies introducing the new Pope, establishing the validity of his election and thus of his coming rule, it was only fitting that the representatives of the nations be there.

They were given an aperitif in the great hall where they waited. Hearth, the British ambassador, sidled up to Morrow.

"You have come to Rome at a timely moment, Mr. Ambassador." Hearth's face looked like the white cliffs of Dover, craggy and pale and topped with a dark fringe.

"This is indeed historic."

Hearth dropped his voice. "It will be a short reign. Benedetto is an old man."

"Surely not old."

"It is said that it was health as much as anything else that lay behind his oft-stated desire to retire."

"I hadn't heard that."

"That desire has not left him, poor man. You can take the boy out of Sicily, but you cannot take Sicily out of the boy. Now he will long in vain for the southern sun, the family vineyards, and solitude perhaps."

It was indeed a melancholy thought that none of that would now be within Benedetto's grasp. Several times in recent years there had been talk of a pope's resigning. Paul VI had been said to be thinking of it after he passed 75; the enemies of the late Pope had talked of it in the hope that it would happen; but the fact was that no pope since Gregory XIII in 1415 had retired. The vast likelihood was that Benedetto, Pope John Paul III, would end his days as his predecessor had, a prisoner of the Vatican, certainly a prisoner of the papacy. Once a new pope could cry, "God has given us the papacy, so let us enjoy it." No one could think of the prospect before Benedetto as one of enjoyment.

Morrow's own duties sat lightly upon him, but even so the contrast between his present life and that spent at his cottage on Powderhorn Lake in Michigan was dramatic. Every morning now McHugh handed him a sheet on which were typed his appointments and doings of the day. Busy people might find it undemanding, but Morrow had spent his life as his own taskmaster, his arduous schedule of research and writing self-imposed, so that he could always in principle give himself permission to take a day off. He seldom had, of course, but nonetheless the psychological difference was there. At the lake, he had just been learning the knack of doing nothing, of accepting a life that held no more great projects, deadlines, publication dates. His major work was done. He would go on writing, of course, but it would be occasional stuff, the flotsam and jetsam of a life of study, by-blows of research already done. He could have gone on the lecture circuit; he could have accepted invitations to visit other universities for shorter or longer periods, but he had turned his face against all that. His intention had been to sit in his cottage by the lake and grow old gracefully, far from the madding crowd.

And here he was in Rome at the center of one of the most momentous events of the new century.

Juan Boxidors of Colombia, the corners of his mouth down turned, stood nodding silently after they had exchanged greetings, then said, "How wonderful for a historian to be present here."

Morrow wondered if it was an advantage. Caught up in these events, he lacked perspective on them; his personal experience would inevitably color any interpretation he developed. In writing the history of the Church in his country, he was dealing with people and controversies and developments that were all at some small distance from himself. He had to reconstruct the past in the usual way, via documents. There were few personal memories to contribute their skewed vision of what had happened. Beyond the unfolding events was the question of what it all meant. This is what the critics had chided him for omitting from his history. Of course they were wrong. Interpretation lay in the sequence of treatment, in the events selected for extended documentation, in the judgments of contemporaries he had selected for quotation. What such critics had wanted was a text punctuated with sermons in which he would draw attention to the overall significance of what had been narrated, as well as an essay at the end in which he would have expatiated on the fate of the Church. Nonsense. His title indicated what he thought the significance of the events treated in the book was. No one, after his history appeared, could any longer pretend that the decades since the Council represented an advance or improvement in any significant sense. Institutionally, personally, the postconciliar years were a tragedy. Every honest observer as well as any believing Catholic already knew that. What he provided was the details.

The diplomatic corps formed up and mounted a wide staircase, at the top of which a passage took them into St. Peter's on the level above the porch. Their dean paid his respects to the new Pope, who wore a melancholy, half-apologetic smile, as if he must seem an imposter in his white cassock. But he accepted the congratulations of each in turn, giving Morrow's hand an extra squeeze before tracing the sign of the cross over him.

For the second time in as many days the Pope went out onto the balcony, and the sound from the piazza was so sustained and loud that it might have driven him back inside again. He went to the railing and extended his arms for all the world as if he meant to execute a dive into the sea of the people.

"We have a Pope, we have a Pope" came the chant from below, and soon the ambassadors took it up so that the Holy Father was sandwiched between two choirs of jubilant chanters. He did not speak on this occasion, but simply gave his pontifical blessing, remaining fifteen minutes more as he acknowledged the acclaim, finally coming inside where he seemed to collapse. A chair was brought, and the pontiff sat, breathing great inhalations and audible exhalations of air. Morrow thought the Pope looked gray.

His eyes met Hearth's to find there an I-told-you-so expression.

Ambrose Frawley accompanied Archbishop Lannan on a visit to the new Pope, and Morrow came along at Lannan's insistence, although he had already been at the Vatican some days before with the ambassadorial corps. Rome was overrun with tourists and others anxious to get a look at this new pontiff, and Frawley had welcomed the opportunity to come along.

"You can interpret for me", Lannan said.

"Oh, he speaks English."

"That's what I mean."

Morrow smiled, but Frawley laughed. It was good to see Lannan taking this turn in his personal fate so well. As they went upstairs, Frawley felt that he had never been there before, that all his experience in Rome was suddenly rendered obsolete. With a surprising absence of ceremony, they were ushered into the papal presence. His predecessor had liked to stand when receiving visitors, but John Paul III remained seated. Frawley saw what people meant when they said the man already looked exhausted.

"Ah, Mr. Ambassador", the Pope said, all but ignoring Archbishop Lannan. "I have been demoted since our last conversation. Then I was secretary of state; now I am the servant of the servants of God."

"*Servus servorum Dei*", Lannan said.

"No doubt you historians are already busy seeking to find out what happened in the conclave."

"Why, Your Holiness? It turned out as everyone expected."

"Did it really?" Sadness flickered in the large, dark eyes. He turned to Lannan. "You might have been there with us, Archbishop, if my predecessor had had the courtesy to live a few days longer."

Lannan made a dismissive gesture. There seemed nothing he

could safely say, and Frawley approved the diplomacy of silence. But the Pope's eyes had come to Frawley. No spark of recognition showed in his eyes. Morrow said, "Of course you know Monsignor Frawley, rector of the North American College."

"Ah, a neighbor. Tell me about your college, Monsignor."

If he had imagined this scene, Frawley would have replied with untroubled aplomb, a few statistics, a couple of anecdotes, a short but indelible performance, before stepping out of the spotlight. Absurdly, he was gripped with stage fright and for a moment had trouble remembering what the North American College was. He had been thrown off his stroke by the need for an introduction from a man who had been in Rome only a few months, whereas he...

"I have been rector for eight years, Holiness."

"Ah."

"It is a privilege to be here in Rome, if only temporarily."

"You do not aspire to permanent residence?"

"No!"

The Pope nodded. "No more did I. But some things are taken out of our hands. Perhaps one day you will sit here, Monsignor."

Frawley felt a blush spread over his whole body, rising up his legs, over his torso, shooting out of his collar until his whole face was suffused. My God, he hadn't blushed since he was a boy. But he felt like a boy, let in among the grownups and asked questions he could not find answers to. A moment earlier he had been observing Lannan's performance with a cold and critical eye. Thank God there were no more witnesses than there were. The only one at ease was the layman, Morrow. But then he was the one first addressed by the new pontiff and, when they were about to go, the Pope indicated that he wanted the ambassador to stay.

Outside the audience hall, Aubrey Taylor, the Australian

cardinal who had been named the new secretary of state, looked surprised.

"Where is the third person?"

"In the trinity", Frawley replied, his wits suddenly restored to him. Cardinal Taylor put back his head, pointed his sharp nose at the gaudy ceiling, and barked a laugh.

Lannan said matter-of-factly, "His Holiness asked the ambassador to stay for a minute."

"They became close, he tells me, in the Pope's last days."

The three of them stood there in the hallway for several minutes, and then Taylor suggested they wait for Morrow in his office. Shown to brocade chairs while Taylor stood at his desk, sighing at the piles of paper there, Lannan and Frawley had little to say. It was a transitional scene in a movie. Taylor was clearly distracted by the chores ahead of him. The two Americans left him to his work.

"What did you make of it?" Lannan asked, leaning toward Frawley with a pained smile.

"Purely ceremonial."

"He mentioned that I would have been in the conclave if the Pope had lived longer."

"True enough."

"He thinks of it as past history. He has no intention of renominating me."

"I don't see that at all. He has hardly got the seat warm; he probably hasn't had a clear thought since he was elected. He's running on nervous energy. I thought he looked completely exhausted. I suspect this Pope is not going to try to rival the activities of the old one."

"I'm surprised he even knew who I was."

Frawley felt anew the sting of Morrow's need to introduce him. "I made an ass of myself."

"It's not just for me, Ambrose. I am Washington."

Lannan sounded like a prince in Shakespeare who was the

360

personification of a county or country. France fought England, and England was advised by Norfolk and Rochester.

"Maybe Morrow will bring it up", Frawley said with an edge in his voice.

"Do you think so?" Hope leapt in Lannan's eyes, and he looked pathetically at Frawley.

"What else could they be talking about?"

Lannan saw no irony in the remark. But Frawley, thinking of his own miserable performance during the audience, did not feel superior to his superior.

Cardinal Taylor frowned at his watch and left the room, excusing himself abstractedly.

"He's been in there longer alone than we all were in there together."

"Cardinal Taylor said it. They became friends."

"If it doesn't come up now, he can bring it up later."

Poor Lannan. His pride and ambition had been under serious assault since he had come to Rome. The trip to Milan had seemed to promise a happy outcome, despite the shock of the Pope's death, but Pavese had gone to the wall for the Twenty without success. Why? Frawley was no historian, unless a gossip qualifies as one, but he was determined to find out what had happened in the conclave. If the Twenty had been admitted, Pavese would be pope today. The few newspapers that mentioned the Twenty agreed on that, but there was no indignation expressed. Except of course by Iggie Wynn and Frank Bailey, who were now talking about the stolen election.

"Twenty of the electors were not admitted to the chapel", Wynn piped in his high voice, interviewed on CNN. "I regret to say that the United States was treated very shabbily. Would it be vulgar to mention the Vatican's dependence on American wealth to keep its nose above water? Why was Archbishop Lannan barred from the conclave?"

"I wish he wouldn't say that" was Lannan's reaction, but he

obviously found it a little heady to be the object of a discussion that was beamed around the world.

3

From the balcony Frank Bailey watched Iggie being lowered from his van in his wheelchair onto the sidewalk below Ben Trovato's apartment. Iggie set the chair in motion, executed a few smart 45-degree turns, then headed for the building entrance, whisking out of sight.

"Wynn has arrived", Bailey said, after going back into the apartment.

Tremblay the Timesman was staring at a large-breasted nude over the mantle, an oil with the colors butterknifed on. It had been done by Trovato's first wife, who was now allegedly living with the model.

Trovato went downstairs to help Wynn up. Bailey felt equivocal about his own resentment of this special treatment Wynn demanded and received. After all, the poor guy had to live in that chair and be carted around in a truck. Think how vulnerable he was. A run-down battery and his chair was immobile, an accident to the van and what would happen to him? Except that Wynn seemed to get around well enough with his crutch when he wanted to. Bailey had it from Wynn's driver that the aging gadfly never used the chair except in public.

Wynn, once inside, accepted the help of Trovato and Tremblay to get to the couch, where he plunked down on the center cushion and looked around like a schoolboy.

"Reminds me of meeting at Robert Kaiser's", he said to Frank Bailey.

Kaiser had been the Timesman back during the Council,

cultivating *periti*, dramatizing reports of the Council by making it a battle of liberal against conservative, the future against the past. Frank wondered if Kaiser had believed anything? Later he lost his wife to an Irish Jesuit. God is not mocked. Trovato was certainly no Kaiser, and he had been reluctant to host this meeting, but the fear of being frozen out of something big had decided him.

"The conclave just concluded was irregular, illegal, and illicit", Frank began. "Its result has no claim on the loyalty of Catholics."

Playing your high card first was good strategy. It tended to define the subsequent discussion. Only Oliver Tremblay reacted with surprise.

"You could rally a lot of canon lawyers to that position", Wynn said, screwing a Nazionali into an amber cigarette holder.

"You could rally a lot of lawyers to any position", said Trovato.

"Well, I can rally bishops and cardinals", Frank replied. "And they are far more important."

"Lannan should be up in arms", Wynn cried. "He was disenfranchised and with him the United States of America."

Trovato, still standing, gave an exaggerated salute. "Drinks are on the table, and you can wait on yourselves."

"Do you have any nonalcoholic beer?" Tremblay asked.

"You'll like this Pironi."

"Does it have any alcohol?"

"About as much as nonalcoholic wine", Trovato said.

Their host was pouring a Scotch. Frank made a bourbon and water.

"Is that for me, Frank?" Wynn asked.

Trovato said, "I thought you drank Scotch. I was making this for you."

"I'd prefer bourbon."

Frank gave him the drink and mixed another. Was Wynn making some kind of power point, wangling his drink out of him? It was hard to have much confidence in this bunch. Like Wynn, Frank was reminded of the good old days when Rome had hummed with journalists, theologians, priests who sniffed around the Council like camp followers, *periti* eager to cut them in on what was really going on while the bishops sat in mitered rows in St. Peter's.

"It's all over by the time a session begins. The deals have been made. When has any intervention at a plenary session amounted to anything?" Thus had once spoken Würner, the portly Dominican from Speyer, now gaga in the order's infirmary.

How the ranks had thinned, whole platoons of the elect wandering away, weary of the endless battle with the forces of darkness, or at least of restoration, winning again and again. The great enlightenment had not come. The champions of the Council were blamed for everything that had gone wrong since. Frank Bailey refused to accept the claim that there was a causal connection between questioning celibacy and the precipitous drop in the number of priests. The answer, he thought, was obvious. The Pope and his *panzerkardinal* had turned off the young. Drop celibacy and hosts of normal men would come charging into the priesthood; he was sure of it. The fault lay in resistance to change. Bishops nowadays were too much like those at the time of the Council, in the grips of an almost pathological prudence, the desire to avoid trouble at all costs, to encourage progressives, yet in the end leave them to dangle unprotected before the winds of power and authority. From time to time, a good bishop, even archbishop, was appointed. They did not last. Frank had written on the pathology of bishops—the subtle change from wholehearted if discreet support from behind the lines, to cautions and caveats, until they stopped taking your calls. The only comfort was the fact that conservative bishops were equally waffling.

The dimple in Frank Bailey's chin was rough with inaccessible whiskers. Thumb to dimple, he pivoted it to sip from his un-iced drink. Courage, strength, one had to work with the materials at hand. And there was work to do, maybe the last chance of his lifetime to make a difference in the Church he loved.... Loved? If nothing else, it was his obsession and had been since he was thirteen years old and showed up at the Hall, the wide-eyed son of a laborer, not believing he was actually going to be a student there. Jim Morrow, Tom Lannan, himself. They were all obsessed with the Church, and now Lannan was as good as a cardinal, Jim was ambassador to the Vatican, and Frank Bailey—what exactly was he? He had fared well enough in Jim's account of the postconciliar years, but they had drifted apart. Liberal and conservative? It was deeper than that. Lannan, being a bishop, was impossible to classify. Like lukewarm water.

Later that night, seated at Trovato's laptop computer, Frank drafted the story that, after discussion, modifications, additions and subtractions, they all resolved to trumpet as loudly as they could: Frank in his column that the CNS would disseminate to the religious press. Trovato in the *Times* and thus to their syndication service, Tremblay to the stateside and international editions of his magazine, and Wynn assigned Europe.

Rome. A week after the conclave, doubt is being cast on the legitimacy of the election of John Paul III. Were eligible electors kept from the conclave? That question is being asked by experts on Church law, Church history, and ecclesiology.

The electors of a new pope are members of the College of Cardinals who have not passed the age of eighty. At the time of the death of the late Pope, the number of cardinals had dwindled to the lowest point since Pius XII. The late Pope, with death impending, appointed twenty new members of the College, clearly with an eye to the election of his successor.

The Pope died, the conclave was called, the Twenty were not permitted entry to the Sistine Chapel where the election took place. Experts agree that if the full body of the electors had been present, it is doubtful that Giancarlo Benedetto would have been elected.

Discussions of an extremely confidential nature are going on as to whether to challenge the election and request that the College reconvene either to confirm what the flawed conclave did or, conceivably, to make a different choice.

Certain nations whose Catholic populations give them a large claim to participation in the election of a new pope, through cardinal electors, were conspicuously underrepresented in the conclave. The United States, for example, with a huge and generous number of Catholics, had only five cardinals at the time of the conclave, and two were ineligible to vote because of age. Nigeria, on the other hand, had four cardinal electors.

Defenders of the conclave argue that the twenty cardinals named by the late Pope had not been officially inducted into the College and therefore were not and are not cardinals. Critics respond that, by that reckoning, Giancarlo isn't Pope because he has not yet been crowned.

"There are no direct quotes", Bailey responded to Tremblay's question as to who was being quoted.

Wynn chirped in, "I could easily produce people who will make those statements."

Trovato showed no unease, but then he had been a research assistant for Bob Woodward for his book on the Supreme Court. Journalistic ethics had changed dramatically in recent years, with considerable leeway granted the writer in his depiction of states of affairs. Imaginary interior monologues had fallen into disfavor once a book on Teddy Kennedy had invaded his psyche and presumed to tell readers what the senator had been thinking and feeling at certain crucial moments.

"Indirect quotations that, as Iggie says, can easily be replaced with solicited direct quotations, are clearly within bounds."

"Oh, I don't have any problem with it, personally. But I don't want to get shot down by the New York office."

Trovato and Bailey just looked at Tremblay.

4

Flying back to Washington from Rome, Thomas Lannan reflected that he had been badly treated by the new Pope in the audience he had shared with Jim Morrow and Monsignor Frawley. He was angry at Frawley and piqued with Morrow and unhappy with himself. Where had the peace he had felt at Gethsemani gone?

Frawley had encouraged the notion that he was familiar with the corridors of power at the Vatican, but it was crystal clear that the former secretary of state had not known who Frawley was. Nor did his post as rector of the North American College draw more than a perfunctory response. It was Jim Morrow who had been the guest of honor, so much so that, having been asked to stay behind, he spent more time alone with the Holy Father than the three of them had been granted.

Morrow, it was clear, was very close to the new Pope. Doubtless John Paul III's vision of the whole Church matched the one Morrow had of the Church in America. Lannan, looking out over the clouds at forty thousand feet, asked himself if he was being personally punished because of the Pope's negative judgment on American culture.

Precedents for his predicament came unwillingly to mind. May had occupied the see of St. Louis, where the traditional cardinal hats of his predecessors hung high in the cathedral, a mute rebuke and reminder that May himself had never been made a cardinal. Lannan gave little credence to the view that he was being punished for libelous remarks about Jim Hitchcock and Fr. Schall, but the fact remained that May had died an archbishop.

Borders of Baltimore had been an earlier instance, though Lannan wasn't sure exactly why the primatial see of the United States was denied a cardinal while Borders was there, not that Baltimore was owed one.

An analogous situation would be found in the men made auxiliaries, who had every hope and expectation of receiving dioceses of their own, but who grew old as second violins.

Oh, it had been a confusing time under the previous Pope. When he ascended the throne, conservatives had rejoiced, certain that the kind of bishop they deplored was now a thing of the past. But the record of the last years was mixed. A few stalwarts in key places—dioceses of New York, Boston, variables like Los Angeles, and Chicago, reclaimed in an apparent reversal of the Bernardin hegemony. Meyer, Bruskewitz, Chaput, George—the number of stalwart defenders of Rome steadily increased. Progressives had bewailed a restorationist papacy, a return of the Bourbons, an attempt to undo all that had been done. In the end, neither side had been happy. How did Thomas Lannan figure in this equation?

There is nothing like an extended flight for unhurried reflection, and Lannan's plight was something he had to think through. He had gone to the monastery to escape the distractions of his life, and there had toyed with a dramatic dream of himself as a monk with a traditional monastic contempt for the world, waiting, in effect, to die. But that had nothing to do with the person he had actually become. Now he had the leisure and the inclination to let his life pass before his eyes, not in a moment, as it is said to do for the dying, but slowly, in pursuit of its meaning and its message for the present in which he found himself. Memory molds as much as it records, but he had no doubt that the years he had spent at the Hall were the most formative of his life and the most keenly enjoyable. There his mind and imagination had opened up, and he had developed a cultural pride in being Catholic.

"Western culture is Catholic!" Uncle Bill Nolan could shout in a whisper; it was his favorite classroom tone. "Catholicism is Western culture." He glared at them. "Belloc. Anyone know Belloc?"

No one said a word. Of course they knew Belloc. How could they have taken a class from Nolan three years running and not know Belloc? But such questions were rhetorical in every sense of the term.

They were doing Virgil, and Nolan had gotten off on a tangent because of the fourth eclogue, which he regarded as the pagan poet's prophecy of the coming of Jesus Christ.

"*Praeparatio evangelica*. Morrow!"

"Evangelical preparation."

Nolan lay his head on his shoulder and closed his eyes. "I am surprised you didn't say Preparation Evangelical." His head snapped up and his eyes opened. "Translation is not the replacement of words. It is the capturing of an idea." He paused as if to think. "Prelude to the gospel", he murmured. "Perhaps Prologue to the good news." He shook that away. "Prelude to the gospel", he decided. It was important to his vision of the West that the Greeks and Romans were part of the Catholic thing that true culture was. Under Nolan's tutelage they developed the sense that they were in the mainstream of Western culture, because of their Catholic faith. ("Potentially only.

Nothing is automatic. Ideas are fragile things.") From being members of a more or less marginalized body, Catholic Americans, they found themselves transformed into inheritors of all that was good and true and beautiful. Their eyes turned toward Europe. Other Americans could live their lives under the chilling Protestant hand of New England; they would remember the French and Spanish missionaries, the culture of the southwest, which flourished long before the austere Quakers and dissenters landed on the cold and rocky coasts of the north.

"What is the oldest American university?"

This was not a rhetorical question. After silence, Frank ventured Harvard.

"I didn't say North American, I said American."

"I thought you meant North America", Frank said.

"Then you are still wrong. Anyone else? What, no one? Not one of you realizes that *l'Université Laval* in Quebec is the oldest in North America?"

Nolan had gone to Laval, a pis aller during World War II when clerical scholars could not be sent to Rome or Louvain or Swiss universities.

"*Deo favente, haud pluribus impar.* Lannan!"

"Could you write it out, Father?"

Nolan wrote Laval's motto in large letters on the board and waited. Lannan began, "To God turning..."

"Stop!" Nolan had clamped his hands to his ears. "Ablative absolute, ablative absolute." He unclamped his ears. "Now."

"God favoring..."

It was too much for Nolan, and he supplied the translation, as he always did, a practice that cushioned the blow of failure. "Equal, by God's grace, to most." He worked variations on it, acknowledging the double negative in "not unequal to many", but what he was after was who those many or most might be?

"The Ivy League, those little Bible-based purveyors of the mere rudiments of learning? They did not yet exist. The universities already flourishing in Central and South America?" Nolan glared at them, obviously wanting to go on about those Spanish institutions in Latin America, but more anxious to make his main point. "The point of comparison was Europe, the mother of universities, of Catholic universities, there being no other kind until a German monk, full of beer, disrupted Christendom with his inadequate learning and deplorable habits."

Outside Lannan's window in business class, there was the blue sky above, clouds below, and through them, far, far below, an ocean where a speck of a ship was visible because of its wake. A metaphor of life: always abandoning the present moment, its past a wake that all too quickly was lost in the great ocean of indifference.

The major seminary had been a new world. Roman collars, cassocks, birettas, and surplices in chapel, the more flamboyant like Frank Bailey affecting capes, they had skidded along the slippery walks between the banks of shoveled snow, the leafless trees like creatures in a German fairy tale, to and fro to class, to and fro to chapel, to and fro to the refectory—an ordered busy life; but just beyond the enclosing hedge, the roar of traffic made known the world they were being trained to serve.

"Husserl is difficult", Rand conceded. "Take this."

Rand had earned his doctorate at Louvain and been an assistant in the Husserl Archives there. The book was by a Jesuit named Krause, scarcely more intelligible than Husserl. On his own, prompted by Morrow, Lannan read Edith Stein.

"Why should I?" he had asked Jim.

"She studied with Husserl, then became a Carmelite."

"A causal relation."

"Quit kicking against the goad. Stick with Thomism."

But Thomism meant Withers who stuttered and was thrown

into a panic by questions. Morrow was being encouraged by Melvin Orr to concentrate on history. The archbishop had no one studying for an advanced degree in Church history, so where was Orr's replacement? He did not wish to grow grizzled and toothless as a seminary professor. Like many on the faculty, he nursed the dream of a small rural parish, near a good Minnesota lake, where he could read to his heart's content.

Melvin Orr had transmitted to Morrow the desire for a place at the lake and a love of history, but not the determination to go on to ordination. Jim left before they began their study of theology. For that both Lannan and Bailey left too— for Rome and the Gregorianum, the Jesuit university, with rooms at the North American College.

Quinn the rector had been what Frawley only pretended to be—perhaps "aspired to be" would be kinder. Quinn had taken young Tom Lannan under his wing. He had a zest for making careers, and his successes were legendary. When Lannan became a member of Quinn's Friends, he and Frank Bailey began to drift apart. Frank spent a lot of time in the offices of the Catholic News Service, located across from the entrance of the Greg on the Via della Pilotta. He parlayed those connections, together with the fact that the editor of the diocesan paper at home was a member of his parish, into a journalistic assignment to cover the Council.

The three of them had never gone home again. Morrow went from the seminary to graduate school and on to two academic appointments before he landed at Notre Dame.

"I thought you didn't want to teach at a Catholic school?"

"Not many other places would let me tranform myself into a Church historian."

Lannan hadn't pursued it. He simply assumed that Notre Dame was more prestigious than one of the other Catholic universities. Had Jim retained the Catholic chauvinism encouraged by Uncle Bill Nolan?

Lannan himself had been seconded by his archbishop to what would soon become the United States Catholic Conference and had taught a course for several semesters at the Catholic University of America, thus qualifying for a room in Caldwell Hall. Quinn had passed him on to Fritz, a profane monsignor who showed him the ropes and made sure he got to know the right people. "Seminaries produce priests; we produce bishops." Fritz became bishop of an Arizona see, the first rung on what was to be his rapid ascent, but he fell ill and died before he had been in Arizona a year.

"I thought people came here for their health", Quinn said, having flown from Rome for the funeral.

What had struck Lannan was that an early death had not been in Fritz' plans, but early or late, that was the way life ended. It was a moment when he first realized what he had always in some sense known. Ambition, even ecclesiastical ambition, has a way of obscuring the facts of life. What would we do without the illusion of immortality, not beyond, but here, as if we will always go on doing what we're doing? During the eulogy, Lannan was assailed by memories of the raunchy stories Fritz had loved to tell. Others dismissed it as therapy, a celibate's defense against the attraction of women. Perhaps. *De mortuis nil nisi bonum.* In his head, Nolan barked, "Bailey!" and Frank supplied a translation that Nolan inevitably would refine. Speak well of the dead was the gist of it. Lannan now saw the dangers in the life he was embarked upon. If he died young, he didn't want his life to seem as pointless as did Fritz'.

The monastery? That now seemed obviously an escape, not the answer.

Then came the fleeting thought that the menacing claim that he had fathered a child was meant to tell him why his desire had been thwarted. He preferred to think that he had been given providential warning. If the accusation was publicly made he was ready for it. Such a thing could not be proved. He would take his cue from Bernardin when that demented lad's charge had withered before a simple, emphatic denial.

To be archbishop of Washington and not a cardinal would make his life as pointless as Fritz', and not just personally. It had been, as the media were insistently pointing out, a species of insult to the United States that he had been kept out of the conclave. Now he doubted that Benedetto would renew his nomination. Nothing in the brief audience suggested that the new Pope shared his predecessor's concern with the size of the College of Cardinals. What he did share with his predecessor, and what talking with Morrow could only encourage, was the belief that Catholicism was in such decline in the United States—and Western Europe—that a pope's energies were best directed to those parts of the world where the faith was on the rise and multitudes were coming into the Church. There it could be like the first centuries of the faith all over again; in the West it was decline and fall.

Why create cardinals in a wasteland? Why give to a regional church with which he was clearly out of sympathy, a larger say than it had now in the future of the universal Church?

Lannan was distracted by the serving of dinner. The wine was surprisingly good, something Frawley might have served. Frawley.

"The story is appearing everywhere", Frawley had said.

"Who's behind it?"

"That's what I came to ask you."

Lannan was unnerved by the story. Did anyone really believe that the election of John Paul III could be declared invalid? The thought was vertiginous, as if great plates beneath the surface of the earth were shifting and would bring down everything. Yet he was flattered by the thought that he could have set off such a barrage of media speculation about the

Pope's election, the validity of the conclave that elected him, and the exclusion of twenty new cardinals. It was the last that must explain Frawley's implication.

"Journalists do not govern the Church."

"But they're not making up the story; they are reporting it."

"No one is cited."

"Of course not. My guess is Pavese."

"Pavese!"

"He sought to seat you and the others and failed. He then lost the election. There is a strict connection between the two events. If twenty eligible electors were excluded, and if they were votes for him, well, of course he has a grievance."

"Has he said so?"

"You've met Pavese. He's an Italian. An Italian can be mute and still communicate. I don't mean the obvious body language. A widening of the eyes, a scarcely lifted brow, a slight movement at the corners of the mouth are enough."

Lannan was incongruously put in mind of a coach signaling a base runner with a pulling of ears, slapping of chest, a whole semaphoric repertoire, most of which meant nothing. But Lannan had known enough, when speaking to Pavese, to watch the cardinal's face. To read that correctly was to decode what the archbishop of Milan was really saying. Of course he could launch the kind of media blitz that was going on. But had he?

"I have also known Frank Bailey most of my life. And Ignatius Wynn."

"The *Times* is involved, and the news magazines."

Lannan found that he was willing to have his doubts dismissed. By the time he had decided to leave Rome, return to Washington, and get on with things, the inquiries about the conclave had become the number-one item in newspapers, television reports, talk shows. And it was safe to say that the tone of the stories was sceptical about what had gone on in the conclave that elected Giancarlo Benedetto.

On CNN, Maurice Plon, a prominent French Catholic layman, looked mournfully into the camera. "The legitimacy of a pope is at the heart of the Catholic system. There must be no doubt about whether a man is pope. When there was doubt in the past, it was resolved by deposing rival claimants and electing another. But today?" A Gallic lifting of the shoulders. His suit coat did not descend, and he seemed about to disappear into it like a turtle. "Today, with instant communications, the whole Church is confused."

"What do you propose?"

Another shrug brought his coat down on his shoulders. "That must be left to those with authority to act."

From Australia the retired Cardinal Micawber, eighty-seven years old, said that he didn't like it. Something was fishy. Why, he remembered...

But the reporter had left the old man with his memories. Sufficient for the day was the expression of doubt about the legitimacy of Benedetto's election.

No wonder Frank Bailey was in orbit with excitement. The election of Benedetto had plunged him into gloom. Now he was emerging with new fire in his eyes.

"We'll get you in there this time, Tom. Who knows, you may come out as the big enchilada yourself."

It was time to go home and consult his brother bishops and find out whether these questions had any real interest for them. Whatever their ultimate judgment, they had to confront the doubts that had been raised.

Thomas Lannan returned to Washington with the sense that he had a work to do, and he meant to do it.

Betty Grauer, in the press office, had been a nun, but activism had drawn her into the world, first to agitate for resident ownership of public housing, next as consultant to the first Hank Whitney campaign, then to her present job. She had a wide mouth, snubnose, and very curly, strawberry blonde hair cropped close to her well-formed head. Janet always felt like a frump with this woman who probably devoted a fast three minutes to getting ready in the morning and ended up looking perfect. Why hadn't she stayed in the convent? You could ask Betty a question like that.

"You make it sound like a fortress."

"What is it?"

"It's not even a place any more. You live where you work, one or two together, sometimes alone."

"Is that why you left?"

Betty's little nose wrinkled. "Some people give that as their reason. Mary Ellen, others—they were let down by it, you know. They didn't leave the convent, the convent left them. I myself just evolved beyond it; my life had taken another turn, and when I realized that, it was all over. Nothing dramatic."

"How do you resign?"

Betty laughed. "By letter. Actually, by fax. While I fed it into the machine, saying good-bye to all that, I realized how instantaneous it seemed. But the decision, the change, was gradual."

It turned out that she was simplifying, about the fax. She had to be released from her vows, and that meant considerable paperwork and letters.

"Just routine. I did it more for the sake of my mother than anything, so she could tell her friends it was all kosher and I hadn't been thrown out or something."

"What are the vows?"

Betty squinted at her. "Don't you know?"

"Betty, I'm a postconciliar Catholic. I don't know anything."

The vows were poverty, chastity, and obedience. Of course she had heard of them from Gene. None of them seemed to have any application to the life Betty had been living, except presumably chastity, but in Washington you never knew. Nor did you speculate. It was presumed that everybody had something going; it wouldn't be healthy otherwise. In this atmosphere, Janet longed for what she had imagined was the otherworldliness of the nun. A bodiless existence. Which is why she had been truly surprised by her non-consanguineous cousin Monsignor Gene Wales in Rome.

"How do priests get out?" she asked Betty.

"It's not as easy for them, at least not lately. Maybe it will be again under the new man."

"If he survives the challenge to his election."

Betty made a face. "You can't just unmake a pope. Not easily, at least. I don't think it's ever been done."

Janet had been reading about it, beyond the newspapers, checking up on the papacy in the *New Catholic Encyclopedia*, which was half a century old. It was slightly shocking to learn about some of the popes, although most seemed to have been what they should have been. The one who wouldn't give in to Henry VIII was not the man you would have chosen to stick to his guns. Every bishop in England had gone with the king except one, the bishop of Rochester, and he was beheaded. St. John Fisher, as he now was, was recognized as a martyr for the faith because he had stuck with the Pope. Like Thomas More. How would Thomas More behave in the present situation? She put the question to Gene Wales.

"He would support the Pope."

"John Paul III?"

"He's the only one we have."

"Don't you take your boss' side?"

Gene was more formal with her now. She sensed that things would never be exactly the same again, not after he had told her he loved her and she had joshed her way out of it, wanting to tell him that it was all overblown; take a look at the people she worked with. Are they happy? But then there were all those millions of families, like the one Jim Morrow's daughter Mary presumably had. How little she knew of all that. But that's what Gene Wales must dream of when he thought of being something other than a monsignor. It had all the attraction of the unknown, and she felt it herself. The papal election was a much safer subject.

"Have you ever met Leach?"

"The skeleton in your office?"

"He's only in my office when he visits. Lovingly known as Holy Toledo. That's his diocese. He would answer you with another question."

"What's his question?"

"How many bishops were at Trent? How many bishops were at Vatican I?"

"That's two questions."

"They have the same answer. Not all the bishops alive at the time and eligible to be at those ecumenical councils managed to get there, for one reason or another."

"What's the relevance?"

"Even if Lannan and the others were eligible to take part in the conclave—and that is a very big if—their not being there does not invalidate the proceedings."

"No one else has mentioned that."

"It's a good point."

"But it ought to be stated. There's such a drumbeat now, as if we all know in our hearts that it was an illegal conclave and its result questionable. What are ordinary Catholics to make of the suggestion that the Pope may not be the Pope?"

"Do you think they really worry about it?"

"Of course they do. How could they not?"

"I'll cite Leach again. He thinks this country could go into schism by sundown, and most Catholics would just fall into line. That's what happened during the Reformation. That's what happened in England."

"Except for John Fisher."

"Except for John Fisher."

"How would Thomas Lannan act if things got that sticky?"

His eyes lifted, as if the answer were written on the ceiling.

She felt they could go on with this topic without danger, and she wanted to talk it out. She realized that she herself felt dizzy at the prospect of a squabble over whether the Pope really was the Pope.

"What are you doing for dinner?"

"Do you mean what am I preparing?"

"No, I'm asking you out."

"Janet", he began, as if he were about to mention Rome.

"I want Italian food so bad I can taste it."

"I was going to make spaghetti."

"I'll take you away from a hot stove."

The Vesuvio was like a movie set—checkered tablecloths, waiters with flashing eyes and mustaches, the girls with breasts ready to roll out of their blouses, an oompah-oompah band playing on a little stage framed in lattice work, chianti bottles stuffed with candles. All it lacked was string sacks of garlic hanging from the ceiling. Wales arrived in civilian clothes. She realized that she was not surprised.

"Traveling incognito?"

"Mustn't cause scandal."

"Here? This is the place where the senator did it under the table with his girlfriend of the night."

His face looked nice in red. His eyes wouldn't meet hers.

"That's why I asked for a small table", she added airily.

That was mean; it brought back Rome and mocked what he had said; for a mad moment she thought he would fold up his napkin and go. He tried to smile, but his mouth wasn't in the mood. She put her hand on his. His expression was so woeful she could have cried.

"Do you know Betty Grauer?"

He shook his head, so she told him all about Betty, just to talk, but when she got going she realized it was not the wisest topic in the world. Still, it relaxed him.

"She did it by fax?"

"Not even the senator could beat that."

He laughed, a good sign.

"Now she's free of her vows, and as far as I can see it hasn't changed her life one bit."

"Because she didn't marry?"

"Marry? In Washington? I don't think she even goes with anyone. So what's the point?"

"I'd marry if I left."

Antipasto was put before them, the band played on, the place filled up, the bread and wine would have been a meal in themselves. She said so.

He said, "Omar Kayam."

"Who does he play for?"

"He owned the Patriots."

"Huh?"

"He liked them so well he bought the company."

She didn't know what in the world he was talking about and told him so.

"A loaf, a jug of wine, and thee."

Their entrees arrived. The waiter emptied the carafe and lifted his brows questioningly. Another? Janet told him another.

"This is my treat."

Later, huddled over the table, they talked about the wave after wave of criticism of the conclave, the questioning of the election. Polls had been taken, which were interpreted to mean that Catholics wanted the situation clarified. If there was doubt, they wanted it resolved. But this seemed to accept that there was doubt. A petition was begun, demanding a new conclave. Wales spoke of all these things with seeming indifference.

"What do you think will happen?"

"Janet, I'm not sure I even care."

"Of course you care. How could you not care?"

"What do you think it's like to realize that someone has taken away the floor you were standing on?"

He put his hand on the basket that had held the bread and moved it around as if looking for its proper place. Only after he said it did his eyes meet hers.

"I'm thinking of pulling a Betty Grauer."

6

After he said it, she looked at him, pursing her lips, eyes filled with tenderness. She put her hand on the bread basket, stopping him from moving it. And then her hand covered his.

"Don't", she pleaded.

"Janet, this is something that..."

She shook her head. "Is it because of me? Because of us, in Rome? Don't do it, Gene. I'd blame myself. You belong where you are."

He realized that he had not imagined what her reaction would be. Thinking of telling her was in itself such a momentous thing that he had never thought beyond it. To say aloud that he was leaving the priesthood would stop the earth from turning, make the sun stand still, interfere with cosmic laws. What in God's name did he expect her to say?

"I'm forty-two years old", he said.

"I am thirty-one."

"Is it too great a difference?"

"Oh, Gene, don't say that."

"Have you ever read Trollope?"

"No."

"In situations like this, when a male character proposes and doesn't receive the answer he wants, he asks, 'May I hope?' "

Her grip on his hand tightened, and she closed her eyes. "Please."

"Please hope?"

"Hope that in a week you won't believe you said these things. I suppose it is awful, with all this confusion. About the Pope, I mean. It'll all work out, won't it?"

To tell her he didn't care would have been to infect her with the doubt he no longer fought. It is not good for one's soul to work with a bishop, let alone an archbishop, and for more than ten years Wales had been with the NCCB, which was like working for all the bishops in the country. For those who took the Conference seriously, anyway. He had not expected to be edified, but he had been shocked, disenchanted, even scandalized. Not by misbehavior—that would have been almost welcome—but by indifference to their role of masters of the faith. Dissenting theologians had the run of the Church, while those who tried to be faithful to the Magisterium were shunned. It made no sense. Or it made sense on only one basis. They no longer really believed anything.

There were John Fishers among them. No doubt of that, but he had not been working for a potential martyr. Only when he met Janet, and they came to see an analogy between their jobs did he realize how cynical he had become. He had lost the right to find Thomas Lannan wanting. He had colluded with him, become like him, hoped to ascend the same ladder. The precedent for him was Richard Rich.

When the Son of Man returns will he find faith upon the earth? But it was not the faith of others that concerned Eugene Wales now. His own had dwindled until he could scarcely stir it from the dark corner of his soul where it lay dormant. That had antedated his feeling for Janet—he would die rather than let her think she was in any way responsible—but the withering of his conviction that his vocation and Christianity and the whole grand story of human history and destiny made any sense had caused him to take a new look around him. And there was Janet, pretty and bright and safe because she was a kind of cousin by marriage.

What if this life were all there is? That was the question that ate at his insides. To be a priest, to be a believer, only made sense if Christianity was true; and if Christianity is true then, no matter how improbable it was, the soul that animated the body survived death and, some day, soul and body would be reunited and a life of glory begin.

How madly improbable it seemed. How many billions had lived upon the earth prior to the present generation? Were all those billions of souls still existent, and would they and all the billions of souls yet to be before the end of the world regain their bodies and live forever, in either heaven or hell? That is what he believed, not only when he recited the Creed, but in the way he lived his life. And what if it wasn't true?

In the seminary they had studied philosophical proofs for the existence of God formulated by Plato, Aristotle, Anselm. Proofs had an appeal if one already believed, but how would they strike the mind of someone who had no religious faith in God or in immortality? Of course Wales could only imagine, or try to imagine. He ended by thanking God that his conviction did not repose on any argument. It was a deliverance of the faith.

But what to make of arguments that the soul cannot meaningfully be said to exist apart from the body—if by soul we mean the organizing animating principle, whatever it is that distinguishes a living breathing human from a dead one? One might as well say that the impression in the wax exists apart from the wax.

For every proof there was a disproof, and for every disproof there was a response, on and on, endlessly. One could not base one's life on so inconclusive a debate. And of course Christians did not. *Do this and you will live. This day thou shalt be with me in Paradise.* One responded to the authoritative voice of God incarnate, linking one's destiny to him, confident that his Resurrection was the sign and proof of ours.

Theologians nowadays not only dismissed such philosophical efforts. They also denied the literal Resurrection of Christ; they denied that he meant to found a Church and a priesthood and the sacraments. How could theologians dispute the very core of Christianity and go on functioning as trustworthy interpreters of the faith? But they were everywhere, notably in the theology departments of the Catholic colleges and universities of the country, unrebuked by bishops, publishing in Catholic papers and magazines, lecturing the bishops at meetings of the NCCB. This could only be permitted because the bishops no longer thought it mattered. And what was that but the loss of faith?

Or cowardice.

Leach told a joke about the consecration of a new bishop. "Why is the new man encircled by the other bishops during the ceremony?"

"Why?"

"So the laity will not see the removal of the spinal column." Leach's reedy laugh needed oil. He nodded toward Lannan's office.

"Leach, I'll set you an imaginary task. What would you do if you were archbishop of Washington?"

The question did not faze Leach. He sounded as if he had been giving the matter much thought, and for a long time. The seminary would be first on his agenda. Out with the homosexuals, both students and faculty, gone by nightfall.

"Of course I would be sued to a fare-thee-well. No matter. I would hire a good Jewish lawyer, someone like the judge that finally rid CU of Charlie Curran. I'd countersue the plaintiffs for using a Church position to undermine Church teaching."

At the Catholic University of America, everyone in the school of religious studies would be examined personally by Archbishop Leach to see if they qualified for a mandate of the kind specified in *Sapientia Christiana* and *Ex corde ecclesiae* and canon 812. The vast majority would not. Out with them. All hell would break loose, of course, but his Jewish lawyer would handle that as well. The religious orders would be next, then the pastors who preached unsound doctrine or left religious education to people trained by the theologians Leach would already have fired.

"No, the seminary would be second, not first. First would be the chancery. Why should I pay people to undermine what I have vowed to do?"

Wales was almost sorry he had asked. "The other bishops wouldn't back you."

"The other bishops will not be my judge in the only judgment that counts."

Clearly Leach would never become a bishop. No one remotely like him would ever become a bishop. Those who did would be like the present ones, neither fish nor fowl. It was difficult not to see the whole organization as doomed. If it survived it would be something totally different. A religion without hope.

Dare I hope? It was unfair to see Janet as an alternative to all he seemed to have lost. No woman could bear such a burden.

"You may be right", he said, in the Vesuvio, putting his

hand over hers. They might have been gripping a bat. Who would get eagle's claws?

"Of course I'm right."

"It's the male menopause."

"At forty-two? And don't make fun of yourself."

It was pointless to expect her to see him as someone other than Monsignor Wales. He found it almost impossible to talk of other things, to round the evening off in lighthearted laughter. When they parted he kissed her on the cheek, just like old times.

The following day an *ad hoc* group of presidents of Catholic universities and colleges issued a statement calling for a new conclave in order that all doubt as to the identity of the head of the Church could be removed.

CHAPTER TWO

I

Jim Morrow watched on CNN as Emery, president of George-town, read the statement.

The undersigned presidents of Catholic colleges and universities request that a new conclave be called because of the serious doubts raised about the conclave recently concluded. Although we are not and do not consider ourselves to be part of the structure of the institutional Church since we are autonomous entities guided only by the pursuit of truth common to all universities, and by the requirements of academic freedom, nonetheless, as institutions in the Catholic tradition we are deeply concerned about the confusion that surrounds the election of the putative Holy Father, John Paul III. Nor has it escaped our attention that the United States was underrepresented at that conclave. Accordingly, a new conclave should assure more equitable representation so that no questions can be raised about its deliberations and all Catholics can be confident in its results.

There followed a list of presidents: first those heading institutions founded by the Jesuits, then Dayton and the two St. John's, as well as the various universities of St. Thomas, the University of Portland, and The Catholic University of America. A reporter asked the question Morrow would have asked. "Why isn't Notre Dame on the list?"

Emery had read the statement with frowning seriousness, then he smiled, the look of a speaker who assumed the media are on his side, now he frowned again.

"Those who signed, freely decided to do so. The same can be said of those who did not."

"Was Notre Dame at the meeting?"

"No."

"No! Weren't they asked?"

For decades the other Catholic universities in the nation had found themselves eclipsed, rightly or wrongly, by Notre Dame. How could they compete for attention with a school every Catholic in the country regarded as his alma mater? Those who weren't alumni de facto, considered themselves alumni *de iure*. The Fighting Irish were followed throughout the country, every game nationally televised. For friend and foe alike, Notre Dame was *the* Catholic university. Under the presidency of Fr. Theodore Hesburgh it had assumed the leadership of Catholic higher education. Hesburgh's phenomenally long presidency, thirty-five years in all, had been followed by predictably choppy years, but now under William Ambler the South Bend school had resumed the even tenor of its ways. The Baxter episode, resistance to the appointment of a member of the Congregation of Holy Cross to the university founded by the Congregation of Holy Cross, had finally wakened a sense of turf among the CSCs. The board turned the university back to the Congregation; unruly faculty proved surprisingly easy to deal with; several bishops and orders were persuaded to recall men who had been at the forefront of the failed coup d'etat; and Notre Dame soon exemplified the ideal of *Ex corde Ecclesiae*. The thrust of the reporter's question was that, without Notre Dame, the statement had no weight.

"You noticed", Emery said, "the presence of The Catholic

University of America, a pontifical institution, on the list. This is the bishops' own university. With regard to the specific point in question, The Catholic University is more important than all the rest of us together. After all, our request is directed to the bishops of the country."

Jim Morrow punched the remote control, turning off the set. He had been made uneasy by the flood of stories in newspapers and magazines attacking the conclave and questioning the election of Benedetto, but it had hitherto seemed destined to follow the pathology of such media flare-ups, which swiftly died of overkill and saturation, abruptly disappearing to be heard of no more. Journalism by definition is the pursuit of the day by day, and day succeeds day inexorably, dragging items out of the sun and into the vast forgetfulness of the past. Thus he had assured Maureen Kilmartin.

"If every publication in the world were in agreement on it, it would make no difference, Maureen. It's not the function of the press to declare conclaves valid or invalid."

"Jim, it's not just the newspapers. Even in Ireland, it's the priests and now a bishop as well."

"There are always priests or bishops ready to be quoted on anything. Sensible people lose their bearings when confronted by a camera or microphone. They know the outrageous is expected, and they oblige."

It was a theory he had developed in writing his history of the Church in America. Much dissent and protest had begun when some theologian succumbed to the lure of the media to distinguish himself by criticizing the Church. He was immediately quoted everywhere and soon was identified with the stand he had taken, perhaps thoughtlessly. In a very short time, to retract would have been tantamount to psychic suicide, ceasing to be who he was, and so, frozen into that mad moment when he had condescended to the Pope, he became a symbol and/or leader of dissent.

What had once been the aberration of a few theologians had come to characterize the Church in America. Soon this bishop or that was calling for rethinking of doctrines that had just been rethought, such as contraception. An archbishop of San Francisco, then president of the NCCB, had suggested that the teaching of *Humanae vitae* be reviewed. Doubtless this was why his career had gone into a tailspin. He had never been named a cardinal, but that, while personally punitive, did little to stem the tide. The original dissenters cited their influence within the hierarchy as validation of their views, and the impression grew that only in the United States was there an enlightened and tenable form of Catholicism, with the Vatican straggling woefully behind. The Pope was patronized, offered lessons in elementary moral theology, and described as a product of an authoritarian Eastern Europe who was unpracticed in the ways of democracy; and the end of his reign had been awaited with ill-concealed impatience.

It had ended, a conclave was called, and the right-hand man of the previous pope was elected to succeed him. There had been an ominous silence after the election, neither joy nor sorrow expressed, but now had come what appeared to be a carefully engineered attack on the legitimacy of the conclave. Here was hardball indeed.

"Jim, it's all very well for you, with your knowledge of history and all, to be so philosophical about it", Maureen said. "But what is this doing to ordinary people, to my children and their children? And yours?"

There was an odd intimacy in this depressing conversation. Was there an *amor theologicus* as well as an *odium theologicum*? "Let's have our tea."

"Only if you let me make it", she said, scrambling to her feet.

"I don't know if that's a comment on the tea I make or commendable feminine subservience."

"Neither." She shot her hip at him as they started for the kitchen, and he all but lost his balance.

"Know what I'd like to do, Jim?"

"Hmmm?"

"Go back to Viterbo and ask that woman what the hell is going on."

Two days later, he was summoned to the Vatican by Cardinal Taylor and was driven over by Luigi, who cut a swath through crowds of tourists, hitting the horn officiously as he did.

The number of people coming to salute the new Pope continued to increase: busloads arriving from the east, chartered planes from various points in Africa, the poor from the south. If Benedetto felt any sadness because of the attack on his election, the view from his balcony had to be reassuring. His Wednesday audiences became so large that they were moved into the open, and he addressed his flock, gathered in the great square, in the same way as he did on Sunday in his Angelus allocution. The equivalent of *Viva il Papa* went up in a confusion of tongues but with a single sentiment. The visible link with St. Peter stood there, a small, fat figure clad in white, speaking to them with the authority of Christ himself, the guarantee that through the ages the saving message of Jesus would come whole and entire to new generations. Luigi had come to a stop, stymied by an unending flow of people crowding into the square.

"Look at them." There was genial contempt in the driver's voice.

"You're a native of Rome, Luigi. You don't know what it's like to see all this for the first time, something you may never see again."

"Hey, I'm all for tourists. We need them. But this bunch is no better than beggars. They sleep outside, right here in the square; they cook their own meals."

And indeed there did seem to be family groups encircling some cooking device or other, avoiding restaurant bills by preparing their own food.

"Did you ever hear of tailgate parties?"

"You mean the Navy?" Luigi perked up, mistaking the reference.

"Gate not hook. Fans at American football games let down the tailgate of their pickups…"

He went on, but Luigi did not understand. Why should he? Football meant soccer. Morrow thought of the parking lots around the Notre Dame stadium, the aroma of charcoal and hamburger and sausage cooking, the smell of beer. High on the wind would be heard the sound of the band, marching through the campus to the stadium, followed by students and visitors, all excited about the coming game. It was the first twinge of homesickness that he had felt for months.

By inching slowly forward, Luigi first bent, then broke through the throng, and they continued to the Porta Sant'Ana and went in to the salute of the Swiss guard on duty.

"Better take this with you", Taylor said, after the swiftest of formalities. Morrow thought of the leisurely chats he had had with Benedetto here when he'd been secretary of state. Taylor was another type, Australian, gregarious, efficient. He handed Morrow a leather portfolio with the pontifical seal on it.

"What's this?"

"Your Viterbo report."

As before, the Pope remained seated and waited for Morrow to reach him before standing and putting out his hand. Morrow kissed the ring and took the chair indicated.

"Thank you, *Eminenza*", the Pope said dismissively, and Taylor left them alone.

"You remember writing that report?"

"Of course."

"What do you think of it now?"

No need to say that he was referring to the Viterbo visionary's prophecies about the conclave just concluded.

And about the United States. Morrow had judged them unlikely in the extreme. The Church was in a mess in America, but to see schism in the offing, a formal break with Rome, while logically possible, had appeared totally improbable.

He opened the leather folder and read his confident account, his impeccably academic assessment of the dire predictions of the alleged visionary of Viterbo. When had he written this? Not three months ago. The lofty dismissal of the report seemed something written in another time entirely, given the events of recent weeks.

"What do you think, Your Holiness?"

"That the night comes when no man can sleep."

2

There were eight messages on his answering device, and Frank Bailey played them back, reordered them according to importance, eliminating two in the process, and settled down to work.

"This is Archbishop Nelligan's office."

"Fr. Bailey, returning his call."

"The archbishop can't come to the phone just at the moment..."

"That you, Gilly?"

"I was trying to disguise my voice. The old man's in the john. He won't lay off the tex mex, and he's paying for it."

"Doesn't he have an extension there?"

"Boyle!" Gilligan said, laughing.

The late Boston cardinal had conducted most of his telephone business from an extension in his private bathroom. The episcopal throne had been an equivocal phrase during his twelve years in Bean Town, and latrine jokes had flourished. Boyle tried to put a stop to this, always a mistake, by pointing out that even moderately luxurious hotels had telephones in their bathrooms. So "according to John", and *sede occupata,* and other scatological witticisms had proliferated. The suggestion that the fastidious Nelligan would communicate in such a vulnerable position was doubly improbable.

"What do you make of the agitation over the new Pope, Frank?"

"What does Nellie make of it?"

"He says it's wishful thinking."

Ah. That was the main thing Bailey was after. The thought is father to the wish. His flight to Philadelphia from Rome had been reassuring. There he had found a definite ally. The other bishops were falling into three groups: allies, leaning, and opposed. Only two fell definitely into the third group, one an auxiliary. Fr. Ambler, president of Notre Dame, having boycotted the meeting of Catholic university presidents ("The last time I looked, I was chairman of the group. I called no meeting. Perhaps this is the way another conclave will be convened") had been lobbying the bishops not to get sucked into a media-inspired fracas. It was the leaners, as usual, who would decide the matter, but leaners followed leaders. Leaders in turn do not like to feel alone and isolated, too far in front of the pack. Bailey was concentrating on allies, recruiting a palace guard for Lannan.

Iggie's long-distance call came after Frank got to Washington. The six-hour difference made it 8:00 P.M. in Rome, not that it mattered. Iggie was a 24-hour-a-day guy, sleep coming with difficulty to him because of his injuries, sleeplessness no doubt increased by the excitement of the campaign.

"Whose side is Jim Morrow on?" Iggie asked.

"Why do you ask?"

"The Pope called him in for a private audience."

"He's an ambassador."

"So are dozens of jealous people the Pope hasn't called in for private audiences."

"Maybe he's taking them one at a time."

"I don't trust Morrow, Frank. That damned book."

"Morrow represents the United States, that is, the President, at the Vatican. If the Pope wants to spy on the church in America, he's got Vilani in Washington."

"Morrow and Benedetto became buddy-buddy before the conclave. I'm told the Pope asks Morrow for evaluations of problems, appealing to him as an historian, and Morrow of course obliges. Their relationship is not confined to his duties as ambassador."

"That why you called?"

"I think it's important."

So did Bailey, but felt no urge to give Iggie the satisfaction of agreement. Joe Wallet, the next call, was available for dinner, and Bailey suggested the Press Club. When he got there, Wallet had changed their table for one in the center of the dining room. Wallet retained the illusion that he was a celebrity because his column was syndicated in 203 papers across the country. But who reads papers any more? It was his infrequent appearances on Sunday news shows that might have provided him what he craved, but his wall eyes and nervous tic diminished the impact of what he said. On the printed page, he came through as a wise and serene man, but on the tube he looked like a nervous freak. Still, the people who counted read him. "Keep Your Eye on Wallet" was the slogan that had led the promotion that got him into all those papers.

"What's new in that old-time religion, Frank?" Feeble jokes were another thing that doomed Wallet as a TV performer. He lifted what looked like a 16-ounce glass, iceless, more bourbon than not. "They ran out of the large glasses."

Bailey laughed, why not? "How's the plagiarism trial going?"

Wallet's brow darkened. A woman in Keokuk claimed Wallet had stolen her ideas about Central America and was suing for attribution as well as punitive damages.

"I've never been in Keokuk."

"It's in Iowa."

"I know where it is." He looked over his shoulder. "Maybe I shouldn't admit that."

A woman judge, Hispanic, had admitted the case, and it was costing Wallet money to counter an absurdity.

"The country's going to hell. The three branches of government are full of saps." Surprised by what he had said, Wallet burst into laughter. Geez.

"Not to mention the diplomatic corps."

"You just mentioned it." Wallet leaned forward.

"James Morrow in Rome is meeting with the new Pope, privately, on matters having nothing to do with the duties of his office."

"Going to confession?"

Bailey talked through the interruption. "It looks certain that the American bishops are going to call for a new conclave. They have a good case, that's pretty widely recognized now. So what's an American ambassador to the Vatican doing putting his oar in with the Pope on a thing like that?"

"I thought it was a private audience."

"Sources in Rome assure me that he and Benedetto got to be big buddies before the election. Morrow poses as an expert on the church in America."

"Poses? His book won a Pulitzer."

"You read it?"

"I skimmed it."

"Morrow is totally out of sympathy with Church leadership. The theme of the book is how bad it's been here."

"Decline and fall."

"Pretty subtle for a historian, right? It's understandable that the bishops don't like our ambassador lining up with a pope whose election they are questioning."

"Politics comes to the Catholic Church", quipped Wallet.

"The Catholic Church is politics. It's always been a question of who wields power, who makes decisions. That's politics."

"I didn't know you could just depose a pope you don't like."

"You can't. It is a very serious thing. What is being proposed has never happened before, not exactly this way. The point is to have it out, get it cleared up, let the chips fall where they may. We don't want the American ambassador to the Vatican encouraging the Pope to stonewall."

"You ought to tell Partridge."

"Someone ought to."

"Anything I write wouldn't appear before next week."

"It would be worth waiting for."

Wallet filled his mouth with bourbon, then let it trickle down his throat as he thought. "Maybe I could get on Brinkley."

The Sunday morning show had retained the name of its originator for those of the vintage of Wallet and was easily the most watched news and discussion program on television. The thought of Wallet initiating an attack on Brinkley, squinting to conceal the wall eye, his face twitching like Dr. Strangelove's, filled Bailey with dread.

"Listen, Joe. Your column is a hell of a lot more influential than Brinkley."

"That's false, but I love hearing it."

"So what if zillions watch Brinkley? Most of them are couch potatoes, waiting for the games to come on. Your column engages minds."

"It would be nice if I could do both."

"Shakespearean actors always want to be comedians; opera divas want to be torch singers; Joseph Wallet wants to be big on the boob tube." Bailey shook his head at this mystery of human nature. Wallet smiled at this sublimated version of his vanity.

"Who should I talk to?"

"The White House."

"The White House!"

Bailey explained it to him. The administration's ambassador was over in the Vatican meddling in domestic religious affairs.

"Church and state", Wallet mused.

"Exactly."

"I'll talk to Senator Partridge. Butterworth the evangelist too. Morrow handled them like a master during his hearings. I wonder what they'll think of what their boy is doing now?"

3

Archbishop Lannan sat in his office with one more advisor than he had asked for.

"Better a formal meeting than an informal one conducted through the media", Wales said when Lannan asked his opinion about convening a special meeting of the executive council of the NCCB.

"Why not a plenary session?" Leach asked.

"Not enough time."

"What's the rush?"

Leach knew that the coronation of the Pope would be delayed no longer than a week. Monsignor Frawley had confirmed that.

"Crowned or uncrowned, what's the difference?"

"What is the difference between a crowned and uncrowned cardinal?" Lannan replied sweetly. "Answer. The difference between taking part in a conclave and not taking part. Don't forget that that is what has raised all these doubts."

"I don't quite understand the doubts."

Why had Wales insisted on bringing Leach into this? Lannan felt like shipping Leach back to Toledo, so he could do his more-orthodox-than-thou act for his own bishop.

Wales said, "The question has arisen whether an election excluding twenty electors is valid."

"But a question had been raised about those electors." Leach brought his palms together and nodded at Lannan. "Begging your pardon."

"A question that was resolved by the very conclave in question."

"It doesn't matter", Leach said. "Say a conclave was called, and several electors were prevented from coming, by weather, say. The conclave begins, an election is held, a pope is elected. Would questions be raised about that?"

"It's not the same thing."

"How many bishops were in Rome for the first Vatican Council? For that matter, how many remained at the end of Trent?"

But Wales had already told him of Leach's analogy. "By that logic, a handful of cardinals could call a conclave to which no one else would be able to come, and elect a pope."

Lannan was pretty proud of that reply, and he saw that Wales also recognized its force. But Leach just smirked, as if Lannan had said exactly what he had expected him to say.

Thomas Lannan had already made up his mind to call a meeting of the executive council, as Wales at least knew. Perhaps that was why he had brought Leach along, as devil's advocate, to see what the best reasons against the meeting might be.

Even so Lannan was glad to get the two of them out of his office.

The meeting to discuss a new conclave was held two days later at a motel in Arlington, that much closer to Reagan National Airport, thus making it more of an in-and-out trip for Meade, Nelligan, Oberman, and Preller, members of the standing committee. The conference room at the motel was a considerable come-down from the facilities at what Morrow had dubbed the Taj Mahal, the huge building behind the Washington Theological College where the NCCB and USCC carried on their work. Leach referred to it as POP—the Preferential Option for the Poor, but this hadn't caught on, although it had shown up in the *Wanderer*, indicating where Leach fed any sensitive information he picked up in the course of his work for the Conference.

"It won't work", Bishop Meade said, hands flat on the table, looking around at the others.

"How can you know that?" Lannan asked, surprised.

"All the Pope has to do is say no thanks. Then what do you do?"

"But the question is whether he is the Pope?"

"That may be your question, but it isn't his."

"Haven't you been reading the paper or watching the news?"

"Where? In Warsaw, Moscow, Tokyo? In Zagreb, New Delhi, and any city you want to name in Africa? This is an American cause."

"Then why did you waste time flying out here?"

"Because I have a better idea."

Lannan did not like this. Meade had given no indication when he talked with him that he had any doubts about the course of action proposed. The plan was for the executive council to commit the bishops of the United States to the call for a new conclave. They might be short on cardinals, but they were three to four hundred American bishops, give or take. It would be hard to ignore such a request from a regional church as large as the American, which Lannan now pointed out.

"But not impossible. The canon lawyers are divided."

"Lots of them are with us."

"And lots of them aren't. It would turn into an endless wrangle, leaving the issue every bit as much in doubt as it is now."

"What's your idea?"

Meade lifted one hand and placed it on the other. "A council."

"A council!"

"A council. We have no power to call a conclave. Cardinals do that. But bishops can call councils."

"You mean the bishop of Rome."

"In recent years, yes, but not necessarily. I had Hawkins prepare this memo."

Meade fished copies of the memo from his briefcase and dealt them around the table. Hawkins was a name to reckon with. Born into a pre-Revolutionary family, cushioned by inherited wealth, educated at Cornell and Cambridge, he had come into the Church and written an account of his conversion that to the astonishment of all became a sleeper in the book trade. The first months after publication it had seemed a well-kept secret. Then George Will did a column on it. Brian Lamb had him on C-SPAN. Sales swelled correspondingly. *Back to Rome* had been likened to Merton's 1948 autobiography, but it was far more cerebral than that. Its chapters had traced Hawkins' odyssey from atheism through agnosticism, from Anglicanism to Catholicism in a style so matter of fact it suggested that entering the Church was the only reasonable thing to do. The question however was, which Catholic church had Hawkins entered? He was not an ultramontane, as new converts tended to be, but equally he avoided such bomb-throwers as Bailey, Curran, or Big Mac and Little Mac who had been eased out of Notre Dame by Ambler.

"Conciliarism", Nelligan said, turning a page of what Hawkins had written.

"Read on."

Hawkins suggested that the National Conference of Catholic Bishops call for a council. This was a suggestion that had been made by people at all points of the spectrum— progressive, middle-of-the-roaders, conservatives—in the years since Vatican II.

"Vatican III."

Meade nodded. "Other conferences may not join us in a revolt…"

"Revolt?"

"Hawkins' word. But a call for a council is a different thing. For the Pope too. It's asking a lot for him to give his consent to a conclave called to look into the legitimacy of his election, but a council to clear up matters generated by the last council and the years since, is something else. Hawkins found this."

Another sheet was dealt around the table. Cardinal Giancarlo Benedetto was quoted in *30 Giorni* to the effect that a century would not go by before the next council was called.

"Is that authentic?"

"He never denied it."

"Maybe he never read it."

"So we give him a chance to deny it now. Not that we want to appear belligerent. The reason this isn't conciliarism is that Hawkins acknowledges that only the Bishop of Rome can convene an ecumenical council."

"But that would be to accept his election as valid."

"Once the council convenes, we will get that on the agenda."

"That's Hawkins' idea?"

Meade shook his head. "No. He just thinks it is time for another ecumenical council."

The main difficulty with Hawkins' proposal, Lannan observed, was that no one had discussed it or even heard of it until Meade distributed the memo just minutes ago. Whatever the merit of the proposal, there would inevitably be a delay in implementing it. They couldn't spring on their brother bishops a proposal for an ecumenical council when there had been no preparation by way of consultation, discussion....

Meade said, "That's a week's work at most. How long did it take to round us up for this meeting? Besides, Hawkins has already tested the waters."

Lannan liked this less and less. The agenda for the meeting he had prepared was being derailed by Meade, and now the whole discussion turned on a novel proposal, which, it casually emerged, Meade had permitted Hawkins to explore even prior to bringing it to the attention of the executive council.

"He has been in correspondence with Joaquin Collins, secretary to the president of the Argentine bishops' conference."

"Argentina", Oberman said and whistled like a schoolboy. Latin America had far more bishops even than the United States, and there were a number of feisty conferences that had run afoul of Rome a number of times.

"Collins translated Hawkins' book into Spanish, and they became friends. Collins has his hand on the pulse of the conference and is certain they will join us in this. And as Argentina goes, so goes Latin America."

Lannan listened to the others rattling off the numbers such allies would give them, his own eye fixed on Hawkins' memo. In it he came to a reference to Cardinal Lannan and felt a little leap of his heart. A hope that had been dealt a blow in Rome revived. A clear assumption of the Hawkins memorandum was that the archbishop of Washington had been named a cardinal by the late Pope and therefore was a cardinal, no doubt about it. He wished he had thought to ask Hawkins to prepare a memo for him on that one specific point.

It would not be fair to say that Lannan's sole interest in the discussions that had occupied him since stories of the legitimacy of the conclave began was his own status as a cardinal. But the fact was that his status was inextricably bound up with everything else, council or conclave, whatever. His best chance of having his nomination recognized as in fact having created him cardinal now seemed to lie in the direction Meade had put before them.

"Make a motion", he advised Meade.

Meade proposed that they, as the executive council of the NCCB, after due but swift consultation with their brother bishops, go on record as favoring the convening of an ecumenical council, the proposal to take the form of a request to Pope John Paul III that he make preparations for and call such a council to be held in Rome and to take the title Vatican III.

Oberman seconded; the vote was unanimous.

"We are all conciliarists now", Nelligan said.

"Read the memo", Meade replied with a frown. He was a stickler for precision. He also wanted to succeed Lannan as president of the Conference.

4

"John Paul III and Vatican III", Ambrose Frawley said. "I can see it on banners strung across the streets of Rome."

"In English?" Morrow asked.

"In all the languages of the Church."

"Maybe a new council will bring back Latin."

"I am sure the notion will be encouraged, to gain support for the council."

"Where did the idea for a council originate?"

"Sao Paulo, apparently."

"The Brazil Nuts." Thus had the then-conservative bishops of Brazil been called by Iggie in his dispatches from Vatican II. In the aftermath of the Council, they were thought to be as flaky a conference as could be found in the Church. Leonardo Boff had been protected by the Brazilian bishops long after it was obvious that the man was heterodox. But he retained his Marxist faith for all the good that did him now. Dissident theology had suffered a more severe blow from the discrediting of socialist economic theory and the appetite of the masses for a consumer society than it ever had from the Brazilian bishops. Of late, however, Brazil had resumed a conservative look.

"The NCCB came in such a close second, it's hard to believe it was just a coincidence."

Frawley had reason to believe that Hawkins was behind it. On the phone Wales had been enigmatic, but his mention of the name Hawkins had clearly been meant to tell Frawley what he wanted to know. From that, he could reconstruct what must have happened at the almost secret meeting in the Arlington motel.

He did not tell James Morrow about Hawkins because the rapidly shifting ground beneath him made him unsure how things would eventually turn out and where he himself would be standing when the day was done. His first, and abiding, reaction to the speculation in the press about the legitimacy of the conclave was horror and disgust. There was of course nothing too sacred for the press to soil with its attention. Frawley had resigned himself to a brief bout of irresponsible speculation followed by a fading of the issue from the secular press. No one could take seriously the suggestion that Pope John

Paul III was not the duly elected and legitimate head of the Roman Catholic Church.

Or so it had seemed. The cranky voices first heard within the Church were predictable perhaps, still it was unsettling to have a bishop, even an auxiliary bishop, seriously propose that there was sufficient doubt about the conclave to warrant recalling it. He, like the press, tied this to the exclusion of the twenty cardinals named by the late Pope.

But the clamor had become widespread, in Europe, in Latin America, and now in North America. Frawley could have believed that the call for a new conclave had been a diversionary tactic, softening up the Pope for a council, which of course only he could call. Moreover, he could give the council fathers their charge, control the preparation of position papers, insure that life in Rome was uncomfortable enough that bishops would soon be dreaming of home. Vatican II had comprised four distinct sessions, stretching over four years. There was no need for anything so extensive now. Better one or two well-defined intensive sessions that addressed some of the most vexing matters that had beset the Church since 1965 when Vatican II came to an end.

"A council is a volatile thing", Morrow said. "The Pope would do well not to cave in to this pressure."

Cave in? There was no doubt where James Morrow's loyalties lay. Of course he was right to be wary. A council was a mere ruse to get the world's bishops together so the question of the conclave could be raised. A council might endorse the election of John Paul III or, conceivably, declare the election null and void and then, acting in concert with the cardinals among them, hold its own papal election. Canon law had envisaged no contingency like this.

"This idea's shelf-life may be no longer than the call for a new conclave."

"What if they called a council and nobody came?"

"I wonder what the quorum for a council is?"

Morrow, just guessing, thought it would have to include a majority of the world's bishops, but he would have to look it up. He said this with little enthusiasm however.

"Who would have thought anything like this could happen?" Frawley asked.

"The visionary of Viterbo."

Frawley looked at Morrow. Of course the rector of the North American College had seen the photocopied sheet hawked about the streets of Viterbo. He had received a photocopy of one from Quigley at Santa Susanna.

"Have you read the gibberish on that sheet?"

"That's not authentic. She brought her message directly to the Pope."

There were links here that cried out for exploration. How did Jim Morrow know these things? Undeniably he had become close to the secretary of state and, to a lesser degree, to the previous Holy Father in a remarkably short time. Frawley felt discomfort at the memory of the audience from which he and Lannan had been dismissed so that the new Pope could have a tête-à-tête with Morrow.

"She predicted this?"

"And much else."

They were dining in Trastevere at Coronari's, a crowded, noisy restaurant but one that Frawley loved. Afterward, they would go up the street to a cinema that showed American films in English. On clement nights the roof was rolled back, and during the by now-obligatory mating scenes Frawley and his flock of clerics could tip back their heads and contemplate the night sky.

"The trouble with prophecy, it seems to negate free will. I mean, if something is going to happen, no matter what, it no longer seems to matter what we do."

"But the prophecy concerns what we will do."

"But are we free not to do what is prophesied?"

"We better not get started on that."

"But it's important."

"Do you know of the dispute *de auxiliis?*"

"I see what you mean."

Once a pope had to order Jesuits and Dominicans to stop wrangling about future contingents, divine providence, and free will. The dispute had become so acerbic and convoluted, promising no successful or agreed-upon outcome, that its continuation simply sapped the energies of the disputants. There remained the central belief that the personal freedom we know we have is compatible with God's causality. How they are compatible is beyond our comprehension.

"Here there is a prior question, of course", Morrow mused. "Has the visionary just been lucky so far or will the rest of her prophecy come true?"

"What is the rest?"

"My lips are sealed."

"Truly?"

"Truly."

"The secret of Fatima", Frawley said edgily. Nothing was more annoying than being told there was something one couldn't be told.

The film was a golden oldie, *Indiana Jones and the Raiders of the Lost Ark*. It was, Frawley commented when Morrow drove him back to the North American College, a biblical thriller, sort of. Morrow thought that apt; but when alone, having a final glass of sweet vermouth and enjoying a pipe, Frawley reflected on the oddness of the times. There were more translations and editions of the Bible in print now than ever before, and they continued to pour from the presses, yet anyone who took Scripture at its word was called a fundamentalist, not a term of praise. Archeologists had located the site of the Tower of Babel; the Dead Sea Scrolls continued to provide historical corroborations; Noah's ark had allegedly been located on Mount Ararat. The Ark of the Covenant had been the inspiration of the movie they had just seen. Despite all the proofs of a kind that seemed peculiarly suited to an age fancying itself scientific, the Bible was widely regarded as a book of myths.

Of course for the believer, there was much more than the sites and historical events that could be established. Once Troy had been considered an invention of Homer. After it was located and seen to have been a real city, Homer continued to be read as he had been before the discovery. Where is the real Troy, what Schlieman discovered or what is found in the *Iliad*?

Frawley's thoughts returned to Morrow's matter-of-fact reference to the Viterbo visionary. Did he actually believe that an illiterate woman had been told what was about to happen to the Church?

"I am glad he could not tell me", Frawley said aloud as he turned off lights and went into his bedroom. "I would not want to know the future."

He repeated this when he was in bed and knew it was untrue. Wouldn't it be something to know the future and, like Morrow, be bound to secrecy?

5

Janet Fortin in her capacity as religious liaison was asked to sit in when Senator Partridge spoke with the President about James Morrow, American ambassador to the Vatican.

"You initially opposed the nomination as I remember, Senator Partridge." The President lapsed into a Southern drawl as he addressed the venerable senator from North Carolina.

"Yes sir, I did. My guide in the matter, apart from my profound belief in the wall of separation between church and state, was Senator Crowe, a very serious Catholic. It was not the nominee but the post, he objected to. That outlook attracted me."

"But Mr. Morrow won your confidence in the end."

"He did. He gave a magnificent account of himself before the committee and prior to that in a televised discussion with Preacher Butterworth."

"I saw a video of that."

"Mrs. Partridge and I visited Ambassador Morrow in Rome during the first month of his service there."

Senator Partridge proceeded in a Southern tempo. Nothing worth saying should be said hastily. Rush into it, and it lost its force. Janet thought he would go on and on about how such matters ought to be discussed and never get around to why he had asked for this appointment. Casey was already sliding back his sleeve and glancing at his watch.

Eventually it came. Partridge wanted to know if the President had authorized the ambassador to intervene in the internal affairs of the Catholic Church. The President widened his eyes and asked why the senator should even ask such a question.

"Well, sir, as you know, considerable doubt has been raised as to whether the present man over there is a legitimately elected pope. There is a lot of disputation going on, and I don't pretend to understand any of it. That's their business, and they're welcome to it. The problem, as I see it, is this. If we have an ambassador to the Pope and they don't know who the Pope is, least ways some of them say this man ain't it, then who's our man ambassador to? When he talks to this one, he is in effect taking sides in a dispute among Catholics, and I don't think you or I or any other American thinks that's what he ought to be doing."

Whortle, the President's counsel, said it was a good point. He would appreciate it if the senator allowed him time to check out the situation.

"You'll let me know right away?"

"Yes, Senator." Whortle had looked at the President and got a nod.

"I mean my subcommittee, of course. This isn't a personal errand, you understand."

While Partridge and the President shook hands for the photographer, Whortle took Janet outside.

"What's he up to?" he asked.

"What he said, I guess."

"Is the Pope in trouble?"

"Give me time to check it out."

"That's my line."

It was because they relied on her access to the NCCB that she had been invited to the meeting, so Whortle would have been surprised if she hadn't offered to get opinions other than her own.

Her own opinion was that she was sick and tired of all the stories about the Pope, the conclave, a possible ecumenical council. In the media, it all sounded like blocs shifting and maneuvering for power. Obviously there were some willing to bring down the Pope if they could. Gene Wales, when she called him, was reluctant to meet. But it was important to go on as if nothing had happened. Janet was certain that if she treated his belated attack of adolescent infatuation lightly, so eventually would he. No matter what he had said in the Vesuvio, he was not the kind of priest who went over the wall; he was not a man who had entered into the life he led without thought. Earlier he had puzzled her with his untroubled serenity that the way he lived made perfect sense. Of course as a Catholic she supposed she should think the same thing, but all around there was talk of doing away with celibacy, ordaining married men, not making such a big thing of the difference between priests and everyone else. And Wales had been a Rock of Gibraltar on those questions.

"Some priests talk as if on the day of their ordination they were handed an envelope containing the surprise message that they must remain celibate. That's nonsense. One reason preparation for the priesthood takes so long is to give you time to see if it is indeed your calling. And what's the magic of marriage? Most people are married, and it doesn't have any predictable effect on them, one way or the other. I mean, some husbands are good and some aren't. I suspect that a man who is a bad celibate priest would be a bad married priest."

That was then. And he had been willing almost to a fault to explain to her the nature of the sacramental priesthood. She had listened, interested enough, fascinated by this man who was both a relative and one whom she needn't worry about possibly having a drink or two and being all over her. And yet, to her enormous surprise, he had made that declaration of love in Rome.

It was almost as important to Janet, as she thought it was for him, to get that into the past, to make it as if it had never been. She was not dismayed simply at his wavering, but even more that she had been the occasion for it. If she had been the ailment, she would be the cure as well.

"Senator Partridge has been to the White House to complain about James Morrow's involvement in Church politics."

"How so?"

"I'd rather not go into all this on the phone."

The place she suggested they meet was an ice cream parlor, bright with whites and yellows and pale blues, 67 flavors available on four kinds of cones, or in cups if you preferred. The tables were classic replicas, twisted iron legs, marble tops. Janet ordered a black raspberry sundae, and he asked for a vanilla cone. His manner was awkward, though he seemed to make an effort to be cheery. The Roman collar and black suit, with immaculate french cuffs emerging from its sleeves, were reassuring. The uniform.

"What about Morrow?"

She continued with her sundae, indicating that talk would have to wait. Good Lord, how delicious it was. He was smiling at her.

"Why don't you have another?"

"Eat your cone."

"What exactly did Senator Partridge say?"

"If I understood better what was going on, I might be able to tell you. But here's his beef, kind of. Catholics are involved in an internal squabble over the legitimacy of the new Pope. Our ambassador, by the very fact of meeting with John Paul III, is taking sides. This means that the United States ambassador is taking sides in an internal dispute."

"Don't ambassadors do that all the time?"

"Touché. He would say the difference is that this is a Church we're meddling in, not another state."

"Separation of church and state in international relations."

"Is the Pope in trouble?"

His expression was one of pain. "He may be. If certain people succeed in what they're doing."

"Should they fail?"

He looked at his cone as if he did not remember that he was holding it. "I hope and pray that they fail."

"Who's involved?"

"In this country? Who isn't?"

"Archbishop Lannan?"

He nodded. She waited, but he said nothing further. It was obvious he was out of sympathy with his boss.

What she took back to the White House was that the American bishops in league with Canadian, Latin American, and European bishops were calling for the convening of an ecumenical council. The ostensible purpose was to address matters that had arisen since the close of Vatican II, but the fact that the new Pope was a clone of his predecessor was the focus of discontent, as well as his alleged failure to embrace the spirit of the Council. Who knew how long this Pope might live? Gene had mentioned Leo XIII, old when elected, but Pope for a quarter-century. Left to himself, John Paul III would conduct business as usual, and the dreams of reform would fade further away.

"They just want to tie his hands?"

"I think they mean to depose him."

6

Cardinal Taylor, the secretary of state, came with Morrow to the papal apartment. Monenem, the Ugandan secretary, poured them each a glass of wine. The Pope drank half of his in one swallow then put down his glass.

"Your countrymen are causing a great uproar, Mr. Ambassador."

"They are not alone."

"It began in Brazil", Taylor said.

"Did it?" the Pope asked. "Perhaps. But without America, it would mean nothing. Do you think I should call an ecumenical council, Mr. Ambassador?"

"Has Cardinal Taylor read the visionary of Viterbo?"

"Do you think I should be guided by her forecasts?"

Morrow looked at the small Madonna in an elaborate frame that hung on the wall behind the Pope. "How is one guided by a forecast?"

The Pope smiled. "Padre Pio predicted that John Paul II

would die after fifteen years in office. He was wrong. There are those who would have considered the saintly Capuchin a more reliable prophet than the woman in Viterbo. Still he was wrong. What if that Pope had made decisions on the basis of the prophecy, assuming he had only fifteen years? He might have done some things he didn't do and vice versa."

"I recall no mention of an ecumenical council by the woman from Viterbo."

"Not in so many words", Cardinal Taylor said.

"You are asking my advice?" Morrow asked.

"I am asking what you would do", the Pope said, wearing a diplomat's smile.

Morrow had been thinking of little else, and he thought he had a defensive move."I would call an extraordinary synod. That could placate the rebels, and it is a meeting over which you could expect to retain complete control."

"You think an ecumenical council would get out of hand?"

"I don't even want to think of it."

"A council can do nothing without me."

"Once it convened, you could do nothing without it."

Taylor murmured that he agreed. Monenem made no sign when the Pope looked to him. Morrow was proud of his suggestion. An extraordinary synod was a far better idea.

"Not a conclave?"

"Holy Father," protested Taylor, "don't even say the word."

"But all this agitation is over my election. They will not be placated with anything less than getting rid of me and installing someone more to their liking."

There was in his voice the suggestion that he would almost welcome that solution. Was his head still full of Sicilian retirement, the direction of the Church relinquished to a successor, himself preparing to leave this valley of tears?

"Do you have any doubt that you were legitimately

elected?" Morrow asked, the words out of his mouth before he realized how presumptuous they were.

"No."

"Then you must not call a conclave."

The Pope reached for his glass, held it under his nose for a moment, then drank it down.

"I will not call a conclave, no." He licked the wine from his lips. "I will not call an ecumenical council." He gripped the arms of his chair. "Nor will I call an extraordinary synod."

"Thank God", whispered the Ugandan.

"Amen", said Cardinal Taylor.

It was the right thing to do; Morrow could see that now. The pressure and agitation had motives that were unworthy. He knew all too well the situation in the United States. But now the dissenters had the bishops with them. Bailey and Lannan, his boyhood friends, were allied again. Morrow was ashamed of them. The Pope was right to make no concessions. But being right did not mean that his decision would not be without repercussions. He would be called intransigent, an obstacle to unity in the Church, a relic of a day long past.

"There are difficult times ahead, Holy Father."

"Can the successor of Peter expect better treatment than Peter received?"

CHAPTER THREE

I

"We'll have to wait and see" became Frawley's standard reply
when one of his young charges asked him what to make of
these unprecedented developments. The rector retained the air
of a man incapable of being surprised, one for whom recent
events had been the unfolding of a script at which he had been
given an advance look, but the truth of the matter was that he
was more confused than any of the students at the North
American College.

Nothing remotely like this had ever happened in the
Church, unless perhaps one went back to the Arians of the
fourth century. The more he thought of it, the more inescap-
able the analogy seemed. He got out Newman's book and read
it, not as he had before, for the author's style as much as the
contents, but poring over it as if perhaps this was the script for
the times through which they were passing.

It went without saying of course that the Church would
come out of this eventually, battered, bruised, bearing one
more wound than Rosmini had counted, but intact.

The Church had survived Arianism, the defection of the
majority of her bishops, but where was the Athanasius who
would guide them through the present troubles?

Frawley reviewed the list of cardinals; he thought of the
bishops whose influence might transcend their dioceses, he

considered theologians. But theologians were the problem rather than the solution: since the close of Vatican II—before that, really—they had been urging an agenda only dubiously related to what the Council itself had done. The formation of bishops' conferences had created conflicting national solidarities and provided theologians with a better-defined target. They need only influence the bishops' conference of their country, and they could bring about what they alleged the Council had been unable to do because of people like the late and unlamented, and much maligned, Cardinal Ottaviani.

The offices of the conference became prime places of influence; new bishops were increasingly chosen from among those who had worked for the conference.... It was difficult not to see how accurate James Morrow had been in his history of the Church in America. Those to the right of Morrow saw what had happened as the delayed triumph of the modernism condemned by Pius X. But Pius X had called Modernism, not just a heresy, but the summation of all heresies.

"It's a question of power", Frank Bailey had growled in a discussion with Morrow that Frawley had sat in on. Bailey had been little more than a prolific journalist, an occasional television presence when the networks needed a priest to criticize the Pope, and had all but faded away until he was resuscitated by recent events.

"Power", Morrow had repeated. "As in political power?"

"Power to control the agenda. The problem with the Pope, the late Pope—" he grimaced, "the very late Pope, may he rest in peace, was that he wanted to control the flow of information."

"You sound like an analyst at a political convention."

But Bailey was undeterred by the implicit criticism; he accepted as fact that they were engaged in a political struggle, in most ways indistinguishable from secular politics. The Church might be more than that—Bailey never denied that it was—but that "more" floated on top of this grubby ongoing struggle. Bailey's main complaint was that he and those who thought as he did had been losing the struggle. Now, unexpectedly, just when all seemed lost, the field was reversed, and Bailey had the air of a winner.

And that was before the American bishops upped the ante by calling for an ecumenical council. There was a scramble among Frawley's wards to read up on how Vatican II had come about. They learned of course that it had been announced to an astounded and unprepared Church by John XXIII.

Frawley's own lines of communication within the Vatican were now better than ever before, with Taylor working with Bukoba, the dean of the College of Cardinals now that Gonsalez was dead.

"He would like to return to Africa", Taylor had said recently of Bukoba. "He does not want to die in Rome."

"He's not that old."

"He is ten years older than his father was when he died."

Bukoba was tall, regal, expressionless, and said to be a very holy man. He had retained a stranger's aloofness and survived long years in the Vatican as prefect for the Propagation of the Faith, growing old without showing it.

"He looks sixty."

"He is approaching his sixty-ninth birthday."

"What of the twenty men the late Pope named cardinals?"

Taylor smiled. "My lips are sealed."

"Would you care to confess it?" Frawley said playfully.

What had Taylor chosen not to say? "Chosen" seemed the appropriate word, since what he had already told Frawley must have been as confidential as any decision about the twenty nominees whose careers as cardinal had been aborted by the death of the Pope who named them.

Not to include them in a new conclave would be to raise all the objections that had arisen about the previous conclave. To include them, on the other hand, would seem to acknowledge that they should have been included before. Perhaps Benedetto meant first to hold the ceremony that had been scheduled then canceled, the official reception of the twenty into the College.

In the event, John Paul III chose a fourth possibility. He named thirty-eight new members to the College, a list including the famous Twenty and adding others from the East and Africa. It had been, Taylor said, Bukoba's idea.

"Africa now has more cardinals than Europe and the U.S."

"Given the success of contraception propaganda, it will soon have more Catholics."

No doubt it was fitting that this great shift in the population and center of gravity of the Church be reflected in the membership of the College of Cardinals. The Church had come to Rome from the Middle East; its Eastward progress had been checked by the Great Schism, and thus it had taken on a Western character. "Europe is the faith, the faith is Europe"; when Hilaire Belloc had written that, it had not been far from the truth. It was true no more. It might more truly be said of Africa, or of those countries, which—after being freed from the cold hand of communism and then having gone through some years of consumerist convulsion—then united with Rome and were pulsing with a renewed and vibrant faith.

"Twenty-nine African cardinals. Bukoba has become the black pope indeed."

"Don't tell that to the Jesuits."

Not long before, the general of the Society of Jesus had been known as *il papa nero*. Morrow in his history had quoted an unnamed theological wag who said that the demise of the

Jesuits was due to the fact that their general had been more *Nero* than *Papa*. It was Bukoba's skin rather than his cassock that gave him claim to the title; that and the fact that he had been among the long shots prior to the last conclave. *Newsweek*'s reference to him as a dark horse had caused a minor rumble about racism that gave more publicity to the possibility than it realistically deserved.

Before the announcement was made, Frawley had been on the phone to Washington telling Lannan to stand by.

"What is it?"

"Just telephoning you could jeopardize access to a privileged source of information."

"So what do you have to lose?"

"The question is, what do you have to gain?"

Lannan was irked by all this secrecy, and who could blame him? At that time, Frawley could not have told him more, so he thanked God he had not succumbed to the urge to hazard a guess as to what it was Archbishop Lannan should stand by for.

It must have occurred to Lannan that he was about to have his status as cardinal made unequivocal, and by the very man who had been blamed far and wide for depriving him of it.

2

"Pull a Sartre", Bailey urged when Lannan stopped dodging his phone calls and Frank was put through to the cellular phone in the archbishop's limo.

"What? Who is this?"

"Frank Bailey, for God's sake. Jean Paul Sartre had the integrity to refuse the Nobel prize when it was offered. George

C. Scott would not permit his name to be even considered for an Oscar."

"What are you suggesting?"

"Look, you've got the satisfaction of his caving in. Savor it for a day or two, why not? Then you turn it into something really big. You say, thanks a lot, but no thanks."

There was no way Frank could interpret the silence that greeted his suggestion as receptive. For a moment, the dissenting theologian had an inkling of what he was asking Lannan to do. To be a cardinal of the Roman Catholic Church, even in a College swollen by rescinding the rule of mandatory retirement at eighty and naming all those blacks, even after the roller-coaster ride occasioned by the death of the previous Pope, was the longed-for acme of Thomas Lannan's clerical career. And Frank was telling him, via cellular phone, to say thanks a lot but no thanks.

"Remember what's at stake."

Lannan said that he appreciated Frank's call, that this was not the way to discuss such an astounding proposal, that he was about to confirm a Church full of converts, and...

Frank didn't push it. As he had said, Lannan should enjoy the renomination for a while, milk it for what it was worth. Who couldn't understand that? Frank could. It was precisely the sweet wine of notoriety he was counting on to persuade Lannan to make the dramatic refusal and ascend into a higher heaven of attention.

"He'll never do it", Wynn said.

"Meaning you wouldn't."

"Me? Ha. Morrow's dog is more likely to enter that College than I am."

"His dog?"

"It's called Wolsey. Maybe that's why he didn't bring him to Rome."

Frank thought of the great, bloated Wolsey that Orson Welles had played in the film. His reaction had been that of Protestant viewers: there was the self-indulgent prince of the Church, with a mistress sharing his bed. No matter that Wolsey had betrayed the Church, swearing fealty to Henry first. But Bailey had blotted out the mistress.

Flo had given up nagging him about pitching the whole thing, resigning the priesthood, taking a position on a faculty where no retribution could reach him.

"Why?"

"So we could marry", she said through her teeth, poking his middle painfully with her finger.

"We are married."

"Are we?"

"What is marriage beyond what we have?"

"You mean beyond what you have."

He did not want a replay of that old argument now. In the heat of it, Flo took evident pleasure in calling herself his whore, his concubine, his mistress, something he used like Kleenex when he felt like it, then discarded. Discarded! Did she forget who paid the rent on the condo above his? The carpenter he had hired to put in a spiral staircase linking the apartments had started some gossip after seeing Bailey in a collar on television, and for some weeks it looked as if, like it or not, he would have to come out of the closet, or whatever the straight equivalent of the phrase was. At the time he had readied a statement, intending to go out with panache, a media event, detailing the ways in which the Church had failed to take up the challenge of Vatican II. He would deflect any criticism his relationship with Flo occasioned, encouraging the view that it was a courageous flaunting of an unjust demand of the Church, thus turning it into an indictment of the popes and bishops who had thwarted the spirit of Vatican II.

The rumors spread then died before a general incredulity that he could really be involved with a woman and go on publicly chiding the Church. Flo loved to read about Talleyrand and the Borgias and Medicis as if she were establishing his pedigree, but Frank Bailey was not really interested. Except to wonder if those men had, like himself, gone beyond the naïve faith that was theirs when they were ordained to a new and deeper understanding of what the Church is. Maybe they had been simply cynics, Borgia anyway; but Frank, like Talleyrand, was convinced that he had transposed his faith into a more effective key for the times in which he lived. The center of gravity, as Tom Sheehan had said, was now orthopraxy, not orthodoxy.

"Not immediately, he won't", Frank agreed with Wynn. "All I ask is a chance to lay it out for him."

Lannan's satisfaction with the new list of cardinals and his renomination could not rival the excitement Frank felt when he realized that this provided the opportunity that the NCCB had sought in demanding a new ecumenical council. The new list represented an adroit countermove, and Frank was the first to admit it, but it did not leave the Church in America without a response. The point of the new council would have been to replace Benedetto or at least to establish that now he was the choice of a council insisted on and dominated by bishops who represented the future of the Church, not the remnants of the old. But the recently enlarged list of new cardinals seemed to check the proposal for a council. There was a new and geographic question on the table.

Was the Church to be led into the future by the backward bishops of the East and those of scarcely civilized Africa? Frank Bailey did not consider himself a racist. He held his black fellow citizens in high esteem; he had many friends and allies among them. It was a cultural not a racial prejudice he felt against all those dusky prelates from the dark continent, against all those flat Slavic faces from the East, against those varied Semites from the Middle East—the Coptics, Maronites, who were enjoying such a rebirth in Egypt, Iraq, Iran, Syria. It had been at Damascus that Fahwi the convert prophet from Islam had been martyred, the event triggering an incredible movement into the Church by former worshippers of Allah who brought with them to the new allegiance all their fanatic fervor.

"They're all the same to me," said Bailey, "theological throwbacks. To call them preconciliar is a compliment, unless the council one has in mind was Trent."

"Florence", Wynn said, and Bailey jumped, but Iggie was referring to the Council of Florence.

Thomas Lannan held the future in his hands. With one exhilarating act he could set the Church in the United States on a new track, showing leadership to the backward regional churches and not permitting them a veto on the direction taken.

First he had to get to Lannan and lay out for him this vision of the future to be realized by dramatically refusing the red hat and declaring solidarity with his fellow American bishops. Fleischhaecker, the other American on the list, had died in a helicopter crash as he was hopping about his huge California diocese. For Lannan to accept would put him in a small group of aging cardinals dominated by his enemies. Frank felt there were so many ways to make his case to Tom that Wales' polite inflexibility enraged him.

"Does Tom know I'm trying to reach him?"

"All your messages have gotten through."

"Gotten through! What the hell is this? Tom Lannan and I grew up together."

"I know that, Father."

Father. You're damn right, Father. The one time a bishop—not his own ordinary—had offered to get him made a monsignor, Bailey had batted down the notion. There were some who had resigned as monsignor in protest when *Humanae vitae* came out. They were Frank Bailey's kind of prelate, not those who could be domesticated by red piping on their cassocks and the glint of red under the lace on their surplices. Not that Frank even owned a cassock anymore. That had been his own form of rejection—away with the collar and the archaic clerical clothes that tried to make every priest look like Bing Crosby in *The Bells of St. Mary's*. If they had made a long-time series of that, Bing would have ended up getting laicized and marrying Ingrid Bergman.

"Tell him it's urgent."

"Of course."

The name of Wales went back on Bailey's enemies list.

It was a rumor retailed to him from the USCC that provided Frank with his opening. The White House was preparing some kind of statement meant to placate Senator Partridge and his right-wing friends concerning Jim Morrow's coziness with the Pope at a time when American Catholics seemed to doubt that Benedetto was the Pope. Lannan's nomination was being taken as a signal that all was now peaceful, and Partridge no longer had a case. Had Joe Wallet followed through? It didn't look like it.

Bailey called the White House and finally was put through to Janet Fortin.

"Frank Bailey thinks I'm acting on my own, Archbishop",
Wales said to Lannan.

"Have you told him you were?"

"Quite the opposite."

"Just a little longer, Gene. I simply don't want to talk to
him yet." Lannan, possessed of a new aplomb since the visit
from the nuncio telling him of his renomination, shook his
head. "Frank is as obsolete as a fire horse, and he doesn't know
it. The death of the Pope brought him out of the firehouse
thinking he heard a bell. He thought he was back in the sixties
again. He has been fading away for years and doesn't realize
it."

"The rumor about him never stops."

Lannan held up a hand and closed his eyes. "I don't want to
hear it. If it was true it would have come out by now. At his
present age, any such accusation would be more farce than
tragedy."

Since Bailey and Lannan were the same age, this suggested
a new and philosophical acceptance of his own place on the
human span. Lannan had not told Wales about Frank's extraordinary suggestion. Had he forgotten that the monsignor stayed
on the line after transferring calls to the limo to make sure that
the connection wasn't broken? Why hadn't Lannan labeled the
suggestion absurd then and there, rather than permit Bailey to
think it was an open question needing only a persuasive visit
from its proponent?

Meanwhile public television decided to devote a segment of
its nightly news show to Lannan's appointment, which was
interpreted as removing all cause for the objections raised by
Butterworth and Partridge. When Wales brought the proposal
to Lannan, the archbishop thought at first the invitation was

for him. But his disappointment was swallowed up in the satisfaction of knowing his nomination to cardinal would be discussed by a distinguished panel for twelve minutes. Of course Monsignor Wales must take part.

"Who else is on?"

"An aide of Pastor Butterworth's and the counsel of Partridge's subcommittee."

Lannan nodded at this roster of second-level people. "The three of you?"

"They're trying to get a fourth."

"Whom did you suggest?"

"They didn't ask for suggestions."

"You should have volunteered a name."

Whether or not they would have accepted his suggestion, it turned out to have been a crucial omission. The fourth panelist was Frank Bailey, and he took the occasion to make his private suggestion a public prediction.

"He won't accept", Frank said confidently when Lannan's appearance on the new list of cardinals was interpreted as oil upon the waters.

Foyle, the interviewer, took the bait as a shark takes to blood.

"Is that true, Monsignor?"

But Frank intervened. "Don't put Monsignor Wales on the spot, Mr. Foyle. I suspect that he thinks a mental reservation denial is in order."

"What kind of denial?"

"Call it a little white lie."

Whatever Wales might have said after that would have been discounted. But Frank had taken Foyle on a little nostalgic trip, recalling that he and Lannan and James Morrow had been in school together.

"Morrow the ambassador?"

"Morrow the historian", Frank said, laughing. "I'm sure Jim

429

Morrow finds being American ambassador to the Vatican as improbable as Tom Lannan would find becoming a cardinal in the present circumstances."

Again Foyle bit, and Frank was happy to lay out for him his vision of where the Church in the U.S. was headed. "This is not the time for American archbishops to become the house pets of a papacy that identifies itself with the most retrograde churches in the backward areas of the world. It is high time this country took a leading role in the universal Church. And I don't mean just as financial contributor."

"What do you think of that, Monsignor?"

"Fr. Bailey is famous for futuristic scenarios."

The Reverend Impasto, Butterworth's right-hand man, smelled a rat. He wasn't sure he liked this identification of the Catholic Church and the United States.

"Housing the United Nations on our shores is bad enough, so far as I'm concerned. But the idea of Vatican City on the Potomac is alarming."

"The head of the Roman Catholic Church is the bishop of Rome, Pastor. There's only one city where he can be."

Partridge's aide Jackson wanted to talk about the asymmetry of the apostolic nuncio in Washington and the American ambassador to the Vatican.

"As I understand it, the papal legate represents the Pope to his fellow churchman in this country, and that is fair enough and none of my business. But Mr. Morrow—and I don't mean this personally, I am talking about the post—represents this country to the Pope. Do we need such a representative?"

"No", said Frank. "We don't."

"You oppose having an American ambassador to the Vatican, Fr. Bailey?"

"I think most Catholics do."

"Well, I know that Senator Crowe does."

Frank made a face. "Maybe for different reasons than the rest of us do."

Foyle wanted to know more about Frank's assertion that Thomas Lannan planned to refuse elevation to the College of Cardinals, but Frank got cute.

"Maybe I should have taken Monsignor Wales' tack and said nothing. I hope I'm not betraying the confidence of a boyhood friend."

Lannan was furious and sought to blame the whole episode on Wales. Even when he saw how irrational that was, he was edgy and fuming.

"The question is, what do I do now?"

"Nothing."

"Nothing!"

"He has put you in the same spot he put me. Whatever you say both gives longer life to the lie and will be discounted as itself a lie."

"He did lie", Lannan insisted. "Shamelessly."

"I suspect that if we read the transcript we would find that he is covered by some subterfuge in moral theology.

"Mental reservation?" Lannan said angrily. "Reserve the truth and utter its opposite?"

"I'm not defending him."

But Lannan acted as if Monsignor Wales was defending himself, something Wales did not appreciate. In recent weeks he had been on half-retreat, trying to find himself spiritually. He had come to see how much he owed Janet for her sensible reaction to his lapse. Dear God, what if she had accepted his declaration at face value? Oh, there was a little leap in his heart at the thought, but it was soon overwhelmed by the realization of how radically his life would have changed. His weakness had humbled him. For years he had lived in the illusion that his priestly character and commitment were so affirmed by time and inclination that any deviation from his life's goal was unthinkable. Then to his own complete surprise, after years of untroubled celibacy, he had become infatuated with Janet, his defenses lowered because of their being cousins of a sort. What previous small chinks in his moral armor had made him vulnerable? He was now engaged in repairing the damage, learning from the episode, and praying daily for Janet in thanksgiving for her common sense. This effort enabled him now not to lose his temper with Archbishop Lannan.

"I can't just do nothing, Gene."

"The decisive answer will be given when you go to Rome to be invested."

Lannan thought about that. He liked it as an ultimate solution. But that called for several weeks during which Frank could be counted on to continue his effort to preempt his decision.

4

"Tom?"

Lannan looked at the receiver. Three people at most had this unlisted number, and Frank Bailey was not among them.

"I don't want to talk with you."

"Don't hang up."

But Lannan had returned the phone to his ear. "You betrayed me."

"The announcement will be easier to make now."

"Will you stop it? What in the name of God leads you to think I would take your advice on such a matter?"

"Let me make my case."

"I heard your case the other night."

"I was sure you were watching."

It had been years since Lannan had felt such a powerful urge to employ obscenity. The alternative was to hang up. He slammed down the phone and removed the cord, disabling it. He would have his unlisted number changed before he hooked it up again.

If only things could be handled so easily. But what Frank had started acquired a life of its own, as commentators and columnists took up the suggestion that the archbishop of Washington would refuse to be created cardinal by a Pope whose face was set toward the past. The majority who dealt with the subject applauded the alleged decision, seeing it as praiseworthy American independence. One or two in the minority argued that, since Lannan's position during the conclave had been that he already was a cardinal, his refusal should have been stated as the refusal of a redundancy. How could a cardinal be created a cardinal?

Lannan raised again with Wales the desirability of a categorical denial of the story Frank had started, but his secretary continued to think that it was best to let the story die.

"But it isn't dying."

"It will if you don't feed it."

But others fed it. Archbishop Meade of St. Louis and Preller of Baltimore said in answer to questions that they would press for a vote of support for Lannan's decision on the part of the executive committee of the NCCB. Of course Meade and Preller were smarting from being passed over on several occasions when new cardinals were named, despite the fact that their dioceses had often been led by cardinals.

"Frank Bailey just made that up", Lannan said to Preller. "He's trying to force me to a decision I haven't made."

"But he's right, Tom. You've got the chance of a lifetime." Meade, vice president of the executive committee, instructed

Wales to convene the committee, something his position entitled him to do.

"He said he realizes it might look self-serving if you called the meeting."

"I don't want a meeting."

"The rest of the committee does."

"Damn it. I told you I should have issued a denial and nipped this in the bud."

Wales did not admit in words that he had given bad advice, but his expression was eloquent.

The meeting was scheduled for the following Monday. Wales told him that the others understood that Archbishop Lannan would not want to be in attendance.

"Archbishop Meade said to count on their support."

Again Lannan fought the impulse to swear. Words he had only heard and never used formed on his tongue, and he had to clench his teeth lest they emerge. What infuriated him was that it was Frank Bailey who was orchestrating this. Only a few months ago, Frank had been on the shelf, a relic of another time; his column, once syndicated across the country and feared by the bishops in whose diocesan papers it appeared, though they dared not risk his anger by having it removed, was now carried by perhaps three papers. He was no longer the mover and shaker he once had been. His vision of the postconciliar Church was cranky and irrelevant. His defenders said that Frank was a victim of his own success. His outlook now prevailed in the chanceries and theology faculties of the nation. Who needs a professional dissenter when yesterday's dissent has become today's orthodoxy? But however it was explained, it was generally recognized that Frank Bailey himself had had his day and that only obscurity awaited him.

Now suddenly he had been resurrected by the death of one

pope and the election of another. The drum he was beating was that of a separate "American Church", one that might pay lip service to the pope as bishop of Rome, but as a practical matter would function independently of control by the antiquated dicasteries of the Vatican. And he had turned Thomas Lannan into a puppet, moving to a script Frank had written and Lannan found repellent, not least because it demanded that he refuse to become Cardinal Thomas Lannan.

He had prepared a written statement for Meade to read to the executive council in which he dissociated himself from Frank's campaign and expressed his intention to accept the honor the Holy Father proposed to confer upon him. He would receive it, he added, as an honor done to the archdiocese of Washington and the Catholics of the United States of America, not as a personal honor.

"Did you give it to him, Monsignor?"

Wales nodded. "He read it immediately."

"And then?"

"He looked at me for a moment, then winked. He said, 'Tell Tom I understand.'"

"I'm going to go to the meeting."

Finally Wales agreed with the necessity for action. They drove in silence to the great building near the National Shrine; they went up in the elevator in silence. Lannan preceded his secretary down the hallway to his office, his heels resounding on the marble floor.

"Good afternoon", Harriet said, smiling over her computer monitor.

"Are they in the conference room?"

Harriet looked blank. Lannan went through his presidential office and opened the door to the conference room. It was empty. He went inside and stared at the polished table, at the leather chairs, at the portrait of the previous pope on the wall. Wales and Harriet came in.

"There is a meeting of the executive council", Lannan said to Harriet. "Where is it?"

"Archbishop Meade's meeting?"

"Yes."

"He said they were preparing a nice surprise for you so you wouldn't be there."

"Where is it being held?"

She had to check her calendar. The address she had given the members of the executive council when she called them was of a motel in Bethesda. Lannan looked at his watch. By the time he got there the meeting could well be over. He looked at Wales. The monsignor's expression was as neutral as he could make it.

Lannan thanked Harriet, assumed a mask of insouciance, and headed back to the elevator. A red-faced man with a white crew cut looked out of an office door and gave him a thumb's-up.

"We're with you, Tom."

Bishop Shreck. Lannan nodded. Schreck stood there grinning at him even after he had gotten into the elevator with Wales. Then mercifully the doors closed, and Lannan could let his face collapse into an expression of gloom.

When Monsignor Wales slowed to turn into the short driveway leading to the garage, his way was blocked by a parked car. Lannan, tense in the passenger seat, needed little more to explode.

"Can't the idiot read?"

A back door of the car opened, and a diminutive figure in black emerged.

"Vilani!" Wales said.

But Lannan, all anger gone, was already on the sidewalk, hurrying toward the apostolic nuncio. He grasped the smaller man's hand and felt his knee buckle, as if he were about to

436

genuflect and kiss the other archbishop's ring. But Vilani would have prevented any such obeisance. His almond eyes searched Lannan's face. "Is it true?"

"No", Lannan said, feeling almost giddy. "It's not true. I have no intention of refusing the Holy Father's great honor." Vilani made a dismissive noise that fluttered his generous lips. Now that he was reassured, he assured Lannan that he had never believed for a moment that the archbishop of Washington would refuse elevation to the College of Cardinals. Was there a wistful note in his voice? But surely Vilani could count on being made cardinal when his diplomatic career was done.

"I have a most confidential message", Vilani whispered.

"Archbishop, you remember Monsignor Wales. My confidential secretary."

Vilani was gracious, but clearly wanted a private conversation. Lannan nodded, and Wales left them.

"Perhaps we could talk in my automobile."

Vilani sent his driver for a walk and carefully filled his pipe, then lighted it with equal care.

"I have a message from the Holy Father." A cloud of smoke emerged from his mouth as he spoke. Lannan had never smelled such wonderful tobacco.

After the turmoil engineered by Frank, it was sweet to hear what the nuncio had to say. Archbishop Lannan would be greeted in Rome a week from this day, and the following morning, along with the other new cardinals, be solemnly inducted into the sacred college.

"While you are in Rome, a conclave will be called."

"A conclave!"

Vilani looked sad and took his pipe from his mouth. "A conclave."

"But why?"

"The Holy Father's explanation is apt, though somewhat surprising. 'It is fitting that one man give his life for his people.'"

PART SEVEN

CHAPTER ONE

I

Iggie Wynn's workroom had been designed for efficiency. Radiating out from his motorized chair was, to the east, a desk used largely just to hold the piles of papers, unfinished letters, magazines, clippings, and the decades of detritus of a popular theologian who could throw nothing away. To the north was the ingenious shelved computer stand, whose wheels had been removed to give it greater stability; to the west, a telephone table cum fax machine; and, southward, a television set and shortwave radio. Iggie rolled into this nest first thing in the morning and remained there much of the day. There was no effective way to fight off the urge to sleep at his age, so he catnapped throughout the day, putting his head on a pillow laid on the reading tray attached to his chair. He had learned to let napping substitute for sleep, by and large, though somewhere between three and four, he rolled into the next room and spent an hour or two in bed before the community Mass. He concelebrated from his chair.

Academic friends had endowed chairs, bishops had their seats, and the pope had his throne, but Iggie operated from an invalid's chair that had made him even more effective, despite the long, fallow period that had been brought to an end with the death of the Pope. Iggie had not hated the Pope. In fact he admired him as a worthy opponent, one who had deftly quelled the opposition through a long reign, outlasting his critics, ignoring them rather than squelching them. They had grown content to wait for him to die, but it was the ranks of the progressives that had been decimated while the ancient pontiff nodded on his throne. Iggie congratulated himself on his decision to save his ammunition and wait for the next man, trusting that the forces of progress and change would stand a better chance with the successor. Iggie had cultivated his sources, recruited a newsman or two, even a few nuns who were not wholly disenchanted, and waited.

Frank Bailey groused and complained, taking on the look of a defeated man. Iggie had given up trying to convince Bailey that they had won. Tom Sheehan had been crazy to publish his triumphalist screed in the *New York Review of Books*, but he had been absolutely right. The progressives were in control of the Church in the United States. Let the Pope scold and admonish, let him write his endless encyclicals, let him jet around the world to be accorded a frantic welcome by crowds who forgot all about him within a week of his departure. The simple truth was that progressives were in control of the departments of theology, of the seminaries, of the chanceries, of the religious orders, of the USCC and NCCB, of what was left of Catholic publishing. Perhaps less control there: led by *Crisis*, cranky magazines had sprung up everywhere, and Fessio's Ignatius Press had dedicated itself to publishing translations of European thinkers of the previous decade. It was not Tom Sheehan's role to claim victory, but the fact remained that victory could indeed be claimed.

But the old Pope died only to be reelected again, in effect, when Benedetto emerged from the conclave as John Paul III. This was intolerable. Iggie Wynn did not intend to tolerate it. He had not waited all these decades simply to face the same old situation for God knows how many more years. They were in control of the infrastructure; they must not be thwarted any longer by a reactionary pope. Archbishop Lannan had emerged as the linchpin of progressive strategy to foil the Vatican and effect an authentic decentralization of power. With a modicum of independence, the Church in America could get on with the business of ordaining women, phasing out celibacy, letting up on all the prohibitions and negatives, and putting the emphasis on Christian love. And now Lannan refused to play his part.

"He's on his way to Rome", Bailey said with disgust.

"Actually en route?"

"His plane left Dulles at nine."

Add five hours and get two o'clock, the flight took maybe six and a half or seven hours, meaning an early morning landing at Fiumicino. It was now 1:30 in the morning, a fact Frank might have taken into account if he were calling anyone else. Frank knew his routine.

"I'll meet him."

"Could you arrange for the Mafia to kidnap him?"

"I never employ a middle man if I can avoid it."

The odd sound coming over the wire was Bailey laughing.

"Is anyone else wavering?"

"Well, they haven't been. Who knows what effect Lannan's collapse will have."

Not much, was Iggie's guess. The American bishops only needed to think of the advantages of greater independence from Rome. The Council had returned the disposition of marriage cases to diocesan tribunals, and this had opened up a far more compassionate practice in the awarding of annulments. The delegate had been effectively defanged since Jadot's tenure. Nothing but Italians since then, but it was already too late. There were still bishops who knew what it had been like to have a Roman spy monitoring everything they did. Of course it had been the bishops' conference and the creation of the USCC that had given the Church in America the bureaucracy and concentration of power needed to assert itself. Not all that great for a bishop in Idaho or South Dakota, reduced to a single vote in an assembly dominated for years by Chicago, but solidarity had been necessary if the case was to be made that the Church in the United States did not need the heavy hand of the Vatican on every move it made. Did anyone realize how much autonomy had been achieved, not by a dramatic coup of the kind Bailey preferred, but by the patient introduction of procedures? Independence was already an unheralded tradition. From that point of view, the defection of one archbishop meant little. The difficulty was that Lannan was president of the Conference and his term had time to run.

"I better get cracking", Iggie said.

"You gonna meet him?"

"I'll have him met."

2

Barry the wire service man came by the embassy, and since he was still up, Jim Morrow agreed to see him. He had with him Julian O'Keefe, an independent producer from California who was making a documentary and wanted to shoot background film.

"You mean record the interview?"

A reassuring smile. He must be in is forties, but he dressed much younger. "No, no. Just film; no sound."

"What do you make of the story that Archbishop Lannan refuses to be made a cardinal?" Barry began.

Morrow had to call on stoic resources he did not know he possessed to conceal his reaction. "Has he himself said so?"

Barry frowned. "I was hoping you could confirm it."

"Where did you hear it?"

The reporter didn't want to say it, but Morrow had the idea that his reluctance was due more to the source's unreliability than to Barry's devotion to the ethics of his trade.

"Sounds to me like a carry-over from the uncertainties when he was first named. I know others have suggested he might or should refuse."

"What uncertainties?"

"I'm thinking of the outcome."

Barry was either dumb or cultivated obtuseness in order to have things explained to him. It hadn't been twenty-four hours since he and Tom Lannan had talked, and there had been no doubt then that the rumors of declining the red hat had not come from Lannan.

"Frank thinks he can pressure me into refusing", Lannan had said.

"Is he jealous?"

"It's not just him. The executive council of the Conference held a rump meeting and announced that they were supporting my decision."

"Which decision?"

"The one I haven't made, and they wouldn't discuss my statement. Frank put them up to it, but they're shrewd enough not to identify too closely with him."

"What's his game?"

Morrow's cigar went out during the lengthy, incredible explanation. The whole thing sounded like a scheme theologians might come up with late at night after drinking too much. Greeley? No, Greeley had his faults, but he wasn't a theologian. The trouble was that there were now bishops, many bishops, who had in the past sat up late with people like Frank Bailey and hatched nutty plots like this. It was one thing for an alienated priest to talk like a rebel and plot secession from Rome. Frank, for example, had published stuff along those lines, speculative, attributing it to unnamed concerned Catholics, and a flare-up of indignant reaction would be followed by a wave of supporting letters. The one thing Frank's friends and foes had in common was the wish that he personally would break with Rome. He had likened the Church to the body of an ailing person frozen until a cure could be found. It was pretty obvious that the cure he had in mind was the death of the Pope and the election of someone who would accept the decline of the Vatican as a major player in the Church in America.

"Have you tried to reach Archbishop Lannan?" Morrow asked now.

Barry just looked at him. "You know a man named Wales?"

"Lannan's secretary."

"He wouldn't tell me where Lannan is."

"The last I heard he was coming here."

"To Rome?"

"Of course, that may be just another rumor. Like yours."

The cameraman had been as silent as the film he took, but now he thanked Morrow profusely.

"Who is the documentary for?"

"That's still undecided. I'm an independent."

"I envy you."

And then he and Barry were finally on their way.

Alitalia confirmed that Lannan was en route to Rome, and Morrow rang for McHugh, waking him up.

"Can you get in touch with Luigi and have him meet a morning flight at Fiumicino?"

A fuddled McHugh asked what time it was.

"After two. I'm sorry to call you so late."

"I was thinking of Luigi."

"Does he have a phone?"

446

"I don't think he's home."

McHugh proceeded to tell Morrow about the chauffeur's domestic battles, particularly since they involved Serena.

"The typist? She's hardly more than a child."

"I told you about Luigi."

"If he can't be found to meet that plane, I'll fire him."

"Could you get me Serena's address from her folder?"

A man answered when McHugh called Serena's number, her father, and he was enraged that anyone would dare call his daughter at such an hour. Morrow on the extension heard McHugh ask if she were home. A terrible silence, then the clatter of the phone being put down, background noises, and female voices, rising in hysteria. McHugh recognized Serena's voice and hung up. Muttering, he called Luigi. The phone was snapped up almost before it began to ring, followed by an anxious "Luigi?" from his wife.

Morrow eased his phone back into its cradle. Listening to his aide's account, Morrow had a sudden vision of a world in moral chaos, but Luigi, whatever his transgressions, recognized them as such. He was an insatiable sinner who prayed daily for the grace of repentance before he died. What would he have made of the ambiguities of moral theologians? Throughout Western Europe, in North America, a generation of Catholics had been persuaded that the old prohibitions were negotiable. No matter that popes said the opposite and persisted in teaching what the Church had always taught, what Christ had taught. Nowadays Catholics could dissent from Church teaching, "form their own consciences", in the phrase. But Catholics who accepted such advice soon drifted away. The appeal of Christianity lay not in its endorsement of sinful behavior but its offering of forgiveness for sins. If there were no sins, if hell were a product of the primitive imagination, if life beyond this one were open to question, what was the point of religion? Morrow had traced such confusions in his book. Compared with that, Luigi was almost refreshing. The embassy chauffeur had no illusions about what he did. He longed for forgiveness—but not yet.

"I'll meet Archbishop Lannan", McHugh said.

"No, no. I will." He had already ruined McHugh's night. Besides he himself was wide awake and was unlikely to get to sleep. "And come in late tomorrow morning."

The sense of magnanimity he felt in saying this dissipated quickly after he had hung up the phone and confronted the prospect of driving to Leonardo da Vinci airport at Fiumicino in the early hours of the Roman morning. Was it really necessary? For all he knew, Lannan had already made arrangements to be picked up, or perhaps they had been made for him. If the Holy Father summoned him to Rome, surely he would want to know his travel plans and would send a Vatican car for him.

Morrow yawned until his jaw cracked. Lannan had always stayed in the Villa Stritch before. Doubtless it was where he would stay now. Were there drivers there? Morrow had no idea.

In the end, against his better judgment, he decided to go to the airport. Sleep all but claimed him now; he was overpowered by tiredness; he was certain that if only he could fall asleep, he would remain in bed for days. Having disrupted the night of McHugh, Serena's family, and Luigi's wife, he could not in conscience lie down and sleep. All the commotion had been over the arriving Lannan and a desire to shore up his old friend now that he had apparently overcome an effort to drive a wedge between himself and the Pope.

So in darkness, using lights, surprised at how heavy the traffic was at this ungodly hour, Morrow drove out the Via Aurelia, past the site of what had once been Notre Dame International (the prep school Ken had attended during one of their sabbatical years), onto the Grande Raccordo Anulare—along which cars hurtled, weaving in and out of lanes, for all the world like the Indianapolis 500 delivered over to rank amateurs—to the highway that would take him to the airport, a narrow chute of a thoroughfare on which, to his enormous surprise, he realized he was hurtling along at 140 KPH. Eighty-five MPH, more or less. Still, other cars shot past him, impatient with his slowness.

At the airport, he parked under the raised track that carried the metro, wishing it had made sense to come on that. The terminal was a good walk from where he had parked, and he might have had the sense of a stroll in the country if it had not been for the whooshing roar above him as trains came and went and the deep guttural sound of jet engines in the thin morning air, tinged yellow now by the rising sun. Halfway to the terminal, he realized he was going to have to ask Lannan to hike this distance in order to be given a ride. Some favor. Luigi would have pulled up to the entrance and parked among the taxis, whisking Lannan into the car with a minimum of fuss. McHugh would have done the same. After all, on his license plate was CD, for *Corpo Diplomatico*. His colleagues in the diplomatic corps might have taken that as warrant enough to drive onto the tarmac and intercept Lannan before he had to confront the nuisance of customs.

His generous impulse seemed a pathetic display of ineptitude by the time he entered the terminal. The smell of coffee drew him, and soon he was restoring himself with a crisp, fresh-baked roll, layered with butter and strawberry jam. He watched people begin to come through the door from customs, looking expectantly at those who held up signs on which were lettered the names of hotels or companies or passengers. He would catch Lannan's attention with a wave.

The plane from Washington was late; and twenty minutes went by before its passengers, having shown their passports, collected their luggage, and cleared customs, began to emerge. The crowd awaiting passengers had grown, and Morrow was elbowing himself toward the front when he saw a sign with "Archbishop Lannan" neatly printed on it. The man holding it was in livery, obviously a professional driver. Morrow stopped and soon was being jostled by others pushing past him. He felt like a fool. Someone had arranged for Lannan to be picked up after all.

3

It had not been a crowded flight, so tourist class had been tolerable, many passengers claiming a whole row of seats and settling in to sleep their way across the Atlantic. Archbishop Lannan wondered what his fellow passengers would say if they realized he was on his way to Rome to be inducted into the small body of men who were princes of the Church and who held in their hands the awesome responsibility of electing popes. He was content with the realization that no one could be as impressed by the thought as he himself was.

Getting out of Washington had been like an escape. Before leaving, he had heard of the ambiguous support tendered him by the executive council of the NCCB, listening to it in the Virginia motel where he had taken refuge before getting a cab to Dulles. The truly incredible Frank Bailey, acting for all the world as if he were the press spokesman for the committee, reminded reporters of Archbishop Lannan's decision to refuse the red hat when asked what it was the committee was supporting.

"Was Archbishop Lannan at the meeting?"

"He is in seclusion."

"Why?"

Frank paused, a man choosing his words carefully. "Let me

put it to you this way. When the colonies declared independence from England, the leaders kept out of the way of redcoats."

This was raw meat to starving animals. Lannan watched in amazement as Frank permitted the press corps to develop his suggestion by way of further questions. By the time it was over, the clear impression had been created that the Vatican might take strong measures to spirit the archbishop of Washington away to Rome and impress him into the College of Cardinals. Frank had always been a man whose resolution was unlikely to be deterred by accuracy and fairness, but this was truly egregious behavior. It slandered the Vatican and made Lannan himself look like a foolish pawn in a game being played by the executive committee, the struggle between the Church in America longing to be free and sinister unnamed forces working on behalf of the Pope.

Wales had been right, after all. The only way to stop this incredible nonsense was to go to Rome and be inducted into the College. When he returned home a cardinal, he would meet the press and sweep away the impression Bailey had created.

In flight, he felt he was moving rapidly away from any temptation he had ever felt to adopt the view that motivated Frank and, seemingly, his colleagues on the executive committee of the NCCB. Had his brother bishops become so confused that they thought they had status apart from union with the bishop of Rome? Paragraphs from *Lumen gentium* rolled past his eyes, making a devastating commentary on the antics of Frank and the committee. Lannan was ashamed for ever having given any comfort to the view they represented. Frank Bailey! It was astounding that he who had been thought dead now roamed the earth again, more powerful than he had ever been. His power consisted in his ability to command time on television and space in newspapers by making false statements. The dream that drove Frank was not of a new Catholicism; it was the Protestant Revolt, indistinguishable from what Luther and Calvin had done, even closer perhaps to Henry VIII's original idea, but in any case a denial that the bishop of Rome was the visible head of Christianity, Christ's vicar on earth. Lannan, whatever else he felt guilty of, was sure he had never himself contemplated that kind of breach.

Grumbling about the bureaucratic and glacial pace of the Vatican was *de rigueur* for an American, of course. The New World did things with so much more efficiency and dispatch. The primacy of the Pope did not entail the heavy-handed way some prefects of Roman congregations attempted to make whatever happened anywhere seem a Vatican initiative. The internationalization of the Vatican had not helped. The truth was that efficiency cost money, and the Vatican had little and thus was unable to hire the number of people it would take to turn a Renaissance operation into a modern one.

Bitching about how bishops were chosen was also understandable, though here justification became more difficult. Lannan thought of some of those whom his brother bishops had urged on Rome who had not been accepted. Dear God, Frank Bailey himself had appeared on several ternas, the short list of three candidates proposed to Rome. Imagine *him* a bishop. Imagination was helped by the examples of several appalling choices who had been allowed to grow old as auxiliaries where there was a limit on the harm they could do. Finally, it was Rome that, through delay, benign neglect, and by overriding the wishes of Americans, had kept wild men to a minimum in the hierarchy. What would the NCCB look like if the choices sent to Rome had been accepted? It was a sobering thought. Whatever flaws one found in Vatican operations paled beside the anomalies of the Church in America in recent decades.

That had been Jim Morrow's thesis, however muted, and he

was right. Most of the difficulties in the Church in the United States were due to defying Rome, not following her. During the long hours en route, Tom Lannan left behind the sense that he had rescued himself from those who would use him as a pawn and took on the conviction of one who expressed in the Creed his belief in the one, holy, Catholic, and apostolic Church. And Roman. Only in union with the Pope did one belong to that Church. It was absurd to imagine that a coequal (at least) branch could be set up in Washington, D.C.

When he became a bishop, he had pledged his loyalty to the Pope. His record since was mottled, he was ashamed to admit. Now that the Pope had chosen to make him a prince of the Church, Thomas Lannan intended to renew that pledge of loyalty and to live it until the day he died.

Despite the delay due to feeble tailwinds, the flight seemed short. Even the ponderous process after landing seemed amusing rather than annoying. And what a relief to see that he was expected when finally he pushed his bags past the indifferent representative of customs and came through the gate into the terminal. He lifted his hand and the man in uniform sprang forward.

"Cardinal Lannan?"

There was a stir around him at this somewhat premature address. But the driver was gathering up his bags and opening a way through the crowd. Someone who might have been Jim Morrow himself was briefly visible in the crowd, but then they were outside in the fresh morning air, and the driver was putting his bags down so he could open the car and get the great man settled in the back seat.

From the outside, the car had not seemed so luxurious, but settling into its suede cushions, he accepted the mineral water the driver poured after Lannan had said no to the offer of cognac. Cognac at nine in the morning after flying all night? It would have knocked him out. Even the mineral water had that effect. He lay his head back on the cushions as the car moved smoothly away from the terminal, and before they had rounded the great statue of Leonardo da Vinci he had fallen asleep.

Traffic sounds, the stops and starts necessitated by semaphores, the Muzak that oozed through the car, all these became part of his slumber, but when the car halted and its motor was turned off, he opened his eyes with an effort. Had sleep ever been sweeter?

The back door was opened, and he was helped out and led through a gate that closed behind him. This was not the Villa Stritch; this was not the Vatican; but the realization did not trouble him. The driver clearly knew what he was doing, and Lannan, eager to get to where he could lie down and give himself up to sleep, allowed himself to be led into a building, into a small elevator that lurched upward. He was shown into a small room, but it contained a bed, and that was sufficient. He stumbled toward it, the driver eased him onto it, and then sleep, blessed sleep, overcame him again.

4

The portiere of the North American College was given twenty thousand lire ($20 more or less, depending on the market) to put the envelope directly into Monsignor Frawley's hands. The rector closed the door of his office, opened the envelope, and took out the note. He looked around after reading it, half-expecting to find the practical joker there to witness the effect of his efforts. He smiled as if to notify the universe that he was not so easily taken in. "Archbishop Lannan is our prisoner. Get ready a ransom of one million dollars and await instructions. Gamma."

The terrorist who bore the *nom de guerre* of Gamma had been suspected in the Aldo Moro kidnapping and subsequent murder but had been exonerated. The name brought back memories of Italy as it had been during Frawley's student days: radical groups bombing, terrorizing, kidnapping. During the awful months while Moro was held captive, armed soldiers were stationed at the major exits from the city, and from time to time military helicopters came suddenly over the rooftops looking for God knows what. Recalling the uneasiness of that time took some of the edge off this joke.

He slid the note back into its envelope, hesitated, then called the Villa Stritch and asked if Archbishop Lannan had arrived. He had not, but no anxiety was expressed. Checking the airline revealed that Lannan had indeed flown in that morning. It was now mid-afternoon. Frawley read the note again. He decided that the person he wanted to speak to was Jim Morrow, and he wanted to speak to him face to face. He would go to the Via Aurelia and take a chance the ambassador was in.

A haggard-looking McHugh told him that the ambassador was napping. "He was up at the crack of dawn to meet Archbishop Lannan's plane."

How swiftly his apprehension went. Frawley sat and looked around McHugh's office with a relieved smile, but then he thought of the note and was suddenly angry. He handed the envelope to McHugh, who looked it over, removed the note, and read it. He looked at Frawley.

"Where did you get this?"

"It was brought to me."

Again McHugh looked at the envelope. Nothing was written on it. Frawley told him that the portiere at the North American College had been handsomely tipped to bring it directly to him.

"A joke?"

455

"I didn't think so until you told me Morrow had met the plane. Some joke."

But McHugh was scratching the tip of his nose. "I think I'll wake the ambassador."

Tousled, yawning, wearing an Indian blanket robe that reached to his ankles, Morrow received them in his apartment. He looked back and forth between McHugh and Frawley when the monsignor put the question to him.

"He came in all right. But they had sent a car for him." He added to McHugh, "So I ruined my own and others' sleep for no reason."

"Who sent the car?"

"The Vatican, I suppose. It was a Lancia, I think, with a uniformed driver."

Frawley handed the envelope to Morrow, who hesitated before taking it. He read it, then sat, and read it again.

"He's not at the Villa Stritch?"

"Cardinal Taylor says he sent no car for him", McHugh reported.

Morrow recalled his early-morning drive to the airport, the waiting crowd, the man holding the card with "Archbishop Lannan" on it. He stopped as if to peer more closely at the remembered face.

"I watched them go. The driver took his baggage and led the way. I came outside just as they drove away." His expression changed. "They were diplomatic plates. I noticed that. Was it CD or CV?"

"Not CV. The Vatican sent no car. It must have been CD."

McHugh asked if they had any idea how many cars with diplomatic plates there were in the city. The question might have concerned the sands of the shore or the stars of the sky.

"I think we should let the consulate and embassy know. After all, he's an American citizen."

McHugh meant the American Embassy in Italy, located on

456

the Via Veneto. Frawley left the letter with the diplomats and excused himself. The day before him required little of him that was not postponable, but he invoked his schedule as excuse for going. He could of course be reached at the North American College should he be needed. Frawley walked along the Via Aurelia, toward the center of the city, and murmured a prayer for Lannan.

The cove in which the terrorists held Aldo Moro prisoner was not far from where Frawley now walked. His captors had released a photograph of the politician, totally humbled, a toy to be played with by people whose notion of what they were doing was mad, an ideological stew. Had Moro known from the beginning that he would never be released alive? He had resisted all pressure to submit willingly to the purpose of the kidnapping; he made no compromising statements, the kind that in such circumstances mean nothing, but still cause pain and disappointment in those who would have preferred heroism. Moro had been heroic. The face in the photograph showed signs of ill treatment—the mouth swollen, an eye discolored. More knowledgeable captors used drugs and subtle psychological pressure to turn their captive into an accomplice. No matter, in the end they too were murdered. The body of Aldo Moro had been found, as a phone call to the police said it would be, in a car parked on a crowded street not far from the headquarters of his political party. The spot had become a kind of shrine since, fresh flowers appearing there each day.

All that had been years ago; Italy had changed, not in every way for the better, but terrorist bombings and kidnappings were things of the past. Nonetheless, if Archbishop Lannan had indeed been kidnapped, those involved could be inspired by memories of earlier events.

Frawley was filled with foreboding when he hailed a cab and was not quite home when he was caught in the middle of a traffic jam. Horns began to sound; the driver soliloquized pro-

fanely, ignoring Frawley's clerical collar; the rector himself felt
an urge to vent his rage at a world suddenly turned unintelligible. After ten minutes of immobility, he left the cab, not without first having an argument with the driver. Frawley paid him
twice what the meter read, but this did not placate the man.
He realized that he was just a target of opportunity for the
man's rage. Imagine having your livelihood depend on maneuvering through Roman traffic?

Back in the rector's suite after a brisk walk, he started to
pour a drink, then stopped. Never drink when you think you
need one. That wise maxim had guided him through his
priestly years. But today he finished making the drink. He had
the sense of being in a unique state of affairs.

At his desk, he sat, put a piece of paper before him, and
wrote at the top, *Novissimae Diei*. He then jotted down the
following numbered points:

1.   Morrow appointed ambassador to Vatican.
2.   Lannan named cardinal.
3.   Pope John Paul II dies.
4.   John Paul III elected, Lannan et al. excluded from
     conclave
5.   Wynn and Bailey begin media firestorm, main-
     taining conclave illegal.
6.   A call for a council.
7.   Lannan again named cardinal.
8.   Agitation for him to refuse as gesture of inde-
     pendence on the part of the Church in America.
9.   Lannan called to Rome to be invested.
10. Lannan kidnapped?

Frawley had also heard a rumor that, with a large number of
the cardinals already in Rome, the Pope would call for a new
consistory in a matter of days, its purpose being to validate his
election and put an end to the absurd rumors that threatened

to affect the Church worldwide. Well, in the West anyway. Africa, Asia, and East Europe gave no serious attention to the Bailey campaign, to the call for a council, or, most recently, to the NCCB urging Lannan to refuse elevation to the College of Cardinals. The weight of numbers was to the East and South, not to the West. Progressives might smile at the retrograde character of these churches, their naïve docility to Rome, but they were as the United States and Latin America had been when the Church flourished in such places. The single most important fact that had been established in Morrow's history was that progressive Catholicism had decimated the Church in America. Why should anyone look to America for direction?

Who had the greatest interest in preventing Lannan's publicly and formally expressing fealty to the Pope, thus putting to rest once and for all that he was part of some independence movement? Clearly, Bailey and company. But Frank Bailey was in the States. Wynn?

Frawley printed the name carefully on the paper before him. Ignatius Wynn. It was ridiculous to imagine that an aged priest in a wheelchair could have donned a chauffeur's uniform and whisked Archbishop Lannan away from Fiumicino and held him incognito since. Personally. But Iggie's connections in Rome were vast and of long standing. Things could be arranged. How easily Frawley could imagine Iggie Wynn resorting to such extraordinary measures if a last and unexpected opportunity to push the Church in the direction he preferred was jeopardized by what he could convince himself was the overweening ecclesiastical ambition of Thomas Lannan. The end would justify the means, as some proportionalist moral theologian would doubtless tell him.

On this hypothesis, Lannan's literal life would not be in danger, of course. There would be no need to harm him. Detention for a few days, until after the induction of the new cardinals, was all that was needed. The Pope himself was in

Palermo, receiving in his native city a wild and enthusiastic reception. Until the conclave, such public manifestations on the part of the faithful made doubts about his legitimacy foolish. The conclave would endorse him, and this would leave his foes no choice but outright schism.

Ambrose Frawley could not imagine the bishops of the United States unequivocally taking such a course. But they might back into it; they might secede by inches, calling what they were doing by some other name, prodded by their advisors, urged on by theologians, applauded by journalists, Catholic and lay. That was certainly imaginable, because it would be a long slide, at no point of which could such a term as schism seem applicable.

Frawley pushed the sheet of paper from him. Here he sat, engaging in speculation, while somewhere his patron, his mentor, his friend, was, well—what? The police had to be told. But by whom? It would not do for the Vatican to learn of the apparent abduction of Archbishop Lannan from policemen or, worse, journalists.

In his bathroom, Frawley rinsed away the taste of bourbon, put on a fresh shirt and collar, and called for the student who served as his driver this month to bring the car around.

"Should I fill it with gas first?"

"Is there enough to get to the Vatican and back?"

The question deserved the laugh it got. The Vatican could be reached on foot in five minutes. But Frawley saw an advantage now in arriving at the Porta Sant'Anna with some semblance of authority.

5

The following day, after a triumphal reception in Palermo and a wildly festive tour of the surrounding countryside in an open automobile, Pope John Paul III was taken to the airport for his return flight to Rome in a chartered Alitalia plane. Halfway up the steps to the open door of the jet, the chubby pontiff turned and smiled radiantly at the distant crowd, whose cheers and shouts carried to him. Written on his face was the confidence that he was loved and honored by the people, recognized beyond doubt as their Pope. The Sicilian crowds, like those that gathered daily in St. Peter's Square, affirmed it as they shouted with triumphant happiness, *Viva il papa, viva il papa.*

Cardinal Taylor took the Pope's elbow and helped him up the remainder of the stairs. In the doorway John Paul III turned once more and stretched out his arms as if to embrace the world. And then he was gone.

The door was closed, the mobile stairway pushed some distance from the plane. The engines had been running for fifteen minutes; the plane stood on the apron fifty meters from the terminal building. It pivoted gracefully and taxied slowly onto a runway that had been cleared for it.

Five leisurely minutes went by as the great plane moved to the far end of the runway where again it wheeled. Before it were several kilometers of concrete, and beyond were the clouds, huddled on the western mountains. Slowly the plane began to move, gathering speed as it went down the runway. It lifted slowly from the earth and began its inexorable ascent into the heavens.

The wheels drew up, and the plane banked to gain altitude to clear the mountains. Perhaps half those who had come to wish the Pope farewell still watched the plane. Among them was Cardinal Ponte of Palermo. Eyes moist with happy tears, he lifted his hand and traced the sign of the cross after the plane.

When the plane struck the mountain, there was at first only a puff of dust, no more, but then flames appeared, which, fed by the full tanks of fuel, suddenly leapt up and engulfed the plane.

Moments ago there had been shouting and cheering. Now there was little reaction, except disbelief. But Cardinal Ponte sank to his knees and began to recite the prayers for the dying.

CHAPTER TWO

I

Peggy was not enthralled with Rome, and there were moments when Julian considered sending her back to California. If that could have been a furlough, he might have done it, but he was sure that once she left Rome she would never willingly return.

"It's like walking through alleys. They're supposed to be streets, but they're alleys—garbage set out on the curb, dog dirt everywhere."

"Rome is one of the most beautiful cities in the world. It is *the* city."

She shuddered. They had moved from the Grand to the Rome Hilton so she wouldn't have to look out on narrow streets. The trouble with her attitude was that it was contagious. How could he defend the Corso when they were driven from it by the noise and, worse, the cloud of exhaust that hovered above the traffic? The life expectancy of anyone owning a shop on that street would be cut in half. Her first view of St. Peter's had impressed her, however. They walked the length of the nave, noticing the markings in the floor indicating how much less lengthy other great cathedrals were. They stood and stared upward.

"There's a pigeon."

One of the architectural landmarks of the Western world

and Peggy's eye unerringly found a bird that had flown in and was fluttering around, looking for a way out. To Julian it seemed a symbol of himself, trying to escape the hold of the Church.

She assumed he had been in Rome before, perhaps often, but this was his first time too. In imagination he had been here, of course; he had carefully prepared for this visit. Now he was familiar with the city, tirelessly acquainting himself with it, while Peggy sat in their suite in the Hilton and watched CNN. Julian had come to know the press corps in the offices on the Via della Conciliazione and was amused by the chatter of the aging rebels who had hobbled into Rome in the expectation that the page of history was going to be turned back. Bailey, Wynn, the religious editors of various papers and magazines— they were all hams. He had endless useless footage of them all. But they were to be unwitting instruments of his plan.

His instinct not to use what he knew of Lannan immediately had proved right. An archbishop became a cardinal, almost. Lannan could not have been more disappointed than Julian when the old Pope who had named him to the College died. That was when he had decided to come to Rome, hoping that the home of the enemy would help him figure out how best to use the proof he had gathered at Karen Christiansen's apartment in Thousand Oaks nearly a year ago.

Lannan's exclusion from the conclave caused open revolt in the press room, but the consensus was that he was even more certain now to be given the red hat by the new Pope.

"It's over, Julian", Peggy whined. "They've elected a new one. You must have enough film for *Gone with the Wind*. Please, let's go home."

He compromised with a cruise through the Greek islands, and Peggy, imagining she was Jackie Onassis, became once more the fawning, docile girl he had known. One evening in Crete, sitting long at table on the terrace of their hotel, he developed out of thin air a movie he planned to be the vehicle that would launch her career as an actress. He actually wrote a treatment and asked her to study it; he wanted her to be thinking on the story line; this was to be her movie.

She looked up from the manuscript with tears in her eyes. "Julian, it's..."

"It is your story."

A young woman, who grows up without knowing who her father is, reaches a point where she must find out. First indications indicate the quest is not without dangers. Her mother objects. But her passion to know who she is is only strengthened.

They returned to Rome without protest from her, and he began working on the screenplay. Entering into the role, Peggy began to think of her own situation.

"I told you she said he was a priest."

"He could be here in Rome, now."

"Oh, my God."

"What would you do?"

"Julian, you're the director."

"Imagine that the man who has offered to help you, takes you to Rome. I could ditch the documentary and use footage I've been taking. He tells you he has found your father."

She listened like a child at bedtime. He should have thought of this before. Meanwhile, he kept an attentive eye on Vatican developments. The press room was not as crowded as it had been, but he continued to stop by. Barry, the AP man who fancied himself an old Roman hand, became a new source.

2

The room was windowless and seemed to be soundproofed as well. Food and water were provided several times a day—Lannan assumed it was day; without his glasses he could not read the face of his watch—introduced into the room by way of a sliding panel in the door. The last human face he had seen was that of the driver who had picked him up at Fiumicino. The sleep that had claimed him in the car must have been drug-induced. He had no clear memories of being put into this room. No one answered when he called out through the opening in the door. It was slammed swiftly shut again before he could push his head through and see something of the world beyond this room.

There was a chemical toilet in a corner of the room, whose operation left something to be desired. Lannan went through a pattern of panic and peace. Finally it was resignation that saved him. He sat on the bed, closed his eyes unnecessarily, and imagined that he was in the guest room at Gethsemani, enjoying a few days of peace and isolation. And nearness to God.

Is that what had been missing from his stay at Gethsemani, attention to the object of the experience rather than to the experience itself? He had meditated on himself meditating in a Trappist monastery; he himself had been at the heart of his soul's attention. *My words fly up, my thoughts remain below...*

Now, unwillingly kept in this small, unlit room, he sat very still and lifted his mind and heart to God. The ostensible point of his life was to serve God, to prepare himself and others for an eternal union with the Father of them all. After some hours—it seemed like hours—he formulated the thought he had been avoiding. I shall never emerge from this room alive.

The room became a cell on death row, he the condemned,

having the inestimable privilege of being able to prepare for death. How infinitely distant from God he felt. He pressed his eyes tightly shut and formed the image of Jesus whose priest he was, in whose name he performed the priestly office. But Jesus, like God, seemed a stranger, a word rather than an image. How wasted his life had been. God had given him a premonition of this at Gethsemani; for a moment he had almost had the truth about himself in his hand, and then the news of his being named cardinal had propelled him once more into the seductively busy world that was his. How could he not be involved in all the duties of his office? But they were a shield behind which he hid. Rather than bringing him closer to God, the services he offered to God had become a barrier.

How much longer did he have? Days, hours? Whatever it was, he was determined to use the time well, to pray that the scales might fall from his eyes, that the ice enclosing his heart might melt, that his tongue would loosen and form acts of faith and hope and love and contrition that would indeed put him in the presence of God.

Meditation had always been based on a conviction of mortality, on the truth that this life is short and eternity long. At least in legend monks had once kept skulls on their desks as a reminder of death. *Memento mori.* It was the reminder with which Lent began when the ashes were traced upon the forehead. *Remember, man, that thou art dust, and into dust thou shalt return.* After all those arguments about the English translations of the liturgy, the prolonged battle over so-called inclusive language, he found that what his mind retained was the English of old.

He had read once that Buckminster Fuller, inventor of the geodesic dome, had learned to survive on naps, forgoing the usual hours of sleep on a bed in a room set aside for the purpose. His pets, Fuller had noted, slept whenever the opportunity offered. The inventor regulated his life like a cat. Work, nap, work, nap. And he had lived to a grand old age. Lannan was not inclined to give himself up to extended sleep now. He might be resigned, but that did not take away apprehension. He did not want to miss any clue as to where he was and why. It had to be Frank's doing. He decided this dispassionately, without any anger or recrimination. No doubt Frank or his friends among the moral theologians could provide a justification for kidnapping and sequestering an archbishop. A cardinal archbishop. He smiled in the dark. Among his new certainties was that Thomas Lannan would never be invested as a cardinal. The thought was liberating. How he had wanted that honor. How he had convinced himself that it was an impersonal desire, for his archdiocese, for his country, that he himself did not matter. But it had mattered greatly to him that he should be raised to that penultimate level in the Church. Now he knew it would not happen, and he thanked God that the realization carried no pain. His captors had done him the great service of freeing him once and for all from his ambition. But it was not for their reasons that he renounced the red hat.

It embarrassed him to wonder if his death, should it come, would be considered martyrdom. The thought was a new temptation, unlike any he had felt before. The scarlet of a cardinal's robes symbolized the blood he was willing to shed for the faith. It would have been merely symbolic if he had indeed been made cardinal. Now the chance that his quite literal blood should flow if his captors did to him what kidnappers so often do attracted him as cloth and vestments never had. Saint Thomas Lannan. He tried to laugh, but couldn't.

He thought of the martyrs of the twentieth century, of the Chinese bishops and priests who had spent whole lifetimes in prison, forgotten by the outside world, indeed few were even aware of them. What had he and his fellow bishops done to ease the pain of those silent prisoners? In the East, it had been the same. A man named cardinal *in petto* had earned his living as a window cleaner; and when liberation came and it was clear that there were hundreds, thousands, whole churches that had suffered a similar fate, it had been an item of news and then faded away. In China all the bishops had to do was take part in the autonomous Catholic Church permitted by the government. They could have gone on saying Mass, ordaining priests, evangelizing the faithful, on one proviso, that they had nothing to do with Rome. Like John Fisher, that one small concession was precisely the one they could not make. To make it was not to become a Catholic of another kind, it was to cease to be a Catholic at all. All Fisher's brother bishops made that concession, swore fealty to the king, and lived. John Fisher had been put to death. How had he seen himself as he waited for the appointed time?

Martyrdom aside, what other purpose did his life have than to attain sanctity? Not a place on the official calendar, not veneration by the faithful of the future, but a response to grace that would earn him union with God in heaven. *Not* becoming Saint Thomas Lannan would mean eternal separation from God, rendering his life wholly pointless and futile.

When he was not sitting on the bed, he knelt beside it, upright, face lifted, the scarcely visible contours of the room an aid to meditation rather than a distraction. Archbishop surprised at prayer. His life had been consumed in ritual, in ceremonies where he officiated, parading up or down an aisle, the curious, wondering faces turned toward him as he cast blessings right and left, the organ swelling while voices lifted in uncertain song. How many sanctuaries had he knelt in, more conscious of the eyes of the congregation on their archbishop than on the God he supposedly addressed?

He had found prayer difficult at Gethsemani. Now he thought he knew why. It came easily here—an overwhelming sense of God's presence, the realization that without God's constant loving attention, he and the whole cosmos would be

469

reduced to nothing. And Jesus seemed to be with him now, a brother, a comrade. *I have not called you servants; I have called you friends.*

Sleeping and waking alternated until it was difficult to distinguish one state from the other. And then he opened his eyes and was surprised that he could see. The panel in the door was open and light flooded in. He stood and tiptoed to the door, hesitating before looking through the opening. He saw a room, hardly more furnished than his own, but with windows. The drapes were pulled, but daylight illumined them. Lannan put his head through the opening. The outer room was empty. He put a hand against the door, to balance himself, and then did lose his balance when the door swung open. He stumbled into the other room and steadied himself on the couch. He realized that he was wearing a kind of pajama suit. Neatly folded on a chair were the clothes he had worn on the flight, and his glasses. Beside the chair stood his bags. Was he free to go?

Beyond he found an unfurnished apartment: four rooms, each as empty as the others. And there was a bathroom. He looked into the mirror over the basin and was almost disappointed at how normal he looked. His beard was shot through with white, and he could imagine it full grown. His eyes had a look that seemed to retain the thoughts that had filled his mind during the terrible time in the dark.

Later he would remember how much time he took getting ready to leave. He shaved and showered, dressed, noticing the dried blood on his arm that had flowed from a puncture in the skin. That must have been how they had drugged him. He had walked about the apartment, drawn back to the room in which he had spent God knows how much time. How different it seemed when he could see it, but he stood in the doorway looking in, imagining himself seated on that bed. It was here that his life had changed.

He picked up his bags, left the apartment, taking the stairway to the street floor. Carrying his bags, the chain of his pectoral cross hitting against his chest, he came onto the sidewalk. The street was lined with plane trees. He had no idea where he was. To his right, a block away, the traffic seemed heavy, and he started toward it. He would find a taxi and go....Where would be go? To James Morrow's embassy.

3

Tom Lannan showed up as if he had just stepped off the airplane and had not been missing for three days. He had no idea who had picked him up or where he had been taken.

"Or why?"

Lannan hesitated. "I thought of explanations, of course, but they are all guesses."

"Why do you suppose you were let go?"

"I don't know that either."

Morrow rummaged through a stack of newspapers and handed one to Lannan. Watching him read, Morrow wondered if his own reaction on learning of the death of the man who had been pope for two months had been any more noteworthy than Lannan's.

"That's twice", Lannan said.

At first Morrow thought he had meant two popes had died, and in a sense he did, but it was rather that for a second time the death of a pope erased his nomination to the College of Cardinals.

"Pavese insisted that all of you take part in the conclave."

"When is it?"

"It's going on now."

Lannan did not spring to his feet; he did not give any indication of being eager to get going.

"My driver can take you to the Vatican immediately."

Lannan shook his head. "No. What you tell me is hearsay. I find it improbable. I would like to be taken to the Villa Stritch, but I might be told the same thing there. Is there any place where I can stay?"

There was of course a guest room in the embassy. Morrow carried one of the bags as he took his old friend up the back stairs. If Lannan wanted privacy, he would accommodate him, but he didn't approve.

"I think you should go, Tom. Have a rest; think it over. If you change your mind, let me know, and I'll get you there immediately."

"Why I should be sleepy after three days of leisure, I don't know."

Lannan was oddly serene. Morrow dismissed the notion that his disinterest in the conclave was feigned. He seemed honestly not to care.

"Does this have anything to do with your refusal of a red hat?"

"I didn't refuse."

"Then you came to Rome to be invested?"

"I did. But the invitation is no longer operative. I think it is a mistake for Pavese to include non-cardinals in the conclave after all the wrangling over the last one. If people don't like the result of this one, the same kind of difficulties could come up."

"If Pavese is elected, there will be no protests."

"I suppose not."

"He's the odds on favorite."

"I don't think he's a good choice."

"Why?"

"He wants it. And he looks toward the West. The future of the Church is not there."

"So what do you intend to do?"

"Just stay on here for now, if that's all right."

If Frank were here they could have a reunion of the triumvirate. Morrow didn't suggest it, of course. It would have been a weak joke, and Lannan's manner did not suggest someone in need of diverting banter. He told his old friend he could stay as long as he liked.

"Frawley has been worried about you."

"I'll give him a call."

So Lannan went into seclusion on the top floor of the embassy building on the Via Aurelia, his circumstances not all that different from the room in which his kidnappers had kept him.

The archbishop was remarkably uncurious about who his captors had been or what their motivation was. Perhaps because he felt he already knew the ultimate inspiration of the deed. The obvious point had been to prevent him from being inducted into the College of Cardinals, an objective rendered pointless after the plane crash in Palermo. Lannan had been insistent on his status the first time this had happened; now he appeared indifferent. If the new pope nominated him yet again, what would he do? Perhaps no Frank Bailey would be needed to prompt him to refuse.

"Did he reach you?" Morrow asked, when Frawley telephoned.

"No! Have you heard from him?"

"He said he intended to let you know he was all right."

"What in God's name happened?"

Morrow told him because he guessed that Lannan would not want to go over his adventures again and again.

Frawley interrupted him. "Are you free for lunch?"

473

They arranged to meet in a little trattoria in the Borgo Pio. Morrow went upstairs and asked Lannan if he would like to come along.

"In the shadow of the Vatican? I'd better not." He shook his head. "I don't mean to dramatize my situation, Jim. But I'd prefer just to stay out of sight until the conclave is over."

"I want to tell Maureen you're all right, Tom."

Lannan nodded. He nodded again at the suggestion that Maureen be invited to have dinner with them there at the embassy that night.

The conclave was into its second day with no indication or rumor that a decision was imminent. Frawley of course had his sources, as seemed clear when he and Morrow met for lunch.

"It should have been a shoo-in for Pavese. He as good as packed the place to insure the result."

"Were the nominees actually seated?"

"There was almost no debate." A thought struck Frawley. "Is that where Archbishop Lannan is?" He muttered an Italian oath. "Of course. He wouldn't miss a conclave."

"You think that's why he was released?"

"They may not have wanted him to be a cardinal. But they surely want him in there electing the next pope."

There had been a ballot late on the previous day, the smoke from the burning ballots indicating that a new pope had not been elected. Was that a good or bad sign?

"For Pavese?" Frawley thought about it. "We would have to know a good deal more in order to answer that question satisfactorily. On the face of it, it looks bad for him. If Pavese had the votes, he should have had them from the beginning. On the other hand, since it is Pavese we are dealing with, he might have seen the advantages of gathering support slowly and arranged for it to happen like that."

"Who else might it be?"

"What about Lannan?"

"Oh, come on."

"As I don't have to tell you, they could elect a layman, as long as he were eligible for ordination. Tom Lannan is an archbishop, as good as a cardinal. It would be a grand gesture, healing, opening the Church wide to the modern world."

"I think Lannan believes the future of the Church is elsewhere."

"An American pope could change that."

"Lannan is not in the conclave."

"That doesn't matter either."

It was unlike Frawley to engage in rootless speculation, but he admitted he had no objective basis for imagining that Thomas Lannan might be the choice of the conclave.

"Who else is there?"

Frawley made a face when he tasted the wine and glanced at the proprietor as if he meant to comment. It was the *vino della casa*, and the monsignor had recommended it, apparently to his sorrow.

"The usual candidates. Perpetual bridesmaids."

"Bukoba?"

"He is only mentioned for diplomatic purposes."

"I have heard a forceful case made for his election."

Frawley nodded. "I know. Those millions upon millions of black and brown and yellow souls, Eastern Europe, Asia. He would represent the postcolonial Church."

"The post-missionary Church."

"Oh, we've become the mission field."

It was one of the genuine surprises Morrow had encountered in writing the history of the Church in the United States. Priests were being recruited from the Philippines, from Ireland, and in recent years from Poland and Africa to man the parishes of America. Dioceses that for too long had ordained only one or two priests a year soon were unable to assign pastors; parishes were merged; or one man said Mass in two or three places. Bare ruined choirs indeed. American Catholics had grown used to hearing the Gospel preached in broken English, much as the Chinese must have suffered through the butchering of their language by American missionaries. It was an ironic fact to put beside the confident claims of theologians that their vision of the Church was what had been intended by Vatican II.

"He's there!" Maureen cried, when Jim called to ask her for dinner.

"Safe and sound."

"Oh, thank God."

It was only when she took Tom in her arms and wept openly that Morrow realized what terrible memories this kidnapping had awakened in her. Tom was taken aback but delighted by her reaction. And she understood when he said he would rather talk about anything else than the three days he had been held captive.

"I feel that way about the conclave too. I just want all this fuss over with, a pope installed, and a return to the usual tenor of things. For months we've been caught up in the strangest maneuverings. I'm sick of it."

"What if it's Pavese?" Jim asked.

She sat more erect. "If he's elected, he is the Pope and that's that."

Morrow liked the uncomplicated simplicity of her faith. When he mentioned the Irish priests recruited for American dioceses, she wrinkled her nose. "The faith flow, we call it. We'll need them all back before long."

To Morrow Ireland seemed a veritable bastion of the faith, but in Maureen's view, acquired from her husband, it had fallen on bad times.

"The universities are full of atheists, the politicians vote for just anything they please, and the priests aren't what they used to be. Maynooth is now coeducational!"

Maynooth was the seminary that once had supplied a surplus of priests, along with the many religious orders. Nuns? They used to trip over nuns. Every girl went to school to the nuns, but why would a girl go into the convent now when nuns were mocked and seemed themselves ashamed of what they were?

"The way they dress!" Maureen said in a singing voice.

"To look pretty?"

"Well, to be noticed."

Tom smiled. Maureen would have been pretty in a wool skirt and a sweater up to her throat, her silver hair brushed back and free, her squinty green eyes loving the world they saw. Tom asked to be excused, and they let him go back upstairs.

"Is he really all right?"

"Fit as a fiddle."

"Thank God. He's so subdued."

"It was a bit of an experience."

She came into his arms at the reminder, and it seemed a perfectly natural move. They got together now as if not doing so would require a decision. He brought her to diplomatic functions, to which she had a kind of honorary perpetual invitation anyway, and saw her several times a week. She stopped by the embassy, just to say hello. She was as close as any friend, as close as anyone had been since Mabel.

Thoughts of remarriage took away some of the contentment from being with Maureen. It made no theological sense, but he would have felt that he was betraying Mabel, being unfaithful, if he should marry someone else. Of course it wasn't just someone else. He had never even thought of such a thing until he met Maureen. And he didn't want to think of it now.

"Do you miss your wife?"

"I'm used to it now", he said carefully.

"Are you? I don't think I'll ever be."

"I know."

"What was she like?"

He had taught all his life, he had written several books, his history had been praised for the eye and ear it showed, but he knew he was incapable of describing what Mabel had been like. After she was gone, when he had indulged himself in terrible self-pitying grief and leafed through the photograph albums she had so carefully prepared, it was the memory of her working over those photographs rather than her image in them that brought her vividly back and made him sob aloud in the empty house. He had always assumed that she would bury him and face years of widowhood alone.

"Thank God, Tom's safe", Maureen said before leaving.

"I thought you didn't like him."

"When did I say I didn't like him?"

"Maybe it was the type you said you didn't like."

"And what type would that be?"

"The kind of bishop you don't like in Ireland."

She had mentioned Lannan, but he didn't want to insist on it. The archbishop of Washington, she had said, was one of those prelates who play to the world as if it is the Church that must change and not the world. "Which is damned foolishness, of course. They're almost ashamed of Catholics who practice the faith and believe it all. They'd rather patronize their enemies."

She didn't know Tom Lannan well, and what she did know was in large part what he had told her of him, filling in those decades when she had not seen him, and Jim Morrow now felt that he had been less than fair to his old friend. Certainly the Lannan who had emerged from captivity to take refuge in the embassy was a very different man from the one Maureen imagined. When he had told her on the phone that Tom did not want to take part in the conclave she made a little disapproving noise. "More defiance?"

But now that she had seen him, such thoughts had flown.

"I wish he were taking part, Jim."

Morrow had been surprised at the indifference Tom had shown, after everything that had led up to this conclave. There was little doubt that he had come away from captivity a very different man.

"I wonder what's taking them so long?" Maureen complained.

It was the third day now, and a total of three inconclusive ballots had been taken. "Monsignor Frawley still says it will be Pavese."

"So do all the newspapers." She added, "I've already said it. He's fine with me. I just want it over with."

During the reign of a pope, the whole hierarchy of the Church along with the one at the top, seemed timeless and unchanging. When a pope died, in the interim before the election of his successor, there was no visible head of the Church, and the process of choosing a new one brought home what a fragile thing the Church was. Usually this was a rare event, but now, as some decades before, there were two conclaves in rapid succession. A pope was elected by cardinals and created new ones, appointed bishops who were consecrated by other bishops, and bishops in turn made priests out of ordinary men who had been raised in ordinary families. Faith did not erase those contingencies or transform into supermen the less-than-perfect humans who made up the hierarchy; this was the shaky process by which the Holy Spirit governed the Church.

4

"Julian, it's as if this is why we came."

"Nothing is accidental."

The boredom that had been Rome evaporated now that they were working on the movie. Sometimes Peggy felt no difference at all between herself and the girl she would be playing, and Julian said that was good, very good; all great actresses became their roles—the line between the real and the imagined simply disappeared.

"They pay a price for that, of course."

"What do you mean?"

"The real is only another role. A husband isn't a real husband, and the man playing the role begins to escape it, and then he has to be let go. After a while make-believe is all there is."

"What stars do you mean?"

"All the truly great ones. There is a magic that takes them out of the world but which makes them strangers. Once I saw Elizabeth Taylor check into a Washington hotel. This was late in her career; she was in her sixties, yet she seemed completely unchanged. She was surrounded by people, six or eight of them, all much younger than herself, and the manager of the hotel was escorting her as quickly as possible to a waiting elevator. Her eyes never stopped darting about, to see if she was seen. Inside the car, she turned and for a moment looked directly at me."

"Julian, what a scene."

"That's exactly what it was. Peggy, sometimes I almost fear for you."

He was more than ever her contact with reality. Either he knew Italian or was able to intuit what was said. Peggy was terrified that someone would speak to her who could not say it again in English. At home there were Chicanos everywhere, in the background, chattering unintelligibly, but they represented no threat. It was their fault if they could not speak English. In Rome there were times when she had felt as a Chicana must. She clung to Julian even more, and he was so busy, and she didn't like to go out with the crew. When she did, she sat in the back seat of the Lancia, protected by its tinted glass, imagining that the people outside were in a film. Only she could not turn it off, and there weren't subtitles. Her movie had changed all that. They were on location, that was all.

Sunday mornings the city was deserted, and Julian would have Aldo drive them around the city. It was a deserted set, except at the Vatican, where they always ended up. The great plaza would be full; and they would leave the car and go in among the people; and at noon high above the square windows would be opened and a white figure would appear, so far away, but his amplified voice was all around them. The people would go wild: cheering, jumping up and down, smiling, tears running down their cheeks.

"What's he saying?"

"Hello."

"Come on."

"That and a little sermon. Peggy," he had added one day, "I know where your father is."

"Tell me." She had hugged his arm and clung to him. She loved it when they talked about her movie.

But he was walking toward the car, head back, eyes half-closed. "We will go there now. I want you to see the scene."

It was all confusing, but what wasn't anymore? In the car he sat in silence as Aldo followed the directions he had given him. He did know Italian. He was so amazing.

After they had parked, he turned to her. "I want you to think of what we're doing. You've come to Rome. The visit has been prolonged, you are impatient, bored, and then suddenly there is a breakthrough. Your friend…"

"Russ!"

He nodded. "Russ tells you that he has kidnapped your father and is holding him in captivity."

"Why?"

He smiled. "That is just what you say."

"What is the answer?"

He pushed open the door. " 'Come', he says, 'I'll show you.' "

They had gone through a little gate and along a passageway that was covered by a flowering vine to the house. Julian had a key. Inside he took her to an empty apartment, and they stood for a moment looking around. He nodded. "This will do. Yes."

When he took her down the hallway and opened an aperture in a closed door and told her to look inside, she could see nothing and said so. He nodded. He opened the door and turned on the lights. The room was all but empty except for the bed. There was a man lying on it.

"There is your father."

He went and knelt beside the bed. He had taken a small kit from his pocket and now rolled back the man's sleeve. He seemed dead, but he winced when Julian inserted the needle and began to draw blood.

"What are you doing?"

He answered without turning. "In the great confrontation he will of course deny that he could possibly be your father." He had finished and stood. He studied the vial of blood. "But we will have a response. DNA."

He turned off the lights and locked the door, and they went back out to the car where he said, "When we film it, I want you dressed differently."

When he drew her blood, he filmed it, though there were just the two of them, but he had shown her what he was able to make from the apparently unrelated snippets of film he had been taking. Peggy realized that in a sense they had been making her film ever since coming to Rome. When he had filmed her pouting in her bedroom she had actually been playing her role. How could she ever have been bored?

"Tell me about the great confrontation."

"He will deny you. You have been searching for him, living to be reunited with him, and he looks at you as if you did not exist. He wishes you did not exist, you sense that. That is why you tell Russ to go ahead. The DNA tests are introduced; it is established beyond doubt that you are his daughter."

"And then?"

"That is what we have to work on."

The next day in the lobby she saw the English-language paper and stopped because there was a photo of a man who looked so much like the actor in that unlit room. It was an American bishop who had been missing but now had been released.

"Isn't that uncanny?" she said to Julian later.

"The make-believe becomes real, Peggy. I warned you."

5

Iggie had been in contact with Frank Bailey via E-mail, but after the plane crash in Palermo, Frank got on a flight as standby and flew all the way to Rome in the middle seat of three, his knees crushed against the seat in front of him.

"Of course the guy in front of me flung his seat back as far as it would go, which was farther than it was supposed to go. His head was practically in my lap. I asked if he'd like a shave."

Iggie laughed. "What did he say?"

"He didn't speak English."

Frank had tried to sleep, but an inane movie was playing, and the silence was punctuated by the laughter of those who had paid for earphones. His feet went to sleep, and the arthritis in his knees was killing him. He was still hobbling when he showed up at Iggie's.

"You got an empty room?"

"We call them cells."

"Ha."

The single bed was not long enough, so Frank put the mattress on the floor and lay down on it. "I have to be able to stretch my legs out."

He was already asleep when Iggie pulled the door closed. No surprise there—when he had been too groggy even to ask questions about the conclave. There wasn't any news to give, except for the inconclusive ballots. Iggie didn't like it. Pavese should have been elected pope two days ago. All Iggie could learn was that the votes were distributed among a number of nominees.

"A number."

"A plurality measured by unity", Pug Lacey, a Thaddeist who worked in the Vatican, had said, little tufts of unshaven whisker sprouting from his smiling Thomistic face.

"Pavese and who else?"

Lacey split his lips with a fat, nicotine-stained finger. He was subject to excommunication if he revealed the proceedings. What he had already told Iggie was not specific enough to be covered by the oath. He probably had a quote from the *Summa* to prove it.

"I'm still betting on Pavese", Iggie said.

Lacey rolled his eyes as if even now he could see the ceiling of the Sistine Chapel.

Frank rose in time for the community dinner and put away two huge platefuls of pasta before taking on the stringy beef. On the plane they had served a cold meal, because the microwaves were on the blink, and before landing passed out juice—still half-frozen—along with a roll that had been hard as a nut.

"What airline were you on?" Frank was asked.

"I think it was Tanzanian."

A joke, but Iggie's confreres only nodded. Most of them didn't know one airline from another anyway. Iggie didn't mean that as a put-down. In a way, he envied their simplicity. He lived here by preference, and because of their generosity, and it did him good to see young men and old living the rule as it was meant to be lived. His participation in the Council had drawn him out of the routine, and then his accident had confirmed his status as a resident-outsider though still member in good standing of the order.

"Any news?"

Everyone knew Frank meant the conclave. He was told there was none.

"Six ballots", the superior murmured. "Has it ever taken so many?"

Iggie could have told him, but he cultivated a species of simplemindedness here, if only as protection against constant questions about what it was really like in the United States. After so long an exile, they knew as much about it as he did, or thought they did, because of the movies they saw.

Iggie took Frank in the van to the press office on the Via della Conciliazione, where Della Boca, the Vatican spokesman, was briefing the scruffy and impatient men and women who had gathered in the certainty that Pavese would be pope within hours and had spent the surly days since filing backgrounders fed them by the Vatican press office.

They were being told that the conclave had adjourned for the night.

"Adjourned", Frank said aloud. "It's going on a week."

Della Boca confirmed that the conclave had been in session five days and would convene again on the sixth.

"Any idea what's taking so long?"

"The participants have not yet reached a two-thirds agreement." Della Boca after years of practice could say such things with a straight face.

"And the sun is due to rise tomorrow."

"At 5:24", Della Boca confirmed, not missing a beat.

Afterward, huddling in the back of the room, trading rumors even their purveyors knew to be worthless, general agreement was reached that all this delay meant trouble for the progressive point of view. Later in a bar, Frank sat preoccupied.

"We could be right back where we started."

Iggie allowed that that was possible.

"I wonder how Lannan will vote."

"He's not in the conclave."

Frank nearly upset his drink as he leaned forward. "You're kidding."

"He was free to join the conclave, but he didn't."

"What do you mean, free to join. He was invited."

Iggie looked at Frank. How to put this? "They set him free in time."

"What the hell are you talking about?"

"Don't you know?"

Frank looked like he might hit him, invalid or not. Iggie told him what he had heard, watching him as he spoke, trying to read his reaction.

"Was this your doing, Iggie?"

"Oh, Frank. Frank."

"Honest Injun?"

"Cross my heart and hope to die."

"I don't get it." And clearly he didn't. That left Iggie equally confused. Who had engineered Lannan's absence when he was about to be made cardinal and then let him go when Benedetto was killed?

"Why isn't he in the conclave, Iggie?"

"That is an answer you will have to get from him."

"I will. Where can I find him?"

"I only know where he is not."

"He's okay, isn't he?"

"As far as I know."

"He double-crossed me."

By flying to Rome for the investiture that had never happened? By not attending the conclave once he was released and was free to do so?

"He might have double-crossed you again in the conclave."

"Yeah."

The following morning white smoke lifted toward an overcast sky. Iggie and Frank saw it on television in the common room, the regular news broadcast interrupted to bring the picture live from Vatican City. A new pope had been elected.

"Want to go down?"

Frank might have been thinking of all the trouble it was for Iggie to get out the van, to get aboard and get going, when he said, "We'll see more of it here."

That was okay with Iggie. Being in an invalid's chair made one vulnerable in the best of circumstances, but now in the crush of St. Peter's Square anything could happen. And he wouldn't see much with happy pilgrims hopping up and down with glee.

The commentator droned on, his message being that he along with the viewers was waiting to see what had happened. That there was a new pope was indicated by the white smoke issuing from the chimney emerging from a window of the Sistine Chapel, but after so long a conclave, even the experts were stumped.

"Turn off the damned sound", Frank growled.

The camera roved over the crowd; there was file footage on the previous conclave, close-ups of the two popes who had died within months of one another, and then the camera lifted to show the balcony above the main entrance of the basilica.

The camerlingo came out and draped the papal colors over the railing. It was the same man who had done this after the election of Benedetto. Microphones were placed and tested, everything moving along quickly. And then some vested figures of cardinals were visible before they stepped onto the balcony. Novak the secretary of the conclave, Llano looking like the ghost of Christmas past and then, to Frank's audible gasp, Pavese. But he still wore the garb of a cardinal.

"Who the hell have they elected?" Frank groaned.

A tall figure now came into view, clad in the distinctive white cassock of the pope. Iggie hit the sound, but all was chaos in the transmission: the roar of the crowd, confused at first, then gathering force, with the voice of the announcer chattering ineffectually over it. More distinctive than the white cassock were the black face and black hands of the new pontiff as he stepped to the balcony railing and acknowledged the plaudits rising from below.

"Bukoba!" cried Frank.

"Bukoba", whispered Iggie.

The man from Tanzania, the first of his race to be elected bishop of Rome, Vicar of Christ, and successor of St. Peter. After the first surprise, he seemed to fill the role perfectly, as if it had been inevitable, or at least providential, that he should be standing there as Pope Timothy, giving his blessing *urbi et orbi*, to all the millions whose spiritual father he now was.

"Jesus", Frank groaned.

"Just his Vicar", Wynn replied.

6

Archbishop Anselm Williams of Detroit, citing implicit racism, appealed to other African-American bishops as well as the BCC—the Black Catholic Clergy; the executive committee of the NCCB voted overwhelmingly in favor of their resolution; and almost immediately the presidents of the majority of the Catholic colleges and universities as well as the Catholic Theological Society of America agreed. The election of Cardinal Bukoba by a conclave even more dubious than the previous conclave was declared a travesty on democracy and, whether intentionally meant to be or not, was an insult to the Church in the New World.

"Cardinal Bukoba", Williams said, pointedly refusing to refer to the Tanzanian as Pope Timothy, "is a product of the inward-turning, incestuous Vatican politics that has put Vatican II on hold for more than a quarter of a century."

The solution? The council that had been called for a few weeks earlier, prior to the death of Cardinal Benedetto.

"It is the only solution", said San Francisco. "This time the United States had only six electors in the conclave."

"*Securus iudicat orbis terrarum*", said Westminster and went on to speak for several minutes of Cardinal Newman. "Only a universal agreement is trustworthy."

"An open meeting is needed, one to which all bishops can come and decide before the eye of the public who shall govern the Catholic Church", intoned St. Louis, whose unctuous manner and felicitous turn of phrase gained him attention. "Secret conclaves are as archaic as the stove pipe coming out of the Sistine Chapel. The modern Church deserves something better. We have preached democracy, let us now practice it."

Mother Arancia Giussini, O.J., president of the Leadership Council of Religious Women, thanked the bishops for suggesting that she be a full participant in the proposed council.

A preconciliar meeting of *periti* was announced, to be held at NCCB headquarters, to draft schemata for discussion by the council fathers.

From Rome, Archbishop Lannan dissociated himself from his brother bishops. "Only a pope can call a council."

"There is no pope", retorted Rochester. "That's why a council is necessary. The bishops of the world can call themselves into session. That is what we are doing."

"The bishops of the world have authority only in union with the bishop of Rome", said Thomas Lannan from Rome.

"There is no bishop of Rome."

"Pope Timothy is bishop of Rome."

Philadelphia acknowledged that there were two sides. "But that is precisely the problem we must meet to resolve."

The Western media found the conciliarists uttering simple common sense. What better way to clear the air and get things straight than the coming together of the bishops of the world in a meeting that could be followed on television by Catholics and all other interested parties?

"It makes sense to me", Senator Partridge said.

"If Senator Partridge wants the secular media to make decisions for the Baptist church, I am sorry to hear it", Senator Crowe said.

"I was referring to Senator Crowe's bishops", Partridge replied.

But the bishops involved were not the bishops of the world. Whatever the official stance of the NCCB, there were voices of "dissent" in the country. Boise said that he and other bishops from the mountain region would shortly make their long-delayed *ad limina* visit to Rome where they looked forward to expressing loyalty to the Holy Father. But the majority of American bishops were in favor of a council, as were those of Canada, Western Europe, Australia, New Zealand, and Britain. In Ireland it was a comfortable majority in favor of a council, and Latin American countries had a bare majority when they were not, as in the case of Chile, dead set against a council. "All our troubles come from councils", Rio di Janero said.

The bishops of Africa and Asia and Eastern Europe were

unanimously behind the newly elected pope. In the Vatican, Cardinal Novak, the new secretary of state, successor to the late Cardinal Taylor, in reply to repeated questions, said that no plans were under way for a council because no council had been called. Pope Timothy, in his first Angelus address, said that the task of the Church remained one of implementing Vatican II. The message was clear. The 1962–1965 sessions were council enough for the present time.

But the conciliarists were undeterred.

The previous two councils had been held in Rome, but prior to that they had been convened in other cities—in Trent, in Lyons, on the very first occasion in Jerusalem. Lyons was out of the question because of the ultramontane cardinal archbishop enthroned there.

"Why not Avignon?"

Once mentioned, the site seemed inevitable. Here were papal palaces and all the appurtenances of Church government. And history made it clear that popes could be elected and reign from Avignon and never lay eyes on Rome. Avignon it would be.

Meanwhile loyal bishops assured Timothy of their support in any move he chose to make to quell the rebellion.

The Pope began a series of talks at his Wednesday audience on faith and its corruptions—infidelity, schism, apostasy. A lifetime of meditation on the *Summa* of St. Thomas came to fruition in these talks, and any Catholic who had ears to hear understood what was at stake in talk of a council to be "called by a few bishops in defiance of the pope and of all those bishops in union with him."

"*Securus iudicat orbis terrarum*", the Pope said, in direct challenge to London. He went on to develop the context of the original remark of Vincent of Lerrins and of Cardinal John Henry Newman's employment of it. From London came only silence.

Budapest suggested that Pope Timothy himself call a council. The number of participants would dwarf anything that Avignon might attract, and the media would have a genuine council to televise. Jerusalem did not concur.

"The battle is not one between rival councils, but between the Pope and some rebellious bishops. The Holy Father has sufficient authority invested in himself to handle the tragic issue before the Church."

If bishops in the rebellious countries wavered before the unwavering confidence of Pope Timothy, they found that their avenues of retreat were clogged by the triumphant voices of dissent. Far from being given pause by the fact that rejection of the recent conclave was confined to what was called the First World, Americanists asserted that this is precisely what was to be expected.

"Where did the documents of Vatican II come from?" Archbishop Meade asked. "From Africa, from Asia, from Vatican City? Of course not. They came from the Rhine, they came from France, they came, in the case of the Declaration on Religious Liberty, from the United States. Let's have another declaration of religious liberty."

The initial solidarity of Archbishop Williams and the other Afro-American bishops began to erode as the rhetoric became increasingly condescending, geographical, colonial, racist. The Black Catholic Clergy wired Timothy that they were with him, united in faith and ministry. The secular media were confused by this development—a minority within a minority—and began to back away from their initial assumption that the NCCB represented fierce American independence and as such deserved support. It was too much to say, as *Newsweek* did, that it was black against white, and not simply because Hispanic Catholics took exception to the proposal of Meade and the others at the NCCB. Notre Dame increasingly became the center of orthodox Catholicism, of those who saw no other

way to be Catholic than to be united with the successor of
Peter, the bishop of Rome.

"Where's their football team?" Leach asked of the dissident
bishops.

7

"Avignon it is", Meade said when the conference call linking
the members of the executive committee of the NCCB was
set.

"On y danse, on y danse", Oberman trilled.

"Who's coming?"

"That you, Nelly?"

"Yes."

"Invitations have gone out to all the bishops in the world,
of course. This will be ecumenical, at least in intent."

"It sounds like a council, not a conclave."

"Maybe a little bit of each. Whatever emerges will be
openly arrived at."

"You're going to televise the election?"

"Why not? Look, this whole thing is a turning point, a
break with the past."

"Has the Pope been invited?" Archbishop Thomas Lannan
asked. Back in Washington again, he was beginning to feel like
a pingpong ball.

Meade did not answer immediately. "A pope will emerge
from those who are invited."

"I mean Pope Timothy."

"Do you think he'd come?"

"No."

"So what's the point?"

"You can't have a conclave when the Pope is alive and well. You can't call a council without his concurrence."

"You sound opposed."

"Of course I'm opposed. This amounts to schism. Anyone you elect will be an anti-pope, not a pope."

"Anybody else share Archbishop Lannan's view?" Meade asked. The question was met with silence. It was clear that the others had caucused before the conference call. "Okay. We're due to arrive in Lyons on Thursday morning, from there we'll take the TGV to Avignon. The French government and the municipal government of Avignon are going all out to make this a memorable event."

"I won't be there, gentlemen", Lannan said softly. "In charity, I warn you against what you are doing. Need I remind you where Dante put schismatics?"

"I know where he put a few popes", Oberman said, his voice oddly cheerful.

It was the excited, almost playful, tone of the others that struck Lannan, as if they were simply arranging for a meeting of the executive committee in some exotic place. When he said he was going to hang up, everyone wished him well. Preller said he hoped he'd change his mind. After all, wasn't this Avignon council what they had all been working for?

That remark echoed in Thomas Lannan's head after he put down the phone. Was this indeed the goal toward which the Church in America had been moving since Vatican II? In 1968, theologians had defied the Magisterium, declaring *Humanae vitae* unacceptable. But if they rejected the teaching of the Church, they had not left it, but remained within, claiming the right to be Catholics while dissenting from the repeated and clear teaching of the popes. Since theologians held posts in universities, their rebellion soon extended to the institutions themselves. Indeed, the universities had led the way with the Land O' Lakes declaration of 1967 when the presidents of the

494

major Catholic universities in the United States announced their complete autonomy from the teaching Church. Academic freedom, the essential mark of a true university, they argued, dictated that the university be subject to no authority external to itself, whether to the local bishop, to the collection of bishops, or to the bishop of Rome.

In retrospect, one could see the beginnings of schism in that *trahison des clercs*. The moral teaching rejected by the theologians was replaced by an ambiguous doctrine that found room for the sexual revolution within the Church herself. As Paul VI had predicted, the severance of sexual activity from procreation, in contraceptive sex, was the acceptance of a principle that was soon extended to premarital and extramarital sex, to homosexuality. The new moral theology for a time agreed that such acts, considered in general, were wrong, but this did not mean that all particular instances of them were wrong.

Confusion about sex led to confusion about marriage, and soon the tribunals were clogged with cases of couples seeking annulments. Priests, muddled about the distinctiveness of holy orders and told that celibacy was a discipline whose time was past, sought laicization in the thousands, sometimes after having entered into a liaison. Nuns adopted radical feminism and accused the Church of systematic persecution of women. *If you won't ordain us, why baptize us?* Lannan had seen this incredible legend on buttons worn by frowning nuns during John Paul II's first visit to the United States. Such women had stopped demanding ordination. They would reject it if offered. It was a relic of an outmoded hierarchical Church, as well as being sexist. Strange rites were practiced in religious houses, led by nuns themselves, and worship of the "Goddess" was allegedly rampant.

Such vocations as there were too often involved young men molded in this rebellious ambiance, vague in what was called their sexual orientation, unsure that a priest differed significantly from a lay person, drawn by the hope of playing a leading role in the liturgy or engaging in social work.

Seated at his desk, as the sunlight waned and shadows lengthened over Washington, Thomas Lannan felt that the scales had finally dropped from his eyes. Who was it who said Frank Bailey and the rest of them should simply declare victory? Despite their grumbling, they had indeed won. Not that Lannan saw himself as an innocent spectator of these past years. He had been at the center of the Church in the United States; he had been a mover and shaker in the NCCB from the beginning of his priesthood; he could not pretend that his own hands were clean. The great difference between him and most of his brother bishops was that he had no more illusions about the state of the Church in the United States. Jim Morrow had gotten it right. They had lived through its decline and fall, and the Church had fallen so low that now its chief bishops were planning to attend a schismatic conclave and elect a rival of Pope Timothy.

He turned on his desk lamp and swung in his chair. "Monsignor Wales?"

The door to the adjoining office was open, but no light was yet on.

"Gene, are you there?"

He got to his feet. His new clarity about what was happening, what had happened, demanded action. He looked into Wales' office, flicking on the switch inside the door. No one was there. He was about to turn off the light when he noticed an envelope propped prominently in the center of the desk. He crossed the room and saw that it was addressed to himself.

He picked it up and looked at his name written in the precise hand of Monsignor Wales. Archbishop Thomas Lannan. He took the envelope back to his desk and opened it.

Dear Archbishop Lannan,

I want to thank you for the opportunities you have

given me, although I do so with some irony. Perhaps if I had been assigned to parish work and kept busy I could have ignored what has happened to the Church. What has happened shouldn't have been able to happen if the Church were what I believed her to be. Just now I am not sure what I believe anymore. If I have any faith left, I know it would not survive going to Avignon with you. Please consider me on leave. This isn't the way to go, of course, but I've reached the point where I don't even want to talk about it.

Lannan threw down the letter and dialed the number of Wales' apartment. He had to tell Gene that he wasn't going to Avignon, that he wouldn't take part in a schismatic council. The phone rang and rang, and as it did he had the certainty that Wales was sitting in his apartment listening to the same ringing. All he had to do was pick up the phone. But the phone was not picked up.

Later Lannan drove to Archbishop Vilani's to discuss with the pro-nuncio the calling of a conclave in Avignon.
   "You're not going?"
   "No."
Vilani took his hand and gripped it tightly. "Thank God. Do the others realize what they're doing?"
   "Yes."
As much as anyone ever realizes what he's doing, that is. The path before us is so distorted by our desires and hopes that we always walk in twilight at best. There was surprise as well as delight in Vilani's eyes, as if he hadn't expected the archbishop of Washington to remain loyal to the Pope.
   "You're still president of the Conference, aren't you?"
   "Yes."
   "What do you intend to do?"

At his instructions, Leach had sent telegrams to every ordinary in the country, denouncing the Avignon conclave as a schismatic act, dissociating the NCCB from it, and asking for an immediate reply, expressing support of the president of the NCCB and of His Holiness, Pope Timothy.

"And what has been the response?"

He had asked that telegrams be sent to his office at the NCCB. His own attempts to call there had been unsuccessful, suggesting that incoming calls were tying up the lines. He told Vilani that he would have an answer for him in the morning.

"You are optimistic?"

"I am hopeful."

A total of fifty-nine bishops wired their support of Archbishop Lannan and rejection of the Avignon conclave. The vast majority of the American hierarchy, over two hundred bishops, all of course appointed by Rome, sided with the schismatics.

It was difficult to feel surprised. The media had welcomed the initiative of the American bishops in calling the open conclave; there were extended interviews with Meade, with Hawkins, and with Oberman, who managed to make the whole thing seem a practical joke they were playing on Rome. The interviewer, Foyle, followed up on Hawkins' mention of St. Catherine of Siena who had prayed and nagged and cajoled the popes to return from Avignon to Rome. Hawkins was suggesting that the American bishops were simply taking a precedented indirect route to Rome via Avignon.

"Perhaps the Pope will send Caterina of Viterbo to nag us", Oberman replied with a merry smile.

"Who is Caterina of Viterbo?"

Oberman threw up his hands and gave a chuckling little homily on the Shroud of Turin, the liquefaction of the blood of St. Januarius, the House of Loreto, the uncorrupted bodies to be found in shrines throughout Italy. "So why shouldn't there be visionaries as well? I am told that she specializes in dire prophecies about the United States."

What had seemed an interesting avenue no longer interested Foyle. Rather he asked if the bishops ordained by the late Archbishop Lefebvre had been invited to take part in the Avignon conclave. Oberman's smile dissolved.

"Only if they first submit to psychiatric tests."

When Senator Partridge was asked for his thoughts on these events, he tucked in his chin. "I hold to the separation of church and state. You might want to ask my esteemed colleague Senator Crowe."

The suggestion was not followed. Thomas Lannan himself refused all requests for interviews. In the light of his newly acquired clarity, it seemed to him that it had been the carrying on of Church business through the secular media that was one of the principal causes of the present difficulty.

Archbishop Vilani came personally to pass on to him the papal invitation. Pope Timothy wished to initiate Thomas Lannan into the College of Cardinals immediately and requested that afterward he remain in Rome for the extraordinary synod to be held in the Vatican.

PART EIGHT

CHAPTER ONE

I

Years before, Archbishop Lannan had heard a talk by Cardinal Law of Boston describing the feeling he had when he arrived in Rome for the Second Extraordinary Synod in 1985. The cardinal had come from a country in which the top items on the Church's agenda were thought to be the ordination of women, the abandonment of priestly celibacy, and the removal of the prohibition on contraception.

"How parochial all that seemed from the vantage point of Rome."

Law quoted a prelate from India saying that in his diocese he was trying to persuade people not to kill their female infants, so of course he found talk of altar girls and women priests somewhat surrealistic. It was the most dramatic contrast of many in the cardinal's remarks, the implication of which was that the United States, seen from the See of Peter, might look more like a withering branch than the taproot of the Church. It was at that extraordinary synod that Cardinal Law had proposed the writing of a universal catechism.

In the years since, the chasm between the declining West and the countries where the faith was spreading like wildfire had widened. Americans were blinded to their condition by their technological leadership of the so-called First World. Feats of genetic engineering won Nobel prizes; the slaughter of the unborn went on despite the billions that had been poured into what was still called sex education; AIDS continued to cut a swath through the homosexual population, whose lifestyle was nonetheless extolled and its rights expanded even as the hideous toll continued. In Africa, on the other hand, AIDS had mysteriously disappeared. Theories abounded to account for this. The Africans attributed it to a miracle wrought by the intercession of Our Lady of Tanzania.

But if Archbishop Lannan now saw his country in much the same way as the last several popes had, it was clear that most of his brother bishops did not. They had set off for Avignon in triumphal good cheer, manifestly certain that they were doing what had to be done.

"You mean, elect an anti-pope?" he asked the Archbishop of St. Louis who came to see him.

Meade pursed his lips and nodded. "If it comes to that. But even if it does, Tom, that's only another move, not endgame."

Meade's mission was to bring Lannan back into the fold. And to chide him for sending out that wire from the Conference.

"We voted to replace you, Tom, but I insisted that before that could take effect I must talk with you. I want to pass on to you some thoughts of Fr. Hawkins."

Meade had mentioned to Hawkins that Archbishop Lannan had raised the question of an anti-pope. ("To tell you the truth, Tom, I knew nothing about all the anti-popes. Or if I did, I had forgotten. I guess I never wanted to look too closely at our claim about the unbroken line.") Hawkins had provided Meade with a memo whose thesis was that it had often been the election of an anti-pope that led to the resignation of an unpopular pope, so that a third-compromise candidate could be elected.

"Is he crazy?"

"He calls it thesis, antithesis, synthesis." Meade smiled

504

indulgently. "But that's what I mean when I say this is just another move. You think I like the prospect of two men claiming to be pope at the same time?"

"Timothy will never resign."

Meade pinched the end of his nose and peered at the ceiling. How to put this? "Tom, he can't afford to ignore us. The Italian government is about to slap a fine on the Vatican that will shut the place down."

"What kind of fine?"

"Back taxes on their business ventures."

"That's just a threat. And it won't be any more effective than a threat from Avignon."

"We'll see."

"Cecil, what if you should die before the game is over?"

A man who has undergone a triple bypass after half a dozen ineffectual angioplasties does not take references to his health kindly. But Meade chose to ignore the question.

"Come to Avignon, Tom. Come as an observer, just be there. You should be with the rest of us."

"Not everyone will be there."

"Boise?" Meade snorted. "Those mountaineers are up too high to think straight."

"I think they're right."

"No, Tom. They think you're right."

"Do me a favor, will you? Before you get on that plane, read Vatican II's 'Dogmatic Constitution on the Church'. *Lumen Gentium.*"

"What's your point?"

"We only have power as bishops when we are in union with the bishop of Rome."

"I accept that! My God, this whole fight is to save Vatican II, not oppose it. The question is who *is* the bishop of Rome."

"You know the answer to that."

"What I know is that if we accept Bukoba we will see a *real* decline and fall in this country. They're breeding like flies all over the dark continent, and he sings the praises of *Humanae vitae*. And he calls the decline in AIDS miraculous!"

"It hasn't just declined in Africa; it's disappeared."

"You can get a pretty good argument on that from a lot of scientists."

"Who haven't taken the trouble to go to Africa and see for themselves."

"But, Tom, a miracle!"

Meade's face contorted in anguished sorrow. Imagine telling their fellow Americans they belonged to a Church that claimed a miracle had wiped out the world's most publicized disease. That was the message on Meade's face. Did he think the dogma of the Resurrection would fare better, or transubstantiation, or the forgiveness of sins? How many articles of the Creed had they stopped talking about because of the concern Meade showed?

"I'm not going to Avignon."

"I'm sorry to hear that." Meade got to his feet, a little edgy because he had had to speak so frankly, and to no effect.

"Are you the new president of the NCCB?"

Meade nodded. "Nothing you've said gives me any cause to set my election aside. You've lost that now. And that's not all."

"Oh?"

"Another proviso was added after I insisted on having this talk with you. You'll lose Washington too, Tom. We can't have someone out of step with the Conference as ordinary of the capitol of the country."

"The Conference didn't appoint me to Washington."

"Your successor will be named in Avignon."

"An anti-archbishop?"

"Oh, it'll be a man." Meade punched him in the arm.

Lannan went with his visitor to the door, where they shook hands solemnly. He watched Meade quicken his pace as he

506

went toward the waiting car that would take him to Dulles.

In his study, he sat in an easy chair and looked around the room illumined only by the lamp on the desk. On the table beside him was a yellowing paperback Fr. Leach had given him, a book of Belloc's. *Characters of the Reformation.*

"He's very good on Clement VII," Leach said, "and on Thomas More."

The ultramontane priest from Toledo was filling in for Wales, at least temporarily. Lannan was not sure he could stand to have so confident and didactic a young man near him permanently. But when Leach asked if he would be accompanying Archbishop Lannan to Rome, the answer had seemed obvious.

"Have you made our reservations?"

"Yes. You in business, myself in tourist."

"That wasn't necessary."

"It was only slightly more expensive."

He seemed fated to be misunderstood by Leach. He explained to him what he meant.

"Archbishop, I would go steerage to Rome."

"When were you last there?"

"Last there?" cried the ultramontane. "I've *never* been there. It has been my dream to go."

2

An informal seminar had been going on in the corridors, refectory, and resident rooms of the North American College. Even in the chapel, it was inaudibly present, like the music of the spheres. Monsignor Ambrose Frawley had stopped trying to divert the young seminarians from discussing the extraordinary steps that had been taken by the bishops of the United States. Out of necessity, he had assumed the role of arbiter, the wise elder who allots time to both sides and prevents rhetorical excesses.

"When I am ordained, I will promise loyalty to my bishop", said a young man from Seattle.

"Who promised loyalty to the Holy Father when he was ordained a bishop", replied a priest from Peoria.

"We were shafted in the last two conclaves. Not a single American voted for Timothy."

"Do we know that?" Monsignor Frawley asked.

"Archbishop Lannan isn't going to Avignon", a bearded black from Chicago announced.

"I don't believe that. He's the one with the real complaint. I mean personally."

"They should have held their meeting in Rome."

"Where?"

"Here!"

And they all looked at Frawley, who held up his hands, disarmed.

On the television in the recreation room a soccer game was in progress, the sound muted. The generally frustrated movements up and down the field seemed a metaphor of their discussion. Frawley, like his wards, was more shaken by recent events than he cared to let on. But he was sure the young men were wrong to doubt that Thomas Lannan was in disagreement with the majority of the American bishops. What he had done was not in doubt, but only why he had done it. A priest named Leach with a high-pitched twangy voice answered Frawley's call.

"Monsignor Frawley calling. From Rome."

"Good morning, Monsignor."

"I would like to speak with Archbishop Lannan."

"Could you give me a number where he can reach you?"

508

"He has my number."

"Even so, it would be better if you give it to me. Things are a bit hectic here at the moment."

"In what way?"

"My name is Fr. Rodney Leach, Monsignor. I'm just learning the ropes as Archbishop Lannan's administrative assistant."

"What happened to Eugene Wales?"

"He resigned."

Aha. A falling out because of Lannan's separating himself from the NCCB? Frawley asked if Leach had a telephone number where Wales could be reached.

"I have a number, but he doesn't answer it."

"That sounds ominous."

"I don't mean to make it so."

It would not have been accurate to say that there was hostility in Fr. Leach's voice. Perhaps it was just that Frawley missed the easy exchange he had enjoyed with Wales.

"I'll be expecting Archbishop Lannan's call." He hesitated. "Don't tell him it's urgent, but there are things he will want to know."

Rome was more alive with rumors than it had ever been—and with pilgrims. They continued to flow into the city, visitors unlike the prosperous, well-dressed tourists with cameras slung around their necks and guidebooks in hand who had been a familiar sight throughout Frawley's residence in Rome. The Bernini colonnade looked like a gypsy encampment; the great square of St. Peter's was alive with color—of fabric and of skin. Black and brown and yellow faces looked up at the window when Pope Timothy appeared for the Angelus, and the chanting that began then had an elemental rhythm that brought a great smile to the face of Bukoba. Frawley had heard him called Pope Pianoforte by a blonde priest from San Diego, an obvious reference to the papal smile that seemed to call into play more than the usual quota of teeth. There was an undeniably racist undertone to many negative comments on the recent election.

"Hey, we're the minority" was the response to Frawley's caution.

"Whites have always been a minority."

"Not in the Church."

"What do you mean by white?"

If the pilgrims filling Rome were a fair sample, whites were now a negligible factor in the Church as well. Like the Romans, tourists from Western Europe and the States were put off by the crowds whose devotion was manifest but who were notable for odors other than that of sanctity.

"Now you know what the world was like before the invention of deodorants."

Deodorants for the masses, that is. Aristocrats had always doused themselves in cologne or some other countervailing scent. But the Catholics who came to Rome resembled the Muslim pilgrims of old, crushing into their holy places; indeed, many of these pilgrims were converts from Islam.

"Now I know what the Boston Brahmins felt like when the Irish took over."

"Or all the big-city machines when blacks became a majority."

By contrast, the bishops who were televised as they arrived in Avignon were predominantly white. And overweight. These jowly, well-dressed men, looking like diplomats or politicians or corporate executives—it could be argued that they were a bit of all three—had the air of stockholders confronting a hostile takeover. Indeed, the parlous state of Vatican finances was a leit-motif of the interviews coming out of France.

"Not very subtle", James Morrow observed. Frawley had stopped by the embassy on the Via Aurelia to escape the feverish discussions at the North American College.

"The Italian government is not being very subtle either."

"Cardinal Novak tells me they are prepared for the worst."

"What is the worst?"

"A ten-billion-dollar penalty."

"Ten billion!"

"I suppose it's negotiable. The amount is pegged to the belief that Americans will come to the rescue."

"The Pope would have to pay dearly for that kind of help."

"Maybe Tom Lannan's decision to stay away from Avignon will have more influence eventually."

On this Frawley would have differed, if he had chosen to respond. His inclination at the moment was to observe a prudent silence until the situation clarified. The bishops in Avignon were playing a high-risk game, but increasingly they seemed to be holding a strong hand. With the help of the Italian government, it could prove to be an unbeatable one. There was open speculation in the Milanese and Roman media about the chances of an Italian replacing the Tanzanian, whose status was generally agreed to be in doubt.

3

If Cardinal Novak and the new Pope were aware of the predictions of the visionary of Viterbo, they gave no indication of it. James Morrow, on a visit to the secretary of state, had made an allusion to the report he had written.

"I am a relative newcomer, Your Eminence, but you are the third secretary of state I've had the honor to deal with."

"We live in changing times."

"As Adam said to Eve on the way out of the garden."

Novak stared at Morrow and then burst into a laughter so

unrestrained that he apparently did not hear Morrow say he had stolen the remark from Dean Inge.

"Of course, of course", Novak said, regaining his composure. "That is a salutary reminder. It is a great temptation to imagine that one's own times are wholly unlike any other."

"There *are* a few unusual things going on."

"The Holy Father has asked me to discuss with you some aspects of reports from our nuncio in Washington. Archbishop Lannan remains loyal, and there are others in his camp. Are there any prospects of the number increasing?"

Morrow still was unsure what exactly Tom Lannan's stand was. The man had been on a roller coaster in recent months—named cardinal twice, kidnapped, absented himself from a conclave in which he could have participated, pressured by his brother bishops, and now separating himself dramatically from the meeting taking place in Avignon.

"My fear is that the number of loyalists will dwindle with time."

"You foresaw this in your history?"

"I foresaw nothing. I was writing history. For predictions you must go to the Secret of Fatima and the woman in Viterbo."

But Novak did not pursue the suggestion.

"I did write a report for Cardinal Benedetto and the Holy Father shortly after arriving here."

"On your country?"

"Yes. But with reference to Fatima and Viterbo."

Novak nodded, but his interest was not piqued.

"It is uncanny how accurate the prophesy has been."

"I understand that you are a friend of Archbishop Lannan's."

"We were in school together as boys."

"The Holy Father would appreciate a supplemental report."

To compare with what they were hearing from Vilani?

"Will Archbishop Lannan be able to gather more loyal bishops to his cause or, as you suggest, is the opposite likely?"

"What does Archbishop Vilani think?"

"We are more interested in what a native American thinks. Particularly one who has made such an important study of the Church in the United States."

"Sometimes I feel I have been away for years."

Morrow had the same difficulty getting through to Lannan that Monsignor Frawley had complained of.

"I am sure he will be contacting you soon, Mr. Ambassador."

"It is very important that I talk to him." Morrow paused before going on. "The Holy Father has given me a little chore."

"He will be speaking to you both very soon."

"Is he coming to Rome?"

Fr. Leach's voice changed, making Morrow feel that he had just solved a charade. "We leave two days from now."

"Tell him I will definitely meet his plane."

"We shall be landing in Milan and driving from there."

"I would never have bet he'd stand fast", Maureen said, picking lint from Jim's sleeve as she spoke. She had leaned toward him to do this, and it was all he could do not to plunge his face into her hair.

"I'm a little surprised myself."

"Will he be able to withstand the pressure?"

"He's coming to Rome."

"Well, that takes courage. After what happened the last time. Where did you get this jacket?"

"It came with the pants."

"It's not wool; it shouldn't catch hold of everything the way it does."

"Like this?"

She came easily into his embrace, devoid of coyness, lifting her face and looking at him steadily. He lowered his lips to the tip of her nose. They had not discussed what their closeness meant, and he assumed she must wonder about her children's reaction as much as he did about his.

Marrying again, taken in the abstract, seemed idiotic. Concupiscence was not what it had been, not so much because of virtue as because of age; but quite apart from that was the seeming impossibility of entering into the drama of someone else's life when it was so far along, particularly when one's own life was already largely what it would be. How totally different it would be from when he had married Mabel and Maureen had married Sean.

"How chaste we are", she murmured, snuggling against him. They were on the balcony of her apartment on Parioli, with the great mosque of Rome just below. As the Pantheon had been long ago, it was scheduled to be converted to Christian purpose. It was Sunday, and Rome was subdued, warmed by an April sun.

"Are you complaining?"

A long silence. Then, "You are the first man who has held me since Sean."

"And the last?"

She looked up at him. "Don't say what you don't mean."

"I want my kids to meet you."

"A test?"

"Not for me. Them. I have two daughters."

Why did he think the girls would consider a second marriage a betrayal of their mother? Ken, he was sure, would accept it or at worst shrug it off.

"I've told my other children about you."

He had met Bridget, a wide-faced girl with pale blue eyes who looked not at all like her mother. Bridget was just sixteen and seemed to think it was great fun that the old people were acting like kids. She had come on a visit from her school in Dublin.

"I was afraid you'd enter a convent", she said to her mother.

"And I'm afraid you won't."

"Don't laugh."

"Now Bridget."

But Bridget gave no indication of whether or not she was joking. "What exactly are my chaperon duties to be?"

"There is a reception at the Argentine embassy."

"Good. They always have the best food."

It was reassuring to have met at least one of Maureen's kids. There were others in the States. The fear that marrying her would be like joining her family, taking someone's place, dissipated. It was obvious that Bridget thought that whatever was going on between her mother and James Morrow was something new and self-contained.

It was companionship rather than passion that drew him to Maureen and, he suspected, vice versa too. He realized that he had been growing quirky living alone, and it was good to have a moderating feminine influence again. Left to himself, he would have become the recluse of Lake Powderhorn. Not all bad, maybe, but thank God he had been rescued from that by Tom Lannan's unlooked-for patronage.

From Washington came requests for regular and extended reports on what was happening in the Catholic Church. Harry Blintz and Emil Coyne at the American Embassy on the Via Veneto told Morrow they were getting the same request.

"What the hell *is* going on?" Blintz asked. His glasses brightened and darkened in response to altering light so that a conversation with him had an episodic quality.

"The American bishops are calling it a second declaration of independence."

"From the British?"

Coyne snickered. He had a face like a fist. "You think they'll elect a rival pope?"

Morrow found discussing these matters with two thoroughly secular minds instructive. These seasoned diplomats assumed that what was going on in the Church was a political struggle between the First World and the rest and that meant it was really an internal struggle in the hearts of the First Worlders.

"Will the power of money overcome the sense of guilt?" Coyne asked. "That's the crux, as I see it."

The news from Avignon suggested that the bishops gathered there also took a political view of the matter. The references to Vatican financial difficulties continued to be frequent and pointed, and this created the impression that they had come together in Avignon to find a solution to the impending judgment in Milan that could break the Vatican bank.

The fact that the Avignon proceedings were carried live on CNN made for the waste of a great deal of time. McHugh undertook to monitor the sessions, but Morrow found himself looking on with dread fascination. Fr. Hawkins addressed the conclave on the subject of the election of Pope Timothy and argued that, because of the unusual character of the conclave, and the unexplained absence from it of a number of key electors, a shadow was cast over the outcome.

Even in color, Hawkins looked black and white; his pale face with its deeply lined cheeks seemed paler because of his shock of black hair and the beard no amount of shaving could keep at bay for long. His bright unblinking eyes looked out from deep sockets. The combination of his appearance and pedantic tone muted the impact of what he was saying. The gist of his argument was that Pope Timothy was not a pope who could claim the loyalty of the Avignon conclave and that this opened the way to an election.

Several participants put questions to Hawkins, not so much

to express disagreement, as wanting more assurance that they were in a position to do what they had come to Avignon to do. They did it on the second day, in a single ballot.

Cardinal Pavese of Milan, who was not present at the conclave, was elected pope, and a delegation, headed by Archbishop Meade, was dispatched immediately to Milan to make the results known to Pavese.

In the interim, Italian banking interests opined that a Pavese in the Vatican could alter the present determination to seek an eye for an eye on the part of those who had suffered from decades of unwise investments by the Vatican.

Pavese was televised celebrating a pontifical Mass in his cathedral. In the homily, he dwelt on the fact that the Church in Milan had been founded in apostolic times, the observation inviting listeners to see him as in direct line with one apostle at least. When he emerged from the cathedral, still vested, wearing his miter and carrying his crosier, he received the delegation from Avignon, and in a sequence that seemed as predetermined as the liturgy he had just celebrated, he read the declaration, folded it carefully, and then, finding and addressing the camera, announced, "I shall be called Pius."

The ovation seemed as confused as it was enthusiastic, and Pavese, accepting his role as anti-pope with an expression made solemn by nearsightedness, looked enigmatically out over the piazza.

"Pius?" exclaimed McHugh.

"Pius XIII", Morrow said, completing the thought. "I hope he's not superstitious."

4

Gene Wales had just disappeared, down the hole like Alice, gone, and that had been bad enough, given the conversations they had been having, but now Janet needed to talk to him, professionally, and she missed him more than ever. Fr. Leach seemed to take delight in explaining that no one knew where Monsignor Wales was. She bypassed him and got to Archbishop Lannan, stopping by his residence and surprising him when he was obviously in a big rush. He was leaving for Rome the following day.

"Gene Wales is my cousin, Archbishop."

"I didn't know that."

"I'm Janet Fortin. I work in the White House?"

"Of course, I know you."

"He was a great deal of help to me. I do Catholic liaison. I'm supposed to know what's going on with Catholics, but right now I give up; I need help."

"How is it a problem for the White House?"

"Everything's a problem for the White House."

He was so obviously being patient with her, bending away as if he couldn't wait to be released and get out of the room, that she felt no impulse to ask him what to make of the so-called pope who had just been elected in Avignon.

"If he went on retreat, where would he go?"

The question had apparently not occurred to him. She had his full attention at last, and he was no longer reluctant to talk about the missing monsignor. A little smile formed on his lips.

"I can tell you where *I* go on retreat."

He gave her the name, then sat down, and wrote directions, as if it was already agreed that she was going to head for Kentucky and find Gene Wales in a Trappist abbey.

"Is there any way I can find out if he's there before taking the trip?"

He called for Fr. Leach and assigned him the chore, then actually sat back, relaxed. Of course. His administrative assistant had gone off to some quiet place to figure out what in the world was going on. Janet herself was not so sure. Gene's idea that he was in love with her had been an effect not a cause, as he himself had said. Something had already been wrong, and he was looking for an excuse to get out. Janet wasn't sure she was flattered to be spoken of as a mode of escape, but once Gene had begun to talk, he hadn't wanted to stop, and just saying all these things had seemed to be good for him.

"I was a target of opportunity?"

"That's not the way I'd put it", he had replied.

Well, she hoped that wasn't the full truth anyway. She liked him too, a lot, but it was a safe kind of liking, because he was a priest, because she was some kind of shirt-tail cousin. Maybe it could have been something else, if he hadn't been Monsignor Wales, she didn't know. But if the doubts about being a priest came before his notion that he had fallen in love with her, it didn't seem likely that he would be off finding himself in a Trappist monastery.

Fifteen minutes went by before Fr. Leach came back. His bald head glittered with reflected light, and his smile seemed meant for another occasion.

"I could try other places. He's not at Gethsemani."

Archbishop Lannan reacted in disbelief. Obviously he had become convinced that Wales had done what he himself would have done.

"Yes, keep trying", he said, but even as he spoke conviction drained from his voice. He turned to Janet. "I'm sorry."

"I'm being asked what to make of Pius XIII."

"There is only one Pope. And he's in Rome."

But he had no intention of discussing these matters with her. Soon he was leaning toward the door again, obviously anxious to get rid of her. Janet wasn't sorry to go. There was no way she could have talked with the archbishop as she had to Gene Wales, and anyway she had found out the main thing she wanted to learn. They didn't know where Gene was either.

He was waiting for her at her apartment, sitting in a car parked at the curb. He got out and came slowly toward her.

"You're right on time", she said, touching his arm.

"On time?"

"I was about to put out an all-points bulletin on your car."

"It's a rental."

"Come on in."

They went upstairs where she took another try at making risotto, recalling as best she could how James Morrow had made it when she first visited him in his cottage at Lake Powderhorn. It ended up more glue than fluff, and the mushrooms sat in it as if they were ashamed.

"Archbishop Lannan thought you might have gone to the Trappists."

"I doubt that."

"But he did." She told him about her chat with his boss ("Former boss", he interposed) and how Leach had made a call to Kentucky to see if they could track him down. "Leach is going to try other monasteries."

He laughed, but it was not a happy laugh. He looked as if he hadn't had a happy laugh in a long time.

"I went over there because I wanted to talk with you about what's happening in Avignon."

"Pius XIII?" He said it scornfully. "What's happening is schism."

He went on, and while things didn't become clear, she no longer felt it was her fault that everything was confused.

"Lannan is probably on his way to Rome because the schismatic bishops have declared the see of Washington open. Meaning they will fill it with one of their own."

"Meaning he has nowhere else to go?"

"There'll be nowhere else for the others to go either."

"What are you going to do?"

"I'm already doing it."

He had been hired by one of the middle-of-the-road Washington think-tanks. "They want me because they aren't sure what's going on in the Catholic Church either. Isn't that ironic? I can earn my livelihood because of my knowledge of what I'm running away from."

"I wonder how far you'll run."

"This is better than the last time." He meant the risotto.

"You can always go into the diplomatic corps."

They seemed to have the same thought at the same time, but Janet said it first.

"I wonder how James Morrow is taking these developments."

5

Unsure whether he would be welcome at the Villa Stritch, Archbishop Lannan went to the American Embassy to the Vatican on the Via Aurelia by a cab, which, because of the traffic, let him out two lanes from the curb. A series of arabesques and pas de deux got him through the intervening vehicles to the embassy door. Dennis McHugh took him directly to Jim Morrow. The two old friends exchanged a long look before shaking hands. McHugh took Fr. Leach to his room before Jim said what Lannan longed to hear.

"I'm proud of you, Tom."

Jim sounded a bit surprised too, as if he didn't quite believe Tom Lannan had broken ranks with his colleagues at the NCCB.

"Because I abandoned ship?"

"Because you didn't."

"Whatever it was, it wasn't heroic."

His motives could seem ambiguous at best. Hadn't he resisted Bailey's brazen effort to force his hand because he wanted to be made cardinal? That ambition as much as loyalty to the Holy Father explained to the cynical his present status.

"Has the NCCB gone mad, Tom?"

"They must know what they're doing, and that seems to exclude madness. God have mercy on them."

"What do they have in mind, a rival church? A national church?"

"It's more complicated than that. Or more confused."

He tried to make the best case he could for what Meade and the others were doing, and that required seeing it, as Meade insisted, as a move in a game, the election of Pavese meant to force the resignation of Timothy.

"And then Pavese resigns?"

"Probably not. He would represent the progressives, and that's what they want. Jim, you know them. They really and truly believe we have to jettison all kinds of doctrinal and moral cargo if we are going to speak to the modern mind. But they would need a compromise candidate.

This was to play into Morrow's hand, of course, since in his history he had dwelt on the chauvinism of theologians in the West for whom the modern mind meant their university colleagues. And of course that modern mind had changed considerably since it was first invoked as a criterion for the acceptability of doctrine.

"Even apart from that, they are speaking of a small segment

522

of the earth's present population and a smaller segment of Catholics", remarked Morrow.

"But they see the others as throwbacks."

"Timothy?"

"What's he like?" If Timothy crumbled under the pressure from the Avignon conclave and the Vatican debt, if he resigned in favor of Pavese, Tom Lannan would have boarded the Titanic rather than stayed with the barque of Peter.

"Surely you've met him."

Bukoba had been in the background during *ad limina* visits, but the Americans had never taken him seriously, perhaps assuming that he was the token African cardinal in the Curia. The attitude was less racist than the result of superimposing the American political experience on the Church. Affirmative action had put many blacks and women and other designated minority groups into positions they might never have otherwise achieved, a fact that led to an almost unconscious discounting of their presence. Thus had Cardinal Bukoba appeared to the American bishops.

"You'll want to get some rest", Jim said, perhaps thinking of Lannan's last visit.

"I was semi-comatose throughout the flight and dozed on the drive from Milan. I doubt I could sleep if I tried."

"Why did you come through Milan?"

"Fr. Leach made arrangements. He claims it was much cheaper."

"If you feel that good, you can come with me."

"Where?"

Morrow was scheduled to visit Cardinal Novak, the secretary of state, and thought it only appropriate that the deposed president of the National Conference of Catholic Bishops should present himself at the Vatican as quickly as possible.

"It's for their sake you were punished."

He had felt less punished than liberated after his conversation with Cecil Meade. When the White House liaison surprised him with her visit, he had been loath to talk about what was happening in the Church. Whatever it was, his immediate responsibility for events was suspended. He was free. When Janet Fortin suggested that Wales might have taken refuge in a monastery, Lannan had been almost overwhelmed by a desire to head once more for Kentucky and the Abbey of Gethsemani.

"They have no canonical right to depose you", Leach said, in his fluty voice.

"They will invoke the authority of Pius XIII."

"Who has no canonical status. The anti-pope has no dominion over you."

He almost resented Leach's insistence. To agree with his new administrative assistant was to face the prospect of a long and murky struggle with Meade and the others, one that would inevitably become public and further confuse the faithful. Rodney Leach reminded him of the kid on the playground always willing to arrange for others to fight. The only solution was to report to Rome and receive instructions there.

In the car, Lannan was impressed by Morrow's rapid exchanges with Luigi in Italian. The driver had begun a running commentary on what was happening to the city, to the Vatican, to everything. Jim told him to pay attention to his driving.

The city was changed; its walks were crowded with people whose dress easily set them off from the dapper Romans. John Paul II had attracted hordes of Slavs, but they were all but indistinguishable from natives of the city. There had always been gypsies in Rome, and Ethiopians, of course, but here were Indians, Asians, Africans, and Turks, as well as former Muslims from the opposite shore of the Mediterranean, all of them crowding up the Via della Conciliazione toward the great basilica of St. Peter for a glimpse of the Pope who was so visibly one of themselves. It was difficult not to sympathize with Luigi when they were immobilized where the street opened onto the square. The traffic stopping them was human traffic, a constant flow of humanity, everyone moving but themselves.

"Maybe we'd better walk."

A protest from Luigi at being abandoned was ignored. Morrow told him to head back to the embassy; they would get home somehow. What Luigi thought of that was clear in his glowering gaze. They got out of the car and pushed through the crowd. Behind them the angry ineffective sound of the car horn began.

"I have brought Archbishop Lannan with me", Morrow announced when they were admitted to Cardinal Novak's office.

The secretary of state came around his desk, a look of surprise giving way to delight. His arms extended, and he moved swiftly toward Lannan and gathered him in a great *abbraccio*.

"Thank God, you're here. The Holy Father has been asking about you."

The suppressed sense of shame at wanting to desert his post and flee into exile dissolved at the warmth of Novak's welcome. Did the secretary of state think he had been in physical danger?

"Physical danger is easy", Novak replied. It was a matter on which he could speak with some authority. As if to illustrate what he meant, he picked up a letter from his desk. He began to offer it to Lannan, then hesitated, looking at Morrow. He decided to read it aloud.

Out of the ornate and orotund prose of the letter emerged

the fact that the government of Italy had secured a judgment of three billion dollars against the Vatican Bank, said sum to be payable immediately in dollars.

Novak's brows lifted above his heavy glasses, and he looked back and forth between the two Americans.

"I had just informed the Holy Father when this arrived."

He flourished another faxed letter. Again he read. It was from Avignon. The first letter had been subtle and courteous and devastating; this letter was vulgar and intimidating. The threat to the Church represented by the debt to the Italian government would be solved swiftly when the result of the Avignon conclave was accepted by John Baptist Bukoba.

"What did Pope Timothy say to that?"

Novak tried to smile.

"He said he would move. They can have Vatican City."

Thomas Lannan's heart sank. If Timothy stepped down, his own stand against Meade and the others would be rendered ridiculous.

"He'll turn it over to Pavese?" Jim Morrow asked.

"No, no. To the Bank of Italy."

It was on that puzzling note that Cardinal Novak took them in to the Holy Father.

The Holy Father extended both his hands to Archbishop Lannan, then drew him to his breast. When he stepped back, there were tears in his eyes.

"Thank God, you have come."

"You are Peter."

All misgivings and doubts were swept away in the presence of Timothy. This man who had been condescended to by American visitors now stood in the direct line of succession from St. Peter. The emotion with which he had received Lannan, the gentleness of his manner, in no way diminished the Pope's recognition of what by the grace of God he was.

"You must stay here in Rome until things clarify in your own country."

"I am not sure that they will."

"Will you stay?"

"Yes."

"Things are not completely peaceful here." His teeth were briefly revealed in a half-smile. "You have heard of our enormous debt?"

"Ten billion dollars!"

If the Pope was concerned, he did not show it.

Cardinal Novak said, "I told them of your alternative solution, Holy Father."

The smile was full now. "Poor Leonard", the Pope said, referring to the prefect of the Vatican museums. "He will go straight to heaven when he dies. Preparing this was the most difficult act of obedience he ever performed."

The sheets of paper the pontiff presented to Lannan were on the stationery of the Vatican Museum. Lannan turned over the pages, then looked at the Holy Father.

"An auction, Archbishop. Even the priceless has a price. We shall sell what we must to meet our debt. The paintings and other works of art will simply go to other museums, so what is really lost?"

6

James Morrow had received instructions from the State Department shortly before Tom Lannan showed up at his doorstep.

It was powerfully reminiscent of Lannan's arrival when he

had been released from the room in which he had been kept for days by people he had never seen. His recollection of the driver who met him at the airport was so fuzzed by the drug he had been given that it was useless. On that previous occasion, Lannan had sought the solace of sleep.

That he had survived the kidnapping as well as he had was impressive, but in itself it seemed external to the archbishop. Nonetheless, Jim Morrow had felt a kind of awe in the presence of his old friend. Frawley had been certain that they would never see Tom Lannan alive again, and his apprehension had not seemed exaggerated. Yet there was Lannan, still woozy, in need of sleep, wearing an equivocal laurel. The thought that formed in Morrow's mind was that his boyhood friend had come within an ace of martyrdom.

The Tom Lannan who arrived in Rome in the wake of the defection of most of his brother bishops seemed unaware of the moral significance of his standing fast. For the first time in his life he had thrown in his lot with the losing side—if a duly elected Pope Timothy could be said to be the leader of the losing side. Like Lannan, Morrow had no doubt that the Tanzanian was bishop of Rome with all that entailed—he was the successor of Peter and the vicar of Christ on earth.

This view was not shared by the State Department, however. In the world of Realpolitik, Timothy was judged to be the illegitimate claimant. James Morrow had been instructed to inform "interim functionaries" at the Vatican that the United States did not recognize Timothy. Morrow was then to proceed to Milan and present his credentials to His Holiness, Pius XIII.

His intention to tell Lannan this in the car on the way to the Vatican was unfulfilled because of the traffic and Luigi. When Cardinal Novak read the two letters, Morrow held back from doing what he had come to do. The warmth with which Tom Lannan had been received made his own mission secondary.

To have made known the State Department's decision at that moment would have piled ashes onto the bad news Novak had read to them. But he had been unable to keep silent at the apparent announcement that Pope Timothy intended to resign. Now all was clarified, and Morrow was elated at the Pope's decision to sell off as much of the treasures of the Vatican as was needed to clear the debt with the Italian government. It was a brilliant move, depriving the Avignon schismatics of what had seemed their irresistible leverage.

"And you too will remain in Rome, Mr. Ambassador?" the Holy Father said, turning to Morrow.

"No, Your Holiness."

"No!" It was Lannan who spoke.

"Holy Father, I have come to tell you that I have been recalled by my government."

The Pope rolled his lower lip pinkly outward and looked at Morrow over his glasses.

"Is that all?"

"The State Department instructed me to present my credentials to Cardinal Pavese."

"That is very grave."

"Jim, you can't do that."

"I don't intend to do it. I have resigned."

This restored Tom Lannan's good cheer, but Cardinal Novak remained solemn.

"I am sorry, Your Holiness."

But Timothy was not as disturbed as his secretary of state.

"I have read the memorandum you prepared for my predecessor, Mr. Ambassador. Are you still as sceptical of the predictions of the visionary of Viterbo?"

"No."

For a moment, he stared into the Pope's eyes. It was clear that Timothy was ready for the trials that awaited him.

"What will you do?" Maureen asked.

"Well, you stayed on here."

She wrinkled her nose. "I just can't see you as a permanent exile. Without a reason for being here, you'll start yearning for your lake in Michigan."

"I thought we'd spend some months of the year there. Maybe another few months in Ireland. The rest of the time we can live here."

"We?"

"That's not the papal we."

"It better not be", she said, and came into his arms.

CHAPTER TWO

I

"Get out now, Nate. The whole thing is falling apart."

"Lorraine, it's the only job I've got."

"You can live on our advance until you get something else. That could speed up production of the book."

Nate Patch could not counter Lorraine's judgement that the Catholic Church in the United States was literally doing what Jim Morrow had said it was in the process of doing. Had there been crewmen reluctant to leave the Titanic? Patch found himself both horrified and fascinated by what was happening, and he had to stay to see how it would end. But he had declined at first to go to Avignon.

"Nate, your stuff out of Rome was the best there was. You've got to go."

"Send Sissy."

"But he's already made up his mind."

"Haven't you?"

Quigley thought about it. "We are employed by the USCC and NCCB."

"So whatever they do is right?"

"Forget about right. We're journalists."

That was a moment when he could have quit. Instead he went to Avignon, renting a car in Paris and driving down the valley of the Rhone. He parked in the vast parking garage, entered at the level of the river, and then took an elevator up, emerging in the square. Rising from below, he might have parachuted in. He had made hotel reservations in Washington, but in the event he had to argue for them; the town was bursting with representatives of the international media as well as the usual tourists. Patch's room was in a rounded tower at the corner of the building, looking out over the square. He dropped the blind, closed the drapes, and slept for five and a half hours.

Holding the sessions of the conclave in the old papal palace was meant to suggest the legitimacy of the proceedings. It was from here that Catherine of Siena had harrangued the self-exiled popes into returning to Rome. The meaning of her mission was clear. The bishop of Rome belongs in Rome, the head of the Church is the bishop of Rome. Did the conclave intend for its choice to return to Rome? Pavese, the inevitable choice, remained in Milan.

"They'll bankrupt the Vatican", Wynn said. He was not finding it easy to get around Avignon in his chair, but he had brought a young Thaddeist with him to help. "That's the plan."

"I thought the Vatican was as unstable financially as it is. And always has been."

"Not so but no matter. Vatican investments are largely in for-profit companies, but its earnings have always been held to be exempt. That will be changed with the result that Timothy will face a bill for billions that he does not have."

"And then what?"

"The Vatican will be repossessed."

Wynn seemed unsure what he himself thought of this. Of course everyone assumed that the threat alone would suffice. With the major financial support of the Holy See taking part in the conclave in Avignon, there was no way in which Timothy could put off the evil day.

"Hard ball", Frank Bailey said, but he too seemed ambiguous about the ploy. Yet one of his themes for decades had been that all the United States had to do was cut off the Vatican's money supply in order to bring the Pope to his senses. The suggestion must have been easy to make when he was certain no one would actually take him up on it

Pope Timothy's surprising response to this pressure had clearly not been anticipated, and there was no doubt that he would do just as he said and do it almost eagerly. There were collectors, private and public, who salivated at the prospect of acquiring some of those treasures, but the overwhelming response was negative. Italians who had not seen the inside of a church since their First Communion reacted as if family heirlooms were at risk; Romans who had no distinct memory of being in the Vatican museums, let alone the basilica, filled the streets in protest. And the target of their wrath was not Timothy, but those who would force him into such a desperate deed. Similar demonstrations took place in Milan, and the mood of the citizenry turned against Pavese. From the pulpit of his cathedral, he explained patiently that it was Timothy, the pretender in Rome, who was threatening to strip the Church of its wealth, of the beauty and art that had accumulated over the years. A man rose from his chair and stepped into the middle aisle.

"Timothy is the Pope!" he said in a solemn carrying voice. "*Viva il papa. Viva, Papa Timoteo.*"

Pavese stared at the man, and then others began to rise, and soon the great cathedral was filled with cries of *Viva il papa!* Not two weeks ago they had greeted Pavese with that phrase. He left the pulpit and returned to the altar to finish his Mass. Before the canon of the Mass was over the cathedral was all but empty.

For the rest of the day, Pavese was on the phone long distance. He had to tell those who had presumed to name him pope that their bluff had been called. There was a note of accusation in his voice when he spoke to Cecil Meade. That afternoon, he crossed the piazza, an anonymous figure wrapped in a cloak, head down as he hurried through the rain. He had to ask Forlani what he should do.

"Go on your knees to the Holy Father", Forlani said. He looked sadly at the man who had deserted scholarship and been further undone by ambition. "Beg his forgiveness."

And so it fell to Pavese, the putative rival of Timothy, to fly to Rome and assure Timothy that the threat was lifted. Perhaps he could be forgiven for calling it an idea of American bishops for whom the western movie provided the basic scenario for human action.

The tall and aristocratic Pavese looked into the eyes of the man whose rival he had presumed to be. He then did what Forlani had advised, walking slowly toward Timothy and then sinking to his knees in a single motion. He closed his eyes and bowed his head. Minutes went slowly by and then he felt the hand on his head and the murmured words of forgiveness. Then Timothy extended his right hand, and Pavese brought his lips to the papal ring in a sign of fealty.

The Pope cited a discussion from the *Summa* as justification for so easily letting bygones be bygones. Pavese returned to Milan shriven and still cardinal archbishop of a city whose first bishop had been a contemporary of the apostles.

For most of Pavese's countrymen, for most Europeans, the dispute among churchmen did not matter. They had defended the Vatican museums because for them all churches were museums, monuments to the past, guarantees that their cities and towns would attract visitors interested in that past, but no longer part of the lives they led. Christianity had flooded Europe, and now ebb tide had arrived.

Nate Patch wrote elegiacally of Europe in his last dispatches, and when he returned home he felt he was returning to the headquarters of the forces of rebellion. Elsewhere the fever passed, and while it was succeeded by no new fervor, bishops who had questioned the validity of Timothy made shamefaced *ad limina* visits to the only vicar of Christ left.

"The Pope isn't important", Cecil Meade said at the press conference he had been trying not to have since his return from Avignon.

"You mean you accept Pope Timothy?"

"I mean that whether or not we do is irrelevant to the task of the American Church. Our guiding star has been and continues to be Vatican II. Our grievance has been the failure in Rome to embrace the spirit of that Council. We took drastic measures to force the hand of Rome and found, not for the first time, that the Old World has lost the spirit of independence and zeal that characterizes the United States."

"So you've become a regional church."

"All churches are regional. Each bishop is head of a church. The Church is a federation of churches."

Pencils moved more and more slowly, then stopped. The media knew when they were hearing the losing side. Cardinal Lannan returned from Rome effectively in triumph, and Nate Patch and his colleagues became employees of the Conference of Catholic bishops that he convened. Archbishop Williams of Detroit was elected first president of the reconstituted NCCB. Lannan held out the hand of reconciliation to Meade and the hundreds of other bishops who had followed him into schism. By and large, the olive branch was declined. Dissident bishops were then formally excommunicated, and this frightened half of them back into union with Rome. Lannan took his clear triumph with good grace.

"You and your wife are writing a book about married clergy?" Julian O'Keefe asked Nate Patch.

O'Keefe had become a familiar figure in Rome, not least

because of his stunning blonde companion who lived the life of a recluse at the Hilton.

"It seems small beer now."

"I have something for you that could make it a best seller."

Julian's manner did not match the excitement of his promise. Mr. Cool.

"It would have to be something sensational."

There was an amused expression in Julian's lidded eyes.

"It involves Cardinal Lannan."

Nate made a face. "That's an old rumor. I got a call..."

"I have his daughter, and I have scientific proof."

He who sups with the devil should use a long spoon. In the circumstances, Lorraine seemed the best equivalent of that.

"I want my wife to hear this."

2

The usually lugubrious Leach was paschal in his joy, murmuring *Resurrexit sicut dixit* at every opportunity, though Cardinal Lannan forbade him to answer the phone with that triumphant phrase. Thomas Lannan now was what he had long dreamed of being, cardinal archbishop of Washington, but the path along which he had come to it had profoundly altered his notion of what he was.

That he must be ready to suffer, even die, for the faith was a thought no longer merely notional but real. The time in captivity had turned into the most profound retreat he had ever made. Earlier at Gethsemani he had cultivated an almost Stoic attitude toward the likelihood that he would not be named. Positions he had taken, things he had done, all for the good of the Church, as he had thought, were judged otherwise and

536

held against him. He was being punished. He would no longer demean himself by checking anxiously with Ambrose Frawley as to the latest rumors from the Vatican. Enough. He had achieved a kind of ataraxy and was prepared to face a future without the red hat of a cardinal. But there had been more.

If the further honor was to be withheld, he would relinquish those that had already come his way. He would resign his see and enter the Trappists and derive pleasure from the fact that his low estate, ecclesiastically speaking, was of his own choosing. At the time he had regarded this as Christian renunciation, but now he could see the subtle pride it was. At that precise moment he learned that his name was on the list of the twenty new cardinals created by the Pope.

How sweet victory had seemed after wallowing in a romantic anticipation of defeat. He had toyed with the idea that the prize had finally come as a reward for his resignation. The monk that might have been left Gethsemani and prepared to be inducted into the College of Cardinals.

Almost at once he had seen the precariousness of his new good fortune. It hung by the slender thread of the Pope's hold on life. Had anyone ever prayed more fervently for the health of the Pope? St. Augustine as a young man, able to admire the idea of chastity, prayed that he might be given that virtue—but not yet. So Thomas Lannan was willing for the old Pope to die—but not yet. Not before Thomas Lannan had knelt before him and received from his trembling hands the red hat that made him a prince of the Church, an elector of the next pope. Then he could work a variation on Simeon. *Nunc dimittat servum tuum, Domine.* Now God might gather the Holy Father unto himself, his culminating earthly act—conferring the red hat on Thomas Lannan—having been accomplished.

But the Pope had died, and those twenty men who were and were not cardinals became pawns in the politics of the conclave. Pavese wanted them included as electors, certain that he could only gain from their presence, but in the event it had seemed more to his purpose to abandon them and go with the electors already in session. Men having maneuvered and made their calculations, the Spirit breathed upon them, and Benedetto emerged from the conclave as John Paul III. Quite soon, not immediately, he named those twenty again along with many more, the largest single list in history, to the College of Cardinals. Having thus tilted any future election, he had been, rumor had it, about to resign from the papacy and retire to the sun and solitude of his native Sicily. Thus would he answer those who had questioned the validity of his own election when the men his predecessor had named cardinals had been excluded on the technicality that they had not gone through the ceremony that formalized the Pope's choice. Meanwhile he had called Thomas Lannan and the other nominees to Rome. And Thomas Lannan had come, his head humming with the politics of the time, escaping Washington where the ineffable Bailey had presumed to announce that the archbishop of Washington would decline the red hat in protest against the questionable election of the man who presumed to name him. It was to clarify the situation and underscore his desire to accept that he had flown off to Rome, only to be taken into custody as groggy with jet lag he emerged into the terminal.

During three days, the truths to which he had dedicated his life finally became his truths. We have here no lasting city. Human happiness does not consist of honor or the esteem of others. A priest—like Christ, whose alter ego he is—is meant to be a suffering servant, a shepherd ready to give up his life for his flock. He is to live, not just as himself, but Christ is to live in him.... All the words, the prayers, the affirmations sincerely made but never profoundly and truly made, became during three days in darkness the limpid truths that were now bone of his bone and flesh of his flesh. Priest, bishop, cardinal—was he ready to enter the Coliseum in the front ranks? He had received the grace of martyrdom, the inner willingness to let Christ use him as he would, to take his life at the hands of... But it had never been clear who his captors were. Their claim to be the terrorists of an earlier time seemed obviously false. Lannan himself had wondered if those opposed to Benedetto had gone to such lengths in order to prevent him from accepting the red hat from Pope John Paul III. Unspoken was the thought that this was a continuation of Bailey's effort to use him in his anti-papal campaign. He had allies in Rome; he would have heard that Lannan was en route.... But he could not really believe that Frank would sink so low. He had accepted the anonymity of his captors. Their deed had been used by God to confer the greatest graces on Thomas Lannan. The scarlet he wore was no longer an emblem of rank, making him a five-star instead of a four-star general. It represented his readiness to give his life.

And then he learned the truth about his accuser.

"Nathaniel Patch is a Catholic journalist, Your Eminence."

"I know that, Monsignor Leach."

"He is a very sober and reliable man."

"What is it, Rodney?"

"He has come to me with the most extraordinary story."

Once again Thomas Lannan sat at his desk and heard discussed events of decades ago, an accusation against which he had no simple and adequate defense. He would of course deny it. There was no way he could appraise such an accusation. What he dreaded was for what was undoubtedly true to be paraded through the press. Yes, he had known Karen Christiansen, while he was still a seminarian, in the early years of the major seminary.... No. He mustn't make it sound like a childish mistake. He had been a mature young man, and he had been infatuated with a girl of impossible beauty, disturbingly untroubled by scruples, demonstrative. If he had ever kissed a girl before it was nothing like this. For years afterward he had to drive away memories of those moments in her summer arms. She became a symbol of hedonism, the mindless pursuit of pleasure, temptation. But eventually she had faded from his mind. Until Maureen came to him to say she had received a letter from Karen's mother saying that Karen had a child and the father was Thomas Lannan.

The drama of these past months was incomplete without the Damoclean sword of that accusation hanging over events, a threat, a menace, a scandal that could turn drama into farce. The information was used malevolently, to the degree that it was used. At any moment, the accusation might have been made, but had not been. He could believe that events in the Church robbed his tormentor of the circumstances he needed in order to harm Thomas Lannan.

"This is not the first time this accusation has been made in recent months", he told Leach, and then told him all he knew. Leach listened with a patience that seemed to cost him.

"The person behind this is someone I know, Your Eminence. He was a seminarian in Toledo."

"Is Patch here?"

"I told him I wanted to speak to you alone. He has gone back to his office." Then Leach told him a very strange story.

"Where is this Julian?"

"He lives in California. He is an independent film producer. I want to go out there and talk to him."

"What is his motive?"

"That is what I want to find out." Leach was seated but had contorted his body as they spoke. He was deeply distressed. "I want to know if I am the real target of this sordid attempt."

"Go. By all means go. The last thing we need at the present moment is…"

Leach was on his feet, hands pressed together, bowing, nodding, he understood. He all but backed out of the room. Cardinal Lannan's eyes dropped to the crucifix on his desk. Christ in his Passion had been stripped of the last shred of human dignity, been mocked and chortled over, derided. Was he ready for a martyrdom such as that? Persecution, death, going out with dignity and grace, Thomas More kneeling before the block and laying his head upon it. That seemed almost easy. But charged with sexual dalliance, a man who had ignored his child for decades while rising in the Church, he would be called a Pharisee, a hypocrite, after all no better than any other sensual man. His cheeks burned at the prospect.

3

Lying beside the pool, embraced by the sun, driving the freeways, taking her pick of dozens of malls within easy driving distance, hours with Julian discussing the film, back once more to food she could understand and that made dieting easy—Peggy felt that she had died and gone to heaven.

"No wonder they call it the old world."

"Don't get too negative. We'll be shooting over there."

Julian lay on his back, his muscular body reclaiming its perfect tan, his eyes invisible behind the large opaque sunglasses he wore. His hands were crossed on his taut stomach; his lips scarcely moved when he spoke.

She forced herself not to ask the questions that annoyed Julian. She still wasn't sure how other real people could fit into the story that was her real story. Particularly when the actor in that dark room in Rome was a real archbishop. She had looked at the photographs in the Italian papers, studying his face. She expected there to be some click, some intuition that this man was her father, but it did not come.

"I have a new plot twist, Julian."

"Hmmmm?"

"Say the man her detective captures turns out not to be her father. She looks at him, she should know if he really is, and..."

Julian pushed his glasses to the top of his head. "He's the man. That's why we took blood samples. His blood, your blood—DNA does not lie."

"I know that. But say the tests come back negative."

He sat up as if he were exercising his stomach muscles. She could not meet his eyes. She wished he would put his sunglasses on again. But suddenly his expression softened.

"The tests have been made. The blood is kept under appropriate controls..."

"What was the result?"

He smiled. "Drama, Peggy. Drama. The results have been sealed. At the great moment, the technician is called to the stand. Not even you and I have seen the results of his testing. But we know what they will be. Thomas Lannan does not know. Silence falls over the courtroom, the suspense builds, closeup of you. My God, you are thinking, after all these years I will know. Close up of him, seemingly unaffected by the suspense: he has spent a lifetime dissimulating. A kaleidoscope of others as in voice-over the technician begins to read out the dry data of his report."

"Oh, I love it."

"The whole world will love it, Peggy. And they will love you." He leaned forward and kissed her on the nose.

Doubts or questions were more difficult to get rid of when she was alone. Sometimes she wished her grandmother were still alive so she could talk about this whole business with her. Not that Margie would have heard a word, but Peggy always

542

felt that she was speaking to someone who understood perfectly and would never be put off by anything. Praying must be like that. Karen had made Margie wary of religion of course.

"Drunks and smokers", Margie used to say.

"Drunks and smokers", Peggy had repeated. The old woman always explained such confusing statements. "Dry out a drunk, and he will spend the rest of his life talking about his drinking days. Now smokers are the same. They know exactly when they quit. Remember it like a religious holiday. Not doing something is the most important thing in their lives." Suddenly she laughed. "I told Karen she ought to be a nun."

"When?" She spelled it out in the air because she wanted to know.

"When? Now."

"Not when she was a girl?"

She laughed again. Peggy would have liked to know her mother then. Obviously she had been fun. But now she was haunted by those days, ashamed, doing penance. Peggy always felt like an albatross hung around Karen's neck. Now she wished she had asked Karen who the priest was that was her father, but it had seemed a reference to a prehistoric period. It had never occurred to her that the man was still alive, that she might actually see and talk with him. The priest, bishop, Julian had chosen for the role in the movie wasn't at all what she would have imagined.

"What are you doing?"

Peggy had found the box under Julian's bed and pulled it out to see what was in it; and then she was certain someone was watching her, but she didn't turn around; and when Julian spoke he disguised his voice, speaking almost contralto.

"Where did you get all these things?"

He sat at the bed and looked down at her as if he were seeing her in another role. "It's background on your father."

543

"This is mother's stuff. I recognize the box."

"Did she ever show you photographs of him?"

He meant the archbishop, only he was just a priest, brand new, in the newspaper clipping she held. Peggy shook her head.

"She doesn't in the movie either. I retrieved that from your mother's apartment after the funeral."

"I wish I had gone now."

He shook her head. "You were right not to."

Julian had thought it would be too hard on her.

"Other things are at the studio. The shrine she had in her bedroom, for instance."

"She gave me a rosary."

He wanted to see it. He was quite excited. Soon he was sketching the scene in which this took place.

"Afterward, when you find out who your father is, you take that out and run the beads through your fingers. Then you stop, think, look directly at the camera. What do you say?"

"What do I say?"

"He did it. It was him. He killed her."

It all made perfect sense. Being her father wasn't a crime, no matter how cruel he had been to her, but for killing her mother he could be punished. They could turn him over to the state.

With Julian you could really believe that absolutely nothing happened that wasn't part of the script. Peggy wasn't surprised when the odd-looking priest appeared at the studio and asked for Julian.

"He's out east. Washington, I think."

He slapped his bony knee. "I've just come from there."

"You know him?"

"Long ago, as it seems now. When he was in the seminary."

She nodded and smiled prettily. There were no surprises.

"I was one of his teachers. Fr. Leach. In the seminary."

"Where men study to be priests?"

"Yes."

It sounded like acting school. She could imagine Julian there. "He would be a good priest."

"What makes you think so?"

"He understands them so well."

"Well, we are not mysteries."

"Did you know my father?"

He seemed so forbidding at first, but his manner was very gentle, and he was very interested when she got out the box of materials and showed him the clippings and pictures of Thomas Lannan.

"Your mother kept all this?" He seemed saddened by the thought.

"I never knew it until after she died."

"She's no longer alive?"

Peggy closed her eyes and shook her head. "It was awful. Someone broke into her apartment and..."

"How long ago was that?"

"A year ago. No, longer. We were doing Wrinklefree."

"Wrinklefree?"

"A cream to take away wrinkles. It really works. Not that I need it. We had to create wrinkles with makeup to show how Wrinklefree removes them. An infomerical. It's still showing on cable."

"Julian made that?"

"Now he is moving on. The film about me and my father will be his first."

"I'd like to hear about that."

"You may be in it."

4

Janet Fortin quit her job at the White House and was taken on as a temporary at the American Enterprise Institute. She took part in some seminars and arranged another, but mainly she sat in her office writing a long memo on her work at the White House. It was kind of like going to confession.

She did go to confession as well, at St. Matthew's, and it was easier than she would have thought. There was daily Mass at the Dominican parish near her apartment, the one she hadn't attended much, always taking her work as an excuse for not going—Caesar getting the lion's share. Going each day now seemed a way of making up for all those misses.

"I am thirty-four years old", she had written when she began her memo and then had sat staring at the sentence, wanting to cry. What was her life all about anyway? Sometimes she thought she could have avoided that question altogether if she hadn't met Gene Wales. Taking this job in another think-tank made her feel close to him again, as if they were two displays in the same aquarium, him blowing bubbles in the tank next to hers.

At Georgetown there had been a black philosopher with a Spanish name who lectured as if he would excuse himself later for wasting their time, and he had the most interesting way of teaching. Ethics, moral philosophy. He said watch it, it corrupts youth. A joke. Once she caught on to his humor she saw that it was meant to cushion the blow of what the course was about. This problem, that problem, what should you do? If you could save ten people by sacrificing one, is that okay? Think about it. And then, "You could be the one." But it was really about what it's all about, life, though he would never have said so in so many words.

Imagine spending your life wondering what life is all about.

Imagine not doing that. She had the time now, and she had no choice; she could not avoid asking herself where Janet Fortin was going. To heaven, she hoped, and it wasn't a joke. The mass of jello that was her faith had firmed from talking with Gene. She decided that that was what it was all about, what he had given his life for and then taken it back. Thirty-one seemed old for lots of reasons, but the basic one was that it made her wonder how many years were left. Which meant she was acknowledging that she was going to die. Like everyone else. Death posed the big question only it came a little late for the one who died. She had never even tried to believe that once death happened there were just so many dollars worth of chemicals lying there, and that was it.

The first time she had talked with James Morrow at his lake place in Michigan she had gotten another jolt. She was one of the people he had written about who had no idea what they meant when they said they were Catholics. No coherent idea.

"What if it's true?" he said once, meaning the faith, when they were walking along the lake.

"Don't you think it is?"

"I'm a Catholic."

"But you think some Catholics don't?"

"I think that if you don't think it's true you're not a Catholic, except maybe in the way I still think of myself as a Minnesotan although I haven't lived there for forty years."

What if it's true? The flip side was, what if it isn't? It had to be one or the other, and it mattered which it was. She thought it was, and what did that make her? A Minnesotan?

The realization that he and Lannan and that wildman Bailey had all been kids together made so much of the commotion in the Church seem like a quarrel between boyhood friends. Of the three she liked Morrow best. She might have asked him for Mary's address and got in touch with her, but no, that wouldn't work. They had always argued in college. Besides, he had shown her a picture of Mary and her family, and it was like a rebuke.

She thought about calling Gene Wales for weeks before she actually did. Trying to imagine variations on that scene in Rome and then at the Vezuvio in Washington convinced her she had been right the first time not to be receptive to his surprising declaration in Rome. Thank God, she had not encouraged him. It would have been easy, in an exciting foreign city, having so much fun together and resenting the pairing off of James Morrow and Maureen Kilmartin.

"They're just old friends", Gene had said.

"They're more than friends now."

"I didn't notice anything."

She opened her hands, claiming the ancient feminine ability to know things the male did not. But she certainly didn't know how to respond to what he said except by joking. She realized that what she had felt with him was safe, the way she had felt with James Morrow at his place in Michigan. Like Morrow, Gene was not to be counted among the predators against whom she could never let down her guard. She had never had a brother, but if she had he would have been like them, particularly Gene, whose age made the fantasy plausible. And all along he had been falling in love.

She blamed herself. She blamed the manner she wore like armor against Casey and the other professional lechers for whom any upright woman, vertical or moral, was a challenge. It was preventive defense, a preemptive strike to immobilize the enemy before he attacked. Gene had taken it at face value. She could cry when she remembered the expression on his face when she kidded away his declaration. Yes, there is no Santa Claus; all that lovey-dovey, flirty stuff was just pretense; let's just be friends. She could not blame his reaction on the male ego. What made it worse was the feeling that she had seduced him in a way that was sacrilegious. He was a priest, and you had to be a lot dumber Catholic than she was not to know what that meant. He stood every day at the altar and did again what Christ had done the night before he was crucified, taking bread and wine and with the power of Christ turning them into Jesus himself. She spoke to Jesus now as she would have to the brother she didn't have. She prayed for Gene, that he would regain his former faith and conviction. She deeply regretted telling him about Betty Grauer, as if that had influenced him. Once she imagined introducing the two of them, but Gene would never forgive her if she did that. Nor would she forgive herself. Finally she telephoned.

"You're in the book", she said.

"I always was."

"Not at this number."

"Is yours the same?"

"Why haven't you called?"

A long silence. Well, it was a dumb question, accusing, plaintive.

"Let's get together", she said. "For dinner or something."

"Good " No hesitation. "The Vesuvio?"

"Sure."

She was almost sorry she had suggested dinner. His selection of the place seemed ominous, but it turned out he wanted to undo what he had done there.

"It embarrasses me when I think of it."

"Well, it should. You could do so much better."

"Don't."

"I'm sorry. It's a habit."

"Actually I'm grateful for it. Janet, don't judge priests by me. Most of them are exactly what they promised to be. Something more, and that's difficult to do in this society. Have you ever watched much television?"

"I never had the time."

"Don't. It's a sewer. Why did you leave the White House?"

"Guilt by association. He's so bad nobody even cares. They expect him to lie, cheat, steal, hold both opinions on any issue, and dye his hair. He gets a pass on everything. Including okaying killing off people when they get too old or useless or whatever."

"Archbishop Lannan has been a surprise."

"Hasn't he?"

"There were times when I thought he was not all that different from Whitney."

"Oh, never that bad."

"Proportionally speaking." He smiled. "A Scholastic phrase."

"Do you know Scholastic philosophy? Oh, of course you would, from the seminary."

"Not at all. Some of us formed a club, Catacomb Scholastics. We got together to read Aquinas when no one was looking. Thomas, Maritain, Garrigou-Lagrange." His voice got wistful. "They were such a refreshing change from the glop we got in class."

"Archbishop Lannan has been a hero of sorts, hasn't he?"

"Janet, I'm going back. I would have called you if you hadn't called me. I wanted to tell you."

"Oh, thank God." She took his hands in hers and pulled herself across the table and kissed him.

"Watch out. I'm celibate."

"Is it catching?"

"Do you aspire to be ordained?"

"Not exactly."

So she told him—why not, he was like a brother, and he wouldn't laugh. She told him what it had been like recently, how her thoughts had been going; she had been almost ashamed to admit to herself what she really wanted to do.

"I thought of talking to Betty, but decided against it."

"Betty?"

"The ex-nun. I told you about her."

"Have you heard of the Carmelites?"

"It sounds like candy."

"It's the order the two Theresas belonged to. Teresa of Avila and Thérèse of Lisieux."

So they sat there like lovers talking about contemplative vocations and what she might do that would be an answer to the question life was. What does it all mean?

"What if it's all true?"

He looked at her and waited, and she went on to tell him of the conversation with Jim Morrow.

"Another hero of sorts. I expected him to make a statement when he resigned as ambassador."

"That's not his style."

"I hope he writes another book."

"When do you go back?"

"Oh, I won't have the same job. Cardinal Lannan said I had been put to the test long enough. Leach has succeeded me."

5

If he had been acting only for himself, he might not have taken this course, Rodney Leach told himself, though what he was doing would vindicate himself as well. Vindicate? Wrong word. The persona he had cultivated, the mordant Savonorola, Grand Inquisitor without portfolio, had involved a raspy, wicked way of noting the faults of others. Most of his complaints had been valid, he had no doubt of that, but he had treated the weaknesses of others as if they were strengths of his. Thank you, Lord, that I am not like the rest of men.

And he had been funny. Even those afflicted by his wit would laugh grudgingly, and humor made it ambiguous. Could he really mean it? It had not occurred to him that anyone would wish to mimic such an acerbic model. But Julian had, and he had been brought down because of it, and that had been the source of this long bitter vendetta to wound the Church.

"I thought you loved the Church."

They were seated in the patio of a franchise food place off the freeway. Beyond the neatly barbered hedge that enclosed the area, the sound of traffic was so regular as to be soothing. Cones of thatched pampa grass roofed each table and rustled in the mild breeze. Julian looked like a man who belonged here. Sandals, white slacks, a lime green shirt opened to display two gold chains and the hair on his chest; Leach had to ask him to take off the sunglasses.

"You're like talking to a mirror."

"I do love the Church", Julian replied. "If I didn't I could not hate these hypocrites so."

"I feel it is my fault you were let go from the seminary."

"Let go." The corners of his mouth dimpled. "Don't think that. At the time, talking of you was the only solace I had. As revenge, I resolved to become rich."

"And succeeded."

He nodded. "It is not enough. I came to see that I could justly punish those who had wrongly punished me. What had I done that disqualified me for the priesthood? True, I recited the Creed with sincerity and believed what the holy Catholic Church teaches, including Christ's vicar on earth, but surely this could be overlooked when scandalous behavior was overlooked in others. My last semester, the man in the room next to mine was nearly killed by a boy he had brought back from town. Rough trade. It was all hushed up, of course."

"And you liken Cardinal Lannan to that kind of thing?"

"What impact would exposing such shenanigans among seminarians have? What is needed is someone prominent. Lannan fathered a child. I know her."

"She lives with you."

"She is my protégée."

"And she told you that Thomas Lannan is her father."

"I'm not sure she realizes it to this day. No, her mother told me."

"But her mother is dead."

"This was before."

"Before she was killed."

A hand went up and lowered the sunglasses. And Leach suddenly thought he knew what had happened to Karen Christiansen. The second thought came swiftly after the first. He would defend the cardinal by exposing the accuser.

The homicide group in the Thousand Oaks police department were not inclined to chat about a murder nearly two years old. A pock-faced sergeant with a nervous squint told him how many unsolved murders there had been in the past month.

"He should talk to Cleary."

"Who's Cleary?"

"He was on that case, but his retirement came up. He wanted to postpone retirement to solve it, but it turned out he had known the woman, and they told him to go sit in the sun; he had earned it."

"Where does he sit in the sun?"

Cleary was a native Californian who looked as if he had just got off the bus from Iowa. He sat in his broker's client room with the ticker going and a newspaper clenched in one hand. He nodded when Leach asked if he was Lieutenant Cleary; then he turned toward him. When he saw the collar he started to rise, but Leach put a hand on his arm.

"I want to talk to you about the murder of Karen Christiansen."

Cleary closed his eyes and his lips moved. "Thank God. And I just finished another novena to St. Anthony."

His prayer had been that her death would not just go down the memory hole. She had been a good woman; seeking a motive for the crime raised dozens of questions; it would take time...

"Time is what we never have, Fr. Most cases, you don't need it. It's not who did it, but where is he and how can we take him into custody. Of course they all plead innocent, but you expect that."

"Can we go somewhere else?"

He glanced at the numbers dancing past on the display. "Why not? I get richer no matter what I do."

They went to a family restaurant, and Cleary loaded up on chicken, mashed potatoes, peas, corn, and apple sauce. "I'm going to have the cherry pie", he explained. "When I choose apple, I skip the apple sauce."

"What did you mean when you said the question of motives turned up ambiguities?"

Cleary held up a hand. "First, we eat. You look like you need nourishment. Then, I'll tell you what kind of person Karen Christiansen was. That way, the case has a context. I knew her."

Could it be considered a penance to eat as well as to fast? Leach managed to do some sort of justice to the food he had selected. He could have spent the day on the chicken alone—chewing it was like gum; it never seemed ready to be swallowed. The iced tea helped.

Finally Cleary took the corner of his napkin from his collar. He had covered his shirt front with it and leaned over his plate while he ate.

"A bachelor? No, Father. A widower. That's what

interested me in Karen. She was living alone in the same development."

"A widow?"

"She wouldn't talk about it. I should say that she did not return my interest. That was a blow. I would see her at Mass; a devout woman, she prayed with such fervor. My wife was a good woman, but she wouldn't have liked Karen. Maud didn't like display. 'God isn't deaf', she'd say. Maud was though, and she said it pretty loud."

"What do you think the motive was?"

"Maud's? She didn't see any reason to go to Mass weekdays."

"I meant the motive of the murder."

He seemed to think Leach thought his wife had been murdered, but then he got on track. The scene of the crime said sexual assault. She was lying on the floor, her undergarments down around her ankles, dead. Only there hadn't been any sexual assault. Her purse was lying there open, and her wallet was found in the wastebasket on the way to the pool, but there were valuables all over the house that hadn't been touched. There was six hundred dollars in cash in a bowl on the kitchen table. Covered, but thieves look into bowls like that. This man hadn't. Theft and sexual assault were both faked.

"So why had he done it?"

"That was my question. The answer I got was, he's just getting started—and she comes home. That makes no sense."

"Did you ever talk about her daughter?"

"It was her daughter she prayed for most. She felt she had failed her completely. She was very hard on herself."

It was Leach's turn to talk. He told Cleary of the accusation that had been made against Cardinal Lannan.

"The guy in Washington?"

"I work for him."

"Well, you tell him for me he's all right. Stick with the

Pope; it's the only way. What do these other guys want to do, start their own religion?"

"I have found who is behind the accusation. He lives here in Thousand Oaks."

He described Julian's background, his ill-fated career as a seminarian, his resentment at being let go.

"The question is, did he make the connection between Karen's daughter and Cardinal Lannan before or after Karen's death?"

Cleary had been interested before, but now he moved his chair closer to Leach's.

"The box he took from the apartment after the murder contained clippings having to do with Lannan's career."

"What box?"

"He brought it to Peggy, as a memento, as proof of who her father was."

"What kind of a box was it?"

Cleary shook his head slowly as Leach described it. "There wasn't any such box in the apartment when the body was found."

6

Julian O'Keefe decided that Leach's effort to save Lannan was not fatal to his plan. He would not waste psychic energy resenting what his old mentor had done. Peggy had been home alone when the police came with the search warrant, and she was the soul of helpfulness when they told her what they wanted. A box of her mother's mementoes? The one Julian had brought from Thousand Oaks? She turned it over without a protest.

"Julian, I thought they were part of it."

He patted her hand, reaching across the divider in the visiting room at the community jail like a loser at tennis. "They are."

Only the plot was not the one he had been working from. No matter. Improvisation is the basis of civilization. Besides, he was not sure he would have been able to orchestrate matters in the way he had planned. He had the proof; he had a target of sufficient eminence, indeed a man whose moral character had shone through during his recent ordeals. Even the secular media found Cardinal Lannan preferable to Meade and his cohorts. They had recently met with Bishop Willa Sayers of the Episcopal church and agreed to acknowledge one another's orders. That had opened the way to a spate of ordinations around the country. Clerical clothes were declared optional, but women priests favored the Roman collar. All this had the effect of increasing Lannan's value to Julian. The other bishops had discredited themselves. Now he would show the world the truth about the apparently impeccable Thomas Lannan.

The scene would be his own trial for the murder of Karen Christiansen. He would insist that his lawyer give him the opportunity to explain why he had acted as he had. The courtroom would resound with the *J'accuse* of the accused. And as the *pièce de la résistance*, he would produce the DNA proof of Lannan's paternity. Q.E.D. What did he care what happened to himself then? Temporary insanity would get him a few years at most. His wealth awaited him when he emerged.

The question was, would Peggy wait?

She proved a little less credulous when he explained why he had chosen the court scene.

"Can't you come home at night?"

"I want authenticity. I have to feel the feeling of someone accused of murder in a desperate attempt to prevent him from exposing your father."

"I wish you could pick someone else for the father."

"The choice has already been made."

"He is too good a man for the role."

"You underestimate yourself."

But he had misunderstood her. She was speaking of his credibility in the role. Even the footage taken in Rome when he was in captivity did not convey a man who had been dodging his daughter for decades.

"Not a word about the film, Peggy. I mean that."

"Is it at the studio?"

"It is safe. Competitors would give a lot for a look at what we have done thus far."

Schlick his lawyer had a baby face and blue eyes that never fully opened. Here was a man nothing could surprise.

"I was doing it for my girl."

"Peggy Christiansen."

"Yes."

"You're not married?"

"She will be a star. Marriage and stars don't mix."

"How would exposing the man who was her father help her?"

"What do you know about publicity?"

"Tell me."

The priest's daughter, the cardinal's child, fruit of an unholy love. Peggy would be the darling of every checkout counter in the country.

"How long will that last?"

"How long does the rocket on the first stage of the Challenger burn?"

Schlick liked it. His pink little lips bowed in a smile. It went away.

"The counter to what you say is that you are seeking revenge for being expelled from the seminary."

"Expelled?"

"Prevented from going on. Blackballed. Whatever. You have been nursing resentment ever since. Finding out about

Peggy was the opportunity you wanted. You would disgrace the Church that had turned you away."

Julian nodded encouragement throughout this. "Exactly. But we let them bring it up. They choose their own poison. I am exposed as the man who could not become a priest. A pathetic figure. We help them; we build it up ourselves. This is meant to discredit the accusation. An obvious ploy. Discredit the messenger. And that's when we introduce the proof."

"Proof."

"DNA proof."

"His blood, her blood?"

"Yes."

"How did you get that?"

Julian's smile suggested insouciant confidence, the anticipation of triumph. But Schlick's question posed a problem he had not before considered. He did not want to be connected with Lannan's three days of captivity in Rome.

7

Nate Patch was there, with Lorraine promising to fly out when things got hot. Already she had decided that Lannan would be the culminating figure in their book, *Down the Aisle: Profiles in Love*. Their editor liked it, and she and Lorraine were planning the promotion tour for which Nate still had not devised an excuse to stay off. He felt badly enough co-authoring the book, let alone advertising the fact in public. His long loyal association with Catholic journalism was an integral part of the planned promotion, however, with the suggestion that he had been somehow betrayed after years of selfless devotion and inadequate pay.

"Even my wife left me", he suggested.

"Let's not get into that."

But he had found that the accusative note was his siren song. Nothing turned Lorraine's mind to tenderness more surely than the reminder of how cruel she had been.

Nate in the innermost chamber of his heart still hoped that Lannan would come out of this all right, but it was a wan hope at best. Adding to the archbishop's bad luck was the fact that Julian's trial took place when there was no other news from coast to coast. The most modest serial murderer might otherwise have eclipsed the California trial that implicated the cardinal archbishop of Washington, so surfeited was the public with religious news. The "American church", the new amalgam formed by Meade and the majority of former Catholic bishops with a number of Episcopalians, Methodists, and Presbyterians in the so-called New Reformation, had added homosexuals of both genders to its hierarchy, made a sacrament of euthanasia, and on the Feast of the Holy Innocents celebrated the courage of women who had given up their children in abortion rather than subject them to life in an overpopulated, underfed, and patriarchal world.

"I would say that human sacrifice is next, but they've already embraced it", Nate said to his wife.

"The joke is that they want to rename Catholic University, Baal State."

It had been wise of Lannan not to fight the confiscation of Church property on the part of the rebels. The Whitney administration, perhaps inspired by the ill-fated Avignon conclave, removed tax-free status from religious enterprises, and the "American church" all but sank under the unexpected burden. The solution had been to turn over churches of any architectural interest to city, state, or federal government for protection as museums and offer to function as custodians. Senator Partridge thus found himself with a problem.

"I say that if it looks like a union of church and state, if it talks like a union of church and state and if it smells like a union of church and state, then by my oath to God Almighty as a senator I have to oppose it." The arrangement was protested by Justice Norman on the contrary basis, that it amounted to the disestablishment rather than to the establishment of religion.

"Then I say that the establishment clause is a disestablishment clause as well."

But the rolling orotund rhetoric of the senior senator from North Carolina was rendered inaudible by the nation's desire to forget all about it.

Across the country in an unreported development, more than fifty percent of Catholics found their way to Mass said by priests and bishops aligned with Cardinal Lannan in what was recognizable as the continuation of the faith passed on by the apostles. Like their countrymen, Catholics were ready to permit anything in the conduct and beliefs of their fellow citizens, but it strained imagination to think that a man in miter and tutu cavorting up the aisle of the national cathedral sprinkling the sparse congregation with newly gathered dew bore any relation to the salvific mission of Jesus Christ.

Thomas Lannan had in his way been the John Fisher of the executive council of the National Conference of Catholic Bishops. Calling James Morrow the Thomas More of the moment seemed to Nate Patch excessive, although resigning political office as a matter of principle rather than under the pressure of charges of peculation or pedophilia did make him stand out. The argument was that, since no successor had ever been appointed, he had in effect thrown effective weight to Pope Timothy at a crucial moment. And moral support to Thomas Lannan's decision to dissociate himself from this brother bishops.

"Brother bishops?" Patch had said in response to Leach's way of putting it.

"Cain and Abel were brothers."

Leach's role in leading the Thousand Oaks' constabulary, as he called them, in the direction of the murderer of Karen Christiansen had not been brought to Nate Patch's attention by the cadaverous monsignor, but he did not deny it when Patch asked him about it.

"The poor fellow was my student. What he has done he did with the distorted notion that I might approve it."

"Good Lord."

Leach sighed. "And he may be the only student I ever influenced. He will be found guilty but sent away for therapy. Could there be a worse punishment? I will visit him then and seek to be an occasion of good in his life to make up for my responsibility in what he has done and what he tried to do."

"You are too hard on yourself."

"In hope that the Lord will be lenient."

Leach flew back to Washington once the trial was under way. It was as if he had wanted to make sure that it would begin before he dared return to his duties. But Julian's lawyer Schlick intimated that the trial was not really the trial of a man who had murdered a woman, but an obvious miscarriage of justice devised by those who would defend the cardinal archbishop of Washington.

"The evidence sounds pretty convincing to me", Nate replied.

"It always does when it is described by the prosecution. I think that members of the jury have learned with the rest of us that the representatives of officialdom are not always to be trusted."

"Planted evidence?"

Schlick just closed his eyes in agreement.

Nate Patch sensed that one way or another Julian would try to put Thomas Lannan on trial. The depth of his obsession was almost impressive in its irrationality. But Lorraine and their editor were hoping that he could bring it off.

"Not to put too fine a point on it", Lorraine said on the phone. "The fate of our book has come to be tied to the case against Lannan. Unless it is convincing that he is the father of that girl, the publisher is losing confidence in the sales value of the book. Some wag in publicity came up with the slogan 'Catholic Priest Called Father'. Humor could be the death of it, Nate."

Patch asked Schlick, once the trial was under way and the prosecution was making its case against Julian, what they had that could counter the case that was being made against their client. The lawyer smiled, exuding confidence.

"Proof?"

"Proof that Lannan is her father."

The smile became more beatific. Nate's heart sank. If there was such proof a lesser lawyer than Schlick could get it admitted into the trial. Criminal trials had been turned into action theater, and the precedents had wrought havoc with the jury system. Patch had a nightmare in which Julian was found innocent because of the vendetta carried on against him by such Catholics as Thomas Lannan. Awake, listening to the prosecutor develop the point that Julian had been unfit for the priesthood, Nate groaned inwardly. But Schlick produced two of the seminary professors who had voted him out. One had undergone a sex change operation and kept making reference to the Goddess; the other was a pathetic figure whose immunal system was unable to fight the disease that ravaged him. In his way he turned out to be a witness friendly to Julian, since he blamed his present plight on such homophobes as Thomas Lannan.

"Do you know Cardinal Lannan?"

The witness made a moist sound before speaking. "I know the type."

Such witnesses seemed to bode well for what lay ahead, and the networks stayed with the trial, helped in their decision by the dearth of other news. In Washington, a Senate committee was holding hearings inquiring into the charge that call girls had been operating from the White House, and in the House other hearings pursued the spoor of Chinese communist infiltration into the Defense and State Departments, but these were routine matters, of little interest to the public, 83 percent of whom were unaware of these events. But then the media had earlier decided that the electorate need not be troubled by such trivia. Thus, the way was clear for gavel-to-gavel coverage of the trial of Julian O'Keefe and its promise to expose the clay feet of yet another churchman.

The day Peggy Christiansen was called to the stand was the day the proceedings were recording unprecedented audiences across the land. That was also the day that for the first time the court heard of the movie she and Julian had been making. Schlick, whispered to by Julian, soon got her off this subject to a description of the kind of woman her mother was.

"I never really knew her."

The stunningly beautiful woman who had been abandoned by both parents soon captured the heart of the nation. Her remarks were as inconsequential as Marilyn Monroe's at her most antic, but the court's inability to follow much of what she was saying became one of her charms. She added a surrealist note to the proceedings as if the truth it sought were beyond logic and coherence.

"Are you a Catholic?"

"Isn't everyone?"

"You think everyone is a Catholic?"

"It means universal, doesn't it, Julian?" she often addressed her answers to her mentor, and the prosecution had stopped protesting since the court did not permit Julian to answer.

"Did you ever meet Thomas Lannan, the cardinal archbishop of Washington?"

"Just the one time, in Rome."

Schlick did not pursue it, Julian having caught his hand and pulled him back to the defense table. It was then that, as Leach might have put it, the penny dropped. Nate got Frank Bailey on the phone and asked if he were following the trial. It had become *the* trial now.

"Why should I?"

"The man on trial is a colleague of yours." Patch thought he could hear the televised hearings in the background at the other end of the line.

Bailey's reaction bordered on the profane.

"And of mine. You'll remember him from the press room at the Vatican. The independent producer from California. Turn it on and let me know if you recognize him."

"I'll call you back."

But he didn't, so Nate called him.

"I wanted to talk to Iggie Wynn about it. He remembers the guy. So do Trovato and Tremblay."

"Did anyone see the girl he had stashed at the Hilton?"

Apparently not. But the manager of the Rome Hilton had assigned someone to follow the trial on CNN, hopeful that his establishment would receive a little free global publicity.

"He remembers the girl?"

"The hotel photographer got some wonderful shots of her. With her permission of course."

That meant that she had been in Rome with Julian and that her remark about having met Cardinal Lannan there was not to be numbered among her enigmatic non sequiturs. The significance of this emerged when the prosecution cross-examined the defense's star witness.

"I am curious about your remarks about the film that you and the accused were making."

Schlick objected, but Veronica Kaufman, the member of the

prosecution team that had drawn Peggy Christiansen, pointed out that the subject had been introduced on direct. Schlick asked if they could approach the bench; the exchange, inevitably called a sidebar—among lawyer jokes now figured admission to the sidebar—was intense and prolonged. The judge said she would overrule, but nonetheless adjourn the court at this time so they could all get a fresh start in the morning. Judge Solomon had a fame of her own, having made a landmark ruling dividing the frozen zygotes of a divorced couple equally between the claimants, and she had a keen sense of how to keep the trial newsworthy. By morning one could have believed that the trial was about an independent production the accused had been engaged in that starred the witness still on the stand, Peggy Christiansen.

"We were discussing yesterday a film that the accused was shooting. Could you tell us more about it?"

Schlick begged to be allowed to characterize the film as a fantasy discussion between his client and the witness, no actual film being involved. Solomon advised him to make this point on redirect. Meanwhile, the prosecutor had placed himself between the witness and the accused, causing an instance of what Judge Solomon, having first looked collusively at the camera, called lunar eclipse, thereby setting off a ten-minute discussion of the difference between lunar and solar eclipses. Schlick asked what's in a name; he did not want the prosecutor blocking the view from the defense table.

"Are you filming this too?" Veronica asked sweetly.

That cost her a fine, but there was repressed mirth at the table of prosecutors all of whom seemed to think the dig worth it. And then Peggy was on, engaging in a free-flow narrative of the way in which her real life had turned into a movie and vice versa, and whatever happened fit in so beautifully, and this would be her breakthrough and Julian's too. There was money in infomericals, but what is money after all? and she herself had not realized at first what was happening, she hadn't even wanted to go to Rome, and yes she had met Thomas Lannan then, the man who played her father...

"Played your father."

"In the movie."

"Is he your real father?"

"That's the point."

"Where did you meet him?"

"On the set where he was being held in captivity."

"Cardinal Lannan was held in captivity in Rome, yes."

"Julian shot footage of him there; he was kept in a dark room, away from everyone else..."

"The girl is crazy", Julian said, standing. "I won't let you exploit her like this. You've heard her testimony. It doesn't make sense. It is a farce to have this introduced into a trial where my life may be at stake."

Judge Solomon had her gavel poised to strike, but she let him complete his statement before bringing it down. A recess was called and eventually adjournment. Nate Patch, seated in the courtroom, would have titled the event, "The Day Peggy Christiansen Lost Her Credibility". But then neither he nor anyone else then knew of Speedy Gazelle, or if they knew of the legendary agent, did not know of his relevance to what had just taken place in Judge Solomon's courtroom. Speedy was in the courtroom, they were soon to learn, but this was to be Judge Solomon's day. She sent the jury out of the courtroom and said she wanted counsel to learn of a new development even as she did.

"I am going to put a man on the stand and ask him a few simple questions. I will tolerate no objections, comments, or demonstrations while I do this."

Schlick asked to approach the bench and was told to keep his chair. He managed to state formally that she was providing a basis for mistrial while he was being gaveled down.

"Would Sidney Gazelle please take the stand?"

He could have been sixty or seventy, the tanned, five-foot-seven man with silver hair and a Roman nose who moved swiftly to and into the witness box, his hand raised to take the oath before he was asked. Speedy Gazelle had represented the giants of the silver screen in the age of the studios; he had made the transition to independents and chaos without missing a beat; he had agreed to act as agent for Peggy Christiansen.

"The kid had talent. Look at her on those infomercials. You have to be blind not to see the potential. So I said yes, if you're not clearing fifty million a year in two years I'll take a full-page ad in *Variety* and admit I've lost it. Because I will have lost it, not you."

At the defense table, Julian had turned and was trying to find Peggy in the audience, but she was not there.

"What is the relevance of this, Mr. Gazelle?"

"Speedy, Your Honor, please. A month or so ago, she gave me some videos, stuff that would clue me into the project she was on with him over there." He hunched a shoulder at Julian.

"What kind of videos?"

"I thought it was a joke. Lots of footage, most of it junk. It was so bad I got fascinated. This was the work of the big genius who had been guiding her career. Then I came on a sequence showing Cardinal Lannan in captivity. We all know that story. No news organization got pictures of that. Where did he get them? The only way that film could have been made was by insiders."

Pandemonium. Speedy spelled it out. "What you got here might be a murderer, Your Honor, but he is also implicated in kidnapping. Now one of my wives was Catholic..."

The debate about allowing the testimony of Gazelle would occupy legal minds for years to come. Motions for mistrial were denied. The videos and a copy of the agent's testimony were turned over to the police, the FBI, and Interpol for investigation. The weekend intervened.

Sunday, on a talk show, Schlick said that his client had scientific evidence that Cardinal Thomas Lannan was the father of Peggy Christiansen, and if this was not admitted at the trial, he would reveal it on the courtroom steps and submit it to the jury of public opinion.

8

Cecil Meade was taken to emergency suffering from a heart attack. As it had in the past, angioplasty proved ineffective, and also as in the past the decision was made to do open-heart surgery, but the problem of where to find a vein arose. Thomas Lannan was at the hospital, visiting Meade, when the doctor came in to lay it out. Having been asked by Meade to stay, Lannan asked if he could help.

"You still have the veins in your legs?"

"Doctor," Meade said weakly, "he's vain all over."

Lannan's leg was examined; the similarity in age was taken to be an advantage rather than the reverse, and soon the two men were being wheeled toward the operating room.

"How long will this take?" Lannan remembered to ask.

"Your part? Not long at all. But you don't come into it until we've done a lot to your friend."

"Want to go to confession, Cecil?"

"And admit I was wrong?"

"That's what confession is for. Think of Pavese."

A full minute went by. "Maybe afterward."

"Cecil, there may be no afterward."

"Are you denying the immortality of the soul?"

"This is an emergency. Are you sorry for all the offenses you have committed against God?"

"Tom, if I say yes, I'm saying that you're right and we're wrong."

Lannan waited.

"Afterward."

Trying to force it would not do. Lannan himself was beginning to feel the effects of the pre-operative relaxant that had been shaken into his hand from a paper cup like a winning number. Meade seemed to be having trouble focusing his eyes. They were ready for the anesthesiologist.

As those who have had major operations will tirelessly explain, there is a time when the operation is going to take place, which is succeeded immediately by a time when the operation has already taken place. Patients in recovery think that they are yet to be operated on. Thomas Lannan's operation was not a major one, but he had a similar experience. As he regained some control over his mind, he asked about Archbishop Meade.

"Let's concentrate on you for the moment. You will soon experience pain. Perhaps much pain."

His left lower leg had been stapled together, and the first time he was shown it he commented that it looked like a zipper. This affected a pool in the cardiac section. The overwhelming odds were that the closed incision would be compared to a zipper. He had made nobody rich by his remark.

The operation had been on Saturday. It was late Sunday that he learned that Meade had not survived the operation. The expression in his old friend's eyes as they both drifted into unconsciousness seemed stamped on his retina. He prayed for his old friend and enemy, repressing the memory of passages from Dante. On Monday, Leach showed up to watch the California trial that came on in Washington early in the afternoon.

"God knows what will happen there next", Leach said. "Did you watch any television yesterday?"

"Certainly not."

Times of solitude were to be cherished, the mind cleared of all the trivia that normally occupies it, the soul made attentive. Lines of Hopkins became the text of his meditation. "The Holy Ghost over the bent World broods with warm breast and with ah! bright wings." Apart from the beauty of the lines, he took comfort from the fact that he held the same faith as the Jesuit poet. There was the view that such comfort in solidarity is foolish, that each must believe by himself alone and the fact that others too believe cannot make the assent less incredible to the worldly. A scandal to the Jews and folly to the Gentiles. But that was wrong. Faith involves other human beings; faith comes from hearing the witnesses of Christ's teaching and their telling of his death and Resurrection. It is their testimony that is believed. That is why the Church involved the living connection with the apostles assured by the body of bishops in union with the bishop of Rome. Rival versions of Christianity are not invented; they are plagiarized and lose in the translation. But each in its own way pointed back to the continuation in time of Christ's ministry in the universal Church, one, holy, apostolic.

He was being granted a time when prayer was pleasure, and he longed to engage in it. That could not last, of course, and he did not want to become attached to the pleasure; on the other hand, he would enjoy it while it was given. He did not feel the anguish he might have over Meade's refusal to admit his error. In justice, so far as one knew, he had gone into the next world in bad shape. But it is mercy we need, not justice, and Thomas Lannan prayed fervently that Meade would find a merciful God. Only God could know what had gone on in his soul during these past months. Or in the moment before the anesthetic took effect.

"Is it all right to pray for Judas?" Bailey had asked in moral theology long ago.

"Why do you ask?"

"I have a great aunt who makes novenas for him."

Waxey looked nonplussed. "We should pray for the faithful departed", he said.

"Does that include Judas?"

"We can't know."

Waxey had enjoyed his own answer. He grinned, stuck a finger in one ear, and began to waggle it, thus justifying his nickname. The question was entered into his notes, and each year thereafter at that point in the course, he would look out over his glasses and with a sly smile ask whether the gentlemen before him in the aula thought it appropriate to pray for Judas.

But Leach was full of the importance of passing things. "Schlick said on Brinkley that they had scientific proof that you are the father." Leach spoke in sarcastic tones. But then he turned from the window and looked at Lannan. "Did they take samples of your blood here?"

"I don't know."

"That's what it would have to be. A blood test, the genetic code, all that."

"I suppose they must have."

"But Schlick doesn't know you're here. No one knows. You said keep it quiet, and I did."

Leach, relieved by his own reassurance, settled down in a chair as the trial came on television. Thomas Lannan wondered if his unknown presence in this hospital would cushion the ordeal that lay before him. For suddenly he recognized his vulnerability to what might be revealed in that courtroom.

Across the continent, Judge Solomon began by noting that she was sure that counsel on both sides as well as knowledgable spectators would agree that the proceeding of this trial had been unusual.

"I have been sailing in strange, uncharted waters. Some of you have let it be known that you think I have made reversible errors. But doesn't that imply that there have been precedents that should have guided my more controversial rulings. I do not know what those precedents might be. A man is here on trial for murder. It is part of his defense that evidence has been manufactured to incriminate him. To that end he has responded to the charge that he has been engaged in a campaign to discredit a prelate of the Catholic Church. Should I say the old Catholic Church? You will know whom I mean. In such a case, great leeway can be granted, particularly when some credibility attaches to the counter-charge. You have heard the claim that an employee of Cardinal Lannan visited Peggy Christiansen and planted the box full of clippings that has been placed in evidence. It has not been easy to maneuver among these accusations and counteraccusations. Today yet another dimension must be gone into. If the defendant was engaged in a campaign to discredit Cardinal Lannan, the principal means was to be the claim that Peggy Christiansen is his daughter. My deepest inclination was to rule out this new direction. I have gone against that inclination because the accused has now made a claim not made hitherto, namely, that he is in possession of scientific proof of the paternity of Cardinal Lannan."

Julian was put on the stand with the repeated stipulation that he was testifying to this point and to this point only and that the court would not permit a wholesale grilling of the defendant. Julian was sworn in and took the witness chair. The usual identifying questions were waived, and Schlick went directly to the point at issue.

"You have scientific proof that Thomas Lannan is the father of Peggy Christiansen?"

"I do."

"What kind of proof?"

"Comparison of DNA based on blood samples of father and daughter."

It would be a cliché to say that a hush fell over the courtroom. Thomas Lannan felt that a hush had fallen over the global audience watching the trial. Some would be watching it in Rome.

"How did you obtain a blood sample from Thomas Lannan?"

"I refuse to answer on grounds of the fifth amendment."

The prosecution would have had to be dead not to object to that, but Solomon silenced the objector. She had decided that this evidence must be heard and they could scruple later about how it was obtained. In any case, that aspect of things had already been turned over to the local, national, and international police forces. She might as well have said that it was obtained when Thomas Lannan was being held captive in Rome. Now, lying in his hospital bed a continent away, his left leg bore the marks of his fruitless attempt to help Cecil Meade. The wound on his arm from which dried blood had run had long since disappeared, gone with so many of the other shocks that flesh is heir to. But Thomas Lannan could see it as if it were still there.

"Where is this proof?" Judge Solomon asked.

"I turned it over to Mr. Schlick in his office some weeks ago."

Schlick produced an envelope from his briefcase. "And which has been in my office safe ever since, until this morning when I removed it and brought it to court."

The judge turned to the witness. "Have you ever opened this envelope?"

"No."

"Do you know what the contents are?"

"It is a report on tests run in Rome some months ago."

"And you do not know the result of those tests?"

574

"The tests are to prove something to others, not to me."

Schlick moved swiftly to the bench and handed the envelope to Judge Solomon. She looked at the envelope and described it in some detail for the benefit of the court reporter. Then she picked up a letter opener and with some drama slit open the envelope.

"I have before me a report from the Galileo Clinic in Rome. There are two forms, filled out in ink, and this." She held up a sheet. "It is titled 'Affadavit from Galileo Clinic'. I will read it. 'The enclosed forms show the tests that were run on blood sample A and blood sample B. A is blood said to have been taken from Peggy Christiansen. B is blood taken from Thomas Lannan. The tests were made to determine whether A contains a genetic code that relates it to that of B, suggesting that A is the child of B. Tests were run under the usual careful conditions; the unused blood samples are retained in this clinic in conditions preventative of their deterioration or decay. Thus our results can be checked by anyone who cares to do so. The results of our tests are...'"

Judge Solomon stopped reading. She looked toward the witness stand, clearly puzzled, then returned to her reading.

"'The results of our tests are negative! There is no biological possibility that A is the child of B.'"

Far off in Bethesda, a great whoop went up from Leach, and he brought his hands together in a clap. He turned and smiled triumphantly at Thomas Lannan.

"It boomeranged, Your Eminence. God is not mocked."

He all but skipped around the room. The television screen was split between the pandemonium in the courtroom, where Julian O'Keefe was being physically subdued, and talking heads who were discussing this turn of events. Lannan pressed a button, and the screen went blank.

"To congratulate you has the implications of an insult, Your Eminence, but I congratulate you nonetheless."

Lannan, the picture of calm composure, smiled at Leach. "I am glad you're glad."

"Of course, you are the one person in the world who could not possibly have been surprised."

Leach left him then, closing the door as the cardinal asked him to do. Thomas Lannan still wore an expression of calm. But his hands gripped the bed clothes tightly. His eyes closed. "*Te deum laudamus*", he whispered. "*Te dominum confitemur.*" He forgot the rest of the words, but it did not matter. "Thank God", he said. "Thank God." And tears ran down his cheeks.

EPILOGUE

Jim Morrow pointed out to Maureen that Dante had applied the devices of scriptural interpretation to his own work, distinguishing levels of meaning in the *Divine Comedy*. Its literal meaning was the state of souls after death, but its anagogic meaning was that human persons freely determined their future condition, whether of happiness or damnation.

"So?"

"You asked what it all means."

"A rhetorical question."

"I'm a literal person."

She nudged him in the ribs. "Well I'm the other. Anagogic. What does it mean?"

"Literally?"

He took her in his arms in self-protection. They were enjoying a species of second adolescence. Could second childhood be far behind? Maureen did not want a large wedding. She did not want to put their many children to the expense of coming to Rome.

"We'll visit them all afterward."

Tom Lannan flew in to be celebrant, claiming to have other business in Rome anyway. The nuptial Mass was in Santa Susanna and the diplomatic corps was there in force. It was in a modest way a social event. Maureen had many friends in Rome, and Jim's resignation when the State Department ordered him to Avignon had won him some notoriety, even praise. It now seemed that he might have been the last American ambassador to the Vatican. Tom Lannan said he would not fight the Crowe-Patridge bill that would eliminate the post.

"We'll have to find another way to get people like you out of the country, Jim."

Tom had come through his ordeals a more relaxed and inward man. Before him lay the task of rebuilding the Church in a country more and more in the grips of the Culture of Death. Criticisms of what Nate Patch had called the "gendercide" going on in China could not be mounted by a country where a million and a half abortions were performed each year, where euthanasia was now accepted and infanticide discussed as if there might be two sides to the question.

The night before the wedding, the three of them— Maureen, Jim, and Cardinal Lannan—had dinner together at Sabatini's in Trastevere.

"That dreadful man", Maureen had said, referring to Julian O'Keefe.

Tom looked at her. "A spoiled priest."

"Spoiled rotten."

"If the Church..." He stopped. "If we were what we should be, that kind of anti-clericalism would have no target."

"Targets can be invented", Jim said. "Thank God you didn't fit the role he cast you for."

Tom looked at Jim and then at Maureen. He seemed about to say more, but all he said was, "Thank God indeed."

They honeymooned in Gaeta, which is below Anzio, and fell in love with it. Perhaps this is where they would live while Jim wrote his book. That was decided now. It would have been difficult not to record the events of the past year. Maybe the act of writing would enable him to understand them. Tom Lannan seemed to have little sense of the heroic role he had played.

"I wouldn't embarrass him by telling him what he was called by the visionary of Viterbo." They sat high above the harbor looking out to sea.

Maureen turned to her husband. "What was it?"

"*Il santo.*"

"A manner of speaking?"

"All speaking is a manner of speaking."

"Not for us anagogic types. Still it fits, doesn't it?"

In the crunch, Tom had acted well. All the wavering and ambition, all the traits that had seemed permanent parts of him as the result of pursuing his career, had, when the chips were down, been set aside, and he had done and said just what a good bishop should. And what else is being holy than doing what one should?

"Anyone else get a mention by her?"

"Let me save it for the book."

"You're going to be difficult to live with."

"Okay, I'll tell you."

"No." She took his hand. "I want you to be difficult."

He still had not settled on the kind of book he would write. *The Decline and Fall* had been objective and scholarly; he was hardly in it at all, withdrawn behind all the documentation, speaking in an authoritative anonymous voice. But he had sat with the seer of Viterbo, he had pondered the message that had been given her, he had seen events unfold as they had been prophesied. Who was the Brentano who had set aside his literary career to record the visions of Catherine Emmerich?

Was it James Morrow's destiny to publicize a private revelation? What the seer had said extended beyond the present time.

Cardinal Novak shook his head at the suggestion that the seer's message should be made public by the Vatican. "The Gospels tell us all we need to know on that score."

Bureaucratic caution? That was scarcely applicable to the Vatican under Timothy. Still, Novak's attitude toward Viterbo was the same as Ratzinger's toward the third secret of Fatima.

"That doesn't mean you can't write about it", the cardinal added. Was that a commission? Novak only smiled when Jim Morrow put that question to him.

"Who owns the lake?" Maureen asked. They were on the path that circled Lake Powderhorn.

"We own land and shore rights."

"But not the lake."

"God owns the lake."

"I love this place."

She meant it, in a way, but only as he had meant he liked the country place near Perugia that she and Sean Kilmartin had been improving over the years. It was there that Maureen had spent much of her time, until Jim was assigned to Rome.

Later, on the veranda, looking out over the lake, its surface spangled by the setting sun, she said, "I thought it was about the end of the world."

He knew her mind was still on Viterbo. "I guess we haven't run out of future yet."

"But we will someday, won't we?" She murmured the acclamation from the Mass. "Christ has died, Christ is risen,

Christ will come again."

"The tenses of the faith."

Silence. Wolsey breathed steadily as he slept at her feet. Tomorrow they would drive to Notre Dame where she would meet Ken. A new generation for a new millenium.

And in the west, the ever-setting sun consumed itself, surrounded by its circling sisters, rushing with the speed of light toward the point systems and cosmoi and galaxies had been fleeing from the beginning, toward darkness and the primordial Fiat. And across the cold ocean of space, audible as the music of the spheres, the defining cry of creation comes. Maranatha! Come, Lord Jesus.

Feast of St. Catherine of Siena
Agrigento, 1997